ENDORSEMENTS FOR PAT SIMMONS

Simmons shines in this godly romance. This avid reader was overwhelmed by the compassionate writing and Scriptures that spoke to my soul. There were points that I identified with each character that led me to further investigate other Scriptures. She uses family history, murder, prison, and postpartum depression along with Scriptures to show God's ultimate sacrifice and constant forgiveness of sins. The character development and storyline pace will have you mesmerized as two families face their demons. Crowning Glory *is a masterpiece of Christian romance which is definitely a MUST read.*

—MONIQUE "DELTAREVIEWER" BRUNER

Talk to Me *is a great book! I am an avid reader and* Talk to Me *is one of the best I've ever read. I found myself laughing out loud—sign of a good book— grinning from ear to ear, and then saying "no she did not"! Once I started reading, I couldn't put the book down. The storyline was intriguing and the characters were well developed. I finished it in two days! You definitely will not be disappointed. Pat Simmons is certainly gifted to write a good story! Thanks, Pat, for sharing your talent with the world!*

—LESLIE HUDSON, BALTIMORE, MD

Guilty of Love *by Pat Simmons was my first experience with Christian fiction and I must admit that I truly enjoyed reading this novel. I thought that Ms. Simmons did an excellent job of inserting the character's spirituality into the dialog in such a natural manner that didn't come across as being preachy and she was also able to interlace a multitude of rich African American history in the process. I felt each and every emotion of the heroine and it touched me deeply within. This story centered on a very difficult, heartbreaking issue, and how Cheney dealt with it came across so incredibly real to me. It was astonishing to find such strong characters in a novel, even with the weaknesses evolved from their past experiences. I advise the* reader to keep a big box of tissues handy because you will need them on numerous occasions. Thanks go to Ms. Simmons for a truly inspirational story.

—NIKITA, REVIEWED FOR JOYFULLY REVIEWED

The author provides great lessons for someone going through any aspect of their life in terms of health, relationships, bearing children, and family values. She truly deserves an encore for Not Guilty of Love as she distinctively uses faith as her theme for the book. I look forward to the continuation she has in store!

—EKG LITERARY MAGAZINE

Still Guilty was a really good and powerful story. Pat Simmons brought it to the line. As I read this book, it was just what I needed. I was going through my own personal struggles and all of the Scriptures that Cheney and Parke recited I jotted down for my own personal use. I have told SO many readers about this series and I'm looking forward to reading more books by Pat Simmons!

—CARMEN FOR OOSA ONLINE BOOK CLUB

I felt as if I was part of this story. I found myself wanting to help the characters. I loved Still Guilty. I want to read other books by this author. She is a talented author. LOVED IT !

—READERS' FAVORITE "BOOK REVIEWS AND AWARD CONTEST"

PAT SIMMONS

the
guilt trip

THE JAMIESON LEGACY

MOODY PUBLISHERS
CHICAGO

© 2012 by
PAT SIMMONS

Scriptures taken from the *Holy Bible, New International Version*®, NIV®. Copyright © 1973, 1978, 1984, 2011 by Biblica, Inc.™ Used by permission of Zondervan. All rights reserved worldwide. www.zondervan.com.

Edited by Kathryn Hall
Interior design: Ragont Design
Cover design: Faceout Studio
Cover image: iStock (3978395, 8114650, and 17790482) and
      Shutterstock (60166576)
Author photo: Naum Furman

Library of Congress Cataloging-in-Publication Data
Simmons, Pat.
    The guilt trip / Pat Simmons.
       p. cm.
    ISBN 978-0-8024-0380-3 (alk. paper)
    1. Man-woman relationships—Fiction. 2. African Americans--Fiction. 3. Guilt—Fiction. 4. Domestic fiction. I. Title.
PS3619.I56125G84 2012
813'.6—dc23

                                2012010381

1 3 5 7 9 10 8 6 4 2

Printed in the United States of America.

In memory of Lorna "Mom" Robnett
for seeing my gifts before I knew I possessed them.

Chapter One

_T_wenty-eight-year-old Aaron "Ace" Jamieson wasn't married and never had been married. In fact, he wasn't planning to pick out a tuxedo and meet a woman at the altar any time soon. To maintain that resolve, Ace displayed the highest level of professionalism when it came to playing the dating game. Early on, his buddies taught him that it's around the three-month mark when a woman begins to fantasize about permanent residency. Therefore, he set a personal benchmark for seventy-two days or less. To maintain his integrity while enjoying the ride, Ace was always upfront with the ladies. He was careful to let them know that he wasn't looking for anything serious.

Standing in the mirror, he snickered while shaving, as he recalled some of the tactics women used to trap him into marriage: lavish gifts, on-demand intimacy, or claiming to carry his love child.

He shook his head in disgust, rinsed off his razor, and methodically massaged aftershave on his face and throat. Women's bluffs didn't make him blink. He would not be lured into any baby mama drama.

But something had happened to his determination several months ago. Lois, a friend of his cousin Cameron, introduced him to the one and only, alluring, Ms. Talise Rogers. She swept him off his feet on the first date. Immediately, Ace was fascinated by her independence and self-confidence. He was mesmerized by her exotic dark features, which were gently caressed by her flawless brown-sugar skin.

"Humph!" Ace let out an affirming expression. If that were not enough, he had to admit their connection was far more than the usual explosive physical attraction. If there was ever a soul mate, Talise was it.

To Ace, she's his Tay. He was convinced she had an invisible grip on him that was about to bring him down—and he wasn't complaining. It took some back-and-forth battling between his mind and his heart, but Ace thought Talise just might be the one he couldn't let get away.

Genuine, honest, and gorgeous is how he would describe her. When she surpassed the one-hundred-day mark, Ace stopped counting. "I'm actually losing my mind over this woman," he mumbled to himself and continued dressing. It was Friday and he was about to pick her up for a night out on the town.

Bobbing his head, Ace slipped his feet into his shoes. *Yep,* he thought. *A man would be a fool to let her go.* He grinned when he thought about their intimacy. It was so full of fire, Ace couldn't even comment about it.

As a matter of fact, before the night ended, he was going to have an out-of-body experience and do something he had never before contemplated: profess that his feelings for her were beyond a mere physical appeal.

Talise was the sole reason why Ace had repeatedly turned down his brother's offer to relocate to St. Louis. Of course, he couldn't tell Kevin, or Kidd, as he was called, that his decision was based on a woman. Despite Kidd's company having two openings in the local area, if his big brother had seen Talise, he would understand Ace's reluctance to be uprooted.

Ace swiped his car keys off the nightstand and jogged down the stairs to the first floor of the condo he shared with his mother in the Hyde Parke neighborhood of Boston.

Sandra Nicholson paused from watching her favorite television show. She glanced over her shoulder and lifted a brow. As youthful and attractive as she was, in Ace's eyes, his mother might as well be eighty years old. All she ever did was go to work, go to church, and return home from either destination.

"Hmm. You look exceptionally handsome tonight. Are you still going out with that Tanya, Tia, Tor—young lady?"

"Ma, just call her Tay."

"I knew it began with a 'T.'" Pointing the remote at the flat screen TV, Sandra muted the sound. She smiled, showing off the same left cheek dimple that Ace inherited.

"Five months with the same woman. When am I going to meet her?" His mother's eyes danced with mischief. "All I can get out of you is her name."

"Which you can't remember. I guess that's why they sent you an AARP card," he teased. Her playful eyes squinted to instill fear. It didn't work. "And it's been four months," he corrected.

"I would like to meet Tay."

That's not happening any time soon. I need to figure out how to define our relationship first. He chuckled. "Good night, Momma Nosy."

Stepping to the sofa, he leaned over and brushed a kiss against her cheek, then sauntered out the door. That was another first with Ace; he never divulged the names of his conquests. It would mean there was some form of emotional attachment.

Getting behind the wheel of his Dodge Charger, Ace grinned in anticipation of what Talise had up her sleeve for the evening. Each week, they took turns planning their Friday night activities. He was sure he would be pleasantly surprised.

A half an hour later, he parked in front of her brownstone. Ace checked his reflection in the rearview mirror. His mustache was perfectly trimmed and his jaws were baby bottom soft after his shave. His skin would have been totally unblemished if it wasn't for the mark on his nose. It was a reminder of the first and last fight he lost. His brother made sure of that.

Next, he rubbed the tamed waves in his hair. Ace still missed his long, thick ponytail that he relinquished when he accepted the job at Healthcare Concepts two years earlier. He had no choice.

Long ago, his mother told him and his brother something Ace always remembered. She said, once they were legally old enough to get a job, if a man didn't work, he wouldn't eat at her house. He and Kidd never wanted to test her on that rule.

Getting out of the car, he glanced up at the third-floor bay window. There she was, watching him. Talise waved then disappeared to come downstairs and let him inside the building. Ace swaggered from the sidewalk to the entrance.

In record time, Talise opened the massive, tall wooden door. Ace's heart crashed against his chest at her glamour. He had dated many women with model looks and figures, but Talise would reign as the top model for years to come.

She had long legs that could stop traffic. A silver dress gracefully hugged her curves. Beaded straps started at her polished toes and continued to wrap upward, stopping at her ankles. Despite her five-eight height, she confidently commanded her stilettos.

Ace whistled. Then his nostrils flared, as he gasped for more oxygen. But that didn't stop his assessment. Talise's hair was naturally long—inches past her shoulders—and it was always glossy, whether hanging straight or in curls. The best thing about it—it was all her hair. She was born with it. He had nothing against hair extensions, except when they looked like hair extensions.

She was a portrait of loveliness with her dark lashes, silky brows, and big, brown doe-shaped eyes. These were just some of her points of overall perfection and his general state of weakness. Yeah, he liked how all of her features—from head to toe—accented her fine, brown frame.

"Hey, baby," Ace cooed, as he stepped closer to her.

Talise's response was to leap into his arms with the force of a hurricane. Her strength would have rocked a man who was unsteady on his feet. But not Ace, he stood at six-three and tipped the scales at 220 pounds.

His buffed body was able to absorb the impact while their embrace lingered, and then she weakened him with her kisses. Ace didn't know who started the seduction, but he wasn't pleased when she regained composure and left him begging for more. He stared at his woman through hooded lashes and watched the longing flash across her face. To his chagrin, a smile chased the passionate moment away.

"Keep that up, woman, and we may not hit the streets and go dancing, or whatever you have planned for tonight."

"What I planned, or hoped, was that we could relax here. Lois and some friends are heading to New York for the weekend. I've prepared a candlelight dinner . . ."

"Then what are we waiting for?" With naughty scenarios running through his mind, Ace scooped her up in his arms and climbed the stairs two at a time. When they made it to the third floor landing, he slowly released her. Jokingly, Ace exaggerated his breathing, as if he was gasping for air.

She laughed. "And what was your hurry, Mr. Jamieson?"

"Let's just say I'm famished." He patted his six-pack. Reaching for his hand, Talise led him into the apartment she shared with his cousin's friend Lois—the one who set them up on a blind date.

The aromas wafting through the apartment teased Ace. Glancing around, he snickered at the dimmed lighting and burning incense. His eyes then settled on the kitchen counter, which served as a table. It was set for two with crystal goblets and china place settings.

Absentmindedly, Ace kicked the door closed. As though in a trance, he followed Talise into the kitchen. Grabbing a serving dish, she turned around and practically bumped into him.

"Here, put that on the table, Ace."

"I'd rather nibble on you." He encircled his arms around her and began to make good on his statement.

Usually, Talise had a witty comeback but didn't take his bait this time. Instead, she busied herself by placing more serving pans on the table. When she seemed pleased with her handiwork, she lit the two candles between their plates.

At the kitchen sink, they played in the water as they washed their hands together. Finished with the task, Ace escorted her to the other side of the open kitchen. He pulled out Talise's stool and took the seat next to her.

Ace had a hard time taking his eyes off her until she insisted. Then they held hands, bowed their heads, and Talise began to say grace.

"Jesus," she said with a pause, as if she was gathering her thoughts.

Opening one eye, Ace squinted. This was not the time for a moment of reflection. *Just pray, so we can eat.* "Baby?" he said softly, studying Talise's troubled face.

She cleared her throat, but never opened her eyes. "Jesus, please bless this meal." Pausing again before mumbling a few more words, Talise finished with, ". . . In Jesus' Name. Amen."

"I'm glad we got through that before our food turned cold," he joked. Lifting his glass, he sipped some water. When she didn't laugh, he proceeded to devour his steak and sautéed vegetables. Then Ace shoved a big helping of twice-baked potatoes, lathered with sour cream, in his mouth and swallowed.

"Baby, this is good." He winked. "And just think, I'll have you all to myself tonight to show you my appreciation."

Talise mustered a faint smile and picked at her food. Usually, they exchanged seductive glances, naughty words, and sassy flirts over a meal. But not tonight. Maybe Ace was reading too much into it because he was about to lay his heart on the table, or maybe she was going through her monthly hormonal thing. He hoped not.

After digesting a second helping of potatoes, he dabbed at his mouth with a napkin. "Tay, I want to talk to you—"

"I have something to say to you also," she interrupted.

Ace snickered and then folded his arms. "Go ahead. What's in that beautiful head of yours?"

Resting her fork on her placemat, Talise pinched at the fabric a few times but wouldn't look at him.

What's going on? he wondered. His lady was usually confident and talkative, not sober as her expression indicated. Once he professed his growing feelings, he knew that would put a smile on her face.

"Tay?"

She bowed her head, as though she was ashamed of something. "I may be pregnant."

His eyes widened when her rushed words finally registered. "What?" he asked to test his hearing.

Lifting her head, she stared into his eyes. "Ace, I may be pregnant."

Noooooooooo. Not his Tay. *She wouldn't do this to me, would she?*

Ace was a gambler. He could count on one hand the number of times he lost. He would never have bet that Talise would set him up like this. But she didn't blink, while she waited for him to say something.

Act normal, be professional and tactful. You aren't going down like this, man, he coaxed himself.

"How?" Ace shook his head. He knew how. *Remain calm.* "I mean, you said you think," Ace struggled for words. "When will you know for sure?"

"I have a doctor's appointment next Thursday," she said above a whisper. Her self-assurance seemed nonexistent. Was it possible that she had aged through dinner?

Nodding, Ace reached for his water. Suddenly, he'd broken out in a cold sweat. Thursday was six days away. He would be packed and out

13

of the state of Massachusetts by Tuesday, if not sooner. Tonight, if he could arrange it.

"Ace?"

"Hmm?" He blinked, as she pulled him out of his trance and back into the nightmare.

"How do you feel about that? I mean, I know we didn't plan this . . ."

He definitely didn't.

Ace didn't hear another word Talise said. He had tuned her out the minute she said two words: *I* and *pregnant*. The word *might* didn't even matter at that point.

Talise was pretty, smart, and definitely made him smile. But that wasn't enough for him to propose. Ace hadn't seen this coming, and he considered himself a seasoned playboy.

All of a sudden, it seemed stuffy in her apartment. He had to get away and quickly told himself to say something. "Okay. You do look a little tired. Why don't you relax on the sofa? I'll clean up our mess here and load the dishwasher."

On the outside, Ace managed a tender smile. He helped her recline, then he removed her shoes. On the inside, he was enraged that Talise thought she could run this game on him. She had already lost. *Women and their games.*

"Are you upset?" she whispered, as she lay back and allowed him to prop her feet on a pillow.

"I'm shocked is more like it."

She sighed. "Me too."

Next, he tackled the cleanup task in record time. He had to get out of there. "Listen, babe, I . . . I'd better go. Why don't you get some rest?" he suggested. Nestling her in his arms, he held her the longest time he could without saying a word.

Shocked, betrayed, and hurt were the only way to describe Ace's emotions. He stalked down the stairs and then used unnecessary force to open the entrance door and his car door.

Ace climbed in as quickly as possible. Without looking up to see if Talise was standing in the bay window, waiting to give him the customary wave sendoff, he sped off.

"You fool!" He was certain he was protected during every encounter. Why hadn't she protected herself? How had he misjudged Talise's honesty?

A red light flashed before Ace's eyes. On autopilot, he stopped and then accelerated when he saw green. Ten minutes or so later, as cars and trucks zoomed by him, he couldn't remember getting onto the Mass Turnpike.

Thank God for GPS. It was automatically activated when he started the motor. By habit, he had punched home. When he glanced at the screen, he couldn't believe he was on Hyde Park Avenue and had already passed Jamaica Plain and Roslindale. It was only a matter of blocks before he would reach his condo.

In spite of his dazed state, Ace made it to the complex and pulled into his assigned parking spot. Cursing, he turned off the ignition and pounded the steering wheel before resting his head on its leather exterior.

Ace couldn't recall one scenario where protection wasn't used. Immediately, as though a warning signal was sounding loudly, he could hear his mother's counsel. Throughout his years of mischief, she cautioned him, "Watch how you live, Ace, because whatever you do under the cover of darkness, Jesus will bring to light. Mark my words. There is no protection for sin. Read it for yourself in First Corinthians 4:5."

As careful as he was, now this. He looked up and stared at the front door of his home. Ace didn't make a move to get out and sat there gritting his teeth. God help Talise if she was pregnant because that wasn't reason enough to make him throw his life away.

His mother called him a late bloomer when it came to gaining the common sense that matched his intellect. Up until he secured his present job two years ago, Ace stayed in trouble. He was arrested for petty things like drinking, gambling, and fighting. For the most part, it took Cameron to convince Ace that jail wasn't the life for a Jamieson. That's when Ace did an instant one-eighty.

Of course, he didn't like the feeling of being caged. And that's exactly what Tay was trying to do, imprison him. Little did she know that it wasn't going to happen.

Maybe he got his free spirit from his father, Samuel Jamieson. Sam had never married his mother. Yet he and Kidd turned out okay. Well, Kidd did anyway. Ace was still rough around the edges from time to time.

Without a father in the home, he couldn't emulate one. So, growing up, he lived his life with an attitude of trial and error. But he had enough good sense to know that mind-set didn't apply to fatherhood. A man was expected to get it right. That's why he never planned to marry or have children—ever—under any circumstances. It was a trap.

Ace pulled his iPhone from his waist clip and speed-dialed his brother in St. Louis. He tried to clear his head before Kidd answered. They were close, and Kidd didn't need to see Ace to read him like a book.

Five years older, Kidd had relocated and eventually married a cutie he met at work. Amazingly, after two years, Kidd and Eva were still happy.

"Whatz up, bro?" Kidd greeted.

"Oh, nothing much." Ace coaxed himself to relax. "Hey, I'm thinking about accepting the opening in the St. Louis office."

"All right. It's about time—" Kidd paused. "Wait a minute. What, or who, are you running from? Please tell me someone doesn't have a mark on your life." He groaned. "Jesus, I know my prayers aren't in vain."

Might as well be truthful. "It's a woman."

"Not another one. Ace?" Kidd groaned, hissed, and mumbled. "You mean a woman claiming to carry your lovechild, like Joy, or that Sheba woman?"

"I didn't need any DNA test to tell you those babies weren't mine."

"What do you expect with your lifestyle? Bro, being a father is a privilege and a responsibility."

"Boy, your wife has you brainwashed."

"What is it going to take for you to stop this bed hopping? There really is a term for your condition, you know."

Ace exhaled. He knew Kidd's answer.

"Fornication," the brothers said together.

"Okay, you can mock me, but you can't mock God. So the question is, could this baby be yours?"

If—and it is a big if—Talise is pregnant, the baby might be his. But responsibility is optional.

"Only the mother knows for sure."

I spooked him." Talise swallowed as she shielded herself from Ace's view. His normal goodbye kiss lacked the luster she had come to expect.

Standing near her apartment bay window, her heart sank when Ace sped off from the curb without giving her his customary goodbye. His hasty exit scared her.

Gnawing on her bottom lip, Talise second-guessed her timing. Maybe she shouldn't have mentioned her suspicions. If only she had listened to her older sister, Sinclaire, and waited until she was one-hundred percent sure before saying anything.

A week earlier, some mild cramping and light spotting had occurred. Talise didn't give it a second thought until the nausea hit. She had been enduring repeated bouts for the past few days. Finally, the unsettling experience prompted her to take a home pregnancy test.

If Talise read it right, she wasn't. But her suspicions lingered. The thought of becoming another statistic as an unwed mother made her bawl like a two-year-old in the middle of a tantrum.

During a Skype call less than twenty-four hours earlier, Sinclaire had tried to console her. "From everything you've raved about Aaron . . ." Her sister refused to refer to Ace by his nickname, saying it sounded too gangster. ". . . I'm sure he'll do the right thing. We can always repent, and God will forgive us, as long as we don't continue in our sins. Even if God doesn't spare you from this situation, you've got to turn your life over to Him."

A tear slid down her cheek as she recalled their conversation. Stepping away from the window, she rubbed her arms and then massaged her flat tummy. Talise turned around and scanned the apartment she shared with Lois. Her roommate was one of a handful of people she could call "friend" since her move from Virginia to Boston.

After responding to a "roommate needed" ad, Talise met with Lois, studied the South End neighborhood, and quizzed Lois about her lifestyle. Seemingly satisfied, she signed the lease. That had been six months ago.

"A good friend of mine—and Cameron Jamieson is fine—has a cousin named Aaron who is equally as fine and unattached," Lois had said when trying to set up Talise on a double date. To her description, she then added, "He's tall and muscular and has a rugged pretty-boy face. Best of all, he's got a good job."

At first, Talise was reluctant. "What's wrong with him? Is he a homosexual?"

Lois had laughed and snorted. "Far from it. He's a good-looking brother who enjoys having a good time—nothing more." She paused. "Just go out one time," she had pleaded. "If he's a jerk, then dump him."

Talise wasn't buying what sounded like a "too good to be true" setup. "If both of these brothers are so fine, then why haven't you dated either one of them?" She questioned, crossing her arms.

Lois could go toe-to-toe with any woman in the good looks department. She had a touch of Puerto Rican in her blood and a whole lot of African American. The woman turned heads as a browner version of Keysha Cole.

"I learned not to date friends or friends' relatives. My relationship with Cameron is for networking purposes only. I keep my friend pool separate from my potential boyfriend pool. Separate and not equal." Lois's voice had been serious.

A few evenings later, during an event at Northeastern University, Cameron and Lois introduced her to Ace. Then they disappeared, leaving Talise and Ace on their own. One night turned into many nights together, phone calls, and now, possibly permanent evidence of those numerous dates.

Ace's personality had magnetism and his presence gave her a sense of completeness in her life. God help her that she would admit it, but Ace had become like the air she breathed. With his early departure, it would mark the first Friday they weren't together until the wee morning hours. The void was almost unbearable.

Alone with her thoughts, she blew out the candles and incense sticks. Talise retook her seat at the counter and closed her eyes. What would her father and his new wife say? Or her coworkers and friends think? She hadn't lived in Boston a year and had already made bad choices.

Imagining the rumors made her sigh deeply. *Talise Shanté Rogers, age twenty-nine, pregnant, unmarried—and a fool.* What was she thinking?

Of course, Ace would want to marry her. But what if he didn't? If he didn't love her, then marriage was not an option, even for the sake of their child. They would share joint custody and live separate lives. That wasn't negotiable.

Aside from being devastated by his rejection, financially, she could probably manage as a single parent. She had her salary as an airline ticket agent and the extra money she earned as a part-time stylist at a trendy salon in Cambridge. Plus, there would be whatever child support Ace agreed to pay. One thing was for sure, she would not be part of any baby drama.

But he loved her. Right? She could see it in his eyes, in his smile, and in the way he kissed her. She no longer wanted to think about any other instances.

Talise stood and picked up her shoes near the sofa. "Why am I torturing myself? A little nausea and a light period don't mean I'm pregnant." The argument sounded good, but Talise just didn't believe a word of it. Tomorrow, she would buy another home pregnancy test.

Sauntering into her bedroom, she tossed her stilettos into the closet. Next, she peeled off her "man teaser" dress. That's what Lois had called the outfit when Talise bought it. After donning a pair of flannel pajamas, she lifted her laptop off a small desk in the corner and climbed into bed.

While she waited for it to boot up, Talise longed for her mother's advice and comfort. But Marilyn, who was only forty-seven at the time, had passed away years earlier from a heart attack. Her father, Frederick, remarried soon after. The new Mrs. Rogers—Donna—was nice, but detached. Her focus was on her husband, leaving very little attention for his daughters. She believed if a person was eighteen, they were grown and should be gone.

Donna had an uncanny way of always making Talise and Sinclaire feel like they were lacking in some area of their lives: looks, education, etiquette, or whatever the topic of the hour. It somehow seemed to slip Donna's mind that they were the products of private education and both were college graduates as well. In fact, the Rogers family was even part of a few elite organizations, such as Jack and Jill. As toddlers, the two sisters had even modeled in fashion shows, print ads, and TV commercials. Yet Donna insisted on overlooking their redeeming qualities.

Not only were Sinclaire and Talise extremely close, they were best friends. With very similar features, their personalities were completely opposite. Two years older, Sinclaire always portrayed maturity as an example for her younger sister. Talise couldn't recall when Sinclaire wasn't grounded in her faith. She consistently prayed before making life-altering choices and thanked God for His wisdom afterward.

Daddy affectionately dubbed her "the family prayer warrior."

On the other hand, even without consulting Jesus regularly, Talise was loyal to her convictions. It was natural for her to treat others the way she would want to be treated. She trusted people at face value, at times, to a fault.

The Rogers sisters loved to travel. Because they were military brats who moved quite often whenever their father was reassigned, it was in their blood. During their childhood years, the girls also enjoyed when the family took lengthy summer vacations at their beach house in Destin, Florida.

As an adult, Sinclaire further fed her hunger to see the world when she joined the air force. Currently, she was serving her country in the Middle East.

In her own way, Talise was following in their father's footsteps too. However, she wasn't about to put herself in harm's way. In her mother's absence, Talise felt there was no reason for her to remain in Richmond, Virginia. Consequently, upon graduating from Hampton University, she had packed up and moved from Virginia to Texas. There she took her first job out of college with a Fortune 500 business consulting firm that required extensive travel.

Three years later, Talise concluded there was nothing glamorous about business travel. It was time to make a career move. When Southwest Airlines posted various vacancies, Sinclaire credited God for Talise beating out the competition. There were only a handful of openings for ticket agent positions. But she landed one and the perks that go along with it. Bags weren't the only thing that could fly free.

Talise took advantage of the travel perks, which were not mandatory. She mapped out an adventure to live in different cities for a period of time. That way she could get a feel for where she wanted to settle down. So far, she had lived in San Francisco on the West Coast and Boston on the East Coast. On her next tour, she planned to move to the Midwest, maybe Chicago.

That was, until she met Ace. Funny how a man could make a woman change her plans. Talise logged on to her email and typed Sinclaire a note. Her sister was the only other person who knew about her suspicion.

In the subject line, Talise typed: *No I told you so.*

I couldn't keep it in. I know. I know. I should have waited, but what difference would it have made? Ace and I care about each other. I would venture to say we're in love, but his reaction was worse than sticker shock. It was a mixture of fear, disbelief, anger, and disappointment. Since your name means prayer, I could use some right now. Email me when you can. Love T.

Talise didn't expect a quick response. In the meantime, she visited pregnancy sites to further torture herself. Almost an hour later, she logged back onto her email account. Sinclaire had replied: Re: *No I told you so. I wouldn't.*

With him or without him, pregnant or not, everything is going to be okay. We'll Skype soon, and p.s., I've never stopped praying for my sister. You're the only one I've got. Hopefully, Donna is beyond childbearing years. LOL. Love, S.

Talise smiled at Sinclaire's dig on Donna. Which situation would be worse, Donna pregnant at fifty-two with a husband, or her pregnancy at twenty-nine with no husband? It would be a draw.

Shutting her computer down and putting it aside, Talise picked up her cell phone and called Ace. She got his voicemail and left a message, "Call me."

As fear crept into her mind, she slid onto the floor and prayed longer than her usual few sentences. "Jesus, please don't let me be pregnant, please. I promise I won't sleep with Ace again—or any man—unless he's my husband. God, this would ruin my life. I'm not prepared for this . . ." She continued to list all the reasons why the timing was all wrong. Once she said, "Amen," Talise climbed back into bed and prayed again. This time that she would be able to sleep.

Saturday morning, Talise woke without a phone call from Ace. It was their routine to talk while she dressed to go to the salon. Either she was still having a nightmare or Ace was sending a strong signal that he was unreachable, indefinitely.

Her imagination and guilt was really working overtime. Since she and Ace had never had a major disagreement, this was a test of how they handled difficult situations. She guessed he needed solitude. There was no way Ace was the type of man to desert her—period.

Talise didn't know how she was going to make it five more days until her doctor's appointment. Mentally and physically, she was a wreck. Knowing this particular Saturday there was a light customer load, she called Sasha, the owner of Sassy's Salon.

"Sasha, I'm not feeling well."

"Too much partying?" she asked jokingly, knowing Talise never missed work or showed up late.

"I wish that's all it was. I'll call my customers and see if they won't mind another stylist doing their hair today. Or maybe they'll want to reschedule."

Sasha agreed and reassured her, "Feel better, hon, we'll take care of your clients. I won't let the girls steal them." She laughed and disconnected.

Next, Talise contacted her customers, explained that she was under the weather and gave them an option. Three decided to reschedule, one said she was going to cancel anyway, and the other two didn't mind a one-time stylist change.

After that task was over, she lay in the bed and stared out the window. Everybody deserved a pity party every now and then. And, at the moment, Talise was suffering with a heartbreak hangover.

The day didn't get any better. Ace still hadn't returned her call and Talise needed to vent. Unfortunately, there was no one available. At least Lois would return tomorrow and she could talk to her.

By late Saturday night, with no word from Ace, Talise was calling him all kinds of names for his uncharacteristic behavior. She texted him: *R U Ok? I missed UR call this morning. Call me.*

Signing on to the Internet, she checked her email account. Sinclaire had left one, suggesting a video chat through Skype at ten o'clock that night. Eastern Standard Time. That was six o'clock in the morning in the Middle East. Checking the time, Talise quickly logged into her Skype account. It was already twelve minutes past ten. Hopefully, her sister was still online.

It wasn't long before Sinclaire peered closer to the monitor. She looked like a dentist checking for cavities. "Are you okay?"

"I wished I had listened to you." It was as if Talise's tears had been waiting for her to connect with Sinclaire. Then, all of a sudden, the dam broke. Sniffing didn't stop the tears from streaming down her face. Laying her laptop aside, Talise got off the bed and went into the bathroom. She returned blowing her nose.

Sinclaire appeared thoughtful. "Sis, regardless of the outcome, baby or no baby, God is there for you. If this man cares about you—"

"He does."

"Then if he loves you . . ."

Recently, Talise thought she saw love beaming from his dark brown eyes, but on the previous night, it was as if a dirty contact lens blocked her view. She sighed. "I hope so." Then she broke down again.

"Hey, sis, hey," Sinclaire coaxed Talise to face the computer. "It's okay. We'll see what the doctor and the Lord says."

"What? So I can cry all over again? I'd rather get it out of the way now."

"You're so dramatic. I'm here to fight a real war with guns and improvised explosive devices, and you're having a tug of war battle with your emotions."

"What are you talking about? This is a battle—a battle within myself. I am truly scared. I wish I could pick up the phone and call Mom. At least Lois will be back soon, and I can get her take on this."

"Don't, Talise. Be discreet about your business. Wait until you see your doctor and you know for sure. Promise me, sis," Sinclaire ordered, as if she was a drill sergeant in the army.

"I miss Mom too," she went on. "But you have me by phone, email, or Skype. And you said you haven't heard from him? Is that like him to be inconsiderate, especially knowing what you're going through?"

Talise shook her head. "This isn't like Ace at all. I've called him and left a message and I texted him. It's like he disappeared."

Frowning, Sinclaire had a thoughtful expression. "I'm withholding my comments until after your doctor's visit. Then I'll start praying that he comes to his senses before I get to him."

Chapter Three

*W*hy is my son packing like he has to get out of town by sundown? Ace's mother wondered. Sitting quietly in a chair watching him, Sandra Nicholson drifted into deep thought as she began reflecting on her life. When she was twenty years old, naïve and in love, Sandra gave birth to Kevin Jamieson. She was an unmarried woman. Five years after that, out of sheer stupidity, she gave birth to another adorable baby boy, Aaron Jamieson. Now, thirty-three years later at age fifty-three, Sandra remained single.

Their father, the man she loved, Samuel Jamieson, played her like a fool. At the time of their affair, he had been married. Of course, she didn't know that until years later when a bill collector called her in an attempt to track him down. Samuel had stayed with them for brief periods off and on.

The scoundrel had been hitched twice and had spawned eleven children, including her two. Sandra didn't know if she was blessed not to have been counted among the wives or cursed because she didn't have even a part-time father for her boys.

At the same time, Samuel was adamant that his boys carry his last name. She gave him no argument on that. However, growing up, Ace and Kidd's given name was always a cause for embarrassment when she had to complete forms or introduce herself. Sandra was convinced it was a source of shame that caused her sons to lash out in negative ways.

Things slowly began to change when their cousin Cameron arrived in Boston to attend MIT. He had tracked Samuel Jamieson down through genealogy methods. Once he earned her sons' trust, Cameron told the story of their shared connections to a royal African tribe. The last name suddenly didn't seem worthless anymore.

Still, to this day, Sandra didn't know what to make of the nicknames their father attached to her children. Where did he come up with the name "Kidd"? She later wondered if it was simply because he couldn't remember the boy's name.

She had learned early on the reason for Aaron's "Ace." Whenever Samuel paid a visit, he played games with the young boy. Ace innocently recited numbers to his dad. Then Samuel would turn around and gamble with those numbers and win.

Unfortunately, this deadbeat dad secured Aaron's future with that silly "Ace in the Hole" nickname that she detested. It seemed as if it influenced her younger son to follow in his father's path in more ways than gambling and winnings.

With God's grace and as much dignity that she could command, Sandra did her best to rear two strong Black men. Physically, she succeeded; spiritually and emotionally, she failed miserably. How could such sweet little boys grow up to become angry Black men?

Regretfully, her definition of a mother's love had been to spoil them. In those days as a young single mother, she worked as many hours as she could. When her children began to grow up, she gave Kidd the responsibility for being the man of the house and protecting his baby brother.

The pressure of having such a big task may have proved too much for a young boy. In hindsight, she realized it was a bad move because Kidd took it to the extreme and developed an unruly attitude. It seemed to work for him, so Ace followed in his footsteps. Both boys resented anyone who tried to exercise authority over them.

Years later, as fully grown men, Ace and Kidd had become as different as night and day. Where Kidd proved he could be tamed, Ace still had to be where the action was—good or bad.

Hearing him upstairs rumbling through his things and packing bags, Sandra paused in her reflections and took a deep sigh. Ace had been out of control most of his life. He was a strong-willed child and bull-headed teenager. It was surprising that she had any hair left on her head because of his drinking, fighting, and gang affiliation. Anything to test the nerves of a single parent—Ace had tried it.

Yes, rearing children alone was a task she wouldn't recommend to any woman—young, middle-aged, or older. Boys need their fathers—period. If only he had given more of himself, even a philanderer like Samuel may have had some redeeming qualities. One would never know since he died several years earlier while living with his third family.

Sandra's mind shifted to the major change that took place after her older son relocated to St. Louis. Cameron had helped to orchestrate the move with the aid of his older brothers, Parke and Malcolm. Two years ago, Kidd married a feisty young woman.

Eva not only put him in check, but she managed what had been impossible for Sandra. Eva had led Kidd to Christ. Before Jesus saved him, Kidd spoke his mind and dared anyone to argue with him. Now he was a level-headed man with a reverence for God and Sandra couldn't be more proud of him.

On the other hand, Ace was close-lipped, preferring to keep people guessing about his thoughts. Included in his everyday wardrobe, he plastered on his poker mask. Since reaching adulthood, Ace has been almost as reckless as his absentee father in his social life.

And the women—typically, she knew about them only after Ace had moved on to the next one. There were a couple of exceptions, though, women who claimed to carry his lovechild. It came out later that those children weren't his. Ace would defy anyone to try and trap him into marriage. Unfortunately, her son had been on the fast track to beat out some celebrities' boastings of sleeping with the most women.

Enough was enough. She needed answers. Standing over Ace with her arms folded, she started, "Let me understand this." Watching him contine to pull clothes from drawers and yank shirts off hangers, she continued, "For two years, your brother has been trying to lure you to St. Louis. You've always had an excuse. Now you're packing up everything you own and some of my stuff too, as if an angry mob was running you out of some racist town before sundown. What's going on, Aaron? Do you owe a gambling debt?"

"You're kidding. Right, Mom?" Ace gave her a dumbstruck look. "I left that kid's stuff behind years ago when I started classes at Roxbury Community College."

She was far from being placated. "I know you still go to that Twin River Casino in Rhode Island."

He didn't break his rhythm and kept packing. "I can play Black Jack without driving across state lines. Pop didn't call me 'Ace in the Hole' for nothing."

Sandra had made up her mind when her sons were small not to badmouth their father. But at that moment, several choice words were bombarding her mind.

"Aaron, don't even think about taking my pedicure kit. Buy your own toenail clippers." She paused. "Have you considered driving? You wouldn't have to cram so much stuff into your suitcase. Take your car."

"Nah, bags fly free, remember?" He kept a straight face while mimicking the Southwest commercials. "Plus, I'm in a hurry to get there. Other than that, I don't want you to drive a rental car for a week while your Kia is in the shop. Drive my Charger. I'll come back and get it later. I don't know why you use that shady mechanic in the old neighborhood anyway."

Sandra refused to get off the subject. "Did you and Tay have a fight?" It was her turn to maintain a poker face. She didn't want to appear overly nosy, knowing she was already on the verge.

That seemed to get his attention. Whipping his head around to face her, Ace stared. He was clearly crafting his response.

"Nope, she's a nice lady, but it's over. It's time for a change and I'm moving on and out."

Read between the lines, she told herself. On Friday night, her son walked out the door relaxed and happy. Surprisingly, he returned a few hours later spooked. His irritability stayed with him throughout Saturday. On Sunday morning, he rebuffed Sandra's invitation to attend church. Now, Sunday night, he's preparing to leave town.

Exasperated, Sandra didn't enjoy this round of twenty questions. "What about your job here?"

"I called my boss at home earlier. Melvin couldn't believe I finally caved in to the enticement to take the St. Louis position. He'll process the paperwork for my transfer tomorrow morning.

"Come Tuesday, I'll be sitting behind a new desk in my own office. It's a promotion with the opportunity for more advancement. Plus, I couldn't turn down the sizeable raise. It's a dream job, Mom." He turned away and mumbled, "And a new hiding place."

Chapter Four

*O*n Monday morning, Talise was near ballistic level when her gynecologist's office called and rescheduled her Thursday appointment to Friday. She had barely been hanging on by a split end.

Plus, she had ruined a recent manicure after a mental meltdown without the comfort of Ace's arms. It was the first time since officially becoming a couple that they hadn't been together during a weekend.

Whether he delivered her lunch at the salon on Saturday afternoons or treated her to entertainment at the House of Blues on Saturday nights, they enjoyed each other's company. It wasn't unusual on Sunday mornings to brunch at Liberty Hotel, the renovated former Charles Street Jail.

Sometimes, for the remainder of their Sundays, they were hole-up in a suite. She sighed, realizing that was how she got into her possible condition in the first place.

When Lois returned on Sunday night, Talise was in the bed where she had pretty much resided since Friday. Her roommate chatted non-stop about her shopping excursion and showed Talise some great bargains she'd snagged. Lois went on endlessly, telling her about the great price she and two other friends were able to get for a Broadway play. Smiling, Talise went through the motions.

"So what did you and Mr. Jamieson do while I was gone?"

This time, Talise followed Sinclaire's advice and didn't say a word about her suspicions. "Oh, Ace and I had dinner on Friday."

"What exotic restaurant did he take you to?" Her roommate's eyes twinkled with mischief.

Talise scrunched up her nose and forced herself to play along. "I cooked a romantic meal here."

"Did you two have a sleepover?"

Picking up her pillow, Talise aimed it at her roommate's head. "You know better. I wasn't about to break our number one rule: no overnight guests."

Lois shrugged and replied, "Just asking." She grinned happily and took her purchases to her bedroom.

Four more days, and then Talise would know whether she had something to tell Lois. Of course, since Thursday was her regular off day, and her appointment was moved to Friday, she would have to make up the missed hours at work.

—⁂—

On Monday, her concentration was at a premium she couldn't buy. Mustering a smile, Talise acknowledged two customers standing at her counter. "Hi, may I help you?" Again, she attempted to banish her personal drama to the wayside.

"I missed my plane to New York. Is there any room on the next flight, and how much extra will I have to pay?" A petite woman with silver hair asked. Talise noticed her generous smile and candy red lipstick.

She tapped into the terminal and waited for the information. A line quickly began to form. It was going to be a busy Monday.

"Good news. There are seats available. Let's see if I can do something about the cost." Manipulating fees, Talise was able to limit the up-charge to twenty-five dollars. The woman and her companion walked away pleased.

On autopilot, she moved to the next traveler. One by one, they kept coming. Whenever there was a lull in passengers, Ace's handsome pretty boy looks came back into her mental view.

He had all weekend to digest the possibilities. Why hadn't he called? Although Talise was attracted to Ace, Marilyn Rogers didn't rear two foolish girls. She didn't chase after men. Never having been a desperate woman, she wouldn't allow the outcome of her current situation to change that.

On the surface, Talise wore the smile and uniform. Mentally, she struggled to focus. The more she tried to take control, the more her mind disobeyed, drifting back and forth with thoughts about Ace. Nevertheless, she was a professional and continued to do her best while working alongside her fellow ticket agents.

Momentarily immersed in her musings, she found herself reliving the memories from the previous month's hour-and-a-half drive to Foxwoods Resort Casino in Connecticut. In eager anticipation, she had rescheduled some regular Saturday clients to free up her time for the weekend getaway with Ace.

Although the man didn't seem to be an addicted gambler, he knew how to play and win. Whether it was Black Jack, Poker, or the slot machines, Ace always seemed to hit the jackpot. Even more interesting, Talise was bewildered by his generosity. During the entire time, he made a surprising, endearing gesture with his winnings. He turned every dime over to her. It had been hers to play or keep.

"This is a lot of money," she had said in amazement. Placing it securely inside the zipper pocket of her purse, her last count was at three thousand dollars. When she couldn't close her mouth, Ace kissed her.

"It's just Benjamins, baby. You canceled your Saturday clients for me. It's the least I can do to make it up to you." The light of excitement in his eyes had shined brightly. Her heart had melted.

Clearly, it would be obvious to any casual observer that Ace was completely at home in the casino environment. The next day, they feasted on the hotel's international buffet and danced for hours in the Sunset Ballroom. In Talise's estimation, they had partied like rock stars. As their weekend drew to a close, Ace wouldn't leave before stocking up on junk food for the road trip back home from his namesake Aces Up Snacks.

With a sudden flash of remembering where she was, Talise caught herself and straightened her posture. It was a good thing the Southwest ticket line wasn't busy at the moment. Only a few travelers had interrupted her thoughts. That was fine with Talise because she was quite preoccupied with her reverie.

Smiling to herself, she reminisced snuggling up to Ace on the drive back to Boston. Their words were few as Gerald Albright and Paul Hardcastle serenaded them all the way to her apartment on Durham Street.

That next morning, instead of hopping on the Silver Line bus to Logan Airport, she had driven to the bank on Mass Ave and deposited her balance of twenty-eight hundred dollars.

Yes, altogether, Talise was smitten. She had begun falling for him not long after they started dating—and she was still falling. Not just because of the things he did or said, but the intense way he looked at her, following her every move. He wanted to spend all of his free time with her and she had no problem with it.

Abruptly, her daydreaming ended when Talise's coworker nudged her. She blinked. Evidently, she had once again drifted off.

"Are you feeling okay?" Kendall McCray asked with a curious frown.

"Yep," Talise lied, as she struggled to suppress a bout of nausea.

Chapter Five

*L*ate Monday evening, Ace shook his head as his beloved Boston Harbor faded from view. To avoid seeing Talise at the airport, he purposely booked a later flight on American Airlines. So despite what he told his mother, his bags didn't fly free.

Not an emotional man, Ace took a deep breath to keep from mourning the loss of those things dear to his heart. Swallowing hard, he whispered goodbye to the seven-time Major League Baseball World Series Champion Red Sox, the National Hockey League World Champion Boston Bruins, the National Basketball Association World Champs Boston Celtics, and so many other places and things he would miss.

At the very least, he was representing Beantown by wearing his Red Sox jersey. Ace's mind went to this coming fall when he wouldn't be there to attend one of the New England Patriots' home games at Gillette Stadium. Hopefully, they were on the St. Louis Rams' schedule to play.

Lastly, he would miss the conniving Ms. Talise Rogers. In the past, Ace had faced guns, survived knife attacks, and spent extended stays in a couple of Boston area jails, but this present situation was foreign to him. Leave it to a gorgeous woman to cause him to run scared out of town. His name might as well be Samson.

Ace exhaled and shook his head at the flight attendant offering drinks. It was Talise's fault that he had to take these drastic measures. He guessed she hadn't heard the rumor that no woman would ever claim this Jamieson man. She might as well dispense with her phantom pregnancy. Her plan to trap him backfired.

With her looks, smarts, and personality, Talise could find another sucker and start the game over. Either she was that good or he'd been too gullible. He had given her the benefit of the doubt because she was possibly the "one," but she blew it, trying to snag him.

As with all the others, Ace wasn't bluffing. He was voluntarily entering into the MIAB program. Unlike a person in the Witness Protection Plan, who always had to watch his back, he didn't have a care in the world as part of the elite Missing in Action Brother club. Ace closed his eyes and reclined his seat.

By the time his plane landed in St. Louis two and a half hours later, he was restless. While dozing, he dreamt he was a father of twenty children. That would have broken his old man's record of the eleven that he knew about.

"Whew," he commented to himself.

Shaking off the nightmare, Ace regained his composure before disembarking the plane. As he strolled through Lambert Airport, he commanded the attention of every woman who made eye contact.

When he approached the baggage claim area, Kidd was leaning up against the wall with his arms folded. His lips curled with a hint of a smile, but his stare was menacing.

Both brothers were buffed, but Kidd had thickened since his marriage to Eva Savoy two years ago. Standing by his side, his wife was all smiles and waves. Eva was pretty, but Talise was stunning.

Within an arm's reach, Kidd engulfed Ace in a bear hug. His brother's grip was as if it had been ten years since they last saw each other instead of six months. Height-for-height and muscle-for-muscle, it was a duel of strength.

"Break it up." Eva separated them before either brother could declare a winner. She swatted at Kidd before giving Ace a welcoming hug. "I'm glad you're here."

"Finally. I can't believe it took a woman to get you here." Kidd barked out, adding a laugh that caught the attention of several nearby passengers. Eva shushed him.

—⁓—

Tuesday, Wednesday, Thursday. Ace sat behind his desk in his spacious new office. He checked his cell phone for the third time—nothing. Talise's appointment with the doctor was sometime that day. Would she tell him the truth if she wasn't pregnant? When her theatrics tugged at his emotions, it bothered him, yet he restrained himself from returning her calls.

Feigning she was scared and worried, Talise had asked him to call her. "I just need to hear your voice," her message had said. Since then, there had been nothing. No more texts or voice messages. Her absence was foreign to him after four months of exclusive dating.

Ace wanted to reach out to her, but he had to break off their relationship cold turkey. He had hoped settling in as a senior accountant at Healthcare Concepts' corporate office would be an adequate distraction. As it turned out, keeping busy worked for his mental faculties, but his heart was empty.

After only a few days, Ace was close to finishing his initial project. Already, he was the center of the office gossip and wore the label "smart and sexy." Undeniably, the variety of attractive female coworkers made a man want to come to work in the mornings. What a selection, with a number of flavors to choose from: Latina, Black, White, Asian, or tantalizing blends.

One would think the beauties would keep his mind from drifting back to Talise. To date, Ace had turned down a lunch offer, a happy hour invitation, and a home-cooked meal. He got his fill of home cooking at Kidd's, and he could go to a sports bar alone to get smashed. As for lunch, he wasn't playing into that so soon.

Later that evening at Kidd's house, he tried to unwind. His transition had gone rather smoothly. The day after Ace arrived, he had settled into his brother's spare bedroom without a hitch.

"It's so good to have you finally move here with your brother," Eva told him. "Make yourself at home. We'll respect your privacy, but a word of wisdom. If any unpleasant odors seep from under your door, smelling like leftovers or unattended clothes, I'm busting in. When I house clean, things sometimes wind up missing," she said, smiling innocently.

His brother had already warned him that Eva was a neat freak. "Word to the wise," Kidd mouthed, standing behind his wife.

An hour or so later, things were cool. Kidd was yelling at St. Louis Cardinals' pitcher Adam Wainwright to change up his swing. Eva seemed to ignore the ruckus, disappearing into the lower level to her hobby room. For some reason, she collected bridal magazines. Did somebody need to tell the woman her wedding was over? Ace didn't even want to know the story behind that one.

The next thing Ace knew, Kidd suddenly leaped from the sofa. He was poised to run toward the flat screen television and coax Wainwright to throw a fast ball and end the dragged out inning. Ace couldn't care less about the Redbirds. His mind drifted to the time he took Talise to the Red Sox's first game of the season. They had dressed alike in the hometown gear.

Why did his day always begin and end with thoughts of her? She couldn't be pregnant. Ace Jamieson always protected himself.

Chapter Six

*F*riday morning, Talise woke at the usual time as though she were going to work. The previous night, she and her sister, Sinclaire, had exchanged sporadic emails.

Sinclaire: *I've been fasting and praying all day for God's will in your situation. So, what did your doctor say?* Nine hours ahead, her sister had sent the message at six o'clock in the morning United Arab Emigrates Time Zone.

Talise: *She rescheduled my appointment until tomorrow, Friday.* Talise had replied hours later when she had a chance to log on to her computer.

Sinclaire: *What! Sigh. Well, I'll keep praying. A person could only fast so long in this desert heat. I won't have time to Skype tonight. Here's a short prayer: O Father, in the Name of Jesus, only You are in control of our lives. Help my sister to trust in You. Regardless of the outcome, let her draw closer to You, Lord. Give her peace, comfort, and forgiveness. Amen. Love you, Sis. Email me as soon as you find out. Claire.*

Although they both shortened their names at times, her sister didn't like to be called Sin, saying it was too creepy. So, other than

Sinclaire, she only answered to Claire.

Forgiveness. Talise's eyes lingered on the word. "Yes, Lord, I know sleeping with a man who isn't my husband is against Your edict. And I know because everybody is doing it isn't an excuse, but somewhere down the road I lost my conviction about it, which is why I'm in this mental torture now. I know it's too late, but Lord Jesus, I'm sorry."

I did not die on the cross to condemn you for your sins, but to save you from the payout of sin, God spoke to Talise's heart. Under her sister's strong influence, Talise had learned quite a bit about salvation and everyone's need for it.

"Thank you, Jesus," she whispered. Gathering a deep breath, Talise fought off a nervous feeling. As she went about dressing, she noticed her breasts seemed a little tender. Wondering about that only added to her anxiety. All she wanted was the time to fast forward, but it was still two hours before her doctor's appointment. It seemed like an eternity.

By the time she finished cooking a bowl of oatmeal for breakfast, she had lost her appetite. Too restless to read a magazine or watch TV, instead she chose to sit and stare out the window. It was a comfortable June day and people seemed carefree as they strolled to one of the surrounding universities, commuted to work, or simply enjoyed the day off.

She quickly tired of the mindless tasks to stay occupied around the apartment and finally gave up. Deciding to leave, it wouldn't hurt if she was a half an hour or more early. So far this morning, Talise had taken three trips to the bathroom. On her last one, she applied her makeup, but it barely camouflaged the dark circles under her eyes. Her flawless skin was beginning to mar from the stress.

Getting in her car, she drove to Dr. Sherman's office on Dartmouth for the moment of truth. The good thing was her doctor stayed on schedule. The bad news was the waiting room was crowded. Talise felt out of place surrounded by other women who were in various stages of their pregnancies. Most wore wedding rings; a few spouses or boyfriends tagged along.

Talise was alone and her heart ached. She longed for Ace to be by her side, holding her hand. But she hadn't heard from him all week, even after she relaxed her rule and left a couple of pleading messages. This wasn't a good sign. He always returned her calls. Maybe he was sending her a message; she feared what his silence meant.

The waiting room was painted in cheerful colors. With a play area set up in the corner, a few busy toddlers were dismantling a wall of building blocks. Finally, two other women entered who didn't have on wedding rings. Ironically, they both wore blank expressions. Did hers mirror theirs?

Right on schedule, at exactly quarter past eleven, Talise's name was called. With her blood pressure checked and temperature taken, the nurse went through a list of questions, including the best estimate of the first day of her last period. After handing the nurse her urine sample, Talise sat on the examining table. As she waited for her results, she prayed for strength.

It wasn't long before Dr. Sherman walked in with a faint smile. "Congratulations, you're six weeks pregnant."

Unable to hold back her emotions, the floodgates opened. Talise burst into tears. She jumped off the table and hurried over to the trash can where she threw up. Her doctor, rubbing her back, assisted her to the sink where Talise rinsed out her mouth and patted cold water on her face.

Back on the examining table, she covered her face with her hands in shame. With a box of tissues in one hand, Dr. Sherman wrapped her arm around Talise's shoulders and squeezed gently. "Everything is going to be all right. Is the father supportive?"

Talise couldn't make eye contact yet. She shook her head and began to bawl again. Her life status had instantly changed. Taking a deep breath only triggered another round of tears. After a hiccup or two, she strained her voice and managed to say, "I don't know."

The room took on an eerie silence and time seemed to freeze. When a few more moments passed, Talise sniffed and was able to wipe her eyes with a tissue. Finally, she looked at Dr. Sherman, who was waiting patiently.

"If you want to keep your baby, I'll go over the regimen of proper diet and exercise and prescribe your prenatal vitamins." Massaging Talise's back, her doctor continued. "On the other hand, if you're not ready to become a single parent, you can elect to have an abortion. I don't perform them, but there are options that don't require an invasive procedure or overnight stay. We can terminate it without anyone knowing besides you and me."

Sinclaire would know and God knew.

"Your lifestyle won't have to miss a heartbeat."

It? She heard the doctor refer to her baby. Does the child have a heartbeat? Talise groaned when she thought about her carefree lifestyle. Someone had to *pay* for her carelessness, either her or the baby—*it.*

Dr. Sherman continued. "Why don't you think about it for a couple of days and then call the office with your decision. We'll proceed from there."

Nodding, Talise was numb as she waited for the doctor to close the door. She suspected she was pregnant, and now it had been verified. Now what? Ace was missing in action. Talise toyed with the doctor's questions as she passed through the waiting room and walked out the door.

The sun was blinding when she stepped outside. Slipping on her sunglasses, her body absorbed the warmth. The weather was far too enjoyable even for her gloomy mood. She seemed lost in space, out of place—and forgotten.

Feeling as if she was the only person standing on the face of the earth whose life was in disarray, she leaned against the building momentarily. Talise was in a state of shock; she watched people passing by, but saw no one.

Abortion. Was it an option for her? Could she go through with it? Did she hate Ace so much that she could destroy what they created?

"Mom, I wish you were here. My baby and I would want for nothing," she whispered. Somehow she doubted whether her father's new wife, Donna, would be as understanding. She sighed at her thoughts and spoke aloud, "You wouldn't like her, Mom, but Dad seems happy. Sinclaire and I know you would've wanted that."

After ignoring a bystander's curious gaze—probably wanting to know who she was talking with—Talise snapped out of it. Clearly, she wasn't ready to return home yet. Afraid of feeling caged and eventually crying the day away, she headed to her car and added more change to the meter.

In her present state, it would be better to be around people. So Talise looked for a bookstore, coffee shop, any public place where she could just think. Walking aimlessly down the street, she rolled the word "abortion" around in her head. Sinclaire's threat immediately came to mind.

"Don't do anything you'll regret later. God forgives, if we ask," Sinclaire had said during a recent Skype conversation.

"Even if I'll regret having a child out of wedlock, being a single parent, and poor?" she had asked her sister.

"I'll risk a dishonorable discharge to come home and help take care of you and my niece or nephew. I mean it. Children are so innocent, even when we aren't. Don't discard them like some people in the Old Testament. They burned their babies as a sacrifice to their idol gods. Children have a purpose. They have a way of teaching us a thing or two," Sinclaire pleaded and then smiled reassuringly before she had to sign off.

Now Talise would have to deliver the official news to Sinclaire. This was way too much for her to absorb and, before she did anything, she needed a drink to dull the pain. Only a social drinker, usually with Ace, she had to tell him there was indeed a baby. Yeah. He needed to know, but first, she needed a stiff drink.

At the corner of Dartmouth and Stuart Streets, she spotted her so-called daytime tavern—Starbucks—and headed that way. Once inside, her stomach growled as she scanned the menu.

"May I help you?" a young man asked, giving Talise a bold and appreciative sweep of her body. Doing her best to keep from rolling her eyes, she ordered, "A Grande Yukon. And please make that with three extra shots of Espresso."

The guy's eyes widened. "Whoa. You must be a serious coffee drinker."

When he gave her the total, Talise handed over the money. While the barista prepared the drink, he tried and failed to coax her into small talk. Finished, he slid the cup in front of her. "To the pretty lady."

"To the pregnant lady," she mumbled under her breath, saluted him with her cup, and walked away. Finding a seat in the corner, Talise said grace. After she ended with an Amen, her hands remained locked in a praying position.

Pregnant. She repeated the word in her mind while taking a sip and wishing she could get drunk on coffee. Who knows? She might get a hangover from the caffeine. Her eyes misted as she stared out the window.

"Jesus, I messed up, didn't I? I'm so sorry," she spoke softly. Closing her eyes, Talise nonverbally confessed what her heart and mind already knew. She would have her baby.

As her lids fluttered open, she stole a deep breath and took another sip. The coffee was strong, just as she preferred it. But would the caffeine harm her baby? She frowned, not knowing the answer. With that thought in her mind, Talise pushed her cup to the side. Before heading home, she would stop at a bookstore and buy some baby books. She was going to be a mother.

When should she begin her round of calls? "I should make a list," she said aloud. Why did she feel like she'd be making death notifications to the next of kin, as though her life was over?

First, of course, she'd tell Sinclaire, the person closest to her. Her sister was waiting anxiously to hear the verdict. Talise would email her as soon as she returned home. Next, she'd tell her dad. She couldn't help but wonder how he would take the news. After that, Talise would have to inform her company and confide in a few close coworkers at the airport. She wanted to hold off on that as long as possible. However, Gabrielle Dupree, her immediate supervisor, came to mind.

Talise had learned when she first entered the workforce after college to watch her back. Every job had friends, enemies, and "frienemies." Observing a few incidents involving various coworkers prompted her to keep people out of her private life. But it was something about Gabrielle that oozed confidence and peace, no matter what went down at work. She was a part of management Talise knew she could trust.

Then, of course, she would have to tell her roommate and Sasha at the salon. Lois should probably know soon, considering she would have to put up with her regurgitations and mood swings.

Oh yeah, the father. *Ace.* As much as she wanted him to know, he probably wouldn't answer if she called him—again. Talise hadn't heard from him since the night he walked out of her apartment—possibly her life.

With too many other issues going on in her body and head at the moment, she wouldn't allow herself to think about him right then. There was no hurry. Soon enough they would have a conversation, either in person, over the phone, or by pony express, with his cousin riding on the horse to deliver the telegram.

On the drive home, Talise's thoughts were focused solely on the baby's father. Ace had never seen her mad. There had never been a cause for it, but Talise planned to unload her mind, in particular, for him not returning her calls or checking up on her.

When Talise arrived back at her apartment, she headed straight for her laptop. Not being able to hold the news until she and Sinclaire could have a Skype chat, she logged on to her email account. In the subject line, she entered, It's official. Then Talise proceeded to type the message, confirming that her suspicions were true. Dr. Sherman told her she was six weeks along.

Talise ended the message, asking Sinclaire to email her as soon as possible. She wanted them to Skype and was looking forward to seeing her sister's face. Her faith needed a boost so that she could actually make it through this pregnancy.

Chapter Seven

*A*ce was number three on the hit list. As customary on Sunday evenings, Sandra called and spoke with her daughter-in-law first, and then Kidd.

Since he hadn't heard an official word from Talise, he concluded the pregnancy thing had been a bluff. He took a sigh of relief and then became agitated that he'd left Beantown in vain.

After her preliminary questions about his new job, health, and general adjustments, Sandra ruined the conversation with a recap of her pastor's sermon. It was becoming another Sunday tradition. Before she started in on him, he had been lounging on the deck without a care in the world.

"I hope you'll go to church with your brother and Eva, since I couldn't get you to go with me. God has a plan that includes you, Aaron."

How many times had Ace heard his mother say that? When Jesus saved her when he was a little boy, Sandra always said God bestowed on her every blessing and gift He promised. Ace was never sure what that meant and how it was supposed to affect him.

"I've got my Bible right here. I'll read it to you from Acts 2:8–40." He heard Sandra flipping some pages. "It was so soul-stirring," she added.

Slowly exhaling, Ace braced himself for her sermonette. One thing he did not do or like to see was a mother being disrespected, so he begrudgingly listened. While waiting for Sandra to begin, he remembered a time when he was barely a teenager. Growing up, he was tall and thick enough to intimidate anyone. Ace had gotten into a fight with his best friend, Quinton Sage, over a girl.

When his friend's mother intervened and broke up the fight, Quinton cursed her out until she cried. Up until that point, Ace didn't know that Black women took such disrespect from their children. His mother didn't. She put the fear of God in him and a belt on his behind at an early age.

Ace would have won the fight had Mrs. Sage let it continue. After that, she banned him from her house because he bloodied her son's nose.

"Are you listening?" Sandra broke into his reverie. She had the sweetest voice, even when she was stern.

"Yes."

One son down, one more to go . . . She read all forty verses, ending with "'*And you will receive the gift of the Holy Spirit.*'"

Sandra paused a moment to reflect on what she had just read and then addressed him. "I'm proud of you, son. You're a late bloomer, but you've matured over the past . . ."

Tuning out his mother again, Ace could thank his brother for this torture. With Kidd surrendering to Jesus, Ace had practically become a marked man in his family.

Just then his cell phone vibrated, indicating a ringtone was moments away. The sound quickly made him grin, literally saving him from further recap of his mom's Bible lesson. Although he didn't recognize the 617 area code number, it gave him an out. For good measure, he made sure his mother could hear it.

"I've got to take this, Mom. Talk to you later."

"I love you, Aaron," Sandra said, hurrying off the phone before her son could reply.

He answered just before the call went to voice mail. "Hello."

"Ace, it's Talise."

His body tensed. Ace's heart pounded and his deodorant failed. It took three seconds for Talise to discombobulate him. Cleverly, she had used an unrecognizable number to get to him. He should have known she would pull something like that since she was so conniving.

Maybe he should call his mother back and let her finish the sermonette . . . anything but talk to a former girlfriend who mercilessly broke his heart.

Act calm. No matter what, don't let her make you feel guilty about not calling, he coaxed himself.

"Hey, how are you?"

"You mean, before I told you I might be pregnant, or after I found out that I'm having a baby?"

Amused by the challenge in her voice, Ace stood from his perch on Kidd's patio and began to pace the backyard.

"Are you going to say something?"

Not really. He cleared his voice. "Are you sure?" When she repeated what the doctor had said, he asked, "So what are you going to do?"

"Don't you mean us?"

"Tay, I did not sign up to be a father."

He felt obligated to give it to her straight. That's when the name calling began. Ace knew she was smart, but he had to commend her on her use of adjectives. Still, he wouldn't be deterred.

"Listen, if you're really pregnant . . ." He paused. It was on the tip of his tongue to ask if it was his. But that would be a low blow, even if she did try to set a trap. "I'm sure you'll make the right decision."

How could he have thought she was different from the others?

"Well, I guess this is a courtesy call." Talise's voice trembled, as she muffled a sniff. "Just know this, Aaron Jamieson: I think you're a coward. But I was the stupid one to think that we loved each other, even if we never said it."

Love? Now that was priceless. His mother drilled into him and Kidd not to swear because no man has the power to fulfill it. But Jesus was his witness. He never loved any of the women he slept with. Well, maybe he shouldn't bring God into this. Still, he had to admit that somehow the word *love* coming from her lips touched him.

Don't fall for it! He warned himself and tuned her out again.

A few times, he had almost been taken by the best of them. There was Janice Dilworth in a top management position. She was also slick. The woman was actually willing to pay him to marry her when, all of a sudden, Janice found out she was pregnant. Unmarried, it could ruin her career.

Ace didn't buy her story either. Nine months after that, he heard through mutual friends, there was no story to tell. As tempting as $50,000 a year would be to become Mr. Dilworth, "The Husband," it wasn't worth it. Ace didn't walk away; rather, he jumped on his motorcycle and sped away.

Talise broke the lull. "I won't bother you again. I won't ask you for a penny," she screamed. Then attempting to calm her voice, she repeated, "Like I said, this was a courtesy call." She whispered a good-bye and hung up.

"Whew. Drama. Why couldn't Tay have been different?" Her tirade was almost enough to make him lock up his libido. Turning around, he headed back into the house, chuckling. "That will never happen."

Chapter Eight

*A*s Talise disconnected, Lois walked through the door of their apartment. Talise couldn't remember the last time she had cursed someone out, probably when she was a teenager. It wasn't her character to lash out at people like that.

"Talise," Lois yelled, as she dumped her keys on some nearby hard surface and kept moving through the apartment.

Without answering, Talise threw her new cell phone on the bed, ran into the bathroom, and locked the door. She turned on the faucet and began to pat cold water on her face. Her nose was swollen and her eyes were puffy.

Looking at her image in the mirror, she was certain her disheveled look would play out over the next nine months. Talise hadn't told Lois yet, but she knew she couldn't hold out too long. After all, they shared the same living space.

At the moment, she needed to regroup. Contrary to her intentions, she didn't push Ace to the bottom of the list and broke the news to him sooner than planned. Now it was a regretful decision. Thinking back to their conversation, Talise wasn't proud of the names she called him, but his nonchalant attitude irked her.

"Talise," Lois repeated again from the other side of the bathroom door.

"Just a minute." That was a lie. She needed longer than a minute to regain her dignity. Without actually saying the word, Ace had basically called her a slut. *God, why was I so stupid?*

"Are you okay?" Lois asked, now knocking on the door.

"Yeah."

"Girl, what's wrong? Unless you're polluting the air in there, open up. I heard you run into the bathroom when I came through the front door."

This would be another moment of truth. Besides Sinclaire knowing, and now Ace, Lois might as well be next to find out about her baby. Turning the lock, Talise cracked the door open. Lois shrieked when she took one look at her face.

"What's going on with you? Spill it! What happened? Did someone die? Oh, God, your sister. She didn't get hurt, did she?" Lois grabbed her by the arm and dragged Talise out of the bathroom.

"Sinclaire is fine, but I'm pregnant," she blurted it out, hurried to her bed, and collapsed.

Lois froze with her mouth hanging open. She blinked and then formed an "O" with her lips, but no words came out. Her roommate had the most comical expressions. Talise would have laughed at her dumbstruck look, but this wasn't the time and she didn't have the energy.

"What did Ace say? Is he happy?" She flopped down on the foot of the bed. "When did you find out? How far along—"

The girl had a Rolodex of questions.

Taking a deep breath, Talise gathered her strength to answer. She was sure to hear the questions again from others. "Ace basically said, 'See ya.' He's definitely not happy. I found out on Friday. My baby is six weeks along. I'm due sometime in January."

Crossing her legs, Lois counted on her fingers. "What do you mean Ace isn't happy?" She slanted her head. "What does 'he's definitely not happy' mean?"

Lois paused. "Okay, I'll let you slide for not telling me two days ago. But let's revisit questions one and two because I'm not feeling this abbreviated version."

"The truth is, Lois, I'm on my own." Talise sniffed. Would she ever get used to saying that? "He acted like he didn't believe me, as if I'm making this up. Why would I do that? Right before you came in, his callousness triggered the ghetto somewhere in my family tree to emerge. I think I created some new curse words while I chewed him out."

"Good for you." Lois bowled over laughing, and Talise chuckled until she started laughing too. Then wiping at a tear, her expression became serious.

"I know Ace doesn't think the baby's not his?"

The question pricked at Talise's heart. "He didn't say it, but sometimes silence is golden."

Lois sprang from the bed, almost twisting her ankle on her stilettos. Once she steadied herself, she wagged her finger. "No man is going to call you a tramp, whether he verbalized it or not. I can't believe Ace! I thought that man loved you. The jerk!"

She bit her lip and continued her line of questioning. "Okay, girlfriend, how do you want to handle this? Hit-and-run, broken bones, what? It's your choice, or all of the above. Say the word and I'm on it. Your footprints on his backside, or it could be both of ours, you call it. I'm speechless."

"I hadn't noticed," Talise attempted to joke.

Lois was geared up. "This is my fault. I never mentioned to Cameron that my roommate was new to the area. It was his idea for us to set you up with Ace. Oooh, the nerve . . ." Lois practically growled, as she balled her hands into fists.

When it appeared that she was on the verge of tears, Talise became the comforter. "You had no way of knowing when you introduced me to him how things would turn out. I fell in love with Ace, although I never told him. He protected himself and I protected myself . . ." God spoke. *Adam and Eve couldn't cover their nakedness. Neither can you hind our sins from My eyes.*

"But the woman always gets caught holding the bag, and the man walks away without a care in the world," Lois added.

Practically ignoring her friend momentarily, her conscience was cutting her to the core. Throwing her hands up in the air, Talise shrugged. "What better time to turn to God, but when I'm in trouble." She sighed in disgust with herself.

"I have thirty-four weeks to prepare for a little one. That's where I need to focus. Ace won't have to worry about any baby's mama drama from me."

"Can I borrow your drama? When I didn't see Ace this week, I didn't think anything of it." Lois pulled her iPhone out of the case hooked onto her belt.

"Who are you calling?"

"Cameron. I'm going to give him a piece of my mind, your mind, and then . . ."

Lifting her hand, Talise was drained from this bout of theatrics. "Let it go, Lois. I can do this. I would prefer to be married to a man who loved me before I had a baby. But this is the bed I created, so now it's time for me to wash the sheets and make it up. Seriously, Lois, let it go."

"Sure," she said with a sly grin. Somehow, Talise didn't believe her.

Chapter Nine

*I*t had been almost a week since Ace gave Talise the cold shoulder. When it came to women, he usually terminated the breakup in a more genteel and polished manner, unlike the heartless jerk he had portrayed to Talise.

The woman had no idea how she crushed him with her lie. If Talise had only known that he was on the verge of contemplating the possibility of saying those three little words, then she would have realized there was no need for her to set a trap. He'd given it a lot of thought. Of the many women he had dated, Talise most definitely could have been the "one." Ace could thank his mother's prayers for keeping him from the clutches of yet another woman.

It was late when he finally arrived in Kidd's neck of the woods of Old Town Florissant. After a long day at the downtown office, he was glad to be on their doorstep. Turning his key into the lock, Ace deactivated the alarm.

The house was quiet as he shut the door and walked into the living room. Kidd and Eva worked at the same affluent Garden Chateau Nursing Facility. No doubt, the pair was together someplace.

Ace would have never guessed his older brother would wind up with a job in a nursing home. According to Kidd, they were paying him big money to boss people around as the resident liaison. Of course, his authority stopped at his wife, Eva, who was an LPN.

The remnants of a home-cooked meal lingered in the air. He headed to his bedroom to change. Grinning, Ace shook his head. His brother definitely got himself a winner. Eva was sweet, nice-looking, and the sister could cook.

Placing his laptop on the bed alongside the folders he brought home from work, Ace whipped his tie from around his neck and unbuttoned his shirt. He twirled them both across the room, but they missed their mark of the chair. Sitting on the bed, he removed his shoes, rolled off his socks, and carefully placed them on the floor by his side. When it came to his footwear, it was a serious matter. Comfort was his goal.

Ace stood up with his hands resting on his waist and surveyed the guest room. It was a mess. Uncharacteristic for him, but that's what happens when you rush in from out of town one night and dive into a new job the next day. Maybe this weekend, he would tidy up before Eva saw it and made good on her threat.

He padded his bare feet across the cool hardwood floor to the even cooler marble tile in the kitchen. His stomach growled. The table was already set, which seemed to be one of Eva's obsessions whether she cooked or served carryout. Ace reached for a plate and walked to the stove.

Lifting the lids, he moaned. "Sautéed vegetables, squash, zucchini, and red peppers. Hmm-mm." Next, he uncovered a pan that revealed some sort of pasta dish and scooped a hefty portion onto his plate. As he added the vegetables alongside, he felt the oven still warm against his leg. Knowing there was more to enjoy inside, Ace bent and opened the door to discover rolls and meatloaf. It didn't even cross his mind to be shy about his serving portions.

At the table, he blessed his food then crammed some vegetables into his mouth. Realizing he forgot something to drink, Ace got up to get a tall glass of water to quench his thirst. When he glanced around the kitchen, he noted more changes Eva had made to Kidd's former bachelor three-bedroom house. His wife simply had a flair for decorating.

Whenever he came to visit his brother during the past two years, there was always something new Eva had done. Whether it was wallpapering or adding more furniture, her creativity was reflected everywhere. This time, it was the colorful cookware and gadgets that complemented the kitchen decor.

Ace quickly lost interest in his surroundings when an image of Talise came to mind. It was the night she had orchestrated a candlelight dinner and the last time he'd seen her face. She looked ravishing and had prepared his favorite—twice-baked potatoes.

Shaking his head, he attempted to erase the memories. He didn't want to think about the four months they shared: the concerts they attended, the New York weekend getaways, or the salsa lessons they took to dance the night away at Havana Saturdays. That was her roommate's favorite spot.

When he finished his meal, Ace cleared the area, rinsed the dishes, and placed them in the dishwasher. The sun was about to set and the temperature had cooled, beckoning him to the backyard deck. It was a showcase for entertaining with its inviting outdoor furniture, movable overhanging umbrella, and strategically placed plants and flowers. His favorite spot, it was like getting lost in a botanical garden.

Getting comfortable in a recliner, Ace closed his eyes and allowed his food to settle. Before it got too dark, he would go jogging through the neighborhood. Maybe Kidd would be back in time and want to tag along. Without his running buddy, Cameron, and . . . his girl, Talise, he was lonely and restless.

When Ace informed his cousin that he was finally accepting the opening in St. Louis, he purposely got off the phone before Cameron could ask questions about him and Talise. Since his arrival in town, he had definitely avoided further discussions with Cameron.

As he tried to center himself, Ace couldn't help but reflect on his current state of being. In the back of his mind, he could hear his mother's words. *This too shall pass,* she would always say when trouble reared its ugly head.

Where were Kidd and Eva anyway? They usually called or left a note with their whereabouts, as if Ace needed babysitting. At the moment, he would welcome a little company.

Alone with his thoughts, he was restless and needed to find somewhere to get into trouble. Maybe he would take a ride as a way to entertain himself. His rental car was equipped with GPS. Besides, he had visited enough times to the point he wasn't a stranger to St. Louis.

Suddenly smiling, he missed being behind the wheel of his fully loaded Charger. Chuckling over distant memories of his prized possession, Ace closed his eyes. No sooner than he had drifted into a peaceful slumber, someone opened the kitchen screen door and let it slam shut. With one eye open, he saw Kidd standing over him with a wide, silly grin.

"Hey, bro, guess what?" Kidd didn't look like he had the patience for Ace to guess. He grabbed a nearby chair and dragged it closer to Ace.

"I'm going to have a baby!" Kidd proudly announced, followed by a hearty laugh. "I mean, Eva is pregnant and we're going to have a baby! I'm going to be a father . . . and a better one than our old man, Sam."

Ace couldn't connect with Kidd's ecstasy. As a matter of fact, he might be having an allergic reaction to the word "pregnant." A sudden queasiness overpowered him that made him feel uncontrollably nauseated. Leaping from his recliner, Ace bumped Kidd out of the way and barely made it to the end of the deck. Promptly, he threw up what seemed to be breakfast, lunch, and dinner.

Kidd hesitantly came to his side. "Man, you okay? I don't want you getting Eva sick."

Resting his elbows on the rail, Ace panted to catch his breath. Since when did he develop a nervous stomach? He knew he hadn't caught a virus. He was fine before his brother dropped that bomb on him. Could it be possible that he escaped a so-called pregnant woman only to be trapped inside a house with another one? The irony of it all.

"Ah, no, I'm fine. I think I may have gotten ahold of some bad food," he said, offering a poor excuse.

"I know you're not blaming my wife's cooking," Kidd said in an accusatory voice.

No, I'm blaming every pregnant woman in the world right now.

Chapter Ten

*B*y the end of the week, Talise had notified her close circle—Sinclaire and Lois—of her condition. Although both women fully supported her, she knew they were concerned about her becoming a single parent. Only Ace could change that status, but he wasn't offering. After his desertion, Talise would have some serious reservations about accepting a proposal from him.

Next had been the dreaded call home to her father and Donna. She rated their response as mixed, but nonetheless it had to be done.

"Hi, Daddy," Talise had said, taking deep breaths to keep her voice steady.

"'Bout time you called your old man," Frederick teased. "I didn't recognize this number. So how's my baby girl?"

She smiled at his warm greeting until she heard his wife's voice—she couldn't bring herself to say stepmother—in the background. "You're not old, honey," Donna corrected him.

Rolling her eyes, Talise rushed her announcement. "Well, Dad, keep this number. I lost my other cell phone, so I changed carriers and upgraded with a better plan," she babbled. Then swallowing, she let it out. "The reason why I'm calling is to tell you that your baby girl is going to have a baby."

Silence.

"What's wrong, dear?" Donna asked from nearby. His facial expression must have spoken volumes.

Frederick cleared his throat and stuttered, "A baby? When?" He paused then fired off a series of demanding questions. "Who is he? Did he ask you to marry him? What does he do for a living? Can he take care of you?"

Tears began to trickle down Talise's cheeks, but she managed to say, "My baby's due sometime toward the end of January and . . ." She gritted her teeth before mumbling, "We broke up." Ace actually walked away from her, but stating *we* broke up left her with some dignity.

"Broke up?" he repeated and then mumbled some choice words. "Well, whatever is broken, he'd better fix it before my grandchild gets here. If that had been your mother, I would have married her in a blink of an eye. I'm not that old where I can't knock some sense into him."

Talise's heart warmed at her father's possessiveness. She felt loved and greatly needed that feeling at the moment. "Daddy, we're talking about your grandchild's father." *An absentee father.*

"A broken leg, foot, jaw, or arm never killed a man," he said with venom in his voice. He sighed as Donna seemed to scold him for his foolish talk.

"I'm serious, baby. He'd better get his act together and be a man. Still, I'm here for you and the baby. Whatever you need, you've got it. You can always come back home so Donna and I can take care of you. I can't believe I'm going to be a grandpa," he said with such awe.

There was a muffled sound and then Donna came on the line. "Talise, I'm disappointed . . . in that young man and your situation. I'm sure your mother would be too. Of course, we'll help and send money to you every month until you can get on your feet."

Donna had already said enough, but as usual, she wasn't finished.

"Perhaps that young man will provide for his child. It's a shame the jams couples find themselves in today. There's all kind of protection on the market. He does believe it's his—"

"I'll call Daddy back later. goodbye, Donna," Talise whispered and hung up. Her heart could only take so many stab wounds before it was completely destroyed. It was clear what Donna thought of her "situation."

How had *she* trapped Frederick Rogers? Talise would never know. Her father seemed totally oblivious to Donna's chilled behavior toward his daughters.

Pregnant or not, Talise could never marry a man if he was controlling like Donna. Reality set in. Of course, that "if" was dependent upon whether a man wanted her with another man's child in tow.

By ten o'clock on Friday night, Talise was exhausted. She had worked her day job and started taking a few clients on Friday evenings. She seldom worked double duty, but without Ace in her life, she had free time now. Plus, her morning sickness had seemed to shift to night nausea.

Desperately trying not to think about Ace, Talise wondered where he was and what he was doing. Did he think about her, or was she already forgotten? She was confused about his complex behavior that Friday night over dinner when she told him of her suspected condition. Looking back, that fateful night seemed like a lifetime ago.

What would be the reason she would explain to her child why his or her parents weren't together? Talise didn't even have closure, so how could she have an answer. If she could have done things differently, what would that have been: never moved to Boston, never agreed to a blind date, or never having slept with Ace? *Bingo.*

Her mind drifted to when Ace had taken her to Velvets Friday at the Red Fez on Washington. The more women tried to get his attention, the more he was determined to focus on her. That night the chemistry between them started to sizzle. They partied hard and she had gotten drunk, but Ace didn't take advantage of her.

Then there was the night he suggested they have a late-night picnic on Boston Common. With a blanket, carryout dinners, and music downloaded to his iPhone, they had set out to enjoy the unseasonably warm temperatures in the month of April. That night had been like magic under the stars.

"Tay, I want you to know my relationship with you isn't like the others I've had," Ace had said with feigned sincerity. "You're special to me . . ."

Her eyes misted now. She sniffed to fight back the tears. What was his definition of special?

Relaxing on the front steps outside her apartment building, Talise shivered in the breeze. She loved Boston's summer nights. With her legs crossed, she sipped on a tall cup of grape juice. Since the baby book said to eat frequent small meals and healthy snacks, her coffee and soda binges had been replaced with juices, water, and milk.

Shifting her body, Talise nodded at a few neighbors as they entered or exited the building. She didn't know most of their names but recognized a few faces. After about an hour of people-watching and taking in the warm air, her relaxed state was beginning to lull her to sleep.

Tomorrow she had eight clients despite working extra time that evening. Sunday would start another work week at the airport. If Talise was going to be a single parent, she might as well get used to providing for two people.

It was getting late. She needed to climb the three flights of stairs to shower and go to bed but kept delaying the inevitable.

"How am I going to be able to stand on my feet all day at both jobs when the baby gets bigger?"

Alone back in her apartment, Talise wished she had someone to keep her company. Lois kept her social calendar full and wouldn't return any time soon from a happy hour with her colleagues.

She longed to talk with Sinclaire, but her sister's schedule still wasn't permitting her time to Skype lately. Talise really could use some positive words of encouragement right about now. Firing off a quick email to Sinclaire, she hoped to coordinate a Skype video chat sometime in the near future. *I just need to see your face a little more right now and hear you pray for me. I miss and love you, Talise.* She hoped her sister would respond soon.

A few minutes later, while she was taking a shower, the only thing on her mind was her new predicament.

"Time for moping is officially over," she told herself. However, her declaration wasn't working. The more she gave herself a pep talk, the more depressed she became. But that didn't stop her from trying.

Talise sniffed as she reflected on her ancestors. Some time ago, her father taught her that the Rogers women were strong and determined. Surely they had faced discrimination yet still thrived in their education achievements and throughout the difficult challenges that came their way. Frederick also pointed out that she had similar personality traits. As Talise grew older, he constantly remarked that her physical features looked more like his side of the family.

On Talise's mother's side, the Skinners were descendants of enslaved and violated people, but the women survived. Because of their adverse circumstances, they developed special gifts on how to hold the pieces of their family tighter. According to their dad, hands down, Sinclaire resembled that side of the family in looks and mannerisms.

Talise recalled the brief conversation she had with her father's wife. Donna was right when she stated her mother would be disappointed. But Marilyn would comfort her daughter in the most loving way possible. She could almost hear her mom saying, "What's done is done. Repent and conquer the obstacles."

Pausing to dwell on her mother a bit longer made her smile. Talise recalled that Marilyn was also a fashion guru. She believed in looking presentable at all times. "You may be pregnant, but you don't have to look ugly and pregnant," her mom would probably say.

Finishing her shower, she smirked at the conversations that could have been. Talise examined her face in the bathroom mirror. It could use some pampering. How could the adamant Ms. Rogers be found guilty of becoming lax in her own beauty regimen? The subject was something she constantly fussed at her clients to adhere to.

For some reason, she couldn't keep her mind off of her mother. Reflections on special times they'd spent together flooded her thoughts. At the moment, the exercise was proving to be some much needed therapy. Nothing succeeded in getting Marilyn down—nothing and nobody. Drawing on her mother's strength, Talise was beginning to shore up critical support for her battle; her memories seemed to supply the encouragement she craved.

After putting on a cozy pair of pajamas, she slid on her knees to pray. Talise had made a promise to strengthen her relationship with God, and it was time for her to make good on that promise.

At first, she was silent, gathering her thoughts. Once she bowed her head and rested her face on her hands, she began, "Jesus, I know You are the one I've disappointed. Lord, I don't know what is going to happen, so I need Your guidance. Please allow me to have a healthy baby. I'm stressed right now and baffled by Ace's treatment, but shame on me for being the fool. I know it's the reason why I should have waited until I was married."

She paused and shed a few tears. "I've made some bad choices, and I don't know how to find my way. Please place people in my path to help me. Amen."

Before she could get up, Talise thought she heard Sinclaire's voice reminding her to pray for Ace. Humph. Indignant, she was about to say Amen again as emphasis that she was finished praying. But the Lord pricked her heart with words from a verse Sinclaire had recently quoted her in an email. Matthew 6:14: *If you forgive others when they wrong you, I will also forgive you.* Sinclaire was trying to get her to understand that God is all about forgiveness. In order to truly move on, it was important that she forgive Ace.

Forgive him? "Lord, Ace hurt me," she said aloud. "I feel used and very foolish. I'm perplexed and ashamed, a bad role model for my innocent child. Jesus, I do love him, but I love my baby more. I'm not at the point where I feel I can forgive him. I can't . . . but help him, please," she managed to say before ending her prayer the second time.

Getting to her feet, a peaceful feeling came over Talise. She noticed that when she prayed, it brought her some much needed peace. Her thoughts went back to the verse on forgiveness. She would have to read more in the book of Matthew. That's where she would begin; maybe there was something God wanted her to learn from it and He was leading her there.

Before she could do anything else, a sudden, belly-wrenching feeling overcame her. Rubbing her stomach, she made her way into the kitchen. A craving for warm applesauce and bread was all she could think about at the moment.

Twenty minutes later when her stomach was satisfied, Talise went back into her bedroom. She opened several boxes stored on her closet shelf, searching for the Bible Sinclaire had given her four years ago on her twenty-fifth birthday. Once she located the blue leather-bound book, it quickly became a telling sign of her lack of devotion to God. The plastic wrapper had never been broken.

Flipping through the crisp new pages, she began reading at the beginning of the New Testament. The first thing that caught her attention was the mention of the fourteen generations between Abraham and David, and then another fourteen before the house of David was carried away to Babylon. She would have to study that—and then the fourteen generations from David to Christ.

Despite her minimum level of understanding, Talise continued reading until the end of chapter two. That is where the details of Jesus's birth were described.

Why was she prompted to read that passage? There was no comparison between herself and the Virgin Mary. Nor was her child the

Christ who would die on the cross for anybody's blemishes, faults, or sins. Her child was conceived of her sin.

Her mind went back to something else Sinclaire had said to her: children are innocent and they have a purpose. Talise knew He regards little children as precious and protects them from harm.

Closing her Bible and turning off the light, Talise scooted under the cover with a smile. God's Word had given her the pep talk she needed most.

Chapter Eleven

S aturday morning, Talise woke ten minutes before her alarm was set to go off. The sun was already shining brightly outside her bedroom window. "I haven't slept that good in weeks," she said, stretching.

After saying a quick prayer of thanks to God for waking her, Talise got up to start her day. She performed her morning ritual and went into the kitchen to prepare breakfast. Pouring herself a tall glass of milk, she took a banana from the basket on the counter. The baby book recommended adding warm applesauce to a bowl of oatmeal. Glad that she had adopted the tip, the cereal gave her a soothing feeling. Talise felt ready for the day when she put together a healthy lunch and quickly cleaned up her mess.

Humming, she returned to the bathroom and applied her makeup artistically. One might have guessed she was going out on the town instead of to work. Lois strolled into her bedroom and flopped down on Talise's freshly made bed. A few curlers were dangling from her hair. Yawning, she squinted.

Talise ignored her and walked across the room to her closet. Standing in her slip, she returned a black and gold printed dress to the rack. It was the third one she had tried on. Seven weeks pregnant. Soon, none of her dresses or clothes would be flattering.

Noticing the way Talise was fussing over her outfits, Lois asked, "Where are you going, looking so cute?" Her eyes were barely opened. "Don't you have to work at the salon today?"

"Yep. And I want to feel and look pretty. I'm moving on. I have to."

"Good. So did you tell everyone you want to know about the pregnancy?"

"Yep, everyone on my list—you, Sinclaire, my Dad and his wife, and the father of my baby. Oh, and Sasha knows too." She twirled around and walked back into the bathroom, closing the door behind her. The baby book said to expect more frequent trips to the bathroom as waste flushed from her body.

"Good. You don't want to jinx yourself before the end of the trimester. Well, I hope you won't be upset that I added one more person who wasn't on your priority list—Cameron," she spoke louder to make sure Talise heard her through the door.

She didn't believe in jinx. Drying her hands, Talise opened the door. "Why did he need to know? I asked you to stay out of it."

Talise's scolding wasn't convincing to her own ears. Deep down inside, she had hoped Lois would give a Jamieson a piece of her mind— even if he was the wrong one. Maybe Cameron would pass it on to Ace.

"Humph!" Lois lifted her chin. "I did stay out of it—for almost a week. When I didn't see Cameron at the university, I hunted him down. His response was rather surprising after I told him what his sorry cousin had done to you. He was speechless and irate. I've known Cam for years. It was a genuine reaction."

"You mean, Cameron didn't know? I thought he and Ace were close."

"Anyway, he wants the two of you to have lunch—today."

"Why? Didn't you tell the man I have to work? I have eight clients, press-n-curls, relaxers, a few colors, and no telling how many walk-ins. I'll do good to get out the door by four. Five o'clock tops. In hindsight, I don't see how Ace and I were able to go out as much as we did on Saturday evenings."

After Talise slipped into a looser fitting summer dress, her roommate stood and zipped it.

"I don't want to see another Jamieson for the next twenty years, Lois. Thank you very much." She dismissed Cameron's request.

Talise gathered some of the hair products she had at home and dumped them into a tote bag. Then grabbing her lunch and purse, she was about to tell Lois goodbye. But it was already too late, Lois had dozed off. It was her friend's nightlife that left her exhausted. Talise covered her with a throw blanket and left.

—⁓—

Sassy's Salon was located on Mass Ave. It was busy when Talise breezed through the door fifteen minutes later. Most of her clients were students from nearby Berklee College of Music, Northeastern, and BU.

On any given Saturday, juicy gossip entertained the stylists and their clients. Talise would hold off as long as she could before she became the next hot topic. She planned to be very careful about to whom she would reveal her secret. So far, only Sasha knew.

"Was it that fine brother who would sometimes bring you those box lunches?" Sasha whispered. Talise nodded. Sasha shook her head in disgust. "But, no doubt about it, you'll have a pretty baby, even if the father is no good. I thought he was one of the good guys."

"Me too," Talise mumbled and walked to her station.

She kept her lips zipped around her clients, especially the college students. As a university graduate with no husband—or boyfriend—for that matter, here she was pregnant. Somehow Talise felt that she had failed them as a role model. It was always her hope to have the traditional family with marriage first and babies later.

Three hours passed and she was able to grab a snack, along with another much-needed potty break. When she came back to her station, munching on grapes, Priscilla Stanford was waiting in Talise's chair. She was there for her regular blow-dry and flatiron press to her natural hair. The woman wasn't just another client, but more like family. She could be trusted. When Talise told her, Priscilla was in shock.

"Baby, if there is anything I can do, just let me know. I can send plenty of customers your way. I get so many compliments about my hair."

"I appreciate it, Miss Priscilla, but I don't know how I could handle the extra load. Already the odors from the chemicals are starting to make me sick," Talise whispered.

"I guess we'll have to think of something else. It's a shame what he did. If you repent and walk away from temptation, the good Lord will forgive you."

Talise nodded. She hoped it wouldn't take her a lifetime to forgive Ace. Just then, a bell chimed, indicating another customer had entered the salon lobby. Suddenly, conversations ceased. Glancing up, Talise recognized the man Lois held responsible for her woes. Removing his sunglasses proved that the new visitor had the handsome face to back up his athletic body.

"What is he doing here?" Talise sighed.

"I hope he's here to take me home," Priscilla replied and waved her hand in the air. She happened to be the mother of three grown children. "Do you know him?"

"Unfortunately, yes. That's Cameron Jamieson, my ex-boyfriend's cousin."

"Why didn't you say so?" Priscilla rolled her neck. "You want me to jump him? Others carry a knife or a gun, but I've got a thick belt in my purse to protect myself." She patted the oversized shoulder bag sitting in her lap. "And I don't mind dishing it out."

Talise chuckled. "Nah. He's supposed to be the nice one."

Without approaching Talise's station, he walked farther into the waiting area. Some of the clients were quickly painting their faces with eyeshadow, blush, and lip gloss. Without him asking, two women parted an opening for him on the sofa.

Besides their first introduction, Talise really didn't know much about him. According to Lois, he was extremely smart, courteous, and family-oriented. Beneath his macho exterior, she described Cameron as a sweet and patient man with a double degree in engineering. Too bad those good genes hadn't been passed on to his cousin.

Talise finished straightening Priscilla's tresses and then trimmed her ends. She had to focus, as she became incensed that Ace's cousin would suddenly come to see her when he found out about her pregnancy. He hadn't bothered to pick up the phone and check on her or visit her.

With the last flip of a curl in place, Talise brushed the excess hair off Priscilla's cape. Standing, the woman dug through her purse for her wallet. At the same time, she glanced over her shoulder to the waiting area and sneaked a peek.

Turning back, she winked at Talise. "I don't mind giving him a spankin'." Priscilla pointed to the object and laughed. "It would be my pleasure," she said in a sultry tone.

"Hush. Come on. I'll walk you to the register, so I can see what he wants."

"Here's something extra." Priscilla handed Talise a twenty-five dollar tip, ten dollars more than usual. "For the baby," she whispered.

"Thank you."

"What are you doing here?" she asked Cameron, after escorting Priscilla to the lobby.

He stood. "We need to talk."

Talise shook her head. "I'm having a good day. I don't want to mess that up. Plus, I'm busy for at least another hour, maybe longer."

Reclaiming his spot on the sofa between his admirers, Cameron crossed one ankle over his knee. "I'll wait."

Jamiesons. Flustered, Talise headed back to her station to service her next client.

Chapter Twelve

*I*t was after six when Talise left the salon with Cameron. Her hefty tips made the long day worth it. When she and Ace dated, she never scheduled eight clients. That way she could leave by one or two to be with him. Saturday evenings were always theirs.

Cameron checked the time on his phone. "Orinoco's just reopened for dinner. Is that cool?"

Talise shrugged. She was hungry. Anything sounded good at this point. "Lois loves that place."

"I know. It was voted the number one Latin American restaurant," he said with a grin. Walking Talise to her car, he said, "I'll follow you." Cameron then jogged to his Audi, parked not far from the shop.

Shawmut Ave was a comfortable walking distance from Sassy Salon or less than a ten-minute drive from Talise's apartment. She could best describe Orinoco's unique décor as whimsical.

The South End neighborhood hangout was cozy. With limited seating, twenty patrons at best probably tipped its occupancy max. Choosing one of only three booths in the place, Cameron waited for Talise to be seated before taking his seat.

Moments later, a server appeared with menus.

"Do you know what you want?" Cameron asked her, since they both had been to the Venezuelan eatery before.

"The Beef Tenderloin Churrasquito, please. And can I get the salsa chimi on the side?" Instantly, she recalled a section in her baby book about spicy food. "Never mind, scratch that salsa."

"I'm not that good. I need to look at my menu." The server waited while Cameron scanned the choices. Quickly, he made up his mind. "I'll have the Parrilla Caraquena and some fried sweet plantains."

After scribbling their orders, the server walked away to do their bidding.

"Okay, what's going on?" Talise anchored her elbows on the table and rested her chin on her linked fingers. Taking a deep breath, she prepared herself. "Did Ace send you with a stake to finish stabbing me in the heart?"

He stared at her with the oddest expression.

She didn't appreciate his scrutiny. "I'm not waiting all night. I can change my order to carry out." Talise started counting down the seconds. She wasn't bluffing. Tired, she wanted to go home and rest. The next morning's work day at the airport would come all too soon.

"Talise, are you pregnant?"

Blunt and to the point. "Do you want to see my pregnancy results?" She lashed out and then apologized. "Sorry, you're not your cousin. That attitude is reserved for him."

Although he and Ace were cousins, a strong resemblance was detected in their facial expressions and proud swagger. Both men were tall, fit, and good-looking. Cameron's smile brightened his smooth, honey-toned face, while the remnants of a small facial scar on his cousin's rich chocolate skin seemed to add to Ace's angular masculinity.

Talise was always attracted to dark chocolate men and considered Ace the "pretty boy" of the two. However, Ace wasn't the only fine man she had dated. Over the years, Talise's looks had garnered the attention of many attractive men. That would change once she started showing.

Cameron asked the question, and then seemed to be shocked by her answer. Stroking his goatee, he frowned. "Does Ace know?"

"Of course."

"When did you tell him?"

"I found out on a Friday and told him two days later on a Sunday."

"This past Sunday? Like almost a week ago Sunday?"

"Why are you repeating everything I say?" Talise had the strangest feeling she wasn't going to like his answer.

"Ace relocated to St. Louis where his brother lives about a week and a half ago. I thought you knew," he said hesitantly, with a grief-stricken look.

Slap! Talise emotionally felt the hit. She fought back a sinking feeling and struggled to regulate her breathing. She refused to faint. Ace had up and moved out of town? "Hmm. He didn't mention that," she heard herself respond with a shaky voice.

Rejected. Could she be any more humiliated?

Cameron leaned closer. He seemed concerned. "I'm so sorry. I didn't know he hadn't told you."

"Ace is his own man. He does and treats people as he pleases," she managed to say, blinking back the tears.

"Are you okay?"

Shaking her head, she couldn't answer. Talise was visibly numb.

"I'm going to change our orders from dine-in to carry-out. You don't look like you can eat right now, but I'm sure you'll be hungry later." His expression was grim as he summoned the server, paid the bill with a handsome tip, and requested their food be bagged to go.

I doubt it, she thought. "He left because of me?" What a drastic move. Was she that much of a threat?

"You are not in this alone."

"I disagree, Ace . . . I . . . I mean, Cameron. I'm on a roller-coaster ride, and the conductor went home and left me hanging. I had no idea I meant so little to him." How could someone fake feelings that way? She had questions that only Ace could answer.

"Do you need me to drive you home? Lois can drive me back for my car, or I could walk back."

"I've changed my mind. I think I'm going to stay here and eat— alone. I'll be all right."

"Are you sure?"

He didn't need to know she wasn't sure. It appeared Talise Rogers wasn't anybody's concern anymore.

The server arrived with their carry-outs. Standing with his bag, Cameron reached into his back pocket and slipped out his wallet.

"Didn't you already pay for our meals?"

"This is for you." Cameron held out a fifty-dollar bill.

She didn't have to make a comment. Her squinted eyes conveyed what she thought of his so-called generosity.

"It's for my little Jamieson cousin you're carrying. Put it in his piggy bank."

Shaking her head, Talise refused. "My child and I aren't charity cases."

"One thing you should know about the Jamieson men. We're stubborn. Ask our mothers," he said, smirking. "You ain't seen anything yet. I'll be in touch."

Nodding, Cameron walked away with the same bowlegged strut as his cousin. She thought Ace owned the copyright on it.

Chapter Thirteen

*H*ave you lost your ever-loving Jamieson mind?" Cameron barked into the phone before Ace could finish his greeting.

What was his cousin's problem? Even-tempered, Ace couldn't recall his older cousin sounding this angry.

"What's wrong with you? I'm in the middle of the game—"

"No, you're in the middle of a life crisis," Cameron spat. "You knew, didn't you . . . about the baby?"

So that's what caused his cousin's uproar. Immediately, Ace was irritated for the interruption. "Oh, so you've heard the rumor? That's what Talise claimed before I left, but protection is a sure thing. Can't believe everything you hear, cuz."

He resumed watching a good matchup on TV between the Yankees vs. Red Sox. When the Yankees cleared the bases, Ace tossed the remote aside in further annoyance.

". . . or see," Cameron added.

That got Ace's attention. "What do you mean? You saw Tay? She looked pregnant?" His nostrils flared. Instant disdain for Talise consumed him.

"Yes, I saw her. Her emotions were real, dude. You played her. As far as her being pregnant, she said she is—and I happen to believe her."

"You're a sapsucker, always believing the best in everybody. News flash . . ."

"I had faith in you while you wrestled with whether you wanted a career change from the streets of Boston to a corporate profession. But I've got to tell you, if Talise was my sister, I would be after you."

"Whoa. Lay off those energy drinks and calm down. She's my ex, not yours. Remember?"

Cameron didn't back down. "That's why you took off out of here as if a tsunami was coming after you. You said the St. Louis office needed immediate help. I can't believe you lied to me."

Ace was seconds away from boarding a plane and finishing this discussion with Cameron eye-to-eye and toe-to-toe. Ace was anything but a chump. He was certain that if he even whispered his brand of choice words, Kidd would hear it and jump into the fray.

As far as he was concerned, the conversation was already out of control. And he wanted to be careful not to get Kidd or Eva involved. That would only mean further torture. Trying to keep his voice down, Ace sucked in a deep breath to freeze his testosterone. It didn't work.

"Do I need to remind you that she isn't the first one to claim she's carrying my love child?"

"You either have a learning disability, you're blind, or on drugs. But from what Lois said about her, and the way she carries herself, I think it's highly unlikely she would lie about something like that. With her looks and personality, she could get any man she wants. Seriously. You need to talk to her, man."

Rubbing the back of his neck, Ace closed his eyes. He hoped he wouldn't regret the day he met her. "Let it go, Cameron," he warned.

"So you're going to sit back and do nothing?" His tone was that of sheer disbelief.

"And what would you like me to do, cuz?"

"For starters," Cameron said, "after you beg her forgiveness, make things right and marry her. Don't act like you don't have strong feelings for her. I know you, Ace. Even if you won't admit it, I will. As close as the two of you were, I thought Talise was the one all along. Don't be a fool and let her get away."

"Yeah, you're right. I did have strong feelings for her. But that was before she tried to trap me with the, 'I might be having your baby' song and dance. She messed it up for both of us with that stunt."

"I love you like a brother, regardless of the ten generations that separate us as cousins. Repercussions from situations like this can affect our bloodline. It's your responsibility—"

Growling into the phone, Ace snapped. "Maybe on your side of the Jamiesons' tree, but according to my old man, Samuel already demonstrated that responsibility is optional. Look, we both know the Jamiesons aren't fools. I'm just choosing to invoke my option clause. Talise is not my concern. If she's pregnant, then that's on her."

"Jamieson men seek the truth and then take action."

"I am so through with this conversation. Let me get you off my back. If she is pregnant, and if I decide to seek a paternity test, I'll support the child. There, are you happy now?"

He was still doing his best not to raise his voice and hoping it wasn't too late. The last thing he needed was for Kidd or Eva to overhear this conversation. His brother's ranch house was spacious, but noise traveled, even with him on the lower level in the game room.

However, Ace was pretty sure Kidd and Eva were probably in bed for the night. If Eva took a nap, so did Kidd. If Eva went to bed early, so did Kidd. If Eva wanted ice cream, so did his brother. Ace shook his head. At least Eva didn't set Kidd up with a baby story.

Cameron shot back. "I'm not happy until Lois is happy, and she won't be happy until Talise is happy. At this point, I don't think Talise likes you, so I don't think you can make her happy."

"I don't care" was on the tip of his tongue, but Ace did care about

81

Talise. It would take time for him to get over the fact that she toyed with his feelings and tried to trap him. "Whatever, man . . . Hello? Hello?" He squinted at his phone. The call dropped or Cameron hung up on him. Either was fine with Ace. He clicked off the television, having lost interest in the Sox's comeback anyway.

Unbelievable. He couldn't fathom why his cousin had turned on him. Cameron was the one who had tracked Ace down on his genealogy chart to begin with. Three years older, Cameron was the one who steered him toward a corporate career in accounting instead of a criminal livelihood in gambling. He once bailed Ace out of jail after a night of drinking and partying, which had led to fighting.

At first, Ace thought Cameron was attracted to Lois because the woman was fine. The fact is, his cousin explained, that Lois had a large pool of contacts who were movers and shakers in the community. It was some of her colleagues who had funded some of Cameron's pet youth programs. Besides, the two business associates tried dating when they first met. There were no sparks.

In a sense, he was Ace's mentor. Early on, Ace shared that he didn't have the dedication or money to attend MIT in Cambridge. Cameron convinced him to start at the Roxbury Community College, and the rest was history.

To further their relationship, his position with Healthcare Concepts had been the result of Cameron's networking. As far as Ace was concerned, orchestrating a professional career was one thing, but his cousin had crossed the line when it came to a woman. That is—one woman—Talise.

His cell phone ring jolted him out of his reverie. *Cameron again.*

Immediately, Cameron picked up where they left off. "It's going down like this. If you're accusing her of setting you up, then I feel your pain. But if you're not denying that this baby is a Jamieson, then I'm setting up a trust fund for my little cousin."

"What!" Ace leaped to his feet. "Now she's blackmailing you?"

He stomped across the room, rubbing his neck. If Ace didn't have a meeting scheduled first thing in the morning, he would be on the next plane out of St. Louis.

"No, I offered and she didn't accept. But I'm just as knuckleheaded and stubborn as you. Oh, sorry about the dropped call."

"Right." Fuming, Ace disconnected. Whatever happened to the saying "Leave your cares behind"? It was a good thing he and Cameron weren't together. They definitely would have come to blows—and over a woman—no less. Jamieson men did not fight over women. There were too many available for their choosing.

Ace sat back on the sofa and dropped his head in the palm of his hands. If he had any artery blockage, it had already worked through his veins. He could feel his heart pumping fast and strong. Then again, maybe that wasn't such a good sign.

He took a few minutes to gather himself. If Talise was pregnant with his child, there wouldn't be any need for his cousin to set up a trust fund. Cameron acted as if he was heartless. Ace would pay child support.

If nothing else, Cameron heard his side of the story. Standing, he stretched his tensed muscles and tidied the game room. He then carried his empty dishes to the kitchen, rinsed them off, and loaded them into the dishwasher. Heading to his bedroom, he realized it wasn't late. However, the blowup with Cameron had drained him. Talise had become a nightmare, wreaking havoc from over a thousand miles away.

Ace hadn't been in his room five minutes when another nightmare stormed in. Kidd's flaring nostrils was an indication it wasn't a social visit.

"What, man?"

"When's the wedding?"

Cameron. He should have figured. His cousin couldn't hold his liquor or water, especially when it came to family news.

Ace flopped on the loveseat in the sitting area of the bedroom. He couldn't guarantee he and Kidd wouldn't argue, but Eva would put them out before she would allow them to fight in her house.

"Cameron is a bulldog when there's a hint of Jamieson blood. What did he tell you?"

"Baby, yours, abandonment." Kidd stared at Ace. "Does that sound about right?"

"I guess he didn't mention phantom baby, entrapment, and gold digger?"

"Your relationships beg for counseling. Let's not follow the crooked path our father created."

"Who says it's crooked? You mean to tell me all of a sudden you know how to be a father?" Ace challenged his brother.

"Of course not." Kidd glanced over his shoulder and walked farther into the room, taking a seat in front of him. "But I love God and Eva more than anything. With those two in my corner, I can't help but do a superb job." His grin was cocky.

"I'm not willing to take that chance, Kidd. I'm not about to play house husband now and maybe never. Tay set me up and now she's stuck with the baggage."

"You've put yourself in those situations."

This wasn't the first time Ace had one of these conversations with Kidd. But this was going to be the last.

"Women are cunning," he retorted.

Kidd shrugged. "No more than a man when he wants to get in a woman's bed."

"Remember the night I had to be bailed out of Randolph jail?" Ace asked him.

"Yeah, for drunk driving."

"Wrong. That's what you thought. It was because crazy Linda Shelton was trying to drug me with that date rape stuff."

"GHB or Rohypnol. Ace, I told you that chick was crazy when I first saw her. I don't care how hot she was. That was too many colors in her hair for me."

Ignoring the dig, Ace continued. "Anyway, it's a good thing that I'm a big man because my body was fighting off that stuff. I was able to get out of her apartment and into my car. Before I could get home, I crashed and woke up in jail.

"They wanted to charge me with driving under the influence. When I tried to explain what happened, nobody believed me. I even got a few jeers and taunts.

"I wanted out of jail, but one punch would have kept me there. By the time Mom bailed me out, I figured she wouldn't believe me either. Now, tell me, that's not desperate measures for me?"

Scratching the hairs on his jaw, Kidd shrugged and remained silent. At first, Ace thought he was dozing off, then realized Kidd was considering what he had said. One thing his brother drilled into his head as they were growing up: Always fess up to the good or bad. If folks didn't like what they heard, then too bad.

"I seem to pick out losers who are willing to sleep with every Tom, Jamal, and Harry."

"Then you need to start turning down Thomasina, Janice, and Harrietta."

"Yeah, I know. I was with Tay longer than with that Thomasina woman."

"There really was a Thomasina?" Kidd snickered.

"Yeah. She was cute too. Sometimes, I get an urge. If a woman's willing, so am I. But I do have my standards. She has to be a looker."

Kidd stood, not looking too pleased from that last comment. "You need to conquer those sexual urges before they lead you straight to a sexual disease hell. Then that hell points straight to the lake of fire and brimstone. Settle down with one woman."

Woman was created for man. Didn't he hear somebody once say that? Ace wasn't about to let Kidd put a guilt trip on him.

Chapter Fourteen

A baby!" Sandra rejoiced when she got the call. She was about to be a grandmother. "Lord, thank You. Please help Kidd to be an exemplary father, to Your glory. Amen," she prayed.

All day long, Sandra couldn't keep the smile off her face at work. A coworker said she was glowing as though she had hit the lottery. Sandra kindly replied, "The lottery is a gamble, but a blessing from God is a sure thing."

God, I must have done something right. Thank You.

A few days later, Sandra almost fainted when she heard some more baby news—this time secondhand. It was a real possibility that Ace had indeed fathered a child too.

A second grandbaby? The first thing that crossed her mind when she thought about her younger son was, *here we go again.*

Cameron supposedly had met the woman and spoke highly of her to Kidd in hopes that Kidd could talk some sense into Ace. What disturbed Sandra the most was that her headstrong, misguided son had to know about the baby before he packed up and left.

Sandra was heartbroken. It had finally happened. Aaron Jamieson had turned into his father, Samuel. If things didn't turn around from here, there would be a second generation of Jamiesons with an absentee father.

Cameron wasn't her nephew by blood, but she treated him as such. Not only was he extremely intelligent, but he was a good judge of character. Considering the way he took Ace under his wing, it seemed as if he could discern a person's worth before they could.

He was an all-around good guy. *If only Cameron would go to church* . . . she left that thought hanging. This was about Ace and that young woman. Surely, it was praying time. Of all days for her to stay late at the office, today wasn't a good one. But there was no way around it. Sandra had to inform her team about upcoming insurance policy changes.

After she returned home, she couldn't wait to close the door and lift her hands in high praises to God. She was so filled with joy over new life coming into the family. Later, upstairs in her bedroom, Sandra fell on her knees and prayed earnestly for Ace.

An hour had passed by the time God's anointing left her presence. Sandra took a few minutes more and read a few passages from Luke. Afterward, she went downstairs and warmed up leftovers, but she could barely eat. Ace still weighed heavily on her heart.

That night before Sandra climbed in the bed, she prayed again. "Lord, I haven't received a word from You. Maybe this is 'much ado about nothing' on my part. Regardless, God, please save my son. Help him to be the man You called him to be." With such mixed emotions, her sleep was anything but restful, so she prayed within her spirit.

At work the next day, she continued praying and spent her lunch break diligently searching the Holy Scriptures. She fasted because she wanted to call her son and calmly verify what Cameron had said. The day dragged on and still God hadn't spoke to her. That evening, after she broke her fast and ate, she was ready to call Ace because he hadn't called her.

Hold your peace, the Word of the Lord spoke to her spirit.

She obeyed and did nothing. At the end of the week, with still no word from Ace, Sandra decided to make her weekly call on Saturday instead of Sunday. She knew her son wouldn't lie to her, but Ace was good at evading the truth.

Saying a quick prayer first, Sandra pressed Ace's cell phone number.

"Hey, Mom."

Taking a deep breath, she smiled to help restrain herself. "How's everything going?"

"No complaints. Eva is feeding me and the job is coming along." Ace chatted about everything but what she wanted to hear.

Finally, her patience grew thin. "Aaron Christopher Jamieson," she said, as calmly as she could. "I hope these rumors about you getting a woman pregnant aren't true. Is that why you packed up faster than a peddler selling bootleg CDs?"

"Mom, I don't know if there is a baby."

"Are you denying this woman is pregnant, or that the baby is yours? And in case the baby is yours, you would be missing in action."

No response. His silence was causing her to have a growing suspicion that he was evading the truth.

"Son, you've always stood your ground with women in the past. This woman wouldn't be the young lady you spent so much time with recently, is it? What's wrong with her? Is she wanted by the authorities, or has an incurable disease, or . . . help me out here, Aaron."

Ace said nothing.

"Don't you see the pattern?"

"No, I don't. You didn't need Pop around to rear us. You know how it goes. You're the strong Black woman who did it all."

Starting to read between the lines, a tear dropped from Sandra's eye. Did it all? *Barely*. For so many years, what she had done deceived her sons into thinking that she could do it all. In reality, she went without lunch, so they could have more than peanut butter and jelly in theirs. She did her own hair and learned to cut theirs. She mastered the art of making secondhand clothes appear fresh and new.

Sandra had no outside monetary help, except from her parents when they could. Of course, she didn't hear from Samuel on a regular basis. But he knew not to come into her house without money for the boys and presents to bribe them. Worst of all, he never stayed long enough for his sons to get to know him. Otherwise, she and her boys probably would have discovered sooner that he had other children.

"If she's pregnant, Mom, it boils down to another woman's attempt to snag me."

Blame it on the woman. "The only snag should've been on your pants zipper. Stubbornness is not attractive or the sign of manhood," she scolded. After a thoughtful pause, she continued, "If that child is a Jamieson, Aaron, please be a real man and take care of your responsibility."

Ace stuttered, "Mom, I can't promise anything right now."

Sandra turned ballistic. "That is not the right answer! Don't make me regret that I'm your mother! I called to pray for you, but right now, I have to get off this phone. I need someone to pray for me, to keep me from hurting you when I see you!"

Disconnecting, Sandra dropped her head into her hands. "That didn't turn out right, Lord. I repent and I'll apologize to Aaron. God, please end this cycle of single-parent homes. Please."

Later Saturday night, Sandra tossed and turned in her bed. Even if her son didn't do the right thing, what could she do about it? How much should she get involved? After all, it might not be Ace's child. What if it was, though? Would he actually walk away like Samuel?

The next morning, Sandra called Cameron to get his take and hopefully the truth. They exchanged greetings and then she got down to business.

"Kidd told me what's going on with Ace. Do you know her? Do you believe her?"

"Her name is Talise . . ."

Talise. What a pretty name. "I guess she's the one he called Tay."

"Sandra, this could turn ugly. I feel somewhat responsible because I introduced them. Her roommate and I are colleagues. When Lois broke the news and chewed me out, I immediately felt guilty. Ace and I share the Jamieson name and so I took it very personally. I really thought Talise was the one to change him."

"No woman wants to babysit a man, sweetie. A man has to want to change if he wants to keep from losing a good woman."

They spoke a few more minutes about the situation. Sandra wasn't surprised to learn that Cameron planned on setting up a trust fund for Ace's baby. She sniffed. But if that was her grandbaby, she refused to let anyone outdo "Nana."

"Do you think Talise would mind if I called her?" Sandra must have lost her mind to ask. She wouldn't know the first thing to say.

"Hmmm. I don't know. You should've seen the blood drain from her face once I mentioned that Ace moved out of state. If she was nine months, she probably would have gone into labor."

"I'll take my chances."

"I don't have Talise's number. I'll have to get it from her roommate, and Lois is still pretty hot."

"Whatever you can do."

———⁂———

Cameron called back a few days later with Talise's number. "Good luck," he said before disconnecting.

Sandra didn't have to imagine herself in Talise's shoes. She had lived it. After saying a brief prayer, she punched in the woman's number.

"Talise Rogers, please." Sandra hoped the woman didn't hear the tremble in her voice.

"Speaking."

"Hello, my name is Sandra Nicholson."

"Who?"

"I'm Aaron Jamieson's mother." Dead silence. She thought Talise was going to end the call right then.

"How can I help you?" Talise was demanding, but still polite.

"First, by accepting my apology for my son's behavior, and . . . hopefully, by agreeing to have lunch with your baby's Nana. I would very much like to meet you, be a part of your life, and tell you my story."

Sandra heard sniffling on the other end.

"I'll have to give it some thought and let you know. To be honest with you, Sandra, I don't think I'm up to seeing another Jamieson in my lifetime."

"Then we should definitely have lunch, because I'm not a Jamieson."

Chapter Fifteen

*T*alise sat dumbfounded after terminating her brief conversation on the phone. She and Lois were camped out in her bedroom, watching health shows about pregnancies and delivering babies on the TLC Network.

"Who and what was that all about? As soon as I heard Jamieson, I knew it wasn't good," Lois said, with a suspicious frown.

Once Talise had relayed to Lois what Cameron told her about Ace's whereabouts, her roommate was livid. Since then, Lois seemed to stick closer by her side. She even offered to go with her to some doctor visits. Talise lost her man, but gained an even better friend.

"Ace's mother," Talise responded. "She wants us to meet for lunch. She says she's not a Jamieson. Maybe she was smart enough to divorce Ace's father before he did too much damage."

"Oh, that's why Cameron wanted your number. I gave it to him with a promise not to give it to Ace. I just assumed he wanted to check up on you from time to time."

"Cameron didn't say it was for Ace's mother?" Talise queried.

"Nope. Besides him and Ace, I hadn't thought about anybody else wanting it. Maybe it's a good thing he didn't tell me it was for Ace's mother. I might have said no."

Talise gnawed on her bottom lip instead of munching on her bite-sized veggies and fruit wedges. "I told her I would get back to her. What do you think?"

"What do I think, or what would I *do*?"

"I'll take both answers."

"Maybe she wants to give you a heads-up." Lois reached over and tore off more seedless grapes from their platter. "Or maybe she wants to threaten you or curse you out. That's where I come in." She thumped her chest, vowing to protect her self-appointed godchild at any cost.

Closing her eyes, Talise fell back on her pillows. "Ace doesn't want to be in my life, so why is his mother concerned? None of this is making sense. His actions are so contrary to those of the man I fell in love with."

"Please tell me you didn't tell him that. It's like a death sentence when men find out a woman loves them," Lois begged with a groan. "Go figure."

"No. Not verbally, anyway. But I thought we shared that love in so many other ways, and I'm not just talking about the baby. When I was with him, I *felt* loved."

"See, love ain't what it's cracked up to be. Stay detached."

"Kind of late for that, don't you think? But thanks for the after-the-fact advice."

Rubbing her stomach, Talise sighed. At eight weeks, she had scheduled her first official prenatal visit the following week. Now, unanswerable questions had begun flooding her mind. What did her baby look like? Was she having a boy or a girl?

"Ace didn't choose me to be his wife, so I'll always be the other woman," Talise explained, regretfully. It was true. She hadn't made the cut.

"One day, a man out there is going to call Ace a fool and snatch you up because you're a good thing."

"Right, me and my big belly."

—⁓—

Talise had a different attitude when she strolled through Dr. Sherman's office. Lois offered to tag along, but Talise felt she could handle the first visit by herself. Without voicing it to her roommate, she knew she had to get used to going solo.

In the examination room, the nurse took her weight and blood pressure. Her blood pressure was normal, but she had lost three pounds.

"Don't be concerned about those few pounds. That's normal at first because you're probably having some trouble keeping your food down," the nurse advised, scribbling notes in her chart. "And you gave us a urine sample?"

Talise nodded.

Next, Dr. Sherman came in the room with a smile. "Well, you look much better than when I saw you last month."

"After the initial shock wore off, and with the support of my sister, father, and a couple of friends, I've accepted that I can do this." Talise wanted to convince herself, so she could convince her doctor.

"So I guess the father hasn't come around?"

Talise shook her head.

"It would be helpful if you could get some of the father's medical history or health conditions, so we'll be aware of what symptoms to monitor. Is there a mother or a sibling of his you can speak with?" Dr. Sherman asked, as she leaned Talise back to check the baby's heart rate. Next, she examined her abdomen for the baby's position and size.

Immediately, Talise thought about Sandra. Before now, she hadn't given the woman a second thought. Maybe this was the time to reach out to her, if for no other reason, but to get Ace's medical history.

"Everything looks okay. Remember to take your vitamins, get plenty of rest and exercise, and I'll see you in four weeks." Dr. Sherman paused. "I'm glad you decided to have your baby." She added in a whisper, "God has a way of blessing us with small packages."

"I'll remember that." Before the doctor left the room, Talise asked a few more questions. Then she got dressed and walked down the street to the bookstore, eager to buy another baby book.

That evening, she shared the good news with Lois that all was well. They celebrated by cooking omelets with plenty of spinach and ham, another quirky craving. Talise washed it down with a tall glass of milk. Lois saluted her with a glass of wine.

Early the next morning, Talise suffered a bout of nausea. She threw up more than once. Hearing the noises, Lois rushed out of her bedroom and into the bathroom.

"You okay? I thought this was supposed to end soon."

"Me too." Talise rinsed out her mouth and brushed her teeth. After she patted cool water on her face, Lois helped her back to bed.

"This is crazy, but until I can settle my stomach, I can't put anything in it. And if—"

"If you don't put anything in it, you'll throw up again, and the cycle goes on," Lois added, glancing at her watch.

"I'm going to be late for work if I don't hurry. Traffic on Mass Ave ain't no joke on Fridays. Are you going to be okay?" she asked with a frown of genuine concern written across her face.

When Talise nodded, Lois added, "By the way, I saw Cameron on campus the other day. He had just finished one of his engineering lectures. Although I ignored him, he made sure he interrupted my day until I paid him attention. He asked how you were doing. He seems concerned."

Yeah. "Everybody, except the father."

"I'm sorry, Talise, but I'm in your corner. Listen, I can pop some bread into the toaster and microwave an instant packet of oatmeal for you before I go."

"Thanks."

She kept massaging her stomach. One more day and Talise could talk to her sister. She would contact her father later that evening and tell him what the doctor said. He called regularly to check up on her. *Thank God for real daddies.*

Friday was always a busy travel day at the airport. Unfortunately, morning sickness caused Talise to be late for work. She made up for her hour of tardiness by staying over. That gave her a few minutes to catch up with Gabrielle Dupree.

When Talise first transferred to Boston from the West Coast, she and Gabrielle hit it off right away and became fast friends. The two had a lot in common, including some physical similarities.

Only a few years apart, Gabrielle had a level of peace about her that Talise wished she could tap into, especially now. Plus, she was the perfect role model of a Christian woman. Gabrielle always said, "I'd better be. One of my brothers is an evangelist, but my whole family would whip me into shape with prayer." Even with her strong faith, she never condemned Talise for her opinions or how she lived her life.

Gabrielle was on her third day of standing in as a ticket agent for a sick employee. In her management position, it was one of many hats she wore. She withheld the option to force another employee to work a double shift; that wasn't her style. Gabrielle wasn't the type of supervisor who abused her authority and took advantage of others.

After clocking in and helping several customers, she turned to Talise. "Have you lost weight?"

"A couple of pounds," Talise replied with a shrug. Trying to appear casual, she was hoping her manager wouldn't ask for details about her weight loss program. When she was ready, Talise was planning to share her news in private. At the moment, they were at the workplace where anyone could overhear them and this just wasn't the time.

"Can you take some of mine?" she joked. "I've picked up five pounds in the last month. If I don't curb my sweet tooth and soda addiction, people are going to think I'm pregnant."

Talise froze, and then blinked. Did Gabrielle know? No way. She had been desperately trying to cover all her bases by keeping up her appearance, apologizing for the times she was tardy—although she never gave an explanation—and blaming the increased potty breaks on adding more water to her diet.

She smiled at Gabrielle's comment, but didn't reply. Truthfully, Talise was too ashamed to mention anything to Gabrielle. She hadn't gathered the nerve yet. Although she knew her friend wouldn't judge her, it was more than the embarrassment of being pregnant without a husband. Talise was humiliated over being dumped. She felt used and then discarded, and that was eating her up.

"Is your boyfriend taking you to see the Boston Pops 4th of July Fireworks next weekend?"

Praying for any distraction, Talise crafted her answer carefully. She was hoping to extinguish Gabrielle's inquires. "Nope, he'll be out of town."

"Too bad. You're welcome to go with me and a couple of my friends."

"Oh, that's okay. I'll watch it online," Talise said, as passengers began to line up at the counter in droves. She was thankful that their conversation had to end.

When the crowd finally slowed down and her shift was coming to a close, Talise was relieved to clock out and bid Gabrielle and the other ticket agent farewell. She knew Gabrielle's questions were innocent, but at the moment she guarded her privacy, at least for as long as she could.

Leaving the airport terminal, Talise caught the shuttle to the employee parking lot. It was a good thing she had driven. Not only were her feet tired, but so was her back. When she arrived at the apartment about forty minutes later, Lois was getting dressed to go out.

"Hey. How're you feeling, hon?" Lois stopped fumbling with the stud in the back of her earring to listen.

"Is that a multiple choice or essay question? I'm beat. I never knew eight hours could be so long. And being on my feet the whole time makes me feel like I've worked twenty hours. Whew!"

The aroma of something Lois cooked tickled her nose, but the only thing Talise wanted was a warm shower to cool her off from the Boston heat."

"The department chair is hosting a mixer for some international dignitaries. I was hoping you felt like mingling. But just in case you weren't up to it, I made cream of chicken and wild rice soup. I also popped some rolls in the oven."

Touched by her roommate's consideration, Talise hugged her. "Thank you for the invitation, but I'm going to shower, eat, and lie down for a nap."

—⁂—

The alarm clock startled Talise. She blinked and racked her brain to remember what day it was. "Saturday?"

Yawning, she looked around her. Evidently, Lois had come in and wrapped her almost in a cocoon. "I can't believe I slept straight through the night." She got up and headed to the bathroom.

Although she looked forward to seeing her favorite biweekly customers, Talise really couldn't wait to see her sister and tell her the latest news. While she went about getting dressed for work, Talise anticipated her next conversation with Sinclaire later in the evening. Her sister would be excited to hear what the doctor said about how the baby was growing.

The downside was she needed Ace's medical history. Talise wanted to get her sister's opinion on how to go about getting that information. Sinclaire would also ask about her prayer life, as usual. Talise still read a few chapters whenever she could during the week, but her mind seemed too jumbled for anything to stick.

Noticing the time, she hurried to the kitchen to grab a quick breakfast and make a snack. She emptied two packets of instant oatmeal into a bowl and added water before popping it into the microwave. Quickly,

Talise cut up some apple slices and placed them into a sandwich bag. Throwing a banana into a paper bag along with the apples, she devoured her oatmeal and downed a glass of milk.

Not wanting to keep her first client waiting too long, she grabbed her purse and keys and headed out the door.

At the salon, "Tammy" was the code name she and her client, Priscilla, had established for when they chatted about baby stuff. "Tammy" was supposedly Talise's friend who was pregnant. Priscilla got a kick out of their secret pact. When it came time to pay, the generous lady always insisted on giving something extra for "Tammy's baby."

With a constant flow of one customer after another, the day seemed to drag on, taking a toll on Talise's body. Between her regular client load and the steady walk-ins, she was going to have to cut back—even if it did put a dent in her savings.

Indirectly, the majority of the money Talise had in her savings account had come from Ace. She frowned. He was so generous in one way and yet so cruel in another. Not expecting him to react the way he did, she really didn't know what to make of his behavior.

When Talise arrived home at the end of the day, she fingered through her mail and smiled when she recognized the Richmond, Virginia, address. It was the second check from her father to supplement her expenses.

The first check had arrived a few days after she gave her dad the news. It wasn't enough to cover her portion of the rent, which was seven hundred-and fifty dollars, but Talise was thankful for the five hundred dollars. It was a big help. Donna had signed the check and in the memo line, wrote "payment #1." Was that her stepmother's way of placing a guilt trip on her? Probably.

She would have to make some long-term decisions about her and the baby's future. From here on out, money would be an issue. Talise had immediately begun managing her income down to the penny. She no longer had extra money. She saved it all.

Boston was an expensive city to survive in. It wasn't unusual for people to have two jobs to make it. Donna had better be careful. She didn't realize Talise could always go back home if it got too rough here.

Surprisingly, the additional check in her hand was for one thousand dollars. Her father had signed this one. She danced around the apartment, sticking out her tongue. "Take that, wicked stepmother," she sneered in a mocking voice.

After Talise fixed herself something to eat and sat down to relax, she called home.

"Rogers' residence," Donna answered.

Talise quickly mustered up a happy voice. "Hi, Donna, how are you?" She didn't wait for her to answer. "Is my dad available?"

"We're in the middle of watching our favorite movie."

"Sorry, but I'm sure my father would want to talk to his daughter," she countered.

"Is this about more money? I sent you—"

"Donna, please put my father on the phone, or I will hop on a plane and talk to him in person."

"Don't you talk to me in that tone, young lady."

Talise had no patience for Donna's uppity attitude. "This is what's going to happen. You either put my dad on the phone, or I'm calling Richmond police and ask them to check on the well-being of a Frederick Rogers because his second wife might have poisoned him."

Weaving her story, she couldn't keep a straight face. "You know what, never mind. I think I'll call the police anyway."

Click.

Turning on her computer, she Googled the number for the Richmond Police department. While she was punching the number in her phone, she heard the call waiting signal. It was her father calling.

She answered. "Daddy? Are you okay?"

"Of course, I am. What is going on? Donna said you were about to call the police. What's wrong, baby?"

"It's Donna. I'm pregnant and hormonal. When I call my dad, I don't want to hear reasons why I can't talk to you."

"I'm sorry, sweetheart. I'll talk to her. I love her and I love you too. She can't replace your mother, but please respect her as my wife."

"I will." There was silence. Then Talise spoke. "Well, I called to say thank you for the money. I really appreciate it, Dad. I went to the doctor this week, and the baby is doing fine. The doctor let me hear the heartbeat."

As soon as Talise mentioned the baby, the tension between her and her father broke. Although she could hear Donna's voice in the background, Talise didn't rush through the conversation. It was only when her battery was about to go dead, that she said goodbye.

"Let me know if you need anything else."

"I will. Love you, Daddy."

"Love you too, baby girl. Take care of my grandbaby," he ordered. They chuckled and disconnected.

Talise couldn't allow a verbal confrontation with Donna to upset her. At best, her father's wife was usually cordial to her. But once she learned about the baby, Donna upped her snobbish attitude. "Lord, help me not to be disrespectful. I want my Dad to be happy."

Checking the time, it would be another hour until her video chat with Sinclaire. This was their first opportunity in a while to actually talk to each other. She made herself a small fruit snack, logged into her Skype account, and waited.

Talise was dozing when she heard a ringing sound come from her computer. Jolting up, she realized it was Sinclaire calling and clicked on answer. Within a few seconds, Talise screamed her delight at seeing her sister on the screen. "Sergeant Rogers, it's about time!"

Sinclaire laughed. "You wanted a video call. Sorry, we couldn't do this sooner. Lately, some of my days have been eighteen-hour shifts. How are you feeling? You look tired." She practically kissed the computer screen, trying to see. Talise angled her laptop to show off a slight bulge.

"Now, what's this about Aaron moving?" Sinclaire asked, frowning.

By the time Talise finished recanting the story, she was in tears. "It's more than about being pregnant; it's about being dumped too," she told her sister.

Talise sniffed, wiped her nose, and vented her feelings. "I feel used. I had no idea that's all he wanted from me. No idea." Her voice faded, as a new round of tears cascaded down her cheeks. Then she told Sinclaire about her conversation with Donna.

"I may not be there, but God is. Father, in the Name of Jesus, we thank You for Your benefits. My sister needs You right now, and regardless of our sins, You washed them away with Your blood, if we repent. Lord, bless her child. There are many women in the Bible who gave birth to great men. Help her child to be great. Let this child be a blessing, in Jesus' Name. Amen."

"Amen," Talise whispered. She reflected on those two chapters in Matthew that spoke of some great men of God who weren't born in the best of situations. Silently, she asked God to help motivate her to read His Word more often.

"In my email, I mentioned Ace's mother wanting to meet with me. I hadn't planned on it until Dr. Sherman said I should try and get some medical history. "What do you think?"

"Off the top of my head? Hopefully, there's only one jerk per household. Secondly, pray. We don't know God's will on this yet."

"Okay, okay, but don't you think it's strange for a mother to reach out to the mother of her son's baby? Someone she's never met?"

Sinclaire shrugged. "I guess there are unbiased mothers out there who are aware of their sons' indiscretions."

"What if it's a setup?"

"At this point, based on everything you told me about the Jamiesons, nothing is making sense. Follow God and your heart."

Lois strolled into the apartment and stopped in Talise's doorway. Talise waved her in.

I heard you talking to someone, Lois mouthed.

"Sinclaire."

"Oh." Lois came around and peered over Talise's shoulder. "Hey, Sinclaire." She greeted her with a grin and a wave.

"Hi, Lois," Sinclaire chimed back with a smile. "Listen, I've got to go. I don't know when we can Skype again. Now you're going to have me worrying about you."

Hearing that, Lois nudged Talise to scoot over and sat on the edge of the bed. "Claire, don't worry about your sister. You just stay safe. I have Talise's back."

Sinclaire nodded. "Thanks, but Talise, you've got to start reading your Bible consistently, not hit or miss. And . . . go to somebody's Bible-teaching, Jesus-is-coming-back church!"

"I work on Sundays," she reminded her sister.

Sinclaire wouldn't accept that for an excuse. "God made seven days. You've got six others," she responded. "Love you. Lois, I'm holding you to that."

Sinclaire and Talise kissed their screens at the same time and made smooching sounds before signing off.

Lois moved the laptop to the small desk near Talise's bed.

First, one tear started and then another. They kept coming, as Lois wrapped her arms around her friend. There was so much to cry about. She couldn't go home because her father's wife would probably make her go into early labor. Although Lois was caring and attentive, Talise craved her mother's arms and wisdom.

Thirty-two weeks. She had to get through it. After her baby was born, she would put in for a transfer, leave Boston, and start a new life with her baby.

Lois stood and went into the kitchen. She returned with a glass of water. "Here, drink this. Do you need anything to snack on?"

Shaking her head, she accepted the glass.

"Sweetie, promise me something. Sinclaire is fighting a war. We both want her to stay safe and come back alive. I'm sure it's hard to focus if she's worrying about you."

Patting her chest, Lois smiled. "I'm your friend and roommate. Stop worrying your sister. I've got your back because I still feel responsible for introducing you to that loser," she reminded Talise, who could hear the remorse in her friend's voice.

"Before you came in, I told Claire about Dr. Sherman requesting that I get Ace's medical history. Claire thinks that's reason enough for me to meet with Sandra."

Talise finished off the glass of water. "A part of me wants to meet her out of pure curiosity. The other part says run the other way. The woman says she's not a Jamieson. Then what is she?"

"Maybe Ace was adopted."

Chapter Sixteen

*I*t had been a week since Ace had the big blowup with Cameron and they hadn't spoken since. Ace knew how to hold out and when to fold up. He wasn't backing down on his claim that Talise tried to set him up. Either Cameron had his back on this one, or he didn't.

His brother was another story. Although his relationship with Kidd was strained, they would eventually hug, fist bump, and be all right. His wife, on the other hand, who was usually sweet, warm, and welcoming, had a few stern words for him these days. Kidd must have blabbed his mouth to Eva about the rumors. Even so, she still cooked enough meal portions to accommodate him, and he was grateful that she did.

On Saturday, Ace could still feel the love within the household, but something was brewing. He could sense it. Unfortunately, his brother and Eva were close-lipped about whatever it was.

The quietness was shattered when the doorbell rang. When Kidd opened the door, loud chatterboxes entered. Cameron's oldest brother,

Parke VI, didn't hang around. He was dropping off his son and daughter for the weekend. As far as Ace was concerned, that was just fine. He didn't want to have to deal with another Jamieson intruding in his personal business.

"Cousin-Aunt Eva, you just have to have a girl! I'll be her big sister and I'll babysit for free. I help Momma change diapers and feed my little brother. Sometimes Daddy and Mommy give me something. They call it a love offering . . ."

Ace knew the high-pitched, whining voice was that of ten-year-old Kami, who talked nonstop.

Pace, the oldest by one year, promptly made his way to Ace's bedroom. "Whatz up, Cousin-Uncle Ace?" He slapped his hand in Ace's. Pace was tall for an eleven year-old and exercised his strength with his strong grip.

Cousin-Uncle. Ace cringed. That was just as bad as calling him by a strange first and middle name, like Johnnie Sue. "You don't have to call me that, man. Ace will do."

Cameron's niece and nephews were respectful; yet they were typical, rambunctious children. Smart kids, they stayed within their boundaries, so unlike Ace when he was a child. He got his thrills from testing the limits on everything.

"Nope, I might slip up around Mom and Dad," Pace said, with a small backpack hanging over one shoulder. Dressed in khaki shorts that reached his knees and an oversized sports T-shirt, he flopped on Ace's recently made bed, sending a few decorative pillows tumbling to the floor.

"Oops," Pace huffed and then gathered them immediately after Ace intimidated him with an evil eye.

"I just got off punishment today for using a permanent marker on one of Kami's doll's hair. But she made me mad for coming into my room without asking. Today is my first day of freedom!"

Ace smirked. Maybe Pace hadn't been inducted into the childhood hall of sainthood after all. Whipping out his stack of baseball playing cards from his backpack, Pace recited stats of his favorite Cardinal players. He was chatting about his idol when Kidd strolled into the room. Pace's eyes instantly danced with excitement.

Kidd had already filled Ace in on the Jamieson offspring. For some strange reason, the boy had latched on to Kidd when he relocated to St. Louis two years ago. At times, Pace preferred spending time with Kidd rather than his own father. Kidd explained that the boy considered him and Ace to be part of the lost Jamieson dynasty nonsense.

Ace noticed that his brother's affection seemed mutual, as he rubbed the young boy's head. "So what are we doing today?"

"How about going to the park and playing catch?" Pace suggested with a hopeful grin.

"You got it. Let's go."

Just like that? Ace snapped imaginary fingers. Watching their interaction, he wondered how his brother could be such a natural.

Kidd and Ace didn't grow up with a father, so where did he pick up the skills to act . . . fatherly? Ace didn't have that type of confidence or instinct. He was sure he would blow it just like his old man had managed to do.

"Do you want to come along, Cousin-Uncle Ace?"

Ace moaned. The boy was going to drive him up a wall before the day was over. Yet he found himself not turning Pace down. "Sure, but for today, just call me cousin."

Shrugging, Pace nodded. "Sure, Cousin—"

Just then, Kidd interrupted. Leaving the bedroom, he yelled to Eva that they were heading out to Bangert Park. Pace was right on his heels and Ace was bringing up the rear. Immediately, the clanging of the pots and pans in the kitchen ceased. Meeting up with them at the front door, Eva stopped Kidd.

Wrapping her arms around him, Kidd returned her embrace. Next, she squeezed a reluctant Pace. After a moment of hesitation, Eva hugged Ace. If he wasn't mistaken, she whispered a prayer and then stepped back.

"Okay, Three Stooges, see ya later. Have fun." Eva saluted them.

"Bye, Cousin-Uncles," Kami yelled from the kitchen.

Bangert Park was about a mile of short blocks from Kidd's home. It contained a water park and was adjacent to the county library. Ace liked the feel of the neighborhood, which featured older bungalows that blended well with the newer construction homes.

Pace practically ran ahead, throwing his baseball up in the air and then catching it in his glove. The brothers trailed him at a comfortable trek.

"What's the story behind all the saints in the names of these streets? St. Francois, St. Ferdinard, St. Jean, St. Charles? Even you live on St. Jacques."

Kidd grinned. "You ain't seen nothing yet. You might as well start counting. We're going to pass by more."

He wasn't joking. They crossed over Washington to St. Marie.

"If I took you around the way, you'd see Sts. Augusta, Baptista, Cheryl, Alicia, and on and on. Parke, the 'anything about history guru,' gave me a tour of this neighborhood after I moved in and we made peace. You know, we bumped heads for months when I first came here."

"That's because you're both pigheaded."

Kidd's steps halted, which made Ace glance over at him. "What? You should talk. It took me a minute, but I learned stubbornness has no place in a Christian man's heart." He paused before adding, "I could have lost so many blessings, but Eva is one special lady. She hung in there with me, demons and all. It's amazing. She's strong and gentle at the same time."

Ace had other words to describe his brother's wife at the moment, like moody. But he wasn't ready to be a patient in the emergency room to get his lip stitched up. As boys, Ace didn't lose all their fights. But when he did need medical care, Kidd would be right there with him, nursing swollen, sprained, or broken extremities.

"Evidently, Old Town Florissant has quite a bit of historical significance, just like Boston. Maybe that's why I like it here," Kidd continued their previous conversation. With a shrug, he added, "More than a few homes were built before the Civil War and in the 1870s. There's a mix of French and Spanish architecture throughout this area."

Once they were on the outskirts of Bangert Park, Pace took off.

"This is the city of Florissant's oldest park. I know you've seen the Sherman Tank when driving by. Maybe we can get Parke to give us a tour of the rest of North County."

"Sounds good." Ace was drawn in by the sounds of children frolicking in the pool and the smell of meat grilling, as families gathered for reunions. Combined with the natural beauty of the park, it was a perfect picture of summertime activities.

"You've got to see this plantation that once had an Indian trading post. It's called Taille de Noyer . . ."

Talise. Ace froze in his tracks and then quickly recovered before Kidd noticed his reaction. Although she had been given the nickname Tallie, he preferred to call her Tay. He sighed. She wasn't a love lost, but a love that almost was. At least, she was out of sight. If only he could keep Talise out of his thoughts before he completely lost his mind.

—⁓—

It was perfect timing when they returned home from the park. The aromas from the kitchen greeted the men at the door. Suddenly, Ace was hungry and thirsty. The familiar scent was coming from Friday's leftovers warming in the oven mingled with freshly baked goods.

Walking into the kitchen, Ace couldn't believe his eyes. Eva and Kami's tea cakes appeared professionally decorated. He hoped they were meant to be sampled.

"Don't even think about touching me or the food. Whew, you all smell sweaty like dogs," Eva warned her husband.

"We're on our way to shower, babe." Kidd bent to place a kiss on Eva's cheek, but she blocked him with her hands.

"What did you expect? How can you stand St. Louis's humidity?" Ace came to their defense.

"Wait until mid-July." Jutting her chin, Eva rolled her eyes and walked out of the kitchen. Mimicking her aunt, Kami followed suit, marching behind her. Head tilted high in the air.

"Why are we mad at Cousin-Uncle Ace?" Kami whispered.

"It's because he doesn't act like a Jamieson." Eva didn't attempt to hush her answer.

Kami's eyes flashed with surprise. "Is he adopted too?"

"He might be. I'll ask his mother," Eva replied.

Ouch. That hurt. Ace groaned and hurried off to his room to shower. He would ask his brother later what was Eva's problem.

While showering, he thought first about the impression Parke's children had made on him. According to Kidd, it was well-known, but seldom believed, that Kami's introduction into the Jamieson clan was first as Cheney's foster child. Then she became the apple of Parke's eye. Parke and Cheney adopted her right after they were married. Kami's features were so identical to Parke, it would take a DNA test to prove otherwise.

DNA. If Talise kept up with her charade, he may have to take a test in less than nine months.

Thirty minutes later, Ace rejoined Kidd in the game room. "Why would she say that?" he asked Kidd while Pace was washing up.

"Just the mention of another Jamieson baby had her floating on air, until she got the full story," Kidd explained.

"What full story?"

"That you deserted Talise. Isn't that her name? Cameron is the only one who's met her. It's a good thing for you that Eva's struggling between praying for you and strangling you."

"Great choices, considering I don't even know if the woman is pregnant."

Kidd shook his head. "Man, Eva is a force to be reckoned with when she's mad. You'd better watch it. She'll take you down. Not only will I let her, but I'll help my baby too. Trust me, you will be overwhelmed." He issued the warning with a grin and then a scowl.

Really? Ace wanted to say, "Her, you, and what army?'

He didn't have to live with a temperamental woman. In fact, he was going to give himself his own going-away party because he was getting out of there. Eva had no business in his business. As a matter of fact, he didn't even have any business with Talise.

Chapter Seventeen

*O*n the next business day, Ace went apartment hunting. Before the week ended, he had narrowed down his choices to a two-bedroom townhouse with a washer and dryer hookup—an amenity, according to the manager.

Without blinking, he laid down the first and last's month deposit. Most of that money came from the company's relocation assistance. Of course, Ace decided to stay in Florissant to be nearby, but far enough away to keep the Jamiesons' clan out of his business.

Ace paused for a second and smiled. One thing Boston had that couldn't be found in St. Louis was Ace's fully-loaded and upgraded Dodge Charger. Ever since he returned his rental, he had been driving his brother's second car. Before he gave Kidd back his vehicle, Ace would see if his company would supply him with a temporary car.

At the moment, he missed his Charger but had to be patient. His plan was to return to Boston and retrieve his dream car once Talise's name had faded into the background.

For the time being, he was quite pleased with himself. Walking through Kidd's door with a grin on his face, Ace planned to tell his brother and his sweet-and-sour little wife of his good news. The couple was sitting in the kitchen having dinner.

"Hey," he greeted, and they returned his greeting. Ace nodded and then headed to the bathroom to wash his hands. He debated whether he wanted to eat alone or share his good news at the dinner table. *Why not?* He thought. It would be the last time the three of them would break bread in the same house.

A few minutes later, he joined them at the table. *Mmmm-mmm-mmm.* Ace sure was going to miss Eva's cooking, even if she was scary. He wasn't quite sure he could blame that on her pregnancy.

It appeared as though Kidd and Eva were waiting on him. They had finished eating but remained at the table, silently watching him eat. Now what did he do? This better not be something connected with Talise. Ignoring their subdued expressions, Ace kept eating.

"Humph. That was good." He patted his stomach. "I'm going to miss this when I'm gone."

Getting up, Ace returned to the stove for a second helping of mac-and-cheddar cheese, baked chicken, and broccoli pasta. Ready to make his announcement, he started, "I found a real cool townhouse not far from here, and I'm movi—"

"We need you to stay," Kidd's voice was flat, cutting him short.

Whirling around, Ace frowned. "Excuse me? Why? I thought you two would have church once the door closed behind me."

"Nah." Kidd fanned his hands in the air. "We'll have church when you answer God's calling on your life."

"That may take a while." Retaking his seat, Ace shoved more food into his mouth and shook his head. "So don't put on your dancing shoes."

"Bro, you may not be ready to be a father, but I am. Eva went to the doctor this morning, and . . ." He paused.

Eva's eyes misted. Suddenly, the strong, sassy, full of attitude woman was gone. Her expression was worrisome.

"She's spotting. I don't want her to lose our baby. The doctor wants her on bed rest as much as possible for the next month or so."

Although Ace swallowed, his food was stuck. "Regardless of the big, bad wolf you think I am, Eva," he managed to say, "I'm so sorry. I would never disrespect you."

"You're right," Kidd said, without cracking a smile. "You wouldn't live to tell about it."

"But you would disrespect the woman who is carrying your child," she mumbled.

"Babe?" Kidd intervened.

"I'm *somewhat* sorry," she confessed, "but I'll be really sorry, if you don't make up with Talise."

"Babe?" Kidd repeated and squeezed her hand.

Eva covered her mouth. "Must be my hormones talking."

"Ace, you know we've got each other's back—and I need yours right now. I hope you'll stay if my wife promises to behave and bridle her tongue." Then, looking directly at Eva, Kidd chided her with a voice of authority, "James 1:26 tells all the saints, 'If anyone considers himself religious and yet does not keep a tight rein on his tongue, he deceives himself and his religion is worthless.'" To that, he added with a confident grin, "And we do consider our faith worth everything. We promise we won't interfere in your personal matters."

Reluctantly, Eva nodded, as Kidd eyed her for confirmation.

Ace grinned. "I thought you were going to pull out that Scripture that tells wives to obey their husbands."

"Ephesians 5:22 says, '*Wives, submit to your husbands as to the Lord*.' And I do love, respect, and submit to my husband. That's my responsibility," Eva checked him.

Kidd looked tenderly at his wife and sighed. "It's an even exchange, bro, because verse 25 is aimed at me: '*Husbands, love your wives, just as Christ loved the church and gave himself up for her*,'" he quoted. "That's easy." Kidd leaned over and brushed a kiss against Eva's cheek.

Maintaining his poker face, Ace experienced a moment of longing. He always brushed a kiss against Talise's lips like that.

"Anyway," Kidd continued, "our doctor says if a woman is going to miscarry, 80 percent of them usually miscarry during the first twelve weeks. Eva's beginning her ninth week now."

Eighty percent chance? It's that high? Ace swallowed, as his mind drifted to Talise again. If she was pregnant, was she spotting? Would she lose the baby?

Kidd kept talking. "During the next two months after that, it's still a ten to twenty percent possibility . . ."

More questions bombarded Ace's mind. Was Talise in danger? Their baby—did he just say *their* baby? His baby? Wait a minute. He wasn't falling for anybody's guilt trip.

"Since you telecommute three days a week, I'm hoping you won't mind sticking around here on those days and checking on Eva while I'm at work," Kidd asked, breaking into Ace's reverie.

Me? Babysit a pregnant woman? Is Kidd crazy? Ace left Boston to get away from one.

Chapter Eighteen

*T*alise now had an excuse. Dr. Sherman's request for Ace's medical history gave her a reason to meet with Sandra. Deep down inside, she wondered if his mother would blatantly state why Talise didn't make the cut to maintain a relationship in Ace's life.

At this stage, it didn't matter whether he wanted her or not, but the curiosity was still lurking in the back of her mind. Making the call, Talise didn't waste time in small talk but got straight to the point.

"Sandra, how about meeting me at the Boston Market on Mass Ave at five-thirty tomorrow evening?"

"I'll be there," Sandra didn't hesitate to reply. There was a hint of relief in her voice. "Thank you."

Silence.

"How will we recognize each other?" Sandra interrupted the awkward moment. She chuckled. "My first thought was to hold a sign, saying 'Ace's mother,' but I figured that would make me an easy target in case you want to shoot darts at me."

Talise smiled at the woman's sense of humor. If it was Ace standing in front of her, then she would use anything she could find to throw at him.

Sandra suggested wearing a shade of green and to wait outside the entrance. What Talise felt like wearing was black to mourn the loss of Ace's presence in her child's life, but she agreed and they disconnected. The woman didn't need to know that Talise wasn't coming alone. Nobody in the Jamieson family was above suspicion. She didn't care if Sandra claimed the last name or not. With Lois present, it would make sure she wasn't caught off guard.

Although mindful of what Lois had advised Talise about bugging her sister, she still wanted Sinclaire to remain in the loop. She booted up her cumputer and signed in to her email account.

Hi, Claire. I've been praying and reading my Bible. I decided to meet with Ace's mother. I don't know what to expect, but I'm hoping there won't be any shockers like he's married or an escaped convict. His moving away was a big enough blow.

Lois is going with me for support. She says I shouldn't worry you. I'll keep my emails short, so as not to distract you on the battlefield. I love you more than anything. I know we both agreed on how we would live our lives and the choices we would make as adults. I'm so sorry I've let you down and fallen short of my career objectives. I'll bounce back, if not for me, then for my baby.

Hitting send, Talise rubbed her stomach. It was becoming a habit whenever she said or wrote the word 'baby.' She didn't care if there was any outward evidence or not.

Sinclaire emailed her back late Friday night: *Talise, you're my sister. I want you to be happy. You've already repented. The sooner you stop beating yourself up over this, you'll have peace.*

I'm paraphrasing here, but the Bible says in Romans 3:23 that we, (including me), all have sinned and fallen short. But then Jesus rectified our shortcomings on the cross. I'm praying that soon you'll want to totally surrender your life to the Lord for all your personal shortcomings.

More on the Bible later. I love you too. And don't even THINK about keeping stuff from me! I want in on every detail about what's going on.

Lois may be a girlfriend and roommate, but big sisters rule! Love you, Claire. Or should I start writing Aunt Claire?

Smiling, Talise rubbed her stomach again and signed off. At only nine weeks, she still had a couple of months to go until she could feel the baby kick. She couldn't wait. That night before going to sleep, Talise read the entire third chapter of Romans.

As she closed her Bible, she prayed and hoped that Sandra would have no ulterior motives. But her main concern was that she wouldn't take out her frustrations on Ace's mother.

The next day, nothing went according to plan. At the salon, hair chemicals dripped on Talise's green dress, despite her wearing a smock. Not only was the mishap noticeable, but her dress was ruined.

"Great." She groaned and called Lois at the apartment. Without any other green garments to wear, she would have to settle for anything. "Bring me something presentable," she asked.

Suddenly, the fumes from a relaxer made her nauseated. She excused herself again from the same customer. Racing to the bathroom, she threw up. After freshening up, Talise took several deep breaths before she went back to her client. Slowly, but competently, she shampooed, conditioned, and then roller set the woman's hair before putting her under a dryer.

Things seemed back to normal. Talise had regained her rhythm with the next two clients when another wave of nausea hit. It came after she applied heat to one of her client's hair to straighten it. Evidence of a rich Italian dish unexpectedly surfaced when the pungent odor of spices, including a strong hint of garlic, seeped from the woman's hair follicles.

Talise was fully aware that it wasn't unusual for the telltale signs of medication or some other intense odor to present itself during a hair appointment. It was amazing that agencies spend a lot of money on DNA testing when hair stylists could detect the same outcome without such a sophisticated process. Just barely finishing the customer's hair, she rushed to the restroom and threw up—again.

After fifteen minutes, a bottle of 7-Up, and some saltine crackers, her stomach settled. Each episode left her weaker and made her move slower. To make matters worse, the next client was a customer referral who decided at the last minute that she wanted curls instead of a bump hair style. The unanticipated change resulted in a prolonged process.

As the day dragged on, Talise went through the motions the best she could. Besides food, her only craving was for rest, which made her contemplate rescheduling with Sandra. Then strangely enough, she experienced a surge of energy that came after finishing her last customer.

Lois arrived at the salon right on time with the change of clothing. Talise glanced at the garment. "Red? You couldn't find anything in the green family in my closet like blue, purple, or even black?"

Shifting her body, Lois angled a hand on her hip. "Hey, you glow in red. Plus, it's my favorite color," she replied with a grin.

"Probably the vitamins." Talise cleaned up her station, took the garment, and went into the restroom. Behind closed doors, she scrutinized herself in the mirror. Her skin had never appeared quite so flawless without makeup. Maybe Lois was right about having "the glow" —whatever that was.

She rinsed any residue from working with the hair products off her face with cool water. After adding a few strokes of blush, Talise sealed her look with lip gloss. Closing her eyes, she mumbled a prayer, "Lord, prepare me for the unexpected."

Minutes later, they left the shop. Lois trailed Talise home to drop off her car. She insisted on driving Talise to her dinner meeting.

"If that woman makes you upset, I don't want you behind the wheel," Lois said, once Talise was fastened in the passenger seat.

"Good point." The thought made Talise feel faint, but there was no turning back now. "Why do you think Sandra wants to meet me? I hope there won't be any 'mother of the son's baby drama,' if there is such a thing."

"You've got money to bail me out, right?" Lois glanced over at Talise with a smirk. When it appeared she didn't get the joke, she cleared her throat. "I don't know if you've thought of this, but could Ace be behind this stunt and is using his mother as bait?"

Why? Ace knew where she worked, lived, and how to reach her by phone. She doubted if he saved her old number. There was no reason for a go-between, unless there was bad news. Talise's heart pounded faster.

"I doubt it," she said, trying to sound convincing. As they were nearing the restaurant, she revealed, "I haven't spoken to Ace since the Sunday I told him that I was definitely pregnant. He dumped me because of the baby and has never looked back. That hurt will last a lifetime."

Lois continued her chatter of possible scenarios, but Talise tuned her out. They arrived at the outdoor shopping area in record time, without her friend racing the cabbies. "Hey, I see a parking spot." Talise pointed.

"Yes!" Lois made it, beating another car to the vacancy. Finished parking, she tried to reassure Talise, "It'll be fine. Cameron says Sandra's cool people."

"Yeah, isn't that what he told you about Ace? And look what happened. I think something was wrong with your hearing that day. Cameron probably said 'Ace fools people,' not 'he's cool people.' Anyway, I'm not blaming Ace for me being pregnant. I should have said no to his seduction and taken the advice of those anti-drug commercials."

"Humph."

Talise dropped the subject. She was already nervous. It felt like she was moving in slow motion when they got out of the car and mingled in with the crowd. Crossing to the other side of the outdoor mall, they headed to the restaurant. People darted in and out of their pathway. Talise's heart began pounding with fear.

Do not be anxious about anything. Pray, give thanks and make your requests to Me for I am God. Talise heard the words from Philippians 4:6.

"Sinclaire must be praying for me," she whispered.

Puzzled, Lois asked, "How do you know?"

"Because God just spoke to me." Talise took a deep breath and smiled. It had to be better than experiencing the baby's first kick.

"What did He say—"

Before she could answer, Talise spotted Sandra. Swallowing hard, she almost stumbled. "That's her."

Chapter Nineteen

*S*andra Nicholson?" a striking woman who was approaching the entrance of Boston Market asked with a slight hesitation. Another woman was a step behind her; neither was wearing a shade of green.

"Yes," Sandra answered with a nod, quickly assessing the woman standing in front of her.

"You're Ace's mother?" Talise asked curiously.

"Yes," she responded again, this time with a chuckle. "Are you Talise?"

Sandra had no preconceived notions about what Ace's ex would look like. But she was instantly impressed with his upgraded taste in women. It wasn't just her appearance but the air of confidence that the younger woman projected.

Caught a little off guard, Talise blinked and then managed to say, "Oh, I'm sorry. I didn't expect you to be so . . . young . . . and pretty." Then feeling a bit embarrassed, she added, "This is my roommate, Lois."

The two women exchanged suspicious greetings. Sandra had hoped it would be only she and Talise.

"Yes, I'm often mistaken as his sister, but I have the gray strands to prove I'm his mother." She laughed nervously, as a few seconds passed. To keep things from getting even more awkward, she regained her composure and motioned toward the door. "Shall we go inside?"

As Sandra reached for the handle, a man came out of nowhere to exercise his chivalry and held the door for them. She nodded her thanks and they stepped inside.

"Hungry, ladies?"

Patting her stomach, Talise breathed in a whiff of the aromas in the air.

"Starving."

"Me too," Sandra agreed. Getting in line, they scanned the menu board. Once they reached the counter, each woman placed her order.

"My treat."

Thanking Sandra, Talise and Lois agreed on water as their drink option. Lois accepted empty cups from the cashier and headed to the drink dispenser.

"I'll find us a table," Talise offered and walked away.

She seems cordial enough, Sandra thought. *So far, so good, Lord.*

As Sandra waited for the staff to complete their orders, she glanced over her shoulder. The two friends were whispering. She hoped Talise's roommate wouldn't hinder her from getting to know Ace's ex. Sandra was starting to have second thoughts about this encounter.

Silently, she prayed, *Lord, I approach Your throne of mercy and grace. I believe Your perfect will to be done in my son and this young woman's life. You know what went on between them. Guide my words for her to look past me and see You. Amen.*

"Miss?" The server called for Sandra's attention.

Suddenly, Lois appeared by her side to help.

"Thanks for coming to the rescue."

While Lois balanced two trays, Sandra grabbed napkins and silverware and carried her own tray. Lois dutifully placed Talise's meatloaf dinner in front of her and then chose a table nearby to eat alone.

"There's plenty of room here," Sandra said to be polite. Secretly, she hoped Lois wouldn't accept the invitation.

"This is fine. I figured you two need some privacy."

Thank you, Sandra mouthed, appreciating the young woman's insight. Taking her seat, Sandra smiled at Talise and then bowed her head, "Lord, in the Name of Jesus, we thank You for Your mercy and grace. We ask that You provide for those who are in need and please bless our food, conversation, and fellowship."

The pair mumbled their Amens. Seconds later, Sandra amusedly watched Talise scoop a helping of sweet potato casserole into her mouth. The satisfied expression on her face was priceless.

As Sandra sipped her water, she continued to discreetly study Talise. *Yes, Ace does have good taste. I could see how he lost his head. I only wish he had Holy Ghost sense to make better decisions,* she thought.

Talise's thick hair was coal-black, glossy, and a few inches past her shoulders. Together with her flawless complexion, she was a stunning picture of health. Her appearance was glowing in the red sundress that complemented her brown skin.

If Talise *was* pregnant, she was wearing it well. Briefly caught staring, Sandra hurried and broke the crust on her chicken pot pie. Whether it was piping hot or not, she didn't hesitate to find out. Taking the first bite, she wondered, *Where do we begin?*

Wiping her mouth, Talise took a sip from her cup and then jumpstarted the inevitable dialogue. "Sandra, I'm sure you could understand my confusion when I received your call. Clearly, your son wants nothing to do with me."

Although Talise's voice was steady and strong, sadness flashed in her brown eyes. Sandra ached for her.

"So why did you want to meet me?"

Sandra exhaled and gathered her thoughts. The correct phrasing of her answer would be key. "Cameron believes you're pregnant, and—"

"I'm not having Cameron's baby. This is Ace's child."

"Yes, that's what he told me." Then attempting to clarify her words, she said, "I'm sorry, what I meant was, Cameron is adamant that you're telling the truth."

Lifting a brow, Talise was poised to challenge her. "Excuse me? I know we don't know each other, so I don't have any credibility with you, but one thing I am not is a liar," she countered. "What has your son said?"

"Nothing," Sandra admitted in disgust and a bit of embarrassment. "Unfortunately, I believe he's in denial, again."

Dropping her fork, Talise stared at Sandra. She squeezed her lips together as if holding in a growl. The sadness in her eyes was gone. Fiery darts were taking aim.

"Again? Denial? Number one, Ace flat-out rejected the fact that I'm pregnant. Number two, he deserted me without a backward glance when my doctor confirmed it. And number three, he broke my heart. That's three strikes. I am definitely out."

She emphasized her words by making a hitchhiking gesture with her thumb. Then Talise's eyes narrowed. "And what do you mean by 'again'?"

Okay, Lord, here it comes, the good, the bad, and the ugly. "Aaron is no saint. I suppose he gets it honestly from his parents. I wasn't exactly close to being God-worthy myself when I got pregnant not one, but two times."

Her confession became easier with her testimony. "Since that time, I've repented and God forgave me of my sins and has given me the tools I need to live holy. With His gifts, I can honestly say I'm striving to live my life as a saint and no longer a sinner."

"Not to be rude, but I didn't realize I was coming for Bible study. What does that have to do with me?"

Sandra wasn't offended by her curt remark; rather, she attempted to explain, "You're going to need Jesus as you go through this." She stalled, picking at her pie. "I'm not trying to be cruel, demeaning, or insulting, but there is no nice way to say this."

Taking a deep breath, Sandra prayed silently and plowed ahead. "You aren't the first woman who has claimed to be pregnant by Aaron. The babies either never materialized, or through DNA testing, weren't his—to my relief."

From Talise's body language, it was apparent she was uncomfortable. The blood seemed to drain from her face. Patting her chest, Talise glanced in Lois's direction.

God, help me to choose my words carefully. Then drawing on her inner strength, Sandra went on, "My oldest son's wife is expecting, and I look forward to becoming a grandmother. God knows I've been praying that Ace would settle down and get married before he fathered a child."

She finished, slowly releasing her breath and hoping Talise received her words with the humbleness intended.

"Great!" Talise raised her voice and slapped her hand on the table. That got her roommate's attention. Lois seemed poised to intervene, but she didn't move.

Sandra wanted to reach across the table, hoping to calm her. But she doubted her touch would be welcomed. Blinking back tears in her own eyes, "Talise," she said softly.

Talise wasn't buying any attempt to be consoled, as her bruised feelings rushed to the surface. "Unbelievable. Ace has set up his own reproductive clinic, a male gigolo who just uses women and then casts them aside. I was no more than a number on his chart," she said more to herself.

A look of horror, disappointment, and shame glared on Talise's pretty face before she covered it with her hands. Moments later, when she removed them, her face was flushed and her eyes wet.

Bowing her head, Sandra began to pray silently as old memories came flooding back. Somehow it didn't seem so long ago when she had to face the reality that Samuel wasn't going to be an active part of her sons' lives. Samuel had no intention of marrying her either.

If Talise was pregnant, then Sandra prayed her situation wouldn't become part of a generational dysfunction. She didn't want this to be "like father, like son," with Ace unwilling to marry Talise. *God, let her see I'm on her side. Help!*

"Let your conversation be always full of grace, seasoned with salt," the Lord spoke a portion of Colossians 4:6 to Sandra.

Leaning closer with her own set of misty eyes, Sandra whispered, "You're not alone."

"Unless your son is crawling through those doors, begging my forgiveness, and putting a ring on every single toe and finger, then I am alone. I'm a twenty-nine-year-old, single, pregnant woman."

"I was a twenty-year-old when I had my first son and became a single mother. Five years later and still single, I had my second son. I didn't know Aaron's father was already a married man . . . but deep down inside, I had my suspicions."

She looked down at her hands. "There were no words to describe how deceived, betrayed, and utterly alone I felt. There was no one to help me out of the hole I had dug for myself—and my children. I lived it."

"Are you telling me that Ace is married?"

Sandra shook her head. "What I'm trying to say is I have been in your shoes. If you're carrying Aaron's child, I don't want you to feel that you're alone."

Talise wore a blank expression. Sandra couldn't decipher if she had broken through to Talise's heart. Anchoring her elbows on the edge of the table, Talise cradled her chin in her hands. "You're ten weeks too late from that happening."

Sandra's heart dropped. Her frustration at failing to convey her heartfelt desire to reach out to Talise battled with the bitterness the young woman had for Ace. She glanced away, trying to regroup her thoughts.

Although she was talking on her cell phone, Lois had her eyes trained on them.

Turning back to Talise, Sandra tried again, "Over the years, Aaron latched on to role models who were irresponsible men. Unfortunately, he has mimicked that behavior."

"I see. So your purpose of this meeting is to give me the heads-up that Ace is a shallow, irresponsible human being. As a result, he's destined to go through life breaking hearts."

Speechless, Sandra bit her tongue in defense of her son. The woman made him sound like a mere dog.

Looking away, Talise nodded her head as if she had reached a decision. Then her expression hardened. "Thanks for the insight. Please don't take this as an insult, but it is what it is—Ace is a jerk. I got that. So I basically could go on Craigslist and find a more responsible father figure. Got it," Talise said sarcastically.

Remaining silent, Sandra continued to take the tongue-lashing that was meant for her son. She connected with Talise's pain.

"Do you mind if I ask you a question? Did you seek out Ace's other false positive baby mama girlfriends?"

"No."

"Why me?

"God stirred my soul the moment I heard about you. If you're pregnant with Ace's baby, I want a relationship with you and my grandchild."

"If?" Talise repeated indignantly. "There's that word again. Evidently, Ace has you brainwashed."

Maybe Sandra's actions were premature and she should have waited for DNA results. Yet she felt God urging her to reach out to Talise. Even if there were too many 'ifs,' such as: *if* Talise is pregnant, *if* the child is Ace's, and *if* Sandra should get involved.

"I'm not trying to hurt or offend you by saying if, but please try to understand this from my point of view. I've gone down this road before with Aaron—"

"And it seems like Ace's GPS has avoided dead ends and he's on a collision course to destroy lives, and I'm just one of many obstacles who got in his way." Talise finished the thought her way.

"Listen, I can understand your anger and hurt, but he is still my son. I reared him right and I'm proud of the good things I've done in his life." Sandra snapped her lips shut.

Temper, temper, she did not come prepared for battle.

"Talise, I'm sorry. The bottom line is, I want all my grandbabies. I promise you that once the paternity test proves Aaron is the father, I won't abandon my grandchild. However, I don't need a test for us to be friends."

"But you're not willing to believe me until then, is that what you're saying?"

Sandra eyed the younger woman with remorse. Slowly, she shook her head. "I'm sorry . . ."

Pushing back from the table, Talise gathered her purse and stood. Lois quickly disposed of her tray and was at her friend's side, as if summoned.

"Ready?" Lois asked.

"Thank you for dinner, Ms. Nicholson. Sweet potato casserole is my favorite," Talise said sweetly. "However, it sounds like I'm on trial, and I'm supposed to prove that I have something that belongs to Ace Jamieson."

Talise grunted. "None of this will matter at the end of forty weeks. Ace already severed the umbilical cord. For the sake of my son or daughter, I am so through with the Jamiesons. Period."

Chapter Twenty

*I*f I knew how to shoot a gun, I would kill Ace." Talise was beyond humiliated. She and Lois strutted out of the restaurant, as though she didn't have a care in the world.

"Stop it before your baby hears you talk that nonsense. If it's a boy, you don't want to give him any ideas about becoming a thug and packing."

Lois was right. Talise exhaled. She wasn't vying to be the next guest on *The Maury Show*. Suddenly, she could hear one of her mother's favorite childhood scoldings, *If you can't say anything nice about a person, don't say anything.* For the rest of the ride home, Talise was quiet.

"Are you okay?" Lois asked, moments after they entered the apartment. "You barely said a word in the car. What are you thinking?"

"About the 'if' word," Talise responded, mumbling and grumbling on the way to her bedroom. Leaving an untidy trail of her belongings—purse, sandals, and keys—across their hardwood floor, she was completely distraught.

"Can you believe the nerve of that woman? Sandra wants us to be friends *if* I'm pregnant with Ace's baby. She would have been less insulting had she requested my friendship on Facebook, whenever I decide to give in to all that social network stuff. I suppose the request would be to meet me in the birthing room." Her voice quivered.

"Actually, I heard her say she wants to be friends, and then after the paternity test, she wants to be the grandmother," Lois tweaked.

"Talk about a superficial relationship. Was it even worth meeting?"

"A free meal—yes." Lois kicked off her shoes, as Talise cut her eyes at her friend. Scooting a chair closer to the bed, Lois got comfortable and then used her roommate's bed to prop her feet.

"You know the saying, 'Momma's baby, Poppa's maybe.' Evidently, with a son like Ace, she's always suspect. Again, I'm so sorry for introducing you to such a low life," Lois offered her ongoing apology.

Lying on her bed, Talise stared at the ceiling. She felt like her identity had been stolen. It would probably be faster to repair a damaged credit report than her life at this point.

"What a mess? I know some women think they can change a man, but that wasn't my intent. I happened to like the man Ace portrayed himself to be." Talise sniffed to ward off a crying spell. It was useless, as her tears began a slow path down her cheeks. This emotional rollercoaster was as bad as physically throwing up. She could never get used to either one.

"I don't know which was more shocking, Cameron telling me that Ace had moved—not moved on, but away—or Ace's mother kindly letting me know that I'm among many who've claimed to carry his love child."

She wiped at her tears. "Can it get any worse?" The dam broke and Talise's mind conjured up everything that was wrong in her life. She bawled for her mother's absence when she needed her most; her sister's noble sacrifice that she was making for her country so far away, her mean and insensitive stepmother or rather, her father's wife. Why did her mind pull Donna into the mix?

She was pregnant, rejected, and a mental breakdown had now been fully activated. This was ultimately about her child, who would need both parents but would grow up with a crucial void in his or her life. Talk about a false sense of security. It hadn't been a good day at all.

Turning to her side when she felt the bed shift, Lois sat next to her and whispered, "It'll be all right."

"How?"

"Because Jesus said so."

The response offered a temporary reprieve, as Talise stared at her roommate. Straining her voice, she asked, "Where did that come from?"

Lois shrugged. "Girl, how would I know? It just popped into my head and sounded like something Sinclaire would say. Did it work?"

Talise mustered a smile. "I hope so."

"Let me get you something to drink."

Standing, Lois first walked into the bathroom and returned with tissues. She stuffed them in Talise's fist and then headed for the kitchen.

Alone with her thoughts, Talise tried to unscramble everything Sandra had said. The microwave buzzed, and seconds later, Lois strolled back into the room. She was carrying a tray with a cup of hot tea, whole grain crackers, and white grapes.

Sitting up in bed, Talise's heart warmed at her friend's thoughtfulness. She reflected on when she asked God to put people in her path. Whether she knew it or not, Lois was definitely a godsend. Talise hadn't made up her mind about Sandra.

"Thanks. I really appreciate you being there for me." Talise took a sip and then sighed.

As she quietly tried to build her resolve, Lois snacked on the crackers and suddenly said, "Women rule."

"You know. I'm so through with the Jamiesons. 'If you're pregnant,' or 'if it's Ace's,' or 'if you didn't trick him like the other one hundred women,'" Talise twisted her mouth, as she mimicked Sandra. "Forget 'if.' I don't need them!"

"Ah, Talise, before you sign up for this 'independent woman retreat,' you do need Ace's medical history."

"Grrrrrrrh. I forgot all about that. Since Ace is emotionally incompetent, I'd better make sure there are no other underlying heartless deficiencies in his genes."

"Here's the bottom line. Your baby is going to be a Jamieson. Period. There are no 'ifs' about that."

"I checkmate your 'period.' My son or daughter will have an honorable name—Rogers. If I have a son, I will do everything in my power so that he won't turn out like his father . . ." Sandra's exact words seemed to echo in her mind. What if Talise's *best* wasn't good enough?

"What blows me away is she never married. I wonder if that was her choice," Lois added to the puzzle.

Talise was lost in her thoughts. She didn't even want to think about that happening to her.

"Sandra Nicholson has it going on," Lois continued to rattle on. "Forget Tina Turner, Halle Berry, or Jennifer Lopez. I want to look like her when my children are grown and gone. She could've snagged a good man and shared the task of rearing her sons with him."

Lois paused. "Did you see that guy checking her out on the way into the restaurant?"

"No, I was too busy calming my nerves to keep from throwing up," Talise replied. She squinted before challenging her friend. "According to you, she's supposed to be the enemy, remember? And you're giving her compliments?"

"I have no shame."

"She is pretty, but I hope that's not me in fifteen or twenty years down the road. Still unmarried because no one wants the responsibility of loving another man's child is not for me. I'm going to borrow Sandra's 'if.'"

Folding her arms, Lois nodded. "It's a free country."

"If Ace thought he was exercising his manhood by walking away from me and his child, then, so be it. One thing I won't have in common with Sandra is my baby's father coming and going in and out of my life. I don't want to duplicate that situation by giving my child a sister or brother."

She and Lois touched and agreed with a high-five.

Chapter Twenty-One

*B*y Ace's calculations, if Talise was pregnant, she would be plus or minus three months. As much as he tried not to think about her, he couldn't escape it. Not with Eva's "in your face" pregnancy.

It was his designated day to babysit Kidd's pregnant wife, who remained on bed rest. Eva looked fine to Ace. Why his brother even asked him to be on standby was a mystery. Kidd came home for lunch, phoned Eva throughout the day, and texted her constantly. Exactly, how much rest could she get with all those interruptions? Besides her bouts of nausea, Eva rested and didn't ask for much.

Ace leaned back in the desk chair. As his mind drifted, he glanced outside the window in his bedroom, where he had set up his home office. Kidd's backyard deck summoned him.

But St. Louis's late morning humidity was stifling and he chose to stay cool inside. Ace missed the East Coast beaches. Actually, he missed Talise—her voice, her smile, and her bright eyes. If the woman was pregnant, how ironic would it be for two brothers to be expectant fathers at the same time?

Ignoring the work that was outlined on his spreadsheet, Ace entertained memories of Talise. He smirked. Whenever one of them missed the other, nothing seemed to deter them from seeing each other. When they were dating, Ace couldn't get enough of her, and Talise felt the same way. Whether it was a late night dinner or taking an early lunch, they wouldn't be denied. Not even with Talise's Saturday schedule at the salon.

A few times, she had juggled her client load so they could enjoy a weekend getaway to New York, Connecticut, or even Rhode Island. He closed his eyes and rubbed his wavy hair. One Friday evening in particular, Ace was waiting outside her apartment when she got home from work. Already packed, she changed into comfortable clothes. Ace grabbed her bags and before they knew it, they were on I-95, headed toward the Big Apple.

"We don't have to race back. I took a vacation day on Sunday." Talise had surprised him.

It was those little sacrifices she made that caused Ace to believe she could have been the one. He thought he felt the clarity of her affections. Was she only catering to his desires as part of her scheme to trap him down the line? Ace frowned. A bird in flight caught his attention.

He preferred to reminisce on fond memories. Ace thrived off Talise's complexities. Once they had gotten settled in their hotel suite, their first destination was to the Empire State Building. The time was early spring and the weather was still chilly in New York. Her boots, skinny jeans, and sweater top with the matching cap caught every man's eye. Ace snickered and shook his head. Talise was his possession and he kept her close.

As she snuggled in his arms at the top of the monument, Talise whispered, "I've got a secret."

"Which is?"

"I'm scared of heights."

Not his fearless woman. He had playfully pinched her. "Right, like a sailor who can't swim? You work for an airline, baby," Ace teased, as he hugged her tighter. Giving him the warmest smile, she had rested her head on his chest.

"I know. But in a plane, I feel protected and safe. Out here in the open, more than a thousand feet above street level, it's scary."

"I gotcha, babe. Trust me, I gotcha."

Closing his eyes, Ace remembered kissing her cold lips. He missed that. Reluctantly, he flipped to the next slide in his mind. Ace smirked when he recalled them standing in a long line in Times Square for bargain tickets to see *Sister Act*. Even at a discount, the tickets were still pricey. Talise had protested, saying it was too much money.

Her complaint had fallen on deaf ears, and they remained in line for him to buy anyway. She had offered him a sip from her cup of hot chocolate. "I kind of like standing in the crowd with you. We can keep each other warm by holding hands," she'd told him.

His response had been some naughty, off-handed comment, but she laughed and scrunched her nose. The intimacy they shared in the moment told him that she was different.

"Ha!" Ace shook his head in major disappointment. Shifting in his chair, he needed to pay attention to the work in front of him. But his stubborn mind craved more memories.

They went shopping at Macys while waiting for show time. Instead of bargain hunting for herself, Talise had been on a scavenger hunt for him. Hours later, they were huddled together in their seats at the Broadway Theatre. It didn't take long for Ace to lose interest in the play that had Talise enthralled. The merriment, passion, and distress all shone through her facial expressions. To him, she was more interesting and he chose to watch her instead.

Finally, Talise had elbowed him, breaking his trance and indicating there was an intermission. "Stop looking at me," she demanded with a laugh. "We stood in line for more than an hour for these expensive seats. At least, you're supposed to pretend you're enjoying this."

"No, babe. My money was well spent because I'm enjoying you."

Talise had rewarded him with an engaging smile that never left his memory.

The next day, on that Sunday morning in April, the only place to be was in Central Park. The moment had been unhurried, as they wrapped their arms around each other. Later he insisted on visiting Ground Zero before heading back to Boston.

As they stood and scanned the thousands of names of those who had perished that fateful day, Ace recalled sniffling. It was a moving experience, and he couldn't remember the last time he'd cried. It had to be in grade school after his mother tore his behind up for some infraction at school.

Since fourth grade, he had developed leather skin on his bottom. Ace was determined his mother wasn't going to get another tear out of him. She didn't. Yet he stood there while Talise used a tissue to dab his eyes that day, and he let her.

"This is why my sister is stationed in the Persian Gulf right now. Yet we can never bring these people back," Talise had whispered.

"Or turn back the hands of time," Ace added.

That statement snapped him out of his reveries. Despite Talise's underlining deceit, he would turn back the hands of time in a heartbeat to be with her again. Maybe if he had confessed his feelings up front, she wouldn't have felt the need to trick him.

When Ace's stomach growled, he signed off the laptop that he wasn't using anyway. Standing, he stretched. "Why do all good things have to come to an end?" He asked himself. Opening his bedroom door, Ace strolled out into the hall. He was on his way to the kitchen and was about to tap on Eva's door to see if she was hungry. Although he had shut down his mind from recalling more memories with Talise, his ears began to play tricks on him.

Standing by her bedroom door, was that Talise's name he heard Eva mentioning? No way. The two didn't even know each other. Leaning closer, he heard Eva giggle. She was definitely on the phone. As he strained to hear the conversation, he was abruptly shoved out of the way.

"What are you doing?" Kidd roared from behind him. Dressed in a suit and tie, his brother didn't look any less intimidating.

Recovering from being slammed up against the wall, Ace scowled. "Well, I *was* eavesdropping, but you put an end to that with your he-man heroics."

"Not on my wife, she'd better not find out. So what are you trying to hear? Is something wrong? Has she stopped breathing?" Kidd was poised to barge into his bedroom.

"Believe me, she's alive and well."

"She'd better be. You're on duty when I'm not here." Aggravated, Kidd cracked open the door to make sure Eva was all right. He waved at his wife and then motioned Ace toward the kitchen.

"What's up with you, dude?" Kidd asked.

"I thought I heard Eva mention Talise's name."

"Oh." Kidd shrugged as if it was no big deal and then opened the refrigerator. Grabbing some bread, lettuce, deli meat, and condiments, he offered, "You want one?"

With an agitated frown, Ace stared at his brother. "Didn't you hear what I just said? Why would she mention her name? Can you ask your wife what's going on, please?"

"Nope."

"Why?"

"Because I don't care who my wife talks to, unless it's another man trying to hit on her." He paused to slap mayonnaise on both slices of bread. "And because you don't care anyway."

"I don't."

"If you don't stop lying to yourself soon, you just might start believing it." Kidd piled slices of turkey and ham on one piece of bread and then topped it off with the other piece. After slicing an apple and pouring a glass of milk, he balanced the dishes on a tray. Kidd then dismissed

Ace and headed toward his bedroom to feed his wife.

—m—

The next morning in his office, Ace stood from behind his massive mahogany desk and strolled to the window. From the twentieth floor of the Peabody Coal Building, he could overlook downtown St. Louis.

Since the previous day, his mind had worked overtime trying not to think about Talise. How could Talise be pregnant—by him? They both protected themselves. In any case, he thought he did, especially after lessons learned from his past relationships with long-legged gold diggers. Now he was more than a thousand miles away, and Ace still couldn't shake his ex. He didn't believe in good or bad ghosts, but the woman was definitely haunting him.

Refocusing, Ace watched the sea of red moving on the streets below. The St. Louis Cardinals were playing a day game and fans were headed to Busch Stadium. Everything was red, including the water in a fountain at Keiner Plaza.

Ace loved baseball and missed the excitement at Fenway Park. He couldn't possibly switch his allegiance to the Cardinals. That kind of defection would be long in coming. Besides, when the coast was clear, he could hopefully return to Boston. When that time came, he prayed that he would never run into Ms. Rogers again.

Ironically, the thought saddened him. Turning around, Ace stuffed his hands in his pockets and perused the large, nicely furnished office. "Not bad for a boy from a single-parent home in a Boston ghetto," he noted.

When his workload was pretty much finished for the morning, Ace wanted to escape. He could go sightseeing or maybe to the game and pretend that he was rooting for the Red Sox. Unfortunately, he had to hang around for an afternoon meeting with new clients.

Instead, Ace took a moment and weighed whether he wanted to

stay in and order a couple of sub sandwiches or test the humidity and run across the street to Imo's. The unique taste of their pizza already had his mouth watering.

There was one more option, which involved a member of the opposite sex. Ace couldn't explain why he hadn't accepted the sexual overtures from several of his coworkers. Simply put, his heart wasn't into the office "cat and mouse game" people play at work.

When his cell phone rang, Ace smiled at his mother's number and welcomed the distraction. Their conversations since the disagreement about Talise had been civil, but strained. In spite of that, every now and then, Sandra would prompt him to discuss his relationship with his ex. She wasn't about to let him off the hook.

"Hey, Mom, what's up?"

"You have good taste, but poor judgment." Sandra's insult was pleasant.

Flattening his tie, Ace settled behind his desk and then frowned. "Huh?"

Just then, there was a light knock and his office door opened. Shala, a woman with a pretty face and enticing body, popped her head in and mouthed, "Lunch?"

Although his stomach said yes, his mind was focused on what his mother had to say. He declined and Shala backed out, pouting. She had been after him since day one. The Jamieson charm. Ace loved it. If Talise didn't still have her handprints on his heart, he definitely would have explored that opportunity.

"Mom, am I supposed to know what you mean?"

"Talise."

Ouch! Just the sound of her name made his heart scream out from the prick. Holding his breath, he attempted to sound casual. "What about her?"

"We had lunch."

Ace gripped the edge of his desk to keep from falling out of his chair. Fully alert, his body stiffened. His nostrils flared at his ex's nerve. She was more aggressive than he had given her sweet self credit for.

"Oh, really? First, she runs to Cameron with her sad story, and now she's after my mother." Ace was livid.

"Let's revisit that conversation we had not too long ago. Talise is the one who is having your baby, isn't she?"

"You saw her. Does she look pregnant?" Pressing his ear closer to the phone, Ace listened intently.

"I couldn't tell. She's probably not far enough along yet for it to be so obvious. Plus, you can't always go by looks. One time, I made the mistake of asking a woman when her baby was due. She wasn't pregnant, but overweight. Believe me, it was an embarrassing moment."

Ace pinched his nose, impatient by his mother's idle rambling when he needed a straight answer. "Mom, what about Talise?"

"Very pretty, but she's divorcing herself from the Jamiesons. You've hurt her badly, and she doesn't want to ever see you again. Aaron, please, if that woman is having your baby, it's time for you to take responsibility. I'm asking you to reconsider your stubbornness and avoid another generation of single parenting in this family."

It's time to do damage control, Ace thought, tuning his mother out. He was going to contact Talise and make sure she put an end to her vicious lies.

Chapter Twenty-Two

*T*alise wasn't expecting the call and had no doubt Sandra was behind it. But by the time the conversation ended, she had to smile and admit that all Jamiesons weren't created jerks.

Without having ever met her, Talise could tell that Eva Jamieson was a gregarious woman who oozed contagious enthusiasm. To Talise's delight, Eva's outgoing personality had made it easy for the two women to engage in an enjoyable thirty-minute exchange.

The woman's timing was uncanny. Talise had just returned from her doctor's appointment. The baby's vital signs were good, and Talise was maintaining a healthy weight gain. She was happy.

Lois had tagged along and fired one question after another at Dr. Sherman, as though she was the patient. Although amused at her best friend's excitement, admittedly, she learned more than she would have imagined.

However, nearing the end, the pleasant visit took a turn—in her opinion—for the worse. The obstetrician was once again harping on needing the father's medical history. Talise voiced her reservations about asking his mother for help. She couldn't believe how Lois betrayed her and sided with Dr. Sherman. Outnumbered, Talise was irritated that she had no choice but to call Sandra again and admit she needed something from her.

After one final attempt to encourage Talise that it would be okay, the doctor's visit was over. The two friends managed to part ways on good terms. Lois had to get back to the campus, leaving Talise stressed and on her own about contacting Sandra.

Since Thursday was her regular day off, Talise looked forward to relaxing the rest of the day. She showered and felt refreshed and pampered after being in the summer heat. Climbing in bed for a nap, she let out a long sigh. It seemed as though she had just crossed over from consciousness to dreamland when her cell phone rang.

"Hello?"

"Talise Rogers, please."

"Speaking." She didn't recognize the number or the voice.

"Hi. You don't know me, yet, but we have something in common. We're both having babies by Jamieson brothers."

Catching her breath, Talise gripped the phone tighter. *What?* The only thing her brain registered was "something in common," "having babies," and "Jamieson." Not another woman deserted and pregnant by Ace. Please.

"I hope you don't mind me calling. My name is Eva Jamieson and I live in St. Louis. My mother-in . . ."

Sandra's daughter-in-law? Talise somewhat relaxed that it wasn't another victim of desertion. But why was she calling her? Groaning, Talise rolled her eyes. It didn't matter. She was not about to have another debate, defending her condition.

"Don't you mean *if* I'm pregnant? Listen, I just came from the doctor and I'm not in the mood—"

"Really? What did your doctor say? Is the baby okay?"

Talise stared at the phone in disbelief. This woman could not be seriously quizzing her.

"Eva, why are you calling me?"

If she came off rude, then too bad. Talise felt cranky and the Jamiesons had an uncanny way of taking her attitude to the next level.

"To be honest . . ." she started, then exhaled. "I'm in baby solidarity with you, girl, because I'm mad at Ace too."

"Get in line," she said dryly. "What's your beef with him?" Talise didn't really care. She wasn't up to another enlightening moment.

"I have a list of them, but the top one is he's cheating me out of a sister-in-law."

Talise almost choked on her own air. "What?" Was it possible to get dizzy while lying down? So far, this short conversation was making her head spin. "What are you talking about?"

"We're both pregnant and we could be sisters-in-law, doing baby stuff together. Instead, his sorry self is hiding out at my house and you're there."

"Ace is staying with you?" So that's where he was. If Talise knew how to contact a hit man, she would . . . nonsense. She had to redirect her thoughts. Despite how badly he had treated her, Talise didn't thrive on that type of drama.

"Yes, and don't think I'm making it easy for him either. The only reason he gets a home cooked meal is because I have to feed my husband. Otherwise, I would starve him."

Talise withheld her laughter. Unlike Sandra, who came at her in a hesitant manner, Eva was a tell-it-like-it-is person. Talise liked her for that.

"I hate to disappoint you, but we'll never be sisters-in-law."

Unfortunately, it was the truth. She swallowed back the hurt. But there was one thing. Talise wished Eva could help get answers to her many questions: what was the real deal behind him leaving? How could he walk away? Yet to ask would make her seem desperate.

"Does Ace know you're talking to me?" she asked, as a tear dropped.

"It's your call. He doesn't at the moment, but I can change that if you want. Nothing's more frustrating than a stupid Jamieson. I didn't take anything off Kevin. Come to think of it, I did hear them arguing outside my door."

"I would prefer he doesn't know." She would die if Ace refused to speak with her. Talise couldn't take another rejection.

"So Kevin is Kidd. Right?" She wanted clarification.

"Yes, ma'am. Oh, I hate that nickname. It sounds too thuggish for me. Plus, I wanted a man who was ready to put away his play toys. Unfortunately at the time, Kevin was an angry Black man. Talise, believe me. I know about rough patches, but it was worth it for Kevin and me to hang in there and make it to our smooth sailing."

Talise teared-up at Eva's happy ending. "Humph. Ace's nickname is fitting. He's a gambler with women's hearts. In trying to explain his pathetic behavior, Sandra disclosed his conquests. I'm just the latest, so I'm sure you'll understand that I'd rather keep my distance from the Jamiesons."

"You're having one in less than nine months. By the way, when is your baby due?"

Grinning with anticipation of that glorious event, Talise rubbed her growing pouch. "At first, my doctor thought the baby was due at the end of January. Now, she estimates mid-January."

"Cool. I'm due around Christmas. Our babies will be first cousins. Do you have any siblings with children?" Eva asked.

"I have one sister, Sinclaire, who is serving in the air force, but she isn't married."

"Oh," Eva's voice softened. "God bless her and keep our troops safe. Please tell your sister thank you."

Talise always sniffed when people said that. "I will. What about you, any brothers or sisters?"

"I have a twin sister who has been engaged for a year."

"Do you know if you're having twins?"

"Nope. Only one, and Kevin and I can't wait to find out what God's blessing us with."

"Well, we both know Ace doesn't care, and I don't think I want to know yet. If it's a boy, then I'll worry about how to do a better job than …" Talise let her words fade so she wouldn't insult Eva's mother-in-law.

"The Jamieson men are a special, stubborn breed. But this is God's world, and things will work out according to His plan. You'll see."

Talise didn't see God anywhere in her situation. Even though she had picked up on reading her Bible, it felt like not much was sticking. It seemed as though every time she read an encouraging Scripture, the next thing she knew, she would turn around and have a bad day.

Sinclaire's last email listed Scriptures about God's will in her life, but Talise just couldn't see it. And now Eva brought God into the conversation.

"If I were to have a little girl, I would still have to break her heart one day. The time will come when I'll have to feed her lies about why her daddy deserted us. I'm not looking forward to that."

The line was quiet. It was the first time Eva didn't have a positive comeback. Maybe she finally comprehended the hopelessness of Talise's situation.

"I hope you don't mind me sharing this. We make mistakes, but God knows. He is in control of everything that happens in our lives. From your last breath, to your baby's first breath, and everything in between—God knows. He is blessing you right now—and me too. And we don't even know the details of what's going on behind the scenes."

Talise listened with tears in her eyes. She needed to hear that God hadn't taken His eyes off of her. A while back, she had prayed that He would put people in her path to help her. So far, He kept sending Jamieson people, just not the right one. Talise didn't realize tears were falling until she heard herself sniffling.

"My mother-in-law and I are praying for you and your happiness. God's going to take care of you and that gorgeous baby, so lean on Him." Eva paused. "If you start crying, I'll start. Then Kevin will be mad and take it out on Ace because he would be the cause of it."

Talise burst out laughing. "Can you ask him to get in a left hook for me?"

Eva giggled. "I'll put your request in." They chuckled. "Say, I've been on bed rest for weeks and I'm pretty bored."

Talise gasped. From reading her baby books, women who were on bed rest ran some type of risks. "Is your baby okay?" she asked, concerned.

"Oh, yes. I had a little spotting at first. Kevin didn't want to take any chances and tried to convince the doctor that I not only needed medical leave, but should stay in bed. That man got on my nerves, so we reached a compromise. The doctor said I didn't need to go on medical leave, just light duty as an LPN. Once the doctor gives the okay, I'll probably be off bed rest too."

How odd that Talise had suddenly become concerned about someone she didn't know. She never had any spotting and, according to Dr. Sherman, she and her baby were fine. Praise God, as Sinclaire would say about the Lord's goodness and mercy.

"I haven't been to Beantown in a while. Maybe I can fly up, so we can go baby shopping and baby eating. I can spend the night at Sandra's. You should come over, so we can have a pregnant PJ party. I'll have Kevin check the air rates."

Where Sandra was extending an olive branch, Eva seemed ready to plant a tree. Talise liked her and would welcome the company of a fellow expecting mother who didn't question the paternity of her pregancy.

She was going to throw caution to the wind. Talise needed a getaway. She had planned to visit her dad and his wife in Virginia in a few weeks, but that could be put on hold. The thought of swapping pregnancy tidbits with another expectant mother was too appealing to resist. Suddenly, it appeared as though she had a Jamieson solidly on her side. Amazing.

"I'll tell you what. Since you've been on bed rest, I can fly to St.

Louis. I work for an airline, so it won't cost me anything. It'll have to be in the middle of the week when I'm off."

"Don't worry about a place to stay because—"

"Oh no, I won't be spending the night. I'll come for lunch and then fly right back."

"Then let's make it a girls' day out."

As Talise listened to Eva's bubbling personality, she was reminded of a high-strung, high school cheerleader. Instead of a nap rejuvenating her, the phone call had not only lifted her spirits, but gave Talise a surge of new energy.

"I'm so excited, I can hardly wait! I feel like jumping up and doing a praise dance," Eva exclaimed.

Talise giggled and reprimanded her, "Don't you dare! You're on bed rest, remember?" For the first time, she actually looked forward to meeting a Jamieson.

"Thanks for not hanging up on me. When Sandra called me, she sounded a little sad. She didn't think she'd made a good first impression with you," Eva confided, "but she's on your side."

Talise really didn't have a problem with Sandra. It was who she represented—Ace. Plus, as the doctor and Lois had sternly reminded her today, Talise needed Ace's medical history. "Do you think Sandra would want to come with me?"

"She'd jump at the opportunity."

Almost instantly, she had second thoughts. "But it'll be in the middle of the week."

"Trust me. Sandra will still jump," Eva assured her.

"Then I guess I'll call and invite her," Talise said. "I'll plan to come next week. But there's one condition."

"Name it."

"Under no circumstances do I want to see Ace or be within ten feet of him."

"Done. That's Ace's mess to clean up, not ours."

When Lois walked through the door later that evening, Talise was all smiles.

"What's up with you?" She eyed her suspiciously.

"I'm going to St. Louis." Talise began to recap the entire conversation while they ate dinner. "So, what do you think?"

Lois didn't answer right away. "Well, I'm surprised, considering earlier today and last night you were adamant about staying as far away from anyone with the last name Jamieson, Jamison, Jemison, or any derivation thereof."

"True."

"My biggest concern is Ace, since he lives there now. What's got me worried is he could upset you. How do you plan to handle that?"

After draining the rest of her glass of milk, Talise gave the question some serious consideration. "Maybe, just maybe, I spoke too harshly about the Jamiesons. It's Ace who's the jerk. His mother and his sister-in-law reached out to me. I don't think they'll let him do that."

"Hmm-mm. One phone call and you did a one-eighty?" Lois pushed away from the table and folded her arms. When she lifted one brow, Talise knew her roommate wasn't convinced.

"When I met with Sandra, I know I couldn't get pass the 'ifs.' But when I spoke with Eva, she jumped right in there. I didn't detect any sign of doubt in her mind that she was suspicious of me. Basically, like you said, my baby will be part Jamieson. No one can change that. Not even me."

Talise had all afternoon to reflect on the last couple of months without Ace. "I have to move on. He isn't coming back and my objective is not to go to St. Louis and get him back. I'm hoping it will lessen the blow to my baby's self-esteem to know that it wasn't the entire Jamieson clan who didn't want him or her, just one bad apple. Unfortunately, it will be the most important apple."

"Sounds like you've really made up your mind. Do you want me to go with you?"

Talise shook her head and smiled. "Thanks for the offer, but I'm going to ask Sandra if she wants to go with me. I'm planning to make it a day trip and come back the same day. Don't worry, I put Eva on notice. If I come face-to-face with Ace, then they've failed my trust test."

"Well," Lois declared, as she stood and began to gather up their dirty dishes. "I'm scared to ask, but what is their penalty if they fail?"

"I don't know, but I refuse to use my child as a bargaining chip."

od bless Eva. Sandra praised the Lord when she accepted Talise's invitation to accompany her to St. Louis.

Her daughter-in-law was able to connect with Talise where Sandra could not. Although it would be a one-day turnaround for Talise, Sandra decided to make it a four-day weekend trip and spend some time with her family. Both of her sons were clueless about what Eva had concocted.

The two-and-a-half hour flight would give Sandra another chance to get to know Ace's ex-girlfriend. She was on a mission, with or without the evidence that Talise was carrying Ace's baby. Sandra felt the Lord urging her to be a spiritual light to the woman. That order took precedence over a possible grandmother-grandchild relationship.

When they were at the restaurant, Talise mentioned that her mother was deceased. Although Sandra wouldn't dare attempt to replace such a coveted position in any woman's life, the most she could hope for would be a lasting friendship.

At nine o'clock on Thursday morning, Sandra and Talise settled in their seats in preparation for takeoff.

"Thanks again for inviting me. I was hoping I hadn't scared you off," Sandra said, as she clicked her seatbelt.

Twisting her mouth, Talise appeared thoughtful before responding. "You didn't scare me off, I felt antagonized."

"That wasn't my intention. I've been praying that we could connect."

"Sandra, I have a sister who is praying for me, a hair client who is praying for me, and for all I know, my obstetrician could be praying for me too. Besides all of that, I'm even praying for me. Still, I'm clueless about what's going on in my life."

Squeezing her lips in frustration, Talise rubbed her stomach. It seemed to relax her. "I'm going to have to eat crow now. I would have called you eventually because my doctor would like to have some basic medical history on Ace to put in my file."

Ace's mother nodded and chuckled. "Tell me what you need. And here I thought my daughter-in-law's engaging personality and the fact that she's also pregnant won you over."

"It helped," Talise responded and grinned.

"Good. Either way, I thank God for giving us another chance at friendship."

"I don't know, Sandra. Friendship is mutually earned. You still have concerns about me. And to be honest, Ace scarred me with trust issues. I admit, after speaking with Eva, my opinion of the Jamiesons moved up a notch, but I'm still leery."

"That's understandable."

"I mentioned to my sister how Eva and I bonded, and she told me to go for it."

Thank God for sisters, Sandra thought.

"Sinclaire has an amazing portion of blind faith. She reminded me that my pregnancy isn't about me, but my baby's future. My child will want and need to know his or her cousins."

Talise went on to chat freely about her sister serving in the air force.

Without Sandra's prompting, she opened up about her family in Virginia, her career aspirations, and her passion as a stylist.

While Talise relaxed, Sandra shared how she coped after the deaths of her parents. She also talked about the joys of motherhood. Although she tried to limit mentioning Ace, it was a struggle.

This time being more upfront about her position, Sandra explained, "I can't change what happened between you and my son. As a mother—Aaron's mother—I don't want to interfere. I just want to see him right any wrongs between the two of you."

"You don't think you're interfering a little bit now?" Talise asked, lifting a brow.

Sandra wasn't sure if she was being teased or challenged. Adjusting her seatbelt, she stalled in answering. *Jesus, allow Talise to warm to me—and to trust me. Help me not take offense to her reaction to me. Amen.*

"I definitely have my nose in someone else's business—yours. Sometimes I think of myself as a poster child for single parents. I've been there, done that, seen that, and survived that. Did I get it right all the time—no, but I'm rooting for you. I want your life to be filled with happiness, not heartache. I can promise you that, no matter what happens, I'll be in your corner as a friend."

Their conversation ceased as the flight crew demonstrated the safety measures. Sandra bowed her head and silently prayed for their safe travel.

"Hey, Talise." She was being greeted by a short, perky flight attendant with big blonde hair and a petite body. "What ya having today? The usual when you fly?" The attendant's eyes twinkled with mischief.

"You've got it, Sal. Cranberry juice on the rocks." Scrunching her nose, Talise leaned closer and whispered, "And make that a double."

The woman laughed and winked. "Sure thing. And you, madam?" Sandra declined.

When the attendant moved on, Talise identified her as an afterthought. "Sally Porter's a doll. She's one of the nicest persons I've ever worked with."

"I'm curious to know what your roommate thinks. Lois, right?

Sally returned with the drink order. Reaching over, she handed Talise her cup. Sandra assisted in pulling back the makeshift table for her.

After taking a sip of the chilled juice, Talise answered in a nonchalant manner. "Lois has mixed feelings, like me. But she has a slight tendency to hold a grudge. Right now, she's barely speaking to Cameron for his role in misrepresenting Ace's character."

Sandra held her tongue. It was okay for her to bad-mouth her own sons. She had to hold her breath when it came from others. *Lord, let her see how uncomfortable it is for me to hear negative comments about my flesh and blood.*

Without letting up, Talise kept talking. "She's under the mindset that one bad apple spoils the whole bunch. And Cameron *is* a Jamieson. Lois has been a good friend to me since I've moved here, and now she's planted that seed of doubt." Talise raised a brow. "I'm hoping this isn't a setup. Sinclaire would like to prove Lois wrong."

"Aaron doesn't know we're coming. Even Eva's husband has no clue," Sandra assured her. "You can trust Eva and me."

"But not Ace ever again, and that's okay. I can do this all by myself."

Talise played with her hands. If she was anything like Sandra, she was probably trying to convince herself that she didn't need the father in her child's life. Rubbing her stomach again, Talise glanced out the window as if something caught her attention.

Sandra stole the opportunity to scrutinize her stomach. In a sleeveless blue top and loose gypsy skirt, there was still no outward sign of a protruding pouch. Possibly because of her frame, maybe five-eight in heels, she might be spared the huge stomach.

As a matter of fact, Sandra recalled the day she went job hunting. She was seven months pregnant with Ace. Without noticing her condition, the manager hired her as a seasonal worker at a department store. She needed the extra money to buy Christmas gifts for Kidd and the new baby. Sandra wondered if she would've gotten the job had the man known about her pregnancy.

"How far along are you?" she asked Talise.

"Twelve weeks on Saturday."

"Are you hoping for a boy or a girl?"

She shrugged. "Either way, the child needs a father. So I guess it doesn't matter," she said sarcastically. Talise sighed and then shook her head. "I'm sorry. Let me rephrase that. What I'm hoping and praying for is that I'll be a good mother."

"God honors unselfish requests," Sandra responded, blinking to keep her tears at bay. She remembered the prayers she prayed in the beginning, basically asking God to severely punish Samuel for deceiving her and using her. It was hard at the time to hold her anger. Once she repented and was forgiven for her sins, she asked God for a pure heart. After that, her burden didn't seem so heavy.

"Jesus is looking for sincerity when we pray. When King Solomon was a boy, he asked for an understanding heart to judge a nation. Because his request wasn't for selfish reasons, God blessed him beyond measure. The story is in First Kings, chapter three. Are you attending church?"

Before Talise could respond, Sally reappeared, offering sample size bags of cookies and peanuts. Again, she lingered at their seats and made small talk with Talise before moving on. Why did interruptions always seem to happen when "church" was interjected into conversations? Sandra tried to hide her annoyance.

Several minutes later, Talise responded to her question, "I work on Sundays, but Sinclaire gave me a Bible."

"Do you read on a regular basis?"

"Not really, but sometimes. Honestly, between working two jobs, I only get one day off. And I've been so tired lately."

Sandra frowned. She was concerned about any expectant mother working two jobs, especially more so with Talise.

Was she hurting for money? Sandra was going to have to figure out a way to bless Talise without offending her. She didn't come across as a woman who took handouts.

Two jobs, not attending church, and becoming a single mother was a troublesome combination. She saw too many similarities between herself and Talise and it deeply concerned her. Ace's ex needed to know that God could supply, meet, and take care of all her needs, according to His riches in glory.

Sandra strongly encouraged Talise to read Philippians 4:19. Besides that, she would pray for her. Talise also needed an opportunity to listen to an anointed man of God preach the gospel. Out of a deep concern, she felt compelled to tell Talise, "God is getting ready to move some things around in your life. Accept them. Remember, He makes no mistakes."

Chapter Twenty-Four

S urprisingly, Sandra was good company on the flight. Nevertheless, as their plane was about to touch down, Talise's mood
soured. Although she'd never been to St. Louis, already she knew
there were two things the city was noted for: the Gateway Arch and
Aaron Jamieson.

Neither sounded appealing at the moment. She wasn't in a sightseeing mood and Ace's name alone was enough to make her stay on the
plane. Wanting to trust Sandra and Eva that he wouldn't be anywhere
near them, Talise hoped the Missouri motto, "The Show Me State,"
would prove in her favor.

As they disembarked the plane at Lambert Airport, Talise recalled
Lois's and Sinclaire's last minute differing messages:

"Personally, you're a better woman than me. I think you're torturing yourself going to a place where the father of your child is hiding
out—the coward. But, in your heart, don't make your baby suffer to
punish the father. The Jamieson family will be important later on when
he or she starts to ask questions. Tread softly." Those conflicting words
of wisdom had come from Lois. Rolling her eyes, Talise didn't quite

know what to make of her mixed message.

Sinclaire's email message had arrived early that morning and was more upbeat: *Just be prayerful. God has some good people that He strategically places in our lives. Let them bless you with their love and support. God knows the future. Trust Him to reveal it.* Her sister's positive message stayed with Talise, bringing her some level of comfort.

Despite any encouraging words, now it was time to face the moment of truth. Under the current circumstances, Talise was suddenly terrified of meeting another member in Ace's family. She would have preferred a formal introduction from Ace standing by her side, such as, "This is my girlfriend, Talise Rogers—no—this is my fiancée." Talise sniffed, as she blinked away her hopeful aspirations.

Hesitantly, Sandra put an arm around her shoulder and squeezed. "It'll be okay." She must have sensed the apprehension Talise was understandably feeling.

Nodding, she doubted it would be okay. She and Eva could swap baby stories, break bread, and what else? They lived in two different states, worlds, and comfort zones—married and single; loved and unloved; committed and deserted. There wouldn't be any marital ties to bind them.

Rounding the corner to the baggage claim area, three women stood out from the crowd. One held a sign: "Welcome, Talise!" A shorter woman cradled a small bouquet of flowers, and the third one bore a gift-wrapped box.

As they got closer, the tearjerker was the little girl dressed with tender care. As a stylist, she couldn't help but notice the straight parts in her hair. The ponytail twists were almost textbook perfection, and the oil sheen gave the desired effect as a crowning touch. Kudos to the child's mother, Talise knew how to groom natural hair.

Jumping up and down and grinning excitedly, the girl held up a smaller sign that read: "And baby!"

Slowing her steps, she wondered, *Who are these people?* Talise was under the impression that only Eva was meeting her. Sandra smiled as the fan club rushed toward them. Their hair, facial features, and attire seemed to blur as the rocks on their fingers blinded her. Somehow, over the past months, Talise had become increasingly sensitive to the presence or absence of a wedding ring on a woman's finger.

The shortest, spunky woman, who was all smiles, had to be Ace's sister-in-law. With a broad grin and no immediate words, she handed Talise a colorful bouquet of mixed flowers. Talise had barely accepted them before the woman quickly pulled her into a tight hug and blew her air kisses.

"I'm so glad you came! I'm Eva."

In Talise's opinion, Eva's most striking feature was her eyes. They were the clearest brown she had ever seen. A rose colored, two-piece outfit complemented her fair skin. While the two women embraced, Eva glanced over her shoulder and taunted the others, who appeared impatient to give their hugs. However, Sandra seemed content to wait her turn for her share of affections.

Talise was shuffled into the next set of waiting arms. "I'm Cheney Jamieson. I'm married to Cameron's oldest brother, Parke." Excitement shone from her eyes. Cheney was the tallest, maybe even six feet. But the height added to her attractiveness. Similar to Talise, she had healthy, shoulder length, jet black hair. Their dark features also mirrored each other, with one distinction. Talise would describe Cheney's complexion as having a dash of lemon flavoring.

"And this is my daughter, Kami." Cheney put her arm around the girl's shoulder. "When I told her we were going to Josephine's Tea Room, she begged to come along. I hope you don't mind. She especially likes the gift shop." Cheney explained her daughter's presence and smiled with a hopeful expression.

"Not at all, considering I don't know what you all have planned."

Kami's eyes lit up. She contained her jubilation to a wide grin. Briefly, Talise wondered if she would have a daughter. Who would she favor, her or Ace?

Pulled into another embrace, the third woman introduced herself. "I'm Hallison Jamieson, but please call me Hali. I'm married to Malcolm, Cameron's middle brother."

Hallison was a stair step between Eva and Cheney. She was equally as beautiful with her golden honey skin tone and almost the same tint in her brown eyes. Out of sheer habit, Talise did a quick assessment of Hallison's hair. There were no split-ends apparent to the naked eye.

Kami bounced on her toes. "I was hoping you had the baby."

"Not yet." Talise surprised herself when she took the liberty and tweaked the girl's nose.

The others laughed. *The innocence of a child.* Finally, Sandra got her turn and received her round of hugs and kisses.

Eva pointed to an older woman reclining in one of many chairs that lined a back wall of the baggage area. "That's Grandma BB. She invited herself." Eva bit her bottom lip. "I hope that's okay too. She's the matriarch of the family, but no men were invited or even know."

Sensing her emotions about to take over, Talise hadn't expected this warm welcome. With new faces, strange names, and loads of unexpected affection, her head was spinning. Tears sprang forth, and then one by one, they trickled down. She had grown weary of surprise emotional outbursts like this one. But the kindness of these women overpowered her. Sniffing, she rummaged through her purse for a tissue.

Immediately, the Jamieson wives encircled her with more hugs. She heard Sandra whispering prayers of blessings and peace. Suddenly, Talise felt an unusual moment of well-being, reminding her of days gone by with her mother and Sinclaire.

"How embarrassing," she said aloud, daring not to look around and see how much attention she was attracting. "So sorry." Talise wiped at her eyes, disregarding her carefully applied makeup.

"Girl, blame it on our hormonal imbalance. I do." Eva consoled her, squeezing her hand.

"I'm a little overwhelmed," Talise explained with a shaky voice. She used her hand to fan herself. Pulling out an envelope from her purse, Cheney used it to give Talise additional cooling. Once she was composed, Talise busied herself by smoothing imaginary wrinkles from her blouse.

"Ready?" Cheney whispered.

Not really, but Talise nodded. She fell in step, as they headed toward their Grandma BB. Sitting regally, the woman watched intently as they approached. Upon closer inspection, Grandma BB didn't favor any of the women. Talise reasoned she had to be a Jamieson. Her glossy silver hair looked freshly done with the curls expertly set on top of her head. Gold looped jewelry dangled from her ears. No wrinkles, moles, or blemishes marred her face.

Hmm, Talise thought, *the Jamiesons must possess good genes.*

Grandma BB was stylishly wearing a white sleeveless dress with bits of red accents. The senior oozed sassy sophistication, and . . . as she scanned downward, Talise blinked . . . a pair of black Stacy Adams shoes with red shoestrings swallowed up her dainty feet. Uh-oh, something wasn't normal here.

Get Ace's medical history ASAP, was the first thought that came to her mind. Every family could be susceptible to mental illness, but she prayed it wasn't a dominant gene in the Jamiesons' bloodline.

Eying her up and down, Grandma BB grunted. "The boy's got good taste, if not good sense."

Caught off guard by the remark, Talise sucked in her breath. Was Grandma BB referring to her grandson, Ace, as "the boy"? The woman's eyes twinkled. Another ally, perhaps? Would the grandmother ask for her pregnancy test results? She hoped not. Talise swallowed and formally introduced herself.

"Chile, I know who you are. I wouldn't be Grandma BB if I didn't know you were Ty, giving her a new nickname. I won't meddle in your business—"

The Jamieson wives murmured and faked coughs. Grandma BB glared at them. "Anyway, my services are for hire. If you need me to roughen him up a little, it ain't a problem." The woman jutted her chin, as if she had made a firm declaration.

Talise released a hearty laugh. That's exactly what Ace needed—someone to knock some sense into him. "I wish."

"She's not kidding," the wives said in a seemingly rehearsed harmony.

"Really?"

"Uh-huh. Grandma BB always says to tell it like it is, and she tells it like it is," Kami chimed in, bobbing her head.

Cheney and Hallison positioned themselves on either side of Grandma BB to assist her in standing. A walking cane with a rhinestone-covered handle rested beside her. Reaching for it, the senior citizen shooed them away, as if she didn't need their help.

"Come on. Sandra's luggage should have made it off the plane by now," Eva reminded them.

Clasping onto Sandra's hand, Kami skipped alongside her. Minutes later, when they stepped up to the baggage carousel, her two small pieces of polka-dot luggage were circulating the ramp. Cheney and Hallison reached for the bags.

Activity around Talise blurred as she focused on the Jamieson family. They were a close-knit, fun-loving bunch. So far, only the grandmother was questionable. Hopefully, Grandma BB's oddity was limited to her sense of style, not her mental faculties.

Talise also noted that none of the women acted as though they questioned her condition. She reasoned that if one were to look hard enough, one could see that she had *something* to show. But, being totally honest, someone might have to first suspect it. Otherwise, she probably looked like any other woman who had a bit of flab around her midsection. Talise had tried to show off her "pouch" to Sinclaire during their last video chat. Her sister had flatly told her she couldn't tell.

Once the luggage was retrieved, Talise and Eva excused themselves to the ladies' room before leaving the airport. Their potty break quickly became a family affair as all the women gathered in the restroom to freshen up. Minutes later, they walked outside toward the parking garage.

"Ugh! It's so humid here and it's barely noon." Talise tried using her hand again as a fan when beads of sweat began to dot her clothes. "How do you stand it?"

"We don't." Cheney groaned. "That's why air conditioning is a wonderful thing."

Talise could tolerate some heat, but this intensity was suffocating. After crossing a wide walkway, they huddled into an elevator and rode to the open parking level at the top. Without the benefit of the lower level shelter, it was almost intolerable, as the sun beamed down on her head.

The lights on a new black SUV blinked. Cheney climbed in behind the wheel. Once again, Grandma BB resisted any help, while she was clearly struggling to climb into the passenger seat.

"The pregnant ladies sit in the middle. Kami and I will get in the back," Sandra announced.

"I'm not pregnant," Hallison reminded them.

"Not yet, but if Malcolm doesn't stop looking at you like you're a doe during mating season, then you'll be next." Cheney snickered.

"Be quiet! Can I help it that Malcolm and I agreed to wait until M.J. was two years old before we started on another baby? And he turned two last month?"

"Oh, it's on, ya'll," Eva teased, while she and Hallison sandwiched Talise between them. Thankfully, the vehicle was roomy enough.

As they travelled along, Cheney and Grandma BB were having their own personal conversation. Kami was a chatterbox, while Sandra politely listened. Eva acted as a backseat tour guide, drawing Talise's attention to several points of interest. Riding east on I-270, they passed the exit to the St. Louis Mills Mall. Eva leaned closer and informed her new pregnant buddy, "They have a Babies R Us. We'll have to go shopping."

"She's not even here for twenty-four hours. You all don't have the sixty you take when we go shopping," Grandma BB chimed in. "Girl, you're like a mouse caged in a maze of cheese."

Scrunching up her nose, Eva laughed. "Give me a break, Grandma BB. Since Kevin demanded I cut back my hours, it's boring just sitting at home," she defended. "I'm so glad that now Talise and I can compare our baby notes." Adding that, she stuck out her tongue. Kami caught her in the act and laughed. It was a good thing Eva was sitting behind Grandma BB and out of her sight.

"Save your money. I keep telling you that you can always come to my house. I've got a big collection of videos," Grandma BB boasted. "And they ain't all Disney movies either."

Talise blinked. She didn't even want to know what that meant. Instead, she reflected on Eva's option to reduce her work hours because she had a husband to support her. That thought caused her to sigh deeply. Talise needed the money and health benefits. She had no choice but to work two jobs. Still, something had to change soon. She was becoming increasingly tired.

At the most, she was counting on her six weeks paid maternity leave to bond with her baby. After that, she didn't have a clue about their future. If her options ran out, she would have to move back to Virginia and start over.

Her eyelids fluttered, as she tuned out the conversations swirling around her. Talise didn't want to think about the absence of a good, loving man in her life. She longed for the kind of man who would pick up the slack and dote on her and the baby.

Soon Eva tapped her on the arm. "We're almost there."

Glancing around at the view, Talise was wowed by an artistically constructed bridge, as they crossed the Mississippi River into Illinois.

165

She didn't realize St. Louis was so scenic. A small casino was docked at its bank. Immediately, it sparked a memory of a getaway weekend with Ace. Shaking her head, Talise refused to reminisce about the good times that had become the prelude to the bad ones.

"This charming town is called Alton. It's known for its bluffs over-looking the river. It's also known as the birthplace of the world's tallest man. Robert Wadlow died here when he was twenty-two years old and weighed more than four-hundred pounds. A medical condition caused him to grow to eight feet and eleven inches tall," Cheney noted, breaking into Talise's reverie.

Impressed by her knowledge, Talise admired the quaint feel of the town.

"Interesting," she commented.

"Paranormal fanatics claim it's the most haunted city in America. I don't believe it," Grandma BB added in dispute. "Supposedly, there're some hot spots of activity where builders used stone from a Civil War prison, and Confederate soldiers had died of dreaded diseases inside the prison walls." Grandma BB grunted. "I'm bad, but I ain't that bad. I've got to sleep at night, and I don't want any ghosts—bad or good— messin' with me."

Squeals of laughter rang out as Grandma BB shivered at the thought of it.

"But for every legion of demons, God's got thousands on thousands of angels ready to be dispatched for battle. All He has to do is speak His Word," Sandra informed the group, with a snap of her fingers.

"Humph. I came along for the food, Sandra, not for the preaching," Grandma BB countered. "If I want a sermon, I'll rent an audiotape from the library."

"Would you be nice, Grandma BB? Don't show Talise how ugly you really can get," Eva scolded respectfully.

"I may not go to church anymore, but I know ain't nothing ugly— but the devil. I looked gorgeous when I went to bed last night. Not to mention when I woke up this morning too."

"We're not going to win against you," Cheney stated, playfully swatting Grandma BB's shoulder.

"This is one crazy family," Eva whispered, nudging Talise.

"No comment," Talise mumbled, as the scenery changed on Godfrey Road.

"Kami," her mother called, glancing in the rearview mirror. "Why don't you tell Miss Talise the historical significance of this town?"

As the girl sat in a rare moment of quiet reflection, Talise felt bad that maybe her mother had put her on the spot.

"Native Americans settled in Alton thousands of years before the Europeans. Artifacts have been discovered here to prove it. Some homes in Alton were built with tunnels and hiding places for enslaved people to run away before and during the Civil War," Kami recited and took a deep breath.

"That's good, sweetie. What did enslaved people call the escape route?" her mother quizzed the girl.

"The Underground Railroad."

Applause erupted in the vehicle and Talise joined in, wowed. With her beauty and brains, the girl would be dangerous when she grew up. Those are traits Talise hoped would be passed down to her child.

"I'm blown away. How old are you, Kami?"

"Ten. My brother's eleven, but I'm smarter because I got all A's last year. I'm going to the sixth grade."

"You are very smart. I'm impressed that your school would teach local history from all perspectives."

Kami leaned forward and rested her chin on the back of Talise's seat. "I didn't learn all that in my school. My dad taught me when we have family game night. We have a lot of fun and food and games. My brothers, cousins, and I can play along with the adults."

"Wow," Talise said.

"We even have team T-shirts. Do you want to come, Miss Talise?"

"We'll see," she said to pacify the girl. But in her heart, she had the strangest feeling that before the day was over, she would regret this visit. Not because they mistreated her. Rather, because she would never be a Jamieson. And at the moment, for the first time since she learned she was pregnant—she wished she was a Jamieson.

*F*inally!" Eva and Grandma BB almost chimed in unison when their destination came into view. Everyone around Talise applauded and cheered as Cheney passed a college campus.

Minutes later, she turned into the parking lot behind an oval sign that read "Josephine's, Est. 1979." Talise's stomach growled. She was surprised her snacks on the plane had lasted this long.

Eva laughed. "Potty break?"

"Yes!" Talise agreed.

As usual, Cheney tried to assist Grandma BB in getting out of the car. And once again, the woman waved her away with her cane. This time, Cheney appeared to be just as stubborn, as she tangled with the old woman until Grandma BB let her help.

"Is she always so feisty?" Talise whispered, as Eva looped her arm though hers and steered her toward the door.

"Yep!" Eva replied with a giggle. "Even in her sleep. She had suffered a stroke when Cheney and her husband admitted her to Garden Chateau years ago. That's the nursing facility where Kevin and I work. Grandma BB didn't last six months in that place before she 'escaped.'"

169

Eva made quotation marks with her fingers. "Since her breakout, her recovery has been amazing. Still, we don't want to take any chances of her falling and injuring herself. Grandma BB sings the praises of Dino, her boy-toy private duty nurse. She leans on him for the most part. But we give Jesus all of His glory. She'd better stop playing with God, if you know what I mean. Anyway, we try to be near her in case she becomes unsteady on her feet."

"Yeah, but she ain't fooling anybody. Our friend Imani, who also happens to be her neighbor, says Grandma BB has woken up the neighborhood more than once with her Janet Jackson workout videos," Hallison mumbled, chuckling.

"I heard that," Grandma BB twirled around and grunted. Cheney almost stumbled, but recovered.

Walking behind Talise and Eva, Sandra stated, "I hope you'll be glad that you came."

"I already am."

Talise felt the cool air when the front door opened to what appeared to be someone's home.

"Welcome, ladies," the hostess greeted them and took their names. "This way to the Garden Room, please."

"Wait," Eva stopped her. "We'd better go to the little girls' room first."

Eva and Talise made a detour around a short corner to the restroom. The hostess waited for them and nodded once they returned. She then walked ahead and motioned for the group to follow.

The place was charming and dainty, like a secret hideaway. Talise couldn't take in the details of her surroundings fast enough. They passed through a large room with snug tables sprinkled all about, a floor-to-ceiling brick fireplace, sun light shining throughout, beautiful chandeliers, and much more. Since it was close to noon, there was a brisk lunch crowd.

The hostess continued on to another enchanting room. Among

the cozy, white wrought iron tables, a section was set apart for their group. As if possible, the ambience in that room superseded the others. Talise was a sucker for airy rooms with enormous custom windows. She smiled in appreciation at the wide shutter-look blinds. Another "wow" escaped from her lips.

Eva chuckled. "We had hoped you would enjoy this experience."

"What woman wouldn't love it?" Talise replied excitedly, quickly scanning the room once more before taking her seat.

"Your waitress will be with you in a moment," announced the hostess. One by one, she patiently handed them their menus and then retraced her steps back toward the front entrance.

As if the moment was synchronized, Eva's stomach rumbled, followed by Talise's. Eva looked at her and grinned. The woman's engaging smile was contagious.

"The babies are hungry, Cousin-Auntie Eva and Miss Talise," Kami said with a laugh.

"Feed those babies," Grandma BB ordered.

Their waitress appeared and introduced herself as Mattie. After pouring hot tea into each china tea cup, she took their drink orders.

Kami unzipped her purse and pulled out white laced gloves. As if she cued the others, everyone but Talise did the same. Eva promptly handed her a new pair of gloves similar to her own.

"Thank you," Talise whispered. "I was starting to feel left out."

"You're always included," Eva reassured her and opened her menu.

By the time Mattie returned with their drinks, they were ready to order. Everyone suggested Josephine's special, the Crystal Bowl Salad, so Talise decided to give it a try. Cheney ordered the small Crystal Bowl and soup for Kami.

During their wait, conversations bounced from babies, to food, to shopping sprees. When Talise mentioned she was a part-time hair stylist, she fielded questions about hair care products, the latest in hair trends, and the best hair maintenance between visits.

"When I go to Boston, I'll have to visit your shop," Eva said. The others bobbed their heads in agreement. "You know," she paused to sip her drink, "we might as well make it a shopping spree."

Grandma BB *tsk*ed. "Don't invite me. If you go into labor while you're on one of your shopping expeditions, I'll be forced to use some of those midwife skills I picked up on the TLC channel."

Talise sucked in her breath, as fear streaked through her bones at the very thought.

"And you'll have to wait until after they ring up my purchases," Eva taunted.

"She'll be like that lady who went into labor while waiting in line to vote for the first Black president. She refused to go to the hospital until she cast her vote," Cheney added.

Eva raised her hands. "That would be me."

When the salads arrived, the conversation ceased.

Bowing their heads, Sandra led the table in saying grace, "Lord Jesus, we are giving You the highest praise for Your blessings, seen and unseen, in our lives. We thank You for safe travels from Boston. We ask You to protect Talise as she returns later today. Thank You for this fellowship and for the next generation of Jamiesons. Please bless our meal, purify it, and sanctify it. And, Lord, please provide for those who have not, in the Name of Jesus. Amen."

As everyone voiced their Amens, Talise sniffed. She enjoyed hearing people pray. She felt Sandra's prayer was sincere like Sinclaire's. As they prayed, Talise heard either Cheney or Hallison whisper something like, "guide Talise through her decisions in her life." Amen to that.

Touched by the prayer, Talise heard a faint voice say The effectual fervent prayer of a righteous man avails much. *I'm far from righteous, God,* she admitted to no one but Him. *I hope my prayers reach your ears. My current condition is evidence of my wrongdoings,* she thought to herself.

Not realizing she had zoned out until Eva's chatter pulled her back into the conversation, Talise sat up and rejoined the discussion.

"My first trip to Boston was when Kevin and I made that friendly wager. He had a suspicion that the ramblings of Grandma BB's roommate in the nursing facility were true. I dismissed her as senile and simply repeating old wives' tales," Eva explained.

"And Valentine could tell some doozies too," Grandma BB interrupted with a faraway look in her eyes.

Agreeing, Eva nodded. With her pinkie poised, she lifted her china cup to her lips and sipped quietly.

"So how much weight have you gained, Talise?" She asked after a brief pause.

Talise finished chewing and swallowed. "Six pounds. I'm following my doctor's orders to watch what I eat. I'm also taking public transportation to work so I can get more exercise."

Plus, I need to save money. Not for a college fund, but for day care, unless I move back home. That would be a last resort—definitely, the last. She kept those thoughts private.

"I hope I don't get as big as a whale," Eva stated.

"I don't know. Your husband was a big baby," Sandra teased.

"That was a joke, remember?" Eva replied, rolling her eyes.

Talise enjoyed the interaction between Sandra and Eva. She hoped that if she did get married one day, she would have the same type of closeness with her mother-in-law. On the flip side, if she followed down the same path as Sandra, then there wouldn't be any wedding bells for her either.

Every now and then, Talise added her two cents in the conversation about clothes and childhood. When the Jamieson wives began to recall their husbands' antics, she withdrew emotionally and remained silent. It didn't take long for them to notice her sour mood and their blunder about her single status.

"We're sorry, Talise. No matter what, you're one of us," Eva whispered and laid her hand on top of Talise's. Sandra's hand followed suit

173

and the other Jamieson wives reached across the table as far as they could. Kami stood and rested her small glove-covered hand on the stack for a few seconds and then retook her seat.

Grandma BB didn't make a move, and Talise was trying to determine where she stood with the odd family matriarch. Maybe the woman didn't like her.

"Girl, you're a Jamieson whether you carry the name or not, like that Jewish law. Remember, Cheney?" Grandma BB interjected.

After displaying a puzzling frown for a few minutes, Cheney seemed to have an answer to what her grandmother was alluding to. "Oh yes. According to the Torah, if a mother is Jewish, so is her baby, even if the father isn't. It's the opposite for the father who marries a non-Jewish woman. Their baby wouldn't be considered Jewish."

Wow. These people were like a walking Wikipedia. "Ah, I'm sorry. I don't see a correlation between a Jamieson and a Jew."

"Girl, there isn't," Hallison said, shaking her head. "That's Grandma BB twisting biblical text to her liking—again," she said, stretching out the last word.

"Humph." Grandma BB leaned across the table. "Ignore her. She's a Jamieson." She paused and squinted at Talise. "Your baby's going to be a Jamie—"

Lord, please don't let any of Grandma BB's defective genes be passed down to my child, Talise thought. Then she spoke aloud, "I'm having a baby who'll be born out of wedlock by no fault of its own. My child will carry my last name, which is Rogers."

Gasps echoed around the table.

"Sweetie, if you're finished, you can go on to the gift shop now," Cheney said to her daughter. Clearly, the calm waters were about to get stormy.

Kami's eyes lit up. "Okay, Mommy," she replied. Giddy, she stood and lifted the long chain shoulder strap of her purse off the back of the chair.

Next, Cheney eyed Grandma BB. Without saying a word, the older woman gathered her walking cane and purse, gripping, "I declare it's more fun babysitting the Jamieson women than the little princess."

In protest, their grandmother huffed and *humph*ed. "I'm going. I hope you gave her a hefty allowance because I'm going to help her spend every last penny."

As Kami led Grandma BB away, the woman suddenly turned around. "Just so you'll know, Ty, I'm down with whatever method you decide for Ace's punishment: abduction, torture, or a simple beat down." She patted her purse. "I pack." Winking, she resumed walking with her granddaughter.

With her mouth hanging open, Talise stared after the woman in shock. When she found her voice, she glanced around the table. "Is your grandmother serious?"

In unison, the Jamieson wives nodded. "Very."

"I don't know how to say this without offending anyone," Talise paused and gnawed on her bottom lip. "But I've got to get this off my chest. Is that woman crazy? Does mental illness run in your family?"

Everyone chuckled. Then Cheney, who appeared to be the spokes-woman for the Jamieson wives explained, "Thankfully, no. Our men suffer from a stupidity gene until they get a good wife, then they're miraculously cured."

"Don't worry about her," Hallison added. "Both Grandma BB and Kami are adopted, but they'll beat you down if you argue they're not part of the Jamieson clan."

Adopted? Not that sweet, well-mannered little girl who could pass as Cheney's biological daughter. Talise's head was swimming with questions. As an outsider, she had no right to ask, so she remained quiet. However, she was relieved that her child was safe from Grandma BB's genes.

"It's a long story. They had to explain it to me too." Eva glanced around the room, as if double-checking their privacy. "Tell us what you

175

want to do to make Ace come around. Although we believe prayer can change things, Grandma BB prefers force—and she will use it."

"Tell me about it. She even played target practice on my dad. But, fortunately, he survived the superficial wound," Cheney added.

Talise gave her a dumbfounded expression.

"I know it sounds crazy. As Eva just said, it's a long story for another visit. But basically, Grandma BB is a widow today because of the actions of my father before I was even born. Dad was the hit and run driver who killed her husband, Henry. He kept the secret bottled up for decades until I returned from college.

"When she learned the truth, Grandma BB shot him in retaliation. Like I said, she wasn't trying to kill him, only scare him. They both served time for the crime. Grandma BB did ninety days shock time."

Talise didn't believe a word of it. The doubt must have been written on her face.

"It's true," Cheney said, as all the women nodded, except Sandra.

Lifting her shoulders, Talise exhaled. "Okay. Well, I didn't expect that. But with me, at this point, she doesn't have to bother. The man walked away from me. He's guilty by desertion. The penalty for desertion in the military is court-marital. My sister is serving in the air force and, despite Ace's treason, she's the one who encouraged me to come today for my baby's sake. Otherwise, I don't know if I would have made the trip."

"Girl, did we not just say we're a praying family? It was a matter of time before we came to you," Eva advised her with a serious attitude.

Mattie returned to their table and collected their plates. "Anyone want dessert?"

Only Eva took the bait.

"Yeah? I prayed that I wasn't pregnant. Since I am, I'm paying for my sin."

"We don't know how to pay for our sins. Plus, we don't have enough clout to eliminate our debt. Christ died on a wood cross to redeem us. For those who repent, He releases the power of the Holy Ghost as the tool to help us live right," Cheney gave her spiel.

Talise withheld her comments. Wholeheartedly embracing Christ wouldn't change anything—Ace's attitude or her condition.

"The Holy Ghost can keep us from falling," Sandra added, raising her arm and waving her hand. "I'm a witness. It's a promise from the Book of Jude, but we have to do our part."

Cheney continued, "I'm not judging you, Talise. None of us are. I was pregnant out of wedlock, and I made a different choice. I aborted my baby over a stupid man. When doctors told me I could never become pregnant again, it was God's grace that gave me another chance to get it right. Now I'm the proud mother of three children."

"Well, Ty's having a baby despite Ace Jamieson's stupidity," Grandma BB added her two cents, sneaking up on them.

Cheney whipped her head around. "Where's Kami?"

"She's coming. I made her max out her allowance. That girl had some serious money saved." Grandma BB beamed.

"Do we really want to have a contest on the stupidest Jamieson man? Because you know Kevin would win hands down." Eva slapped the table.

Talise watched their interaction with humor, interest, and longing. The Jamieson wives were a harmonious group. However, there were no whimsical thoughts dancing in her head that she would ever be part of the team.

"Do you go to church?" Hallison asked her, seemingly out of nowhere.

That was the second time in one day someone asked her that. "No, I work on Sundays."

"God will make a way," Eva said with a nod, and then stuffed the last bite of dessert in her mouth. "We'll pray on it."

It was close to two o'clock, and the crowd at Josephine's Tea Room had thinned considerably. Their group seemed to be a handful of the last remaining guests. When they left Josephine's stuffed, Cheney drove to historic downtown Alton to shop.

Not wanting to haul a big bag on the plane, Talise refrained from going overboard on souvenirs and other purchases. The hours passed quickly, until it was four o'clock and time to head back home.

Arriving at Lambert Airport, Talise assumed she would be dropped off. Instead, Cheney parked and everyone, including Grandma BB, escorted her inside. With her purse and bouquet in one arm, Talise accepted their goodbye hugs.

"This has been fun. You all are some special ladies. Eva, I appreciate you honoring your word and not ambushing me with Ace."

"Hey, whether you accept your ties to the Jamieson name or not, we've got your back. Ace will never know you were here." Eva said it with a smile, as she winked in triumph.

Chapter Twenty-Six

*A*ce had a one-track mind. He had to get home to see what was brewing in Boston. Besides, he missed the months he'd been away from his beloved Beantown. Not only would he surprise his mother, his main objective was to confront Talise.

On his way to Lambert Airport, Ace couldn't stop thinking about the nerve of his ex-girlfriend. Whatever shenanigans she had up her sleeve, he would put a stop to it once and for all. He wouldn't allow her to keep dragging his family members, especially his mother, into her web of dishonesty. He knew how to wear his game face when he threatened to put the fear of his fist upside an opponent's head.

Threaten. Ace groaned at his bad choice of words in association with Talise. He would never lay hands on his ex or any woman. At the same time, he knew he'd need a game face. Staring into Talise's mesmerizing brown eyes would be a huge challenge.

Unable to ever admit it, he shuddered at the thought of confronting a woman who could make him weak in the knees. However, at the end of the day, no matter how tempting Talise looked—whether she was pregnant or not—Ace couldn't give in. Above all—whatever she said or however enticing her voice may be when she said it—Ace had to stay strong.

"Don't fall for her charm, man," he coaxed himself. Parking his car on the park-n-ride lot, he boarded the shuttle to the airport. While in Boston, he also planned to patch up things with Cameron. Very much like a brother, Ace's cousin was the closest person to him after Kidd.

Minutes later, the Super Park shuttle dropped him off at the Southwest terminal. He was more than two hours early for his 7:05 flight home. Although he preferred an earlier flight, it was booked. But there still might be hope for him to fly stand-by. If that didn't work out, Ace figured he would hang out in the sports bar.

With his mind elsewhere, he bypassed the curbside check-in and headed for the door. Then something got his attention. From a distance, Ace squinted and blinked when a woman who reminded him of Eva caught his eye. It couldn't be. What reason would she have for being at the airport?

Earlier, when he informed Kidd that he was going home to surprise their mother, his brother had joked with him. Kidd had told Ace that he'd better be glad Eva wasn't home. If she'd been there, she would have handed him a list of items to bring back from her favorite places.

"Eva, the other Jamieson wives, and Kami are spending the day together shopping," Kidd had said. So there was no way the person he just saw could be his sister-in-law.

Funny how women have such peculiar ways, he thought. It baffled him how Eva could side with a woman she had never met. Ace shook his head in disbelief. Blood was thicker than water, though, so Eva might as well forgive him for whatever imaginary transgression she thought he caused.

For some reason, he wasn't able to dismiss the woman's uncanny resemblance. So, angling his head, Ace decided to get another look. When he turned around, the woman in question was nowhere in sight. Evidently, his eyes and mind were playing tricks on him.

Inside the terminal, he looked straight ahead at the line of Southwest ticket counters. The familiar sight caused Ace to envision Talise in her uniform, smiling and greeting passengers. Knowing that Thursday was her day off, there was no chance he'd run into her at the airport when he arrived in Boston.

Already holding a ticket, he stood in line, impatiently waiting his turn. The six o'clock flight to Boston would be boarding soon. Hopefully, someone canceled and he could fly standby. He was anxious to get there and, just in general, hated to waste time. His preferred flight was going nonstop without a layover in Baltimore.

As he approached the counter, the agent standing at the desk gave him an appreciative stare. Ace upped his charm, wondering how many men flirted with Talise.

"May I help you, sir?"

Handing the woman his ticket, he said, "Yes, are there any seats available on the six o'clock flight to Boston? If so, I would like to make a change."

"Let me check that for you," she said politely.

Ace stood there tapping his foot and waited for what seemed like hours. Finally, the agent said, "Sir, I'm sorry, but that flight is booked solid." She slid the boarding pass into the pocket of his ticket and returned it to him with a polite smile.

What else could he do but thank her and move on? He'd tried. Ace proceeded to go through the security checkpoints. The line inched along from the TSA workers checking IDs to those manning the scanners. Once he put his shoes back on and grabbed his keys and change, he checked the monitor for his flight.

> BOSTON   4376   7:05p   8A   ON TIME

"Great."

Ace was still glad he got there early. As planned, he'd spend the time watching the game in the lounge area. Walking down the lengthy corridor, he weaved his way through the crowd of travelers. Looking for the sign with his gate number, he scanned the passageway. Just past his waiting area, there was a restroom and beyond that he spotted the lounge.

Heading to his destination, he felt hunger pangs. Although airport food wasn't the greatest, he was thinking he might also grab a bite to eat while waiting for his flight. When he passed Gate 8A, Ace glanced over in that direction. A group of people were forming a line near the ramp to the plane entrance. Evidently, they had just started boarding the one through thirty "A" group for the flight before his. Then something made him stop abruptly in his tracks. This couldn't be.

Talise? Suddenly, out of the corner of his eye, Ace thought he saw her. As part of the line formed for group "A" passengers, a woman had just handed over her boarding pass to be scanned and was poised to enter the ramp. He twisted his body around to get a better look.

First, he thought he saw Eva. And now, his ex?

In fact, if it wasn't her, the woman could pass as her twin. Talise did have a sister, Sinclaire, who was in the military. The last he knew before they broke up, her sister was stationed somewhere in the Middle East, not the Midwest.

Moving quickly to get a closer look, he said to the other passengers blocking his way, "Ah, excuse me just a minute, please." Barging his way through the line, he shouted, "Talise!" Ace was desperately trying to catch the woman's attention, who was wearing headsets and oblivious to his calls.

"Tay!" He shouted again.

To the other travelers' annoyance, he had pushed his way to the front of the line. He just had to know if it was her. Shouting down the ramp, he yelled out, "Tay!" The agent who was scanning tickets held out her arm to block him from going any farther.

"Excuse me, that's my girlfriend," he said, pointing frantically.

"Sir, unless you have an 'A, one-to-thirty' seating ticket, please wait until your turn is called. I'm sure she'll hold you a seat."

"You don't understand. We had an argument. She might not. I'm on the next flight. Can I speak with her a minute?" He had begun to rattle on anxiously.

"Sir, you're holding up the line," the woman tried to reason with him.

"But I only want to talk with her," he explained. By this time, Ace had broken into a sweat and his behavior was beyond making a scene. With growing irritation and confusion, he couldn't fathom what Talise was doing in St. Louis. Even in his frazzled state of mind, he knew his efforts were futile, and they'd never allow him to get on that plane without a boarding pass.

By now, another agent joined the one who had been trying to get through to Ace. Instead of a smile, he was met with a suspicious glare.

"Sir, can I help you?"

"Yes, I just need a minute to get on that plane and talk to my girlfriend." He pushed his ticket at the agent, thinking it would somehow prove his right to be there.

"I'm sorry, sir, this plane—"

Snatching his ticket away from her, Ace was out of control and thinking irrationally. "Listen, I just need five minutes." This time, not waiting for an answer, he tried to shove his way through.

The next thing he knew, he was overpowered, tackled, kissing the ground, and being threatened not to move. Handcuffs were slapped on his wrists and a barking German shepherd rounded out the incredible scenario.

"Police!" they shouted. Tightening the grip on his arms, the officers tried unsuccessfully to yank him to his feet. Ace was solid muscle. It would take more than two men to lift him.

Finally, Ace assisted them by pushing his body up from the floor.

183

"I'm not a threat. I just wanted to talk to my girlfriend." That wasn't entirely true. Talise was his ex and he was planning to threaten her to stay away from his family.

Gawking passengers made room as the officers carted him away. Right before they led him down a long hallway, he noticed several travelers with smart phones aiming their devices his way. Making the best of an embarrassing situation, Ace presented his favored facial profile.

"Hi, Mom," he said with a terse smile while inwardly groaning.

Talise was doing it to him again. If he hadn't been on his way home because of her, he wouldn't be in this jam.

—⁓—

Talk about a terrible travel experience. Wait until he had the opportunity to fill out a survey. Almost an hour later, Ace was still pleading his case. In a back room somewhere in a secluded area of the airport, his answer remained the same.

"Listen, I've told you. I'm not a terrorist. I was just trying to get to my girlfriend. It's the honest truth."

"The next time you have a lover's quarrel, do it before you get to the airport. Let's go," one officer ordered.

While being ushered to a police car, he took some comfort in the fact that the coast was clear of a curious crowd or the relentless media. However, his relief didn't last too long. Moments after Ace was shoved into the back seat, reporters and camera equipment were on his trail. Cowering lower, he bowed his head and closed his eyes. Adding insult to injury, the officer didn't seem to be in any hurry to avoid a media circus.

"Just great." Ace groaned.

"Did the suspect pose any threat to security?" he could hear a female reporter ask.

"No, we were able to subdue him with little effort."

"Right. I'm six-three and weigh two-hundred and twenty-pounds.

It took more than a little effort to bring me down," Ace corrected under his breath.

He hadn't been in jail since . . . the last time he was in jail. Actually, it was two years ago after that stint for disorderly conduct outside a bar. That was when he vowed to his mother, brother, and cousin that his childish behavior was behind him.

Cameron had harped on Ace's wasted potential, going as far as using his connections to secure his cousin several job interviews. Ace landed a position with his current employer and his business acumen soared.

With his mind finally made up, things began to change. He cut his association with guilty parties and unsavory relationships. Now his income, for the most part, came by legal means. Surprisingly, Ace's social calendar didn't suffer when he cleaned up his bad boy image. Then he met Talise and his life seemed to get even better—at least until a few months ago.

Chapter Twenty-Seven

He what?" Sandra led the chorus. She, her son, and daughter-in-law couldn't believe the phone call Kidd had received less than ten minutes earlier. Adding the brief news report from the local station, it verified that a man at the airport had momentarily lost his mind. Without a photo, his mother, for one, didn't really want to accept that it was her son. One thing for sure, they couldn't deny he was in some kind of trouble.

Kidd was fuming. Sandra was bewildered and disappointed. "What was he doing at the airport?"

"He was on his way home to surprise you, Ma."

"Me?" Sandra sucked in her breath.

"Yeah. Ace said he was homesick and he wanted to go home and check on you."

"Well, his timing was off. That's for sure," Sandra replied in exasperation. "Why does your brother seem to be a magnet for craziness?"

Surfing the Internet on her phone when they got the call, Eva was about to sign off when a headline grabbed her attention. "Hey, look at this. A video is going viral on YouTube." She read, "'A lover's spat brings a St. Louis airport to a halt.'"

Then Eva tapped "play" and the three of them squinted to watch the video play out.

"That can't be Ace. He didn't know—" Sandra caught herself. Kidd wasn't privy to their whereabouts during the day. She was hoping to keep it that way.

Peering over Eva's shoulder, they continued to watch the footage. Sure enough, two men were straining to lift a muscular man off the floor. Both women gasped when they saw the man stand up and a German shepherd ready to pounce. It was Ace.

"Thank God, he didn't resist." Sandra patted her chest to console her pounding heart. The potential aftermath of what could happen if her sons resisted when they were growing up, kept Sandra praying at night. Instantly, this scene became a stark reminder of those days.

Apparently, she should have never stopped praying. Turning away, she couldn't watch anymore. Then she heard Ace's muffled voice say, "Hi, Mom." Sandra glanced over her shoulder in time to see Ace's engaging smile and shuddered.

Kidd mumbled, "Fool." He clutched a fist.

"Come on. You have to admit it's funny. For Ace to be so arrogant in his moment of unfavorable international notoriety is amusing," Eva commented.

Sandra exchanged glances with Kidd when he looked up. Staring each other in the eye, neither of them could contain it any longer. They laughed harder than Eva.

There was a brief intermission when Cheney's husband, Parke, called. Malcolm followed and somehow, Cameron knew about it all the way up in Boston.

"I guess I've let him stew long enough. I'll be back." Kidd dug in his pants pockets for his car keys. He kissed Eva and was about to kiss his mother before she interrupted him.

"I'm going with you. No wonder Talise doesn't want to be bothered with him," Sandra said in disgust.

Kidd froze in his tracks. He glanced from his wife, who could keep a straight face no matter what, to his mother who wore an angelic expression—her game face.

"Somehow you two know something I don't," he announced, folding his arms and towering over them.

The women didn't back down. One thing Kidd forgot was Sandra never let her sons, regardless of their size, intimidate her. She was the momma, and if anybody was going to instill fear, it would be her. Sandra lifted a defiant brow.

"Okay, I see you two have the mother/daughter-in-law pact going on. That's all right. Don't worry. I'll figure it out. I'll be waiting in the car." With that said, Kidd walked out the front door.

The two women looked at each other. "Do you think we should say anything to Talise?" Eva whispered. "The video is pretty funny. She may get a good laugh. I promised her that Ace wouldn't be within ten feet around her. And . . . look what happened." Eva exploded into giggles again. "The Federal Marshals took care of that."

"I think those were local police," Sandra corrected, shaking her head. "Either way, she's had enough excitement for one day. With all of us and Grandma BB, we were a handful."

"You're right."

"Besides, Talise reminds me so much of myself when I was pregnant with Kidd and realized I was on my own. That was a challenging time to endure. Then after I got pregnant with Aaron, I took the 'I am woman' pledge and haven't been with a man ever since."

"You cheated yourself out of happiness."

"And my sons out of a father figure. Samuel wasn't available to fulfill his role, but I should have tried to make sure there was a male role model in their lives. They needed someone to help them grow into manhood," Sandra admitted.

Reaching for her purse, she wore a somber look. "I recognized the longing in Talise's eyes when she watched all of you. I pray she doesn't miss out. She's such a pretty girl—intelligent and independent too. As Aaron's mother, I can't believe I'm saying this, but after his stunt today, he may not be the best man for her."

Blinking away a tear, Sandra's heart was doubly heavy for Ace and Talise, as she headed out to join Kidd.

Come to me, all you who are weary and burdened, and I will give you rest . . . For my yoke is easy and my burden is light, God spoke from Matthew 11:28, 30.

"Sandra!" Eva called quickly, just before she closed the door.

Glancing over her shoulder, Sandra noticed Eva's reverent expression. "God just spoke to me. It's praying time."

"I know."

Chapter Twenty-Eight

*T*he next morning, Talise settled in a seat aboard the Silver Line bus that would take her to work at Logan airport.

With a faint smile, she recalled the memories from her time spent in St. Louis. Talise couldn't believe how much she enjoyed the Jamieson wives and the little girl. However, the jury was still out when it came to Grandma BB. She was scary.

After returning home from her trip, she couldn't wait to type a long email to Sinclaire last night. Had it been written on paper, it might have filled a book. Carefully, she attempted to outline every detail about the Jamieson women: their warmth, personalities, and support.

Maybe, if they ever invited her again, Talise would go. Hopefully, the next time she wouldn't care if she came face to face with Aaron "Ace" Jamieson.

Before leaving for work this morning, she checked her inbox and Sinclaire had replied.

Hey Sis, I'm glad everything turned out okay. I was praying for you. I'm glad you opened up and admitted your mixed feelings about seeing/not seeing Ace yesterday.

*Somewhere deep in your heart, your feelings haven't changed for him.
I know that frustrates you because of how badly he treated you.*

*God puts people in our path to help us see Him despite the dark days
and darker nights. Those people may be Ace's people, which might not
include him. You have to brace yourself because the hurt could take a long
time to heal. Just remember that Jesus is a Healer of all things, including
the heart.*

*I need you to promise me that you will either read your Bible every-
day for five minutes or pray for five minutes. I guarantee Jesus will listen
to your prayers and pay attention to your dedication. He's got your
roadmap laid out. DON'T BE A SLACKER. Be consistent!*

Much love and smooches to the baby, Claire.

Five minutes, huh? Every day? Talise had already tried to take her
sister's advice. This wasn't the first time Sinclaire attempted to drill that
in her head. In fact, Talise had given it a try this morning. As she
skimmed through 1 Peter, chapter 5, the only verse she remembered
was about casting all her anxiety on God because He cares for her.

Well, in a rush for work, maybe it wasn't quite five minutes. Nevertheless, those words continued to revolve in Talise's head until she
arrived at the airport. Smiling, she felt rejuvenated. Was it from God or
the Jamiesons? Talise remembered the wives saying they were praying
for her too.

Once she cleared the security lane for employees, she strolled to
her assigned ticket counter.

Her coworker, Kendall, was greeting one passenger after another.
The woman's smile masked a variety pack of personalities. Hopefully,
she would be in a good mood for most of the shift.

Before Talise could get settled behind the counter and power-up
her computer, Kendall was spilling the latest gossip.

"Did you hear about what happened in St. Louis yesterday?"

Talise's fingers paused on the keyboards. Frowning, she gave Kendall
her full attention. "No. What? I was in St. Louis yesterday, visiting..."

What would she call them—her baby's family? Kendall didn't know yet, but the way she was starting to put on inches and pounds, her coworker would suspect something soon and broadcast a newsflash that might be close to the truth.

"I was there with friends. What happened?"

"Girl, YouTube is calling it a lover's quarrel, but the only thing you see in the video is the bodybuilder image of a Black guy being forced to the ground. Apparently, he'd been trying to get to some woman who, I guess, had already boarded the plane."

"That's scary." Talise held her breath. Why did Ace come to mind just because he lived in St. Louis? There were more crazy men out there besides her ex.

Kendall instantly switched to her professional mode when a passenger approached the counter.

"Hello, are there any available seats on the next flight to Philly? If so, I would like to change." The man asked more questions while her coworker checked.

Talise tried not to be impatient, but she wanted to hear what else Kendall had to say. She was curious about the St. Louis incident. However, that curiosity was put on hold as a steady trail of passengers stopped at their counter.

Soon the day was becoming a nightmare. When a plane was grounded for mechanical problems, Talise and Kendall had to scramble and rebook all the passengers. Dealing with the crisis at hand, while toying with a suspicious thought at the back of her mind, was beginning to weigh on Talise. Just before Kendall was about to take a lunch break, Talise stopped her.

"Hold on a sec," she said, while assisting a customer who was constantly being distracted by her small child.

Checking her watch, Kendall obliged with a professional smile. Talise pretended not to notice that she was impatiently tapping her shoe. After the passenger finally went on her way, she turned to Kendall.

"You never finished telling me what happened in St. Louis."

"Oh," her coworker said with a shrug. "Girl, I forgot all about yesterday's news. My ears are waiting for the latest going on around here."

Resting one hand on her narrow hip, Kendall leaned on the counter. "Anyway, some Black guy, who was pretty-boy fine, seemed bent on talking to this woman before that plane took off. Someone caught his antics on a video phone. You would think the brother enjoyed the attention because he sure didn't seem fazed by it."

"Really?" Talise hoped no one would come to the counter until after Kendall completed the story.

"Yeah. Mr. GQ stared directly into the camera with a crazy, sexy smile and had the nerve to say, 'Hi, Mom.'"

"Sounds like a fool."

"Yep, a fool for love. Check it out on YouTube. It's hilarious. Now my feet are killing me. See ya after break."

Men only acted a fool for love in the movies. That was too much to ask from Ace. Talise lost faith in undying love months ago.

God, has love passed me by? Was it too late for her to find her true love? Especially having someone else's baby? Talise shivered. She didn't even want to think about another relationship. Focusing on her child would keep her busy for a lifetime.

By late afternoon, most of the flights were back to normal and the rest of her Friday was uneventful. She only thought about that crazy video once more.

With one hour to go before her shift was over, Talise couldn't stop yawning. The good sleep she experienced the previous night was long gone. Plus, her body had begun to serve notice that she'd been standing too long. That feeling had become the norm during her shift. Between an aching back and swollen feet, she was hurting all over. Talise craved her bed and comfy cover. A glass of milk and then a nap would round off her day and make her a happy camper.

Forty-five minutes and counting, then she'd be off. It just wasn't coming soon enough. Looking up, a smile of relief stretched across her face. Her body relaxed when she spotted Gabrielle navigating through the terminal, working her way around the passengers.

This was the last day for Gabrielle to wear her ticket agent hat. Hopefully, for her supervisor's sake, Talise's regular replacement would be back on Sunday. She watched Gabrielle detour into a gift shop for some snacks.

With fifteen minutes to go, Kendall's replacement so far was a no show. Jessica was notorious for running late and then blaming it on traffic. When she did arrive, she was usually flustered and Kendall was less than understanding.

"Hey, Talise," Gabrielle said, resting her items on the bottom shelf behind the counter. "You're free to move around the cabin," she repeated her standard greeting.

"You're early," Talise said with a big smile. "Thanks for coming to my rescue."

"That's my job. Go ahead and sign out. I'll take it from here." Then turning to face the next customer in line, with a genuine smile, she addressed the gentleman. "I'm sorry for the delay, sir. We're in the middle of a shift change. Give us thirty seconds, please."

The man's flared nostrils seemed to deflate. "Sure. I have a few minutes." He returned her smile, looking like a prince who had just discovered his princess.

Talise bit her lip to contain her grin. They often teased each other about the impact their attractiveness had on the male species. Gabrielle always seemed to win hands down.

Mouthing her thanks, Talise gathered her things. Before she could walk away, Gabrielle touched her arm and whispered, "Get some rest this weekend. You've looked tired lately, but you're still a diva." She winked and lightly bumped her out of the way.

"Yeah, right."

Covering a yawn, Talise nodded and patted Gabrielle's shoulder.

Waving goodbye, she escaped under Kendall's watchful eye.

Talise had a full schedule the next day at the salon. Immediately after that, Sunday would begin her new work week back at the airport. She couldn't fathom how she could squeeze in any "extra" rest. Except for the previous night, her sleep was routinely interrupted with multiple trips to the bathroom.

How did she manage to spend so much time with Ace between the two jobs? It saddened her that what she had with him was so superficial. It was a still a mystery how she had become pregnant, despite their safety precautions. Of course, it goes without saying, if she had never slept with him in the first place, then she wouldn't be in her current predicament.

Talise was almost out of the airport when Kendall's relief came rushing through the door. Jessica didn't even notice her. Talise shook her head. The woman knew what she was up against. Kendall would curse her out in two languages, all the while smiling.

The Silver Line bus seemed to be waiting for her the moment she stepped to the curb. Although her body was tired, her mind hadn't forgotten what Kendall said about the incident in St. Louis. She wondered if it happened before, during, or after her plane took off.

"Thank goodness for airport security," she mumbled, as she thought about a possible workplace disaster. Employees were trained to react swiftly to any threat, no matter how insignificant it may appear at the time.

Collapsing in an empty seat, Talise pulled out her phone and accessed the Internet. Kendall had mentioned it was about a lover's quarrel. On the YouTube site, she entered "man," "Southwest," and "lovers" in the search box.

The shaky video started with two smaller men tackling a man the size of a football player, as if to keep him from scoring a touchdown. The commotion would have been slapstick comedy if it wasn't happening in an airport, her place of employment. Once in handcuffs, it was comical watching the men attempting to stand the suspect up on his feet.

From the rear, the guy was nicely dressed. She couldn't yet make out the "pretty-boy fine" face, as Kendall described him. Scrutinizing the side view, he did favor . . . when his face came into full view, Talise gasped.

Her hand flew to her mouth, but the sound escaped anyway. With enough clarity, there was no doubt in her mind that it was Ace being escorted away. She blinked several times. Immediately and unexpectedly, her heart longed for him.

It had been over two months, and Ace Jamieson was more handsome than her memory could ever paint. Fearless and not easily intimidated, he still possessed the same aura that had attracted her.

"Are you all right?" A female rider asked, peering over Talise's shoulder, who was instantly startled. Once the woman realized the cause of Talise's behavior, she laughed. "Girl, isn't that hilarious! It's all over the Internet. Isn't that man fine?"

Ace. Talise mused before she found her voice. "Ah, yeah, it is, especially the part where he's being thrown to the ground."

"He sure didn't go down easily."

Talise wanted to be left alone to her thoughts. It was good she wasn't far from her South End apartment. Replaying the clip, she paused on Ace's close-up.

"It didn't take you long to move on," she mumbled, as her eyes misted. So Ace was already involved in another relationship with someone in St. Louis.

Eva was pretty adamant that he wouldn't be anywhere near her. But Ace was family, and Eva's alliance would be to him. Talise swallowed. Her mind was running wild. *Why couldn't he fight for me like that?*

The bus stopped a block from her apartment. Getting off, Talise began walking on autopilot. Her refuge seemed miles away. She prayed

Lois wasn't home. In her emotional state of misery, she didn't want company.

By the time she made it to her door, Talise was on the verge of tears. Seeing Ace's face was upsetting. She entered, listening for her roommate.

"Lois?"

When there was no answer, she shut the door and released the flood gates. Making a beeline to her bedroom, Talise tossed her purse in a corner and kicked off her shoes. With tears blurring her vision, she quickly disrobed. The only thing on her mind was going to bed and crying herself to sleep.

Unfortunately, her stomach growled as she turned back the cover. Then she froze, feeling something unusual. *What was that?* She waited to see if she would feel it again. *A flutter.* It was subtle, but she felt it.

Jubilation immediately replaced the pity party Talise was about to have. She was almost thirteen weeks. Her baby books said she could expect to experience flutters after week fifteen. Talise grinned, wiping at her tears. Evidently, her baby was saying otherwise.

"Okay, little one, let me feed you."

She put her emotional breakdown on hold and made her way to the kitchen. Opening the refrigerator with gusto, she took out the makings for a hamburger and a salad. Twenty minutes later, she was enjoying a small meal and reading a baby book.

Afterward, Talise stored the leftovers for Lois's lunch and cleaned up the kitchen. She couldn't wait to relax in bed. With one hand on her stomach, she lay there, waiting for another flutter. But after the initial two quivers, her baby ignored any request for more.

It seemed like she had just dozed off when Lois came into the apartment, disturbing her peace.

"Talise." Her footsteps brought her to the bedroom door, which was partially closed. She tapped.

"Talise?"

"Hmm?" Rolling over, she slurred, "Come in."

"What's wrong? Are you feeling okay?"

Talise grinned. "I think I felt the baby. It wasn't a kick, more like a flutter. I was lying still, so maybe I could feel it again. Then I dozed off."

Lois sat gently on the bed and smiled. "I hate to break up your moment of utopia, but a video is going viral on the Internet, and—"

"I've already seen it. Ace having a lover's spat."

Lois lifted a brow. "Humph. They never showed the woman. Personally, I think it was a setup. It was your flight, Talise. According to an article I dug up, it was the same flight as yours. It looks like the Jamieson wives had you fooled after all."

Bracing her hands on the mattress, Talise shook her head and scooted to sit up. Her conflicting emotions from earlier returned with a vengeance. In a twisted way, Lois's theory about a setup gave her a slight amount of comfort that another woman wasn't involved. But it didn't take long before reality set in and she became outraged at the potential embarrassment he could have caused her.

Lois stood. "It doesn't appear that any Jamieson can be trusted. After I saw that video, I confronted Cameron. He denied knowing about Ace's travel itinerary or motives. But all my trust was maxed out after he knowingly withheld information that his cousin was a scumbag."

Talise smirked. It was a waste of energy for her to get mad when Lois was mad enough for the both of them.

After Lois left her, she reached for her cell phone. First, she had to prepare herself for a reality check. She had no right to demand the Jamieson wives pick sides. They seemed like the kind of people who, once they made up their minds about something, they couldn't be swayed. Yet, days after meeting them, Talise was already testing their truthfulness about wanting a genuine friendship. Her interrogation began the moment Eva said hello.

"Did you know that Ace was at the airport yesterday?" Talise's heart pounded, waiting for the answer she hoped.

"None of us did, until his stupidity went viral on that video."

Talise breathed a sigh of relief. Thank God there was no setup as Lois hinted. She genuinely liked Eva and her in-laws.

Eva chuckled. "I can't remember the last time I was so entertained by something on YouTube."

"Do you know why he was there?"

"You."

"Me?" Talise frowned, confused. "You just said Ace didn't know I was there." Something wasn't adding up. The seed of Lois's suspicions was taking root again.

"Evidently, he planned a surprise trip to Boston this weekend. When he thought he saw you, he was calling out and trying to get to you. The rest, as they say, is viral."

"Hmm." What was Ace up to? Thank God for iPods and headsets. She was glad she didn't hear him or else she would have been on YouTube right along with him. Talise didn't know how she would have reacted, seeing him after his betrayal. She could hear Sinclaire clearly telling her to watch and pray.

Chapter Twenty-Nine

Unbelievable!" Ace roared, pacing in Kidd's living room.

His brother, Eva, and his mother seemed unfazed by his tirade. Their eerie calmness irked him more. He felt betrayed when his mother admitted that it was indeed Talise at the airport.

"A girls' tea day, huh? She flew a thousand miles to sip tea. Come on, people. How idiotic is that?"

Ace twisted his lips. It was too simplistic to believe. Talise definitely had other motives. What nerve she had to try and brainwash his mother, just so Sandra would help her to string the others along. He had to admit she was clever, though. What better way to infiltrate the family?

"You should talk, bro," Kidd said, snacking on a sandwich Eva had prepared for him. "You're the one who clowned on YouTube."

When Kidd replayed the incident captured on video, Ace groaned at his brother's scowl. Sure, he could have done without Kidd's smart remark. After all, his reaction was merely his way of feeling in control in an out of control situation. How was he to know that it would turn out to be such a big deal?

All weekend long, Ace had held his peace and accepted his mother's tongue-lashing about his behavior. Compounded with Kidd's glare and Eva's shun, he felt like a naughty grade-school boy.

Once the clamor over his YouTube celebrity status had blown over, his suspicions grew that something else was going on. His mother and Eva had one too many hushed conversations when they thought he was out of hearing range. When Talise's name and the mention of a baby were repeatedly used in the same sentence, Ace demanded answers. She was none of their business and no longer his. How could they go behind his back and welcome her with open arms?

"The woman is lying, I'm telling you. Did she even look pregnant?" Ace demanded.

"A woman doesn't have to look pregnant to be pregnant," Eva retorted, rubbing her stomach.

"Hmm-mm. That's the wrong answer in my book. The woman is lying and she has all of you feeding into her deceit."

As hard as he tried, Ace couldn't believe how his mother and Eva came to Talise's defense. Nothing he said could convince them otherwise. It was part of her plan to use them to lay a guilt trip on him for a baby that didn't exist.

"You walked out on her, Ace," Eva snapped.

Finishing his sandwich, Kidd wiped his mouth and stretched his arm around his wife's shoulder. His expression dared his brother a rebuttal. Whatever words he was ready to spew from his mouth, it was certain that Kidd would take it personally.

He and his brother had never fought over a woman, but somehow, it appeared things were about to change. They were going to have to step outside because Ace didn't want Eva and his mother to witness him getting the upper hand on his older brother.

Ace barked, "Do you know how many women I've walked away from, Eva Jamieson? Talise is no different." He experienced a sour taste in his mouth after spewing those words.

Standing, Kidd folded his arms and he lifted a brow. He didn't say anything, but his stance was threatening enough, which annoyed Ace. Whose side was he on, anyway?

"Then that's your loss. Men like you give all Black men a bad rap . . ."

"Babe, watch it. He's still my brother."

Ace didn't blink. His brother had called it right because, at the moment, Ace was beyond angry. His family had interfered enough. It was time to part ways.

"What do you people want from me, blood?"

"You don't need to give your DNA until after the baby is born," Sandra spoke up. "But then what do you plan to do?"

"I'll decide when the time comes." Ace headed for the front door. He needed fresh air and didn't care if the summer heat was still stifling at night. With his hand on the knob, he glanced over his shoulder.

"Have a safe flight home, Mom." Opening the door, he was gone.

———

Ace walked the neighborhood until he was sure Kidd and Eva had left to take his mother to the airport. When he returned to their house, he packed as much of his things as he could.

He was going to a hotel room. The next time he set foot into their house, it would be to get the rest of his belongings. Eva was no longer on bed rest, so no sob stories could sucker him into staying longer.

Once he checked into the Hilton Garden Hotel off I-70, Ace didn't bother unpacking. He lay on top of the bed and stared at the ceiling.

"When did my life become so complicated?" he wondered out loud.

Give Me all your worries because I care about everything in your life, God whispered in the wind, ending with First Peter 5:7.

He heard that and now he could hear his mother's voice when he was a teenager. "Don't lead these young girls on, Aaron," she would say to him. "If you want to be friends, then keep your conversation friendly and don't spend so much one-on-one time with them. Otherwise, a girl will begin to think something more is going on between the two of you."

Ace grunted. As far as he was concerned, he had listened to his mother and never led a woman on. They simply followed and he didn't stop them.

Recalling a time when he was just turning nineteen, trouble seemed to be dogging him everywhere he turned. Between girls, school, and peer pressure, Sandra had told him to give it all to God. She said that God wanted Ace to trust Him with all of his problems because God cared about everything in his life. Ace had dismissed her advice then just as he had done this time.

How could God care about him when he wasn't reading the Bible, going to church, or even had a desire to live right? Nah, Ace could handle his business himself.

Closing his eyes, he heard his brother's voice. It was after he proposed to Eva. "She is there for me," Kidd told him. "Eva has helped me put my life in order. Now I understand Genesis 2:24, which basically says that a man will leave his parents and cleave to his wife. I would die to protect her."

What a drastic declaration, Ace thought at the time. But Ace loved his brother and was behind Kidd 100 percent.

Finally, he recalled Cameron's words. "She's not like the others, man. I get the feeling she doesn't have an agenda. She doesn't appear needy like those women with multi-colored hair you dated. I think you can trust her from everything Lois has told me about her."

"Trust," Ace spat out with disgust. He couldn't even trust his family. He continued to stew until finally, he dozed off.

When he woke up the next morning, his clothes were wrinkled and his head ached from the lack of a good night's sleep in a comfortable bed. His muscles were tense from so much inner turmoil.

Through his uncomfortable state, he thought about what he would do that day. Besides getting some work done from his hotel room, Ace had to contact the manager at Whispering Breeze apartments. After putting his move on hold, now he was ready. Hopefully, there would be an immediate vacancy.

One thing was for sure. As soon as he could retrieve the remainder of his belongings from Kidd's house, Ace planned to have a showdown with Ms. Rogers. From what he could see of her at the airport, Talise's body could still grab a man's attention. It didn't appear there was an ounce of baby fat on her. A phone call was his only option at the moment.

He rolled off the bed, showered, dressed and went downstairs to the hotel lobby to see about breakfast. While he chewed on the food he couldn't remember tasting from the buffet, he pondered over the stuff in his head from the previous night.

After eating, he returned to his room and turned on his computer. Slightly taken aback by the number of unopened email entries in his inbox, he addressed the immediate work-related emails and ignored those messages from coworkers about his stunt on the Internet.

Relieved that his boss thought the video was entertaining, he was warned not to let something like that happen again. Regardless of Ace's talent, he was expected to abide by the company's code of ethics. Ace assured Dale he had nothing to worry about.

Logging off a few hours later, Ace called the apartment complex.

"Whispering Breeze apartments, how can I help you?" The same woman who had helped him weeks earlier answered. Alma had two apartments available for immediate occupancy. Both had two bedrooms, but only one had a balcony. The other she described as a first floor with a walkout to a small patio. It led to a luscious flower garden with a manmade waterfall in the center of a pond.

The choice was a no brainer. The patio—large or small—hands down. Since his paperwork was still on file as well as his security deposit, the only thing Ace had to do was pick up his keys. Pleased with himself, Ace chuckled.

"I'll get the rest of my things and see you soon." After disconnecting, he grabbed his car keys and prayed that Eva wasn't at home.

Pray. He thought about the word and grunted. With the way his family was siding against him, he doubted God had his back on this one.

When he arrived at Kidd's, the house was empty. Ace quickly packed up his possessions and made return trips until his trunk, back seat, and front seat were stacked with his stuff.

In the kitchen, he raided their refrigerator one last time. Pivoting on his heels from side to side, Ace canvassed his surroundings. It turned out to be a much needed temporary hiding place. His brother and sister-in-law had been good to him.

But he and Kidd saw things differently when it came to relationships. Kidd believed in commitment. To Ace, responsibility was optional—and a man had to chose when and where to apply it.

Finished with his snack, he cleaned up his mess. Then, grabbing a pen and pad, he wrote, "Sis and bro, I appreciate your hospitality. Eva, I'm glad you're feeling well enough . . ." Ace's pen was poised to write "to get in my business," but he refrained. "I decided it was time for me to move into a place of my own. I'm taking the apartment at Whispering Breeze. I'll be in touch. Ace."

By late afternoon, Ace had settled his matters in the complex business office. With keys in hand, he began to transfer his stuff from the car to his first floor, spacious apartment. He could really spread out with two bedrooms, a living room, kitchen nook, laundry room, and a bath and a half.

Checking his watch, Ace had to bide his time. A few more hours and Talise would be off work and at home. He didn't want to affect her livelihood by getting into it with her over the phone at her place of work.

Surveying his new home, Ace didn't realize until now that starting from scratch meant beginning with nothing. To survive, he reasoned that he needed three pieces of furniture: a high-def flat screen TV, a king-size bed, and a dinette set. Everything else could come later.

The shopping trip took longer than expected. Making a decision on the furniture in less than an hour, it was the TV that took the most time. Ace made the salesman go over every feature twice before he decided.

Since the furniture wouldn't be delivered for a few days, he made another stop to buy an inflatable mattress, a microwave, and a few groceries. When he returned to his empty apartment, he got settled and then took a deep, deep breath.

It was time. Ace wasn't looking forward to having the "talk" with Talise. But if he didn't put a stop to it, she might permanently move to St. Louis and torment him for the rest of his days. Talise needed to face the music. Whether she would have a life after Ace Jamieson or not, Ace Jamieson was definitely going to have a life post-Talise.

After blowing up the mattress, he made himself comfortable. Although he had erased her number, he knew it by heart, or so he thought. When a recording came on that the number was disconnected, it caught him off guard.

"What?"

Okay, it had been months since he'd called her, but he was sure it was the right number. He tried two more times. Ace took a deeper breath. How did it get past him that she changed her number? Was it because of him? "She's good," he uttered to himself with a smirk.

Come to think of it, actually, it was his fault. He hadn't bothered to save the number she'd been calling him from. Like that was going to stop him. For sure, Eva and his mother had her number. However, he was smart enough to know that asking them was out of the question. Cameron was his best choice.

There was only one slight problem. He and Cameron were not on the best of terms. Maybe he could tell his cousin that he was reaching out to Talise in an effort to reconcile their differences. Cameron didn't have to know that his reconciliation included officially terminating any contact between the two of them—and his family.

"What's up, Ace?" Cameron answered, annoyed. Clearly, the air between them was still stuffy.

"Hey, cuz, how are things in Boston?"

"Well, if you hadn't cut up at the airport, you would be here and wouldn't have to ask. Would you?"

That was old news. "I was coming home to make things right, man." Cameron didn't bite.

"Anyway, since I can't go near the airport until my court date next month, I . . . wanted to set things right with Talise. I see that she changed her number and I was hoping you had it."

"Liar. You can lie to her, but not to me. You know we feel each other. Man, if you get caught, you pay. You got caught and now your girl is having a baby. It's like a speeding ticket. You have to obey all the traffic signs . . ."

"Save your lectures for the classroom, Cam. Do you have her number, or not? I know you two have become chummy lately."

"I'll break your jaw for that remark when I see you. As for her number, I don't have it and I can't get it. When I see Lois on campus, which I try to avoid, I get chewed out because of you."

Now what? It was obvious that Cameron wasn't going to help him. "Write her a letter, tweet, email, or find her on Facebook, but I can't help you with this. It was easier bailing you out of jail. I don't have enough money to get you out of this one."

Write a letter? Right. Knowing Talise, she would have the post office return it. As for the social networking sites, neither of them had bothered to set one up. Talise did have an email account, but he wasn't sure he knew her address. It was some cutesy name like tatolrod@ymail, or gmail, or something like that. Trying to pinpoint her correct email address was definitely not worth his frustration. Besides, there was no reason to email her when he could text instead.

Annoyed, Ace gritted his teeth. He loved his cousin, but if he too was going to hold a grudge against his own flesh and blood because of a woman, Ace was going friend shopping.

"She's ruining my life. It's as if she's running a scam on me from an offshore country."

"That's your doing, dude. You were wrong to leave her like that," Cameron scolded.

"Listen, man, I can understand your loyalty to Talise because you introduced us, but it's over. Face it."

"It's over, huh? Then why do you want her number?"

"So I can remind her of that fact and order her to stay away from my family."

Cameron laughed. "Man, I'm so glad that I don't choke when I'm in a relationship."

"Ha! Your relationships consist of networking, seminars, and lectures. Only when we started hanging together, did I loosen you up."

"Keep believing that." Cameron snorted.

"How long has it been, seriously? You may not love them and leave them only because you turn away women you could easily have. You're too choosy."

"We have different definitions of love, but this isn't about me. You want her number? Then you'll have to get past lioness Lois to get it and here's her number."

"Sure. What's one more angry Black woman?"

"Good luck. May the force be with you—and better you than me," Cameron said and disconnected.

Ace knew Cameron couldn't stay mad at him for too long because of Talise. Unfortunately, when he called Lois ten minutes later, she was beyond hot. The woman cursed him out like she was reciting from Webster's dictionary or had created her own thesaurus. A third party would probably think he and Lois had broken up before she called Talise to the phone.

"It's . . ." Lois continued manipulating his name in choice ways. "He wants to talk to you. Girl, I wouldn't give this slimy, tattooed snake-head the time of day. He ain't going to do anything but upset you . . ."

She was calling him out for the Ace of Hearts tattoo on his knuckle? Really? Ace was fuming. He didn't let a man talk to him like that without leaving his signature somewhere on the dude's body. He sure wasn't going to let a woman get away with it. At least, that's how he felt. Yet he was fully aware she was untouchable.

"Get his number. I'll call him back," Talise said in the muffled background.

Get my number! She knew it. So . . . she still wanted to play her game. Little did she know that the cards were always in his favor.

He was about to tell Lois to forget it. His inflatable mattress was seeping air anyway. Ace was slowly sinking to the floor, as if he was on a see-saw. Suddenly, Talise's voice came on the line.

"Hello, Aaron," she said softly.

Catching his breath, Ace's anger began to dissipate and he felt his heart shattering. How could he confront Talise about her lies and deceit when his fight was oozing out, along with the air in his blowup bed?

"Tay?"

"Talise, Aaron," she corrected.

Ouch. The formality stung. Talise's eyes would light up whenever he called her his pet name. Her coldness threw him off.

Knowing what he wanted to say, he wasn't prepared to say it now. Ace cleared his throat. Fearless, he was no Samson. No woman was going to bring him down.

"You changed numbers." *Why all the small talk? Get to the point,* he chided himself. What was wrong with him?

"You called me to tell me that?" her voice cracked.

"Yes." A piece of his heart cracked too. He steadied his breathing and gathered himself. "Tay, you didn't have to try and trap me with this baby story. My feelings were already strong for you. I gave you my heart and your heart's desires."

"Excuse me?" she snapped. "Trap you? Is that what you think I did? I didn't drug you to sleep with me."

"Stranger things have happened," Ace stated in a matter-of-fact manner. "Are you pregnant with my child?"

"If you had stuck around, you could have read the results yourself. In my twenty-nine years, I've never desired, tried, or needed to trap a man. If a man doesn't want me, like you, then I move on."

Through all her ranting and raving, it didn't escape Ace that she hadn't answered the question. "Are you pregnant with my child?" he repeated.

Silence. Ace had her cornered. So the truth was finally about to be told.

"Yes," Talise whispered and then sniffed.

Was that the truth? "So what do you want from me, Tay?"

"Absolutely nothing. Not your money, not your name, not you!"

That's when her bawling began and it started to rip Ace apart. A few seconds later, the call was disconnected. Ace bowed his head in cupped hands, as his bottom actually slid to the carpet. When did his life become such a guilt trip?

Chapter Thirty

*I*t was one week since Talise's argument with Ace. She was still shaken by his mean-spirited and pompous attitude. The five minutes of praying routine that she was trying to adapt into her lifestyle only caused her to cry more.

When Lois escorted her to her next doctor's visit, she blurted out possible causes for Talise's mood swings and forgetfulness. Finally, Talise gave her the eye to be quiet.

Dr. Sherman paused in examining her. "You're fourteen weeks now, so you'll experience more of your hormones being out of control. Just try and keep your stress level down. Have you talked to the baby's father about his medical history?"

"That's the major part of her stress. The loser," Lois spoke up.

"I asked his mother, but never followed through. I'll call her today."

"Good. On your next visit, I'll have Kathy take your blood so we can test for any birth defects. It's nothing to cause alarm. Just routine. But if your baby is having any problems, we want to know early enough so we can intervene. The father's medical history is important."

When the doctor left the room, Talise snapped at Lois. "You're a bad pregnancy partner."

"I'm better than Ace. I just want her to know you're having a rough time, that's all. You know I'm here for you."

"I know, but the next time I come, will you please be the elephant in the room and remain quiet."

Lois shrugged. "Just trying to help."

They left the office and grabbed a bite to eat. Lois headed back to the campus and Talise drove to the apartment to take a nap. After an hour of twisting and turning, she gave up and got out of bed.

She didn't think it was possible, but basically, Ace called her a tramp. Where was the Ace she fell in love with? Booting up her computer, Talise fired off an email to Sinclaire.

I'm not a tramp! She typed in the subject line, with tears streaming down her face. *How am I going to make it? I have twenty-six weeks left. I'm definitely getting fat now. Lois is irritating me. I'm irritating myself. I'm losing my mind. I'm venting. T.*

Talise had upset herself to the point where she was nauseated. Hurrying to the bathroom, she regurgitated everything, including last night's dinner. After freshening up, it wasn't two minutes before she started crying again. When she finally came out of the bathroom, her cell was ringing. Hurrying across the room to answer it, to her pleasant surprise, Sinclaire was calling.

Taking a deep breath, she answered. "Hello," she was able to say before the flood gates opened.

"What's this about a tramp?" Sinclaire was hot, as Talise repeated the phone call she had with Ace.

"Maybe you need to go home where you'll have a better support system. It'll be another nine months before my tour is up. I dislike very much that Ace is making you feel that way. He needs God to intervene in his life—quick."

"I need Jesus more than he does. How am I going to get through

212

this? How?" Talise sniffed, as she curled up on the bed. "I feel like my life is over. Who would have thought when I moved to Boston, my life would have gone downhill?"

"Okay, it's time for me to get military tough with you. You are a woman soldier who has been injured on an emotional battlefield. You're not the only one. Others have been on the front line and injured too. God is sending His angels to pick you up. I've been praying for God to send good people your way."

Talise nodded through her sniffles. "He has. Sandra has called a few times to check up on me. I really like her, so has Eva."

"Only God knows why those people are in your path. But if they're lifting you up and not letting you fall, hang on to them."

"That sounds good, but being with them is a constant reminder that I'm not part of them."

"We don't pick our friends, Talise. But in the end, we value true friendship. I love you, sis, but I've got to go. Remember, give God five minutes and your investment will pay off. I promise you."

Sinclaire said a heartfelt prayer before they disconnected. Talise only felt peace when others prayed for her. God seemed so far removed from her situation. He hadn't given her any assurance in a while to let her know He was concerned. It was hard to be strong when she felt all alone.

Her mind was confused. Talise craved company. She thought about calling Eva, but that wasn't the same. Then her stomach growled. She was hungry but didn't feel like cooking. After wrestling with herself for long enough, she gave in and called Sandra.

"I was just thinking about you. How are you, now?"

"Hungry." She put on a cheery front.

"I'll bet you are," Sandra teased her.

"I am and so is the baby. Do you want to keep me company? Maybe you can tell me about my baby's father's childhood illnesses."

"What ya got a taste for?"

"Boston Market." Talise couldn't get enough of their sweet potato casserole.

"Okay, I'm leaving work in ten minutes. I need to stop by the house and then I'll meet you at the one near you. Wear some flat shoes too. Maybe we can do a little window shopping afterward, if you feel up to it."

Talise smiled. "I would like that." Then she added in a whisper, "Thank you for being a friend to me."

"I thank God you allow me to."

Sandra brought along Ace's baby pictures and grade school photos. They gave Talise an idea of what her son or daughter might look like. Either sex, her baby would be beautiful. Ace was one of those pretty baby boys with long lashes—an unnecessary asset for a boy—a head full of curly hair and an adorable smile.

Sandra described him as an inquisitive toddler, happy and very sociable. She also made a list of some of his childhood illnesses. He suffered with childhood asthma and was allergic to fish and peanuts.

"Besides that, Aaron was a normal, hard-headed little boy."

Yeah, a little boy who grew up to be a cold-hearted man, thought Talise.

When they finished their meal, she declined a stroll, but Sandra accepted a rain check for the next evening. It was ironic that Sandra would be replacing her son. Usually, Talise and Ace were always together on Fridays after work.

The next day, Talise found out that she and Sandra had very different definitions of window shopping. Sandra was like a caged pet set free at Faneuil Hall Market Place. Talise looked, but didn't spend.

The older woman splurged without hardly giving an item a once over. It didn't escape Talise that most of the things weren't for Sandra, but keepsake gifts like a snow globe, a picture album, and knickknacks for a child's room. Talise assumed they were for Eva's baby, until she noticed many of the articles Sandra purchased were two of the same thing.

By the time she got home and climbed into bed, Talise had no doubt in her mind and heart that Sandra was a gift from God. As she laid her head on the pillow, it was as though God seemed to whisper in her ear.

"Where you go I will go, and where you stay I will stay. Your people will be my people and your God my God."

Talise blinked, recognizing the words were from something she'd read in the Bible. It had been a while, yet she sensed God's presence. The only thing is she didn't exactly know where to find the Scripture. That bugged her, yet it intrigued her.

Suddenly, curiosity got the best of her. Talise got up and pulled out her Bible, sandwiched in between a stack of baby books. As she began to flip through the pages, she realized she was clueless.

Gnawing on her lip, she asked, "What did You mean, God?" Frustrated, she logged on to her laptop to Google it. Once she typed in as much as she could remember, the search engine directed her to www.biblegateway.com, the Book of Ruth 1:16. Bingo, or maybe she shouldn't say that in the same sentence with a Scripture.

The entire chapter was about a daughter-in-law whose husband died, and the young widow was determined to follow the religion and customs of her mother-in-law. That night, Talise didn't doze off while reading. She actually read the entire story. In the end, Ruth's mother-in-law, Naomi, had led Ruth to her blessing. Talise realized that once trouble came Ruth's way, if she had turned back, she would have missed the blessing of a new husband and baby.

"Jesus, what does this mean? Is Ace going to die? Are we going to get married and Sandra will be my mother-in-law? What does it mean?"

Talise closed her Bible and held it to her chest. She wished God would just write what He wanted her to know. Sitting there in deep thought for a moment, she then chuckled at herself. "I guess that's what the Bible is—God's Word on a lot of paper."

She would email Sinclaire later and get her take. In the meantime, maybe she might up her prayer time to six minutes. Turning off the lamp, Talise snuggled under the covers.

Saturday morning, she woke up happy, content, and hopeful. Perhaps, she was experiencing a different type of mood swing.

Talise showered and ate in record time. It was the dressing that had become challenging. She wished she would have purchased some articles when she and Sandra went "window" shopping the previous night.

On her way to the salon, she phoned Sandra. "I know it's early for me to call, but I was wondering if you want to go shopping with me later today."

"Nonsense, I'm up and doing my morning workout. Shopping? Did you say mall?"

Talise laughed. "Believe it or not, I need a few maternity clothes."

"I would love to go with you."

"Great, I'll call you after my last customer."

"Okay, sweetie."

Talise disconnected with a smile. Ten minutes later, she parked across the street from Sassy's and strolled into the salon just ahead of her first customer.

After finishing three clients, Talise waved her favorite client back to the shampoo area. They exchanged a quick hug, and then she whipped a plastic cape across Priscilla's shoulders. Once she was reclined in the chair, Priscilla sighed in contentment as Talise massaged warm water through her hair.

"So how's Tammy?" She asked about Talise's alias.

Glancing over her shoulder, Talise scrutinized the few clients and stylists milling around. "Although I wouldn't want to be in her shoes, I think she's starting to handle her situation better."

"Good for her. Does she need anything?"

"Nah, except to cope better with her mood swings. I think Tammy will be glad when it's all over."

"It goes slow in the beginning. And then once she reaches four or five months, that precious baby really begins to grow. I've been through it three times and, believe me, I was a force to be reckoned with.

"My husband said I was downright hateful. Couldn't nobody stand me, but once I held little Stella in my arms, I promised to be the sweetest mother ever. That was, until I got pregnant with Macie, and then I was back to my mean self again."

Talise laughed so hard, she had to race to the bathroom to relieve herself before she had an accident. Once she returned and rinsed the conditioner out of Priscilla's hair, she wrapped a towel around it.

"So how many more customers do you have today?" Priscilla asked, as she sat in Talise's chair at her station.

"Two." She turned on her blow dryer and began to comb through Priscilla's hair.

"How are you going to make a living with doing only three heads on a Saturday, girl?"

Talise whispered, "I had to cut back. The fumes from the chemicals make me sick. If I move too fast, I get dizzy. Plus, my feet are starting to swell."

"Get some good support shoes," Priscilla whispered back and reached for a magazine. She didn't utter another word as Talise began to flat-iron and then bump her hair. An hour and a half later, when she was about to spray oil sheen to top off her style, Priscilla lifted her hand.

"Nah. Not today. I like the bounce."

Talise frowned. "You complain when it looks dry."

"Then I'll oil my scalp." Priscilla stood and removed her own cape. As she rummaged through her purse, Talise could see the woman's thick whipping belt.

"How much I owe ya?" she asked, as if it changed from her last appointment.

"Seventy-five."

Priscilla handed Talise a one-hundred dollar bill, then added a twenty. "Keep the change."

"Is this extra money a down payment on a hair weave or something? This is way too much."

It's for Tammy's baby, she mouthed.

The light bulb went on. Talise was starting to recognize the people whom God was placing in her path.

Chapter Thirty-One

On Sunday morning, Talise felt like she picked up another pound and inch overnight as she dressed for work at the airport. She reflected on the shopping adventure with Sandra for maternity clothes.

Sandra raved about a bronze-colored, sleeveless dress. "Don't look at the price tag. Do you like it or not?" She held up the garment on the hanger.

"It's nice if I had somewhere special to wear it." After spying the price, Talise gritted her teeth. "Besides, it's out of my price range anyway." She had set an allowance and wasn't budging.

"Well, it's not out of mine. You can wear it when you go out on a hot dinner date or to church," she teased and scrunched her nose. Her eyes sparkled with mischief.

Talise snickered. "Then you'd better save your money. No one wants to date a pregnant woman. Plus, I work on Sundays, remember?"

"Humph. God is in control of your life and schedule."

She sighed. "And that's a little scary for me right now. I feel like I'm walking around blindfolded. I have no idea what to expect."

Sandra perused the sales racks and tables. Talise gasped at the price of a good maternity bra. She would rather use her money on a pair of shoes that would give her better support.

"Do you have one?" Sandra lifted another maternity bra.

"I think I can hold off a little while longer. I need to stop by the shoe department before I leave."

Sandra eyed her chest and then the table. She guessed Talise's size and then searched through the assortment. Talise's mouth dropped open. The woman was making her feel like a charity case.

"That's too big."

"You'll fit into it."

God whispered, *Let her bless you.*

He immediately reminded her of the passages in the Book of Ruth. She resolved not to put up any more objections, so Sandra bought the purchases and Talise accepted. Next, they headed to the shoe department. Sandra offered to pay for those too, but this time Talise refused. She pulled out the hundred dollar bill Priscilla had given her and handed it to the clerk at the register.

As she recalled that experience, another Scripture came to mind. *I will supply your every need according to My riches in Glory.* It surprised her when she remembered reading the words from Philippians 4:19. Talise found herself marveling at the truth of God's Word and how it was applying to her life in a real way. Wasn't God using people to meet her needs? Both Sandra and Priscilla had blessed her, and she had no doubt He had something to do with it.

Sinclaire had prayed that God would put people in her path and Talise was beginning to see them. Although she wasn't near welfare assistance level, saving money was an issue. Being a single mother was new territory for her. She had no idea what financial state she would be in when the baby arrived. If she worked, there would be day care expenses. If she stayed at home, bills had to be paid. It was starting to look more like a move back to Virginia was in her future.

Talise cleared her mind of worrying about the future. She ate breakfast, got dressed, and thanked God for her new fashionable shoes with better support. They were definitely worth the money. And Sandra had been right. The bra did fit after all.

After applying her makeup, she headed off to work. On the way, her mind returned to the issue of money. Her father had been faithfully sending her funds. Twice, he added a bit more, but her expenses would skyrocket when her baby was born. She tried to figure out ways to be more frugal.

At work, Talise walked from the parking garage to the terminal with a slight pep in her step. Once she cleared the employee security check in, she smiled when she saw Gabrielle at the ticket counter. This time her supervisor was working in Kendall's place.

"Hey, Gabrielle, what are you doing here?"

"Kendall's off on her Alaskan cruise, so you're stuck with me, if that's okay." She smiled and scrunched her nose.

"Sounds like fun to me," Talise said, putting her things away and then logging on.

The Sunday morning airline traffic was light and the two made small talk in between customers. Talise watched Gabrielle's face light up every now and then. Several families paraded the terminal in their Sunday best. It looked as if they were heading to church as soon as the plane landed at their destination.

When Gabrielle wasn't looking, Talise scrutinized her hair: thick, thick, and thick. Talise was glad she didn't have to detangle it. Physically, Gabrielle had the legs men always noticed, along with her other assets. Personality wise, Talise's friend and coworker downplayed her intellect and beauty.

That was most endearing and made her wonder what her own assets would look like once she delivered her baby.

"You're glowing today. Did your boyfriend take you out last night?"

"I got some rest. Plus, I'm single again."

"Do you mind me asking if it was mutual?"

"Let's just say, I never saw it coming," Talise said, before they both turned to someone approaching them.

"They must save the pretty ladies for the weekend," a male passenger flirted when he stepped up to their counter. Peering through quarter-pounder thick glass lenses, the man appeared old enough to be someone's great grandfather.

Gabrielle giggled. "We're here to make sure you get to your destination on time. How can I help you?"

After the crowd diminished at their counter, Gabrielle revisited Talise's taboo topic. Actually, she welcomed the discussion with someone who was unbiased. Lois couldn't make up her mind if she was looking out for her best interest, or simply ready to release revenge on a Jamieson.

"Break-ups are hard, especially if it's one-sided." She held up her hand. "I'm not saying it's this, but sometimes God has to work out the kinks in a man."

It was on the tip of Talise's tongue to say it was too late for her and Ace, but she didn't interrupt.

"Men have baggage just like women. Once they're willing to unpack it, God can fill them with His wisdom, His power, and a fire for Him. That's the kind of man worthy of a woman's love."

Nodding, Talise leaned on the counter. She looked away and watched as passengers headed in their various directions. "That sounds so beautiful and encouraging, but I don't believe a word of it."

They laughed. "I have three wonderful brothers. I've been taught well," Gabrielle explained.

"I wish I had brothers, but I have a great sister who I miss hanging out with." She straightened her body. "Oh, I need a potty break. Can you handle it?"

"Go while the coast is clear." Gabrielle shooed her.

Hurrying away, Talise couldn't believe how much of a difference her new shoes made. While in the restroom, she examined her face. Her skin was still flawless, but her face was starting to fill out around the cheekbones. What would people say once they learned she was dumped and pregnant?

"Did you read this email?" Gabrielle asked when Talise returned.

"What email?"

"Southwest is cutting back. The president says it's in response to the struggling economy. She read, 'We, at Southwest Airlines, are restructuring our goals and priorities. To avoid a massive lay off, effective immediately, it is necessary for every employee to . . .'"

Talise didn't wait for Gabrielle to finish. She hastily tapped on her keyboard, searching for the company's Outlook mail. Talise scanned the email and continued reading, "'Scale the work week to thirty-two hours. This furlough will remain in effect until further notice. Thank you for your sacrifice. Please advise your immediate supervisor of your preference for which day you would like off.' Oh, no," she said, deflated.

Sniffing, Talise prayed that she wasn't about to lose it. She couldn't handle a crying spell at work.

"I know. Since I'm in management, I've heard the rumors for months. I guess they decided to go through with it. I've been hoping they wouldn't. Don't think this doesn't affect management. Who do you think is supposed to pick up the slack? I've been contemplating a career change lately. The airline industry has run its course in my veins," Gabrielle confided. "Please don't repeat that last part."

Talise bobbed her head and felt a sinking feeling in the pit of her stomach. Why did it seem like a bad day always follows a good day? She dabbed her eyes with her finger.

Gabrielle smiled and attempted to console her. "It's good that you already have a part time job at the salon to help pick up the slack."

"I have rent and expenses to split with my roommate."

"Yes, the South End is pricey. Well, at least you don't have any small ones to feed."

"I'm pregnant," Talise whispered.

Forming an *O* with her mouth, Gabrielle was speechless. Her eyes darted to Talise's stomach and then back to her face. She nodded when the realization seemed to hit.

"When I noticed your weight loss and then a slight gain, I thought you were suffering with some kind of gland disorder. I started praying for you. Then today you walked in here glowing. I thought everything was okay."

"I'm sure rumors have been circulating about me."

"I stay away from rumors. They have a tendency to cloud a person's opinion of others and that could cause me to cast judgment."

Talise listened in awe. *Could a person be that neutral?* She frowned. "That sounds impossible. How can you do that? Rumors about my baby's father have made my life miserable, but without those rumors I would have nothing to go on. It's not like he's been upfront with me."

"There's a wise saying and it happens to come from the Bible: '*In all your getting, get an understanding.*' Is there any way you and your boyfriend can come to an understanding?" Gabrielle gave a hopeful look.

"That would be too much like the right thing to do. It's too hurtful for me to talk to Ace, especially in my condition. He seems so cold and I can't bear his chilly attitude." She twisted her lips. "Anyway, I have a more pressing matter. I'll need to make up for the lost income."

She worked the rest of her shift on autopilot. That evening, back at her apartment, Talise was heavy in thought when Lois came home, dumped her keys and purse, and headed to her bedroom.

Sitting in the bay window seat in the front room brought back memories for Talise. She would wait there and watch for Ace's Charger to pull up. That spot always made her feel like a damsel locked in a tower, and the only person who could rescue her was Ace.

She spoke to Lois and continued to stare out the window. So far, she had yet to come up with a way to cut more corners on her living expenses. Refusing to touch the thousands of dollars that had accumulated from Ace's winnings on the boat, Talise had designated that money as his one-time child support payment.

Lois came back to the living room, wrapped in a bathrobe. "Hey, you feel like going out tonight? We haven't done that in a long time, and—"

"We need to talk," Talise cut her off.

"What's wrong? Is the baby okay? Are you okay?" Lois went into panic mode, as Talise advised her to have a seat.

"I'm in trouble—financially. My day job is cutting back hours to keep from laying off workers." She *tsk*ed. "I've already cut back my client load at the salon. Talk about bad timing."

Lois didn't interrupt, as Talise gnawed on her lip, thinking.

"Daddy's already been sending me money. I'd feel guilty asking for more to meet the high cost of living here. I've thought about moving back home until I have the baby."

"There's no way you're going back to Virginia, not after you've complained about your evil stepmother's lack of sensitivity and charisma."

Rolling her eyes, Talise corrected her, "Please refer to Donna as my father's wife. And I didn't call her evil."

"And you didn't say she was nice either. I haven't met her, but I can't stand her already."

"You've got to get over this obsessive, compulsive disorder against people."

"Maybe. I happen to enjoy holding a grudge, just for the fun of it. We'll figure something out. Don't go getting desperate on me," Lois advised. "I guess we're both staying in tonight."

For the next few hours, they lounged in the living room, brainstorming. "I guess it's too late to take your clients back from other stylists, huh?"

Shaking her head, Talise answered, "Besides treating them like a yo-yo, standing on my feet is taxing, even with comfortable shoes. I guess I can find a sit down job to supplement my lost income at the airlines."

Lois worked her neck and lifted a brow. "Three jobs? Your hormones are already out of whack. That ain't happening. I'll think of something." She stood and stretched. "In the meantime, do you want to watch some movies, or the TLC channel?"

"No, I'm going to email Sinclaire to see if we can Skype." Whenever Talise's judgment was cloudy, which always seemed to be the case since she learned she was having a baby, she depended on Sinclaire to think with clarity.

Before the night was over, Talise was staring into her computer, video chatting with her sister.

"I feel like I'm on family and friend welfare. I hate to say it, but going back to Virginia is starting to sound more appealing," Talise said, hoping to talk herself into it.

"Nah, I just don't think that's a healthy situation for you and the baby. It's not like Donna welcomed us with open arms when she married Dad. She tolerates us because of him." Sinclaire glanced over her shoulder and spoke to someone behind her.

"Sorry. Anyway, how Daddy didn't see through Donna's fake façade baffles me . . . Ooh," Talise complained and held her stomach.

"What's wrong?"

After catching her breath, she smiled. "Your niece or nephew just kicked me."

Sinclaire laughed. "I hope it's a girl. That way she can ditch the name Jamieson when she gets married."

"She won't have it at all. I'm not putting Ace's name on the birth certificate."

Chapter Thirty-Two

S andra would never get accustomed to the so-called "empty nest syndrome," as she walked through the door after Sunday morning service. A three-bedroom condo was simply too big for one person.

Even Cameron's visits were less frequent now that Ace was gone. He still called and asked if she needed anything, and dropped by occasionally, but it wasn't the same as having another person living in her house.

Talise had no idea how happy she had made Sandra when she invited her to dinner and shopping. Although Sandra didn't lead a boring life between church and work, she missed Talise after that brief time they spent together.

She didn't fool herself into believing that Talise accepted her friendship blindly. Being in the company of her ex-scoundrel of a boyfriend's mother couldn't be easy. Sandra hated how Ace handled the situation, but if he really thought that the child wasn't his, she could understand his reaction.

Ace's defense was his refusal to believe she's pregnant. Shaking her head, the boy was pitiful. He knew about the birds and bees. God turned Kidd around, so she still held out hope for her youngest.

Her mind went back to Pastor Lane's sermon on faith from Hebrews, chapter 13. "The prophets had faith because God told them things. What things has God told you that you refuse to believe?" he had asked the congregation.

His question had lingered on her mind since she heard it. After she slid a pan of leftover casserole in the oven, Sandra sat at the table and folded her hands in thought.

"Jesus, I believe that You will draw my son to Your salvation! You told me so, God." Sandra lifted her arms in praise. She needed a distraction, as she stood and strolled into her living room. Glancing at the time on her violin-shaped clock that sat perched on an end table, she had an anxious feeling.

It was a little after seven. She wondered if Talise had made it home from work and was resting. Picking up the cordless, Sandra called her.

"Did I wake you?"

"No, I've just got a lot on my mind. That's all."

Sandra frowned. Talise seemed in a good mood on Friday evening. "Anything you want to talk about?"

"I'm having a pity party right now. I don't think you'd want an invite."

"Honey, I know how to be the life of a party," Sandra joked, masking her concern.

"I don't feel like I have any control over my life any more . . . my body, or my mind . . . and now my job is cutting back."

Sandra went on alert. "What does that mean? Do you still have a job?"

"Yes. But I now have an extra off day. Management is cutting our work week to four days instead of five. At least, I'll still have my full benefits, including medical coverage."

"Are you worried about the money? Because—"

"My dad has been helping me out financially. Before I found out,

I'd just reduced my client load at the salon. If I'd known, I wouldn't have turned away new customers and transferred some of my regulars to other stylists. My choices were between Friday and Sunday. Of course, Friday was snatched up by people with more seniority, and I can't do hair on Sundays."

Sandra's heart pounded, as she pumped her fist in the air. Now Talise had no excuse not to go to church. *I see You working this out in her favor, Jesus.*

"Well, God knows you need the rest."

"Yeah, but He knows I need the money too. I have to think in terms of two now."

Sandra had increased her savings deposits weeks ago, just in case Talise was carrying Ace's child. Once God revealed her purpose in Talise's life, she banned the 'if' word from her mind and lips.

"I'm here if you need me, and the invitation to visit my church is still open."

"Thanks." Talise ended the conversation not long after that.

—⁂—

Throughout the following week, Sandra increased her fasting and prayer time. Making intercessory prayer for Talise, she went before the Lord. "Jesus, please let there be a breakthrough in her life. Give her hope for the things she can't see."

Of course, she never stopped crying out for God to call Ace to repentance. And when He did, she prayed Ace had better answer.

The next Saturday morning, Sandra gave Talise a call. They weren't at a place in their relationship where they could chat for the sake of chatting. Still, without forcing her friendship, Sandra wanted to remind Talise of her presence if she needed her.

"Did I catch you at a bad time?"

"I'm finishing up on a favorite customer. Right, Miss Priscilla?"

"The best," Priscilla confirmed in the background.

"Well, I won't keep you. I was calling to remind you that the invitation to church is open for tomorrow." She paused. "Do you have time to take one more customer?"

"Who?"

"Me."

"Ah, yeah, but I'll have to tell you about Tammy before you get here," she whispered.

Sandra frowned and asked, "Who is Tammy?"

"Me," she whispered again.

Then without warning, Talise handed the phone to her customer, who practically spoke in a secret code. She instructed Sandra on how she should inquire about Talise's condition while in the shop.

Chuckling at the humor of it all, Sandra agreed and scribbled the time Talise had given her for an appointment. An hour and a half later, she strolled into Sassy's Salon.

The place was sleek from the gold and black awning outside to the marble flooring inside. In the waiting area, there were three groupings of cozy chairs huddled around coffee tables. Each table was artfully decorated with books and magazines. A well-organized receptionist's desk separated the manicurists' and stylists' stations.

Talise appeared from a back area, carrying a large cup of water. As soon as she saw Sandra, her eyes lit up and she beckoned her new customer to come back. Making her way to Talise's chair, Sandra was impressed by each stylist's station she passed by. They were extra roomy and appeared to be equipped with every latest hair styling tool known to Black women. Talise greeted her with a hug that warmed Sandra's heart and made her feel welcome.

Once seated, she slowly twirled Sandra around and started to massage her scalp. "Your hair seems slightly over-processed. Have you been doing it yourself or using a stylist?"

"I used to put a relaxer in myself. Then last year, I started to let it grow it out . . ."

"You know, chemicals don't grow out. I have some new products I would like to try on you. They'll give your hair more moisture . . . and you're going to need a shape-up."

Sandra nodded. She had plenty of hair and could stand to lose an inch or two.

"I have a style in mind to complement the shape of your face. It'll make you look younger and even more beautiful."

Sandra blushed. She was about to become a grandmother. Without a husband or a man friend, there was no need for any enhancements. But she agreed. "Sure."

With efficiency, Talise whipped a cape around Sandra's shoulders and escorted her to the shampoo bowl. From the fragranced shampoo, to the stimulating conditioner, to the gentle care exhibited when Talise washed her hair—Sandra had no complaints.

Back at her station, Talise proceeded to blow-dry Sandra's hair. Thoroughly enjoying the experience, she relaxed and let her mind wander. Yet all of her thoughts seemed to lead her back to Talise and the baby's wellbeing.

"So how's Tammy?" she asked, as Talise used a flat iron to straighten her hair.

"She's going through some rough patches, but as my sister—I mean, her sister tells her," Talise slipped and corrected. "This too will pass."

The conversation turned toward the Jamieson wives, Grandma BB, and Kami. They laughed until Talise focused her attention on trimming Sandra's straightened hair.

"Your ends aren't bad, but you still need a slight trim." She turned Sandra's face to the left and right, analyzing the shape of her hair. Once Talise was satisfied with an imaginary style, she heated her curlers.

Amazingly, a short time later, Sandra didn't realize Talise was finished until she handed her a face shield. With one hand, she covered her own nose and sprayed oil sheen and holding spray on Sandra's hair. Once she finished and turned the chair around to the mirror, Sandra gasped at her reflection. Blinking several times, she practically stuttered, "Is that me?"

Laughing, Talise removed the cape. "Yes, and you are more beautiful than ever."

In a state of awe, Sandra turned her head from side to side. She fingered her hair, unable to remember the last time it felt so soft.

"You're definitely talented," she complimented, unable to keep her eyes from misting.

At that moment, the woman who Talise had introduced as Sasha, the shop owner, walked by. "The girl is bad, ain't she?"

Speechless, Sandra could only nod.

Sasha chuckled and mentioned it was a shame Talise was turning away customers.

"I'm reducing my roster," Talise explained.

"I hope you keep me on your list," Sandra said, as she reached into her purse for her wallet.

"It's my treat," she said. Her smile was genuine.

There was no way Sandra wasn't going to pay. "Thanks, but no thanks . . . and here's a tip," she insisted, while jamming five twenties in Talise's smock pocket. "How about a late lunch?" Sandra asked, still wearing her determined face.

"I'll have to pass. Sasha's going to wash and set my hair, so that's a minimum of two hours. Before you go, let one of the girls wax your brows. And then, look out, you'll be fighting the men off." Talise chuckled, with a faraway look in her eyes.

"Not tonight. I'm going home and then to church tomorrow. Speaking of which, don't forget, you're welcome to come." Sandra hoped her invitation was subtle.

Following Sasha to the shampoo area and settling herself in the chair, Talise didn't answer right away. Sandra waited patiently. "I don't know," she finally said. Then with a sigh, she added, "Okay but, Sandra, if the pastor gets long-winded, I'm leaving and probably won't come back."

"Great." Sandra was thrilled but would pray for a short and sweet sermon. "It's called Faithful Church on Woodrow Ave. Service starts at ten thirty." Smiling, she said goodbye and walked to the other side of the shop to get her brows waxed. "Thank You, Jesus," she whispered.

Twenty minutes later, Sandra was surprised to see Cameron swagger in as she was about to leave. The proud walk, arrogant air, and good looks were definitely Jamieson traits. Hugging her, Cameron brushed a kiss on her cheek and stepped back.

"What are you doing here?" he asked in surprise.

"I had a hair appointment," she answered, proudly shaking her head from side to side. "What are you doing here? Are you getting your brows waxed?" she teased him.

Cameron grinned. "Never. I'm just checking on Talise to see if she needs anything. After she left St. Louis, Kidd, my brothers, and I made a Jamieson pact. We're going to be there for her, even financially, whether Ace faces his responsibility or not."

With her hair tucked under a plastic cap, Talise snuck up on them. "Sorry, Cameron, I can't take any more walk-ins for the day, nor will Ace ever walk back into my life."

Chapter Thirty-Three

I would go to church with you, but that's one habit I don't plan to develop," Lois informed Talise. "I work all week long, go out on Saturday night, and regroup all day Sunday. Sorry, I'm sticking to my schedule."

Talise felt obligated to go to service this morning after she stood Sandra up the week before. She really enjoyed Sandra's company, and at times, it slipped Talise's mind that she was Ace's mother.

Seeing Cameron yesterday was another matter. His walk and some of his facial expressions reminded her of Ace. Ironically, his generosity clashed with Ace's callousness.

Being around his cousin filled her with regret for falling for the wrong Jamieson. Unfortunately, there was never any chemistry between them. It's too bad because Cameron seemed like a genuinely good guy.

Nevertheless, his visit had flooded her mind with memories of Ace. She had come home and cried that evening. It also happened to be bad timing. Her father had called while she was in the middle of her distressed moment.

Frederick could tell right away that something wasn't right. "Hey, sweetheart, what's wrong? Are you crying? Did you and that no good young man have another fight?"

Whenever they talked, she evaded the subject. She never told her dad outright there had been no relationship—period—since she learned of her pregnancy.

"Daddy, Ace and I didn't break up." She paused to gather strength. "He dumped me as soon as he found out about the baby." Talise braced herself as he exploded.

"What! You mean to tell me that he deserted you? What kind of animal is he? That's it," he practically growled into the phone. "I'm coming to get you and bring you home," he yelled.

She held the phone away from her ear while her father continued his tirade. He kept it up so long that Talise thought he was going to hyperventilate. By now, she was sure Donna was somewhere near him with a brown paper bag.

"Daddy, calm down."

"Don't tell me to calm down. I have a problem with you not telling me this until now, Talise." He took a deep breath. "I want you to give me this gambler's legal name and address. It appears this Ace and me need to come to some kind of understanding. You should have told me this sooner . . ."

Even though her father was causing her head to pound, she welcomed his anger. It mirrored her own bottled-up rage. He was right. It was time for her to go home where there would be no reminders of a Jamieson. Talise had to give this some serious thought.

She could have her things packed up by the end of the week. Her dad could fly in, they could rent a U-Haul, and then drive back to Richmond. Of course, she would have to turn over her remaining clients to Sasha. Talise could trust her to distribute them among the stylists, according to her clients' preferences. She would definitely miss her friend Priscilla, but they would stay in contact.

Next, was her major employer. Hopefully, Talise would be able to work out an arrangement with the airline so that she wouldn't lose her medical benefits. If allowed, she would take a leave of absence and probably have to pay a higher premium.

Although she hadn't made too many friends on her job, Talise would miss her chats with Gabrielle. There was calmness about her that Talise wished she could emulate. They would definitely have to stay in contact.

With a deep sigh, the thought of choosing another obstetrician at five months was daunting. Talise didn't realize she had zoned out until her father mentioned Donna's name.

"I'll have Donna book our flights and we'll be there . . ." When he paused, Talise could hear his wife in the background.

"We can't go this weekend, dear. You have that golf tournament benefit and . . ." Donna sounded like a dutiful secretary giving the boss his weekly schedule. Talise huffed.

Taking the phone, Donna came on the line. "Talise, can you hold off a bit? We really have a full schedule for the next few weeks. Plus, I'm going to have to rearrange the guest bedroom to accommodate your things and the baby. By the way, it's a shame the way that boy used you like that and moved on . . ."

Nope. She made up her mind right then. Going home was not going to be an option after all. Donna just reminded Talise how annoying she could be. She was going to have to stick it out twenty-one more weeks.

If her mother were living, Marilyn would have been on the first plane out of Richmond. She would have practically moved in with Talise and seriously pampered her. That thought made her smile at the same time the baby kicked softly. She rubbed her stomach.

Frederick returned to the conversation at the same time a call from Sandra had beeped in. "Dad, we'll talk about it later. I have to get this other call. Love you." She disconnected and answered the other line.

"Hi, sweetie, I'm just checking to see if you're up to some inspiration in the morning?"

Talise could hear the happiness in Sandra's voice. "I could use some, but," she hesitated. "I'm drained." An emotional wreck was more like it after seeing Cameron had forced flashbacks of her and Ace. "Maybe I should stay home and rest."

Sandra had done a poor job of masking her disappointment. "Okay, perhaps when you're feeling up to it. Remember, once your soul finds rest, your mind and body will follow."

That had been her drama last week. Now, this morning, she decided to go to church. Could God give her some rest from her emotional turmoil?

Rest. Lord knows she needed some. The question triggered her to recall a Scripture that she read a few days ago. It had brought her comfort at a time when she was feeling down.

Come to me, all you who are weary and burdened, and I will give you rest. She was pleased with herself, this time remembering it was Matthew 11:28.

Determined to press on, she gathered her strength. With Lois uninterested and steadfast under the covers, Talise would go by herself. Hoping it wasn't too early, she called Sandra. Not realizing she had been holding her breath, Talise exhaled when Sandra answered.

"I'm going this morning," she announced.

"Praise the Lord." Sandra sniffed. "That's wonderful. I'll wait for you outside at the entrance."

Her baby shifted during Sandra's jubilation. Smiling at that occurrence, Talise rubbed her stomach. They chatted a few more minutes before Sandra hurried her off the phone.

Perusing through her closet, it didn't take long for Talise to find something to wear. This was the perfect occasion to put on the dress Sandra insisted on buying her. As she lifted the elegant dress off the hanger, surprisingly, Lois was up and wandered into her room.

Making herself comfortable lying at the foot of Talise's bed, she squinted. "So you're definitely going, huh? Well, you'll look gorgeous in that color. Instead of having a sugar daddy, you've got a sugar mama."

"Lois," Talise warned. Her roommate had no idea about the internal tug of war she had going on when it came to accepting Sandra's generosity.

"Okay. Okay. Wear those bronze strapped sandals. They'll go well with it and your nail polish. Plus, the heels aren't too high." She yawned and sat up. "Okay, praise the Lord, pray for me. I'm going back to bed."

As Lois stood and trotted back to her own room, the baby moved again. "I guess the baby book was right. You *can* hear." She patted her stomach. It was the first time she felt this much movement. Maybe the baby was getting excited about going to church.

Just then, another Scripture came to mind: *"Before I formed you in the womb I knew you, before you were born I set you apart."* It was a portion of Jeremiah 1:5.

Talise was beginning to see that Sinclaire was right. Her Bible reading was beginning to make a difference. Her eyes misted. She loved how the Word spoke to her heart. "Lord, please don't let it stop," she thought out loud. The feeling of being close to God kept her in an exceptionally good mood throughout the time it took her to eat and get ready for church.

Finishing with plenty of time to spare, Talise liked her reflection as she studied herself in the mirror. Although she had noticeably picked up weight, it was proportioned throughout her body and not all stomach. Grabbing her keys and purse, she left the apartment.

Fifteen minutes into the drive, Talise realized two things. She forgot to bring her Bible, and Sandra's church was farther away than she had expected. Nevertheless, she stayed focused. At last, her GPS had her turn off of Blue Hill Ave. On the corner of Woodrow Ave., a tall, white structure stood majestic like a beacon.

True to her word, Sandra was waiting for her, as she pulled into the adjacent parking lot. She stood poised by the door, wearing an outfit in her favorite color. Sandra looked pretty in pastel sage and adorned in a flirty hat. In Talise's opinion, she was, in fact, striking. How could a man not chase after her, especially with her sons grown and gone?

Waving when she spotted Talise, Sandra left her post near the door and met her halfway. "I'm so glad you came," she said, engulfing Talise in a hug and grinning like a proud parent. It was almost as though Talise could see her mother's face reflected in Sandra's expression.

"So am I, and the baby too. He or she's been busy this morning."

"That's so exciting, isn't it? May I?" Sandra grinned again, as she carefully placed her hand on Talise's stomach. The baby didn't do any somersaults, but Talise felt a slight movement. After moving to three positions on Talise's stomach, she removed her hand. Shrugging, she looped her arm through Talise's and they strolled to the main entrance.

"When are you going to find out about the sex of the baby? Then you won't have to keep saying 'he or she.'"

"My next doctor's visit is on Thursday. But I'm not sure I want to know."

Sandra faked a pout. "Eva is saying the same thing. I need to know, so I can go shopping."

Talise laughed. The woman was so endearing. "Would you like to go with me to a doctor's appointment? Lois has already made arrangements to go with me this time. But I have an ultrasound coming up soon. That would be the perfect time for you to go. There's one stipulation, though. If you find out, you can't tell me if it's a boy or girl. I don't want any hint or even see you buying all pinks or blues."

"I would love to! I can leave work and then return after the appointment," she responded. Sandra looked like she was about to cry, but she smiled instead. Talise noticed her slight dimple that was similar to Ace's.

"Sandra, I have one more stipulation. Please don't pass on any of my personal information to Ace. In my heart, he's no longer the baby's father. Just a reproductive donor."

Chapter Thirty-Four

*B*efore they reached the double doors of the church, someone opened them. Talise followed Sandra inside.

"Wow, Sister Nicholson. Don't you look beautiful today! You're going to give the deacons around here a fit." Someone with a deep voice complimented Sandra before Talise could see his face.

When the tall, dark and handsome face materialized, Talise had to look the other way to keep from drooling. However, it wasn't fast enough and he caught her staring.

"Minister Thomas, I'm going to tell Pastor about your flirting," Sandra teased and they both laughed. She turned to Talise.

"Minister Richard Thomas, this is Talise Rogers, my . . ." Sandra's words faded, as a frown appeared to replace her smile.

Right then, it dawned on Talise that the two of them had never been in a situation where they had to define their relationship to someone.

"My good friend, almost like the daughter I never had," she quickly recovered, giving Talise a warm glance.

"Oh, very nice to meet you." He bowed his head slightly. "Talise, is it?"

"It's Talise"

"Lovely," Minister Thomas acknowledged. "My apologies. I stand corrected. Please forgive my unprofessional manner in which I teased Sister Nicholson. We have this routine exchange on Sunday mornings."

Before he could say more, Sandra reached for Talise's hand and tugged her toward a staircase. "The music has started. Come on, so we can find good seats."

Smiling, Minister Thomas nodded and hurried off in another direction. Talise whispered, "Sandra, you're a cougar." They both laughed.

"I wouldn't be opposed to dating younger men, but eight years is my max. Richard is young enough to be one of my sons. He's a sweetheart and a dynamic youth minister," she rambled on, as they reached the second floor.

The sanctuary was filling quickly. Somehow, Sandra spied out two empty seats among the thick of the crowd. Without waiting for an usher, she made a beeline for them. Talise humbly followed, wondering if she stood out as a sinner among saints. Was it obvious that she was an unwed mother dumped by her baby's father?

As they entered the pew, no one gave her scolding stares, only warm smiles. Sandra knelt, whispered a prayer, and then took her seat. Talise sat and watched while the high energy of worship began to draw her in. Within minutes, Sandra was on her feet, engulfed in the praise.

Talise couldn't remember the last time she had attended church. For the past ten years or so, it had been a hit-and-miss occurrence—mostly missing. She also stood and put her hands together in sync with the music.

As the pastor walked to the pulpit with his Bible in hand, the music gradually ceased. "Praise the Lord, church!" After he thanked the praise team, Pastor Lane welcomed the visitors and made a few announcements. Talise was glad he didn't waste any time opening his Bible. The congregation joined him in a short prayer before he began preaching the Word.

"Amen, Amen, and Amen. I'm excited about Jesus today and the mission He accomplished. In the Old Testament, God guided the Israelites with a cloud by day and fire by night, leading them to the Promised Land. In your private study time, read about their journey throughout the book of Exodus, and especially Exodus 13:21 and 22. Now fast forward thousands of years. You may not know what road you're on, or how long your journey will be, but trust God to put a light in your path.

"Don't take lightly the people you meet or the situations you encounter along the way. Get in a good Bible study and apply God's Word so you can stay on the right path. Dress for the storm with the wardrobe God gave you in Ephesians 6:10 to 18. Watch and pray like the rapture is coming tomorrow. As Jesus stated in Revelation 22:12, He is coming back to take us to His Promised Land."

Talise leaned over and whispered, "Will you help me write down those Scriptures? I forgot my Bible and I can't keep up."

Sandra nodded and whispered back, "Sure. Pastor Lane purposely does that to make us read our Bibles."

They both turned their attention back to the sermon. "Some people make the mistake of believing Jesus' sole purpose for coming here was to save us from our sins by dying on the cross. And, thank God, He did do that." He paused, as if he was waiting for his statement to sink in. "But I'm talking about His main purpose. If you think I'm wrong then you need to spend more time studying your Bible. Jesus came to get us out of here! That's where all paths will end on the Day of Judgment . . ."

Talise's mind began to rebel and wander, as she battled to stay focused. When the baby moved, that served as a reminder for her. She rubbed her stomach and smiled, knowing it was time to get her life together. If for no other reason, Talise wanted her child to do right before God—unlike his or her parents.

The pastor continued to preach with a warning message until he seemed to run out of steam. "Will the congregation please stand," his booming voice broke into her reverie. Talise blinked when she watched him close his Bible.

"If you're a visitor today, you may have thought your presence here is because someone invited you. But it's the Lord who sent out the invitations. Your salvation is His priority alone," Pastor Lane explained.

"Take a quick assessment of your life. If you're completely satisfied, then I'll come back to you. However, for those of you who will admit you're lacking in one or more areas of your life, I'm advising you to repent. You can't go any further without taking that first step. Tell God you're sorry for what you know you've done against His commandments. He'll forgive you for that and even the stuff you can't remember."

He began to pace the pulpit. "Now back to those persons who have no complaints, wants, needs, or desires. The bottom line is—you still need to repent."

I've done that, Talise thought to herself.

"We've all sinned. As a matter of fact, we were wrapped in it like a diaper when we were born. Again, I say repent from where you are standing. I have no words for you to recite as you talk to God. That's a personal conversation. If you want to take another step, then we have ministers ready to talk to you."

Talise's feet would not budge, although some did take heed to the invitation. As they walked down the aisle to the altar, she noticed that several received prayer only and returned to their seats. She watched as others followed a minister through a doorway.

Talise had seen, heard, and felt enough for one Sunday. This type of intense praise was foreign to her. Ready to go, she gathered her purse, quickly waved to Sandra, and left the pew. The most important thing was she kept her word and had come.

Just before she reached the sanctuary's exit, Sandra caught up with her. The hat was gone and she sniffed while dabbing at her tears. Reaching out, she engulfed Talise in a hug. "I'm so glad you came. I hope the Word gave you some comfort."

"Yes."

"Good, I'll talk to you later." Sandra kissed her cheek and returned to her seat.

Talise stopped before exiting the sanctuary door and reached into her purse for an offering. She pulled out a ten dollar bill and placed it in the usher's gloved hand, who tossed it in the offering plate.

After a polite nod to a few people scattered throughout the hallway, she held the banister and walked down to the lower level. As she made her way through the foyer, Talise wondered if something was wrong with her because she didn't go down to the altar with the others. But in all honesty, she didn't feel ready.

Stopping and digging in the bottom of her purse for her keys, she couldn't find them. Talise sighed and prayed that she hadn't left them on the pew. She didn't want to go back into the sanctuary. One by one, Talise pulled out her wallet, checkbook, cell phone; and finally, she tangled with her car keys that were caught on an inside zipper.

With a sigh of relief, she stuffed her things back inside and turned to leave. Before she could make it to the door, Minister Thomas spotted her and headed her way.

"Talise, you're leaving already?" he stopped her and asked.

Already? Two hours was her limit and service had already gone over by fifteen minutes. She nodded.

"Did you enjoy the message?"

"I did," she replied. It was hard not to stare. He was a good looking man.

"Will you come back?"

It was on the tip of her tongue to say she doubted it. But one look into his eyes changed her tune. "I might give it another try."

"Whew. That's good." He grinned and wiped imaginary sweat from his brow. "I'll escort you to your car."

"Oh, there's no need. I'll be fine."

"That wasn't an invitation, sister. The brothers in this church see after the sisters."

"Hi, Minister Ricky!" Two small children chimed, as they ran ahead of their parents. He acknowledged them and promptly opened the door for her to go first.

Chivalry. It no longer impressed her. Ace had mastered the technique and look where that landed her.

Once they were outside, Talise slipped on her sunglasses. As the wind fussed with her hair, she squinted to see her car in the distance. Relieved that it wasn't too far, she wanted to limit her interaction with Minister Thomas.

Walking alongside Talise, he commented, "Sister Nicholson is a sweetheart. How long have you known her?"

Talise began counting the weeks since their first meeting at the restaurant. "Several months," she responded.

"She was the first person who reached out to me when the Lord saved me a few years ago. When I became an ordained minister, she encouraged me to keep walking with Jesus. I couldn't ask for a better cheerleader. She kinda adopted me as her son."

Nodding, Talise smiled in agreement. She felt the same way. "Sandra has a way of doing that."

He continued, "I remember when she told me about her two sons and how they gave her the blues when they were younger. But she kept praying and I think her oldest repented and Jesus saved him."

Minister Thomas frowned. "The other son . . ." he started then exhaled. "Unfortunately, he's lost in the wilderness, but Sister Nicholson and I are still praying."

At that moment, they approached her car. Talise deactivated the alarm and he opened her door. "Have a good day, Minister Thomas," she said, tossing her purse in the back seat.

"And I wish you the same. By the way, how do you know Sister Nicholson?"

"As you can see, I'm pregnant—and it's by her *other* son." If she stunned him, he didn't show it. She slid behind the wheel and turned the ignition. As soon as he closed the door, Talise drove off without a backward glance.

Chapter Twenty-Five

*A*re you ready for your court date tomorrow?" Kidd asked Ace over the phone.

Rubbing his head, Ace exhaled. "Yeah. I might as well get this over with, so I can move on."

Sitting behind the desk in his downtown office, Ace welcomed the interruption. Before Kidd called, he had been staring at a client's spreadsheet countless times without computing any summaries. At the same time, he wasn't thrilled that Kidd's purpose for calling was to remind him of a regrettable event. It wasn't like he needed to recall the day he clowned before the world.

Too often his apartment left him alone with his thoughts. Quietness chased him away from its bare walls most days. Being in the thick of things was his preferred defense mechanism. Of course, his coworkers still enjoyed riling him about his three-minute debut on YouTube.

"I'll meet you there," Kidd said.

"There's no need. I'll probably be fined and 'set free.'"

"Ace, you're already free. Besides, I'm there for you in the good and bad times."

"How did my life get this messed up?"

"You want the truth?" He didn't wait for Ace's yea or nay. "Your 'responsibility is optional' attitude has backfired on you. We're both about to become fathers. We can do this and Jesus will help us. If you don't want to marry Talise, at least be man enough to be an active father in your child's life—"

Ace cut him off. "If I wanted advice, I would pay for it." That's where Ace drew the line. He knew how to handle his business. Changing the subject, he asked, "So is that the only reason you called?"

"Nope, wanted to remind you about family game night tomorrow over at Parke and Cheney's. You don't have to be a stranger just because you moved out. It's like a monthly party." Kidd added, "The invitation also still stands for you to visit our church. Just because you don't live with us doesn't mean we'll stop inviting you to church."

"First of all, there's a church on every corner. I'll get to one, eventually. Second, your game night is not my idea of a party—"

There was a slight knock on Ace's door and his administrative assistant peeked inside. "Don't forget about your conference call in ten minutes with Money Express," Nina said softly. With a cheerful smile, she backed out.

Any other man would be so lucky to garner this much attention from almost every woman on his job. Ace had flourished in his heyday with so much interest. But the hunt, the chase, and the capture game had played out in his life once he met Talise. Or rather, it had gotten him into emotional trouble.

Ace sighed, thinking about her smile, the perfect grin. Her seductive eyes sparkled and lit up when she saw him. Boy, he missed the Talise he thought she was. It was disgusting to even think about her.

"Look, man, I've got to go. I'll probably stop by Parke's tomorrow night, but I don't want to hear Talise's name mentioned—or I'm out of there."

"Have you *heard* us say her name around you?"

"Don't play games, Kidd, those Jamieson wives have been scheming behind my back all along. If Talise hadn't been invited, or if she hadn't invited herself to St. Louis, I never would have seen her at the airport and tried to talk to her. The rest is history."

—⁓〰⁓—

On Friday morning, Ace hadn't expected the courthouse to be in such frenzy. The sight reminded him of a circus or a church convention. His only consolation was that he didn't see the media anywhere in sight.

From a distance, Ace spotted Kidd standing in the lobby in a sea of red. Women of all ages decked out in red and purple hats were everywhere. Kidd had been chatting amicably with one of the ladies before Ace saw him step away. He squinted. It was the woman notoriously known as Grandma BB.

He tried to infiltrate the crowd to get to his brother. At least twice, a fierce-looking, petite woman blocked his path.

"Friend or foe, handsome?"

"Neither." Evidently, Ace's height and build wasn't intimidating her. The woman matched his step to the side. "Sorry, this party is reserved for supporters of the YouTube sensation, Ace Jamieson."

"I'm ... Ace."

Stretching her neck, the woman peered up through her thick glasses. "It is you! Sugar, you should have said somethin'." Putting two fingers between her lips, she forced air through her mouth and whistled. That action seemed to make her dizzy.

After leaning on Ace, she panted until Grandma BB came over. "Ethel, you know you have bronchitis," Grandma BB fussed. Looping her arm through Ace's, it was unclear who was escorting whom to Kidd.

Grandma BB mumbled, "I hope we won't have to call the paramedics again. Humph! I told her to take her medicine this morning." She shook her head.

"Grandma BB, why are you here? I thought only my brother was coming."

"No, chile, being in the courtroom is second nature to me. For some reason, criminals are attracted to me, and it ain't for my looks." She winked. "But I don't know if I can help you in this case. I don't know the judge."

They finally met up with Kidd near the doorway to the courtroom.

"Hey, man, what's up with this red convention?" Ace asked.

"She insisted on coming. The funny thing about it is she wants the judge to give you the maximum sentence."

"What!" He squinted at the woman.

"This is bigger than YouTube, Acey. Talise should have—"

"Preach to him later. We've got to get inside," Kidd said, ushering him through the door where there were even more ladies in red.

"Seriously, who are these people?"

"The Red Hat Society, St. Louis chapter. They backed Grandma BB when she was on trial for shooting Cheney's father," Kidd said nonchalantly.

"What!" Maybe he was still asleep and this was a nightmare.

"Yeah, she got ninety days shock time."

"Was it an accident?"

"Nope. When Grandma BB aims, she hits her target. I think Parke told me it was Dr. Reynolds' shoulder, or some other extremity. Anyway, that's a long story or maybe even a book. Come on. Let's see if we can squeeze into some seats."

First, Ace needed to locate his attorney. They shook hands and then took their seats. Judge Cahill went down the roster, calling those who had committed petty crimes, from peace disturbance, animal cruelty, to shoplifting less than a hundred dollars.

Finally, it was Ace's turn. Standing with his attorney, Ace approached the bench. Judge Cahill recited the same spiel he used with the other defendants and then named Ace's charge of resisting arrest.

"How do you plead?" the judge asked Ace's attorney.

"Not guilty."

A soft chant floated throughout the courtroom, "Guilty, guilty, guilty."

In disbelief, Ace whirled around. The judge pounded his gavel. Were they serious? He glanced at Kidd for an explanation. His brother shrugged.

"Mr. Jamieson, since you did not actually enter the aircraft and no weapons were involved, I order you to one hundred hours of community service. You are also banned from the airport for the next ninety days." Judge Cahill handed down the sentence and dismissed him. The clerk called the next case.

"What! All I was trying to do was get someone's attention," he said to his attorney, who quickly nudged Ace outside the courtroom. There were some important matters to resolve, such as details of court costs and the date his name would be removed from the "no fly" list.

Dissatisfied with the outcome, Ace asked his lawyer, "Can't I appeal this?"

The attorney responded, "Yes, you can. But you'll be off the 'no fly' list by the time that could take place."

—m—

"Great." Ace threw up his arms in disgust. When he didn't want to go home, he had the privilege of flying. Now that he wanted to go back to Boston, he couldn't. Fate was not on his side. He was doomed to St. Louis.

Fed up with the whole court fiasco, Ace went back to the office. Trying to take his mind off his troubles, he turned his attention to what he'd do with himself that evening. Somehow it was hard to believe it was a coincidence when a female coworker seductively strutted into his office. It seemed more like a setup, but still he had to contain his drool. Lana was wearing a black, form-fitting leather vest, skinny jeans, and stilettos.

"Want to hang out tonight?" she asked. "There's an ethnic festival going on in Forest Park this weekend. It started today."

Ace declined. The possibility was tempting, but since his last blowup with Talise, his family jewels were on lockdown with a padlock. The only other option was the family get-together at Parke's.

Well, he thought. He might as well hang out with his folks in the Gateway City. Cameron had raved about family game night. Even Kidd mentioned it when he first moved to St. Louis. Personally, Ace didn't see what the big deal was about sitting around a table for hours playing board games. But it beat spending the evening alone in his apartment.

After work, he showered, dressed, and then gladly left his lonely surroundings. Driving to Parke's turn-of-the-century, massive house that was often the center of major family activity, he exited off of I-170. Ace weaved his way through the neighborhoods until he came to Darst Street in Old Ferguson.

The cars were lined up in front of the mouse-gray, three-level house. Lights were shining brightly in almost every window. Ace parked and got out. Strolling down the winding pathway to the front door, he could hear happy voices before he stepped foot on the porch.

Ace didn't bother knocking or ringing the bell. He doubted they would hear him anyway. Turning the knob, he walked in unnoticed. As he paused by the door, he took in the cheerful scene in front of him. The younger children were squealing and running around and the adults were huddled in groups, laughing. Everyone was wearing bright T-shirts, as if they were at a sporting event. Each family had a different color shirt with the word "Team" on it, followed by their leader's name. And Ace thought the Red Sox fans were fanatical.

"Hey, you made it!" Eva said, coming toward him with arms opened. She actually started a receiving line of greetings as others followed. Soon Cheney announced the food was ready and everybody made a beeline to her spacious kitchen. There they formed another line to serve themselves pasta, hot vegetables, meatballs, and pigs-in-a-blanket.

The toddlers ate in the kitchen under the supervision of Kami, who took her role as boss seriously. She even made Paden and M.J. stand as she clasped her hands for prayer, rather than blessing the food sitting down. Her older brother, Pace, ignored her.

In the other room, the adults gathered around the dining room table. They were coupled off: Parke and Cheney; his parents, Parke V and Charlotte; Malcolm and Hallison; Eva and Kidd.

Parke's father, known as Papa P., offered the blessing over the food and everyone dug in. Everyone chatted as they enjoyed the fellowship. After the meal, the dining room table was cleared. As soon as Cheney cleaned the smudges from the glossy table, Hallison set out the game board and pieces. Pace shuffled a stack of cards like they were about to play blackjack.

"What are we playing here?" Ace asked Parke.

"The game is called 'Fact or Fiction Black History.' The object is simple. We go around the table and everyone pulls a card from the deck. One team asks another team a question. If they answer it correctly, they'll win the number of points on the card."

Malcolm took over, "The first team to score one hundred wins. But if you answer incorrectly, then your team's score is deducted the number of points on your card." He smirked. "Since this is your first time, we'll loan you our children to be on Team Ace. Next time, wear your own T-shirt."

"You may not want one after we whip you up. You might be too scared to come back next month," Kidd taunted him.

"I see ya'll talkin' trash. Put children on my team. I can win, with or without them. Bring it on." Ace had his game face. He told the older children, "Let's do it." The preschoolers, M. J. and Paden, he considered extra bodies.

Papa P. and Charlotte pulled the first card and glanced around the table, looking for which team to challenge. Kami waved her arms frantically by Ace's side. Ace groaned. He was definitely going to lose if his little cousin volunteered before a question was asked.

"Pick me, Grandma. Pick me!" Kami begged.

Charlotte smiled at her granddaughter. "This might be a little rough for you, baby. But if Team Ace wants to start us off, I will."

"Sure." Ace huffed and eyed his little cousin. "I don't play to lose, so you'd better bring your A game," he told her.

"Okay." Charlotte chuckled. "For ten points, what is a contraband camp?"

Already, Ace was stumped. What kind of question was that? They were going to be the first group in the negative. "You'd better make up something," he mumbled.

Kami and Pace whispered in each other's ear. *Great, they're stalling for time,* he thought. If he could get away with it, he would use his phone.

Nodding, Kami cleared her throat and grinned. She had a pretty smile, but Ace doubted that it was bright enough to score any points.

"The Contraband Camps were formed by enslaved African Americans during the Civil War period. Thousands on thousands escaped when Union Army forces invaded . . . wherever they settled on the way . . ."

Impressed, Ace had to sit up. He had underestimated the child. When he had children, he wanted them to be just as smart. *Whoa. Did I just say that?* He mentally collapsed.

The last time he checked, he didn't have any children. And, up until this point, from hearsay, no one could verify that Talise even looked pregnant. When the adults cheered, Ace snapped out of drifting off.

"That's my grandbaby! When you come over this weekend, I'll give you something extra." Charlotte winked and the girl beamed.

Next, it was Team Malcolm/Hallison's turn. Hallison pulled from the stack and scanned the card. "Okay, Papa P. and Momma C., for twenty points, name two states that held Negro State Fairs."

Where were these questions coming from? Ace wondered.

"Texas and Oklahoma," Papa P. answered without hesitation.

"You can't let us hang like that. The question should have asked for a definition," Hallison said.

"It's like the name implies. Thanks to the Jim Crow laws, separate, but equal was a way of life in everything. The laws didn't just apply to swimming pools, water fountains, transportation, and education. Think about the Negro League and Black beauty pageants," Papa P. explained.

Charlotte picked up where her husband left off. "That's right. Even back then, African Americans made lemonade out of sour lemons. They added some sugar to their own fairs. One was held at a man's ranch. His name was Coody Johnson in Wewoka, Oklahoma. It was a yearly event that lasted four days with rodeos, parades, and festivals."

Ace couldn't believe he actually learned something. Team Parke/Cheney pulled next and directed the question at Kidd. Ace hid his smirk. The St. Louis Jamiesons might have the upper hand on these family nights, but his brother was no dummy either. *Sic 'em, bro,* Ace taunted under his breath.

"Eva and Kidd, for ten points, what were 'resurrection men,' also called 'resurrectionists'?" Cheney asked.

Ace stroked the hairs on his chin. He was considering growing a beard. *Was that a religious question?* "I didn't know we were playing Bible games," he mumbled.

"We aren't," Kami whispered.

"They were also called 'body snatchers' because they dug up graves under the cover of night. The grave diggers stole bodies for medical experiments. Segregated gravesites were targeted, whether the deceased were freed Blacks or enslaved," Kidd answered and met Eva's waiting lips for his reward.

"Body snatchers also hit the White cemeteries too," Papa P. added. His son's team, Team Parke, was the first group to lose twenty

255

points when Parke stated that there were two periods of the Great Migration of Blacks from the South in 1910 and 1940.

"Big bro, did you forget about the exodus of Blacks at the end of the Reconstruction? Bam!" Malcolm argued.

Pace chimed in, "But Uncle Malcolm, what about the American Colonization Society that shipped freed Blacks back to Sierra Leone? That's a migration, but to a different continent."

Ace gave him a high-five. His team was on a winning streak. Then Eva yelled and jumped. All activity ceased. Kidd, who was sitting next to her, was poised to act.

"Baby? What's wrong?"

Massaging her stomach, Eva smiled at her husband. "Your child kicked me."

Laughter and chuckles filled the air, as the toddlers and Kami took turns rubbing her belly. Pace didn't seem interested.

The conversation then shifted to how many weeks along she was and what the baby was doing. Ace racked his brain. When could Talise have gotten pregnant?

The evening was going well until Eva mentioned Talise's name. Immediately, he eyed Kidd, who shrugged. A man of his word, Ace called it quits. Despite their pleas for him to stay, he declined and headed out to the casino. He would try his luck there.

An hour after he'd arrived, Ace stalked out. His winning streak was over. He had just lost five-hundred dollars. Strangely, he never lost—until now.

Chapter Thirty-Six

I've got great news!" Lois announced with a grin, as she drove Talise to her doctor's appointment.

"Okaaaay," Talise said, drawing out the word. Eying her friend suspiciously, she added, "And please don't tell me that sorry line, 'you just saved a lot on your car insurance.'"

"How did you know? No seriously, I've got a solution to the rent problem."

"Sinclaire said she would work it into her budget to—"

*Tsk*ing, Lois shook her head. "Didn't I tell you to stop worrying your sister? One of my coworkers needs temporary shelter, and I offered her our apartment."

Somehow, Talise had the strangest feeling she wasn't going to like hearing the rest of her roommate's idea. Unable to ignore that she was the cause of the problem, Talise had to hear Lois out. Her choices were definitely limited, so she asked, "Okay, for how long does she plan stay?"

"Six months."

That's temporary? It sounds like she's a day away from permanent to me. "Six months!" Talise exclaimed in protest. "Our shared living space is large enough, but our bedrooms aren't."

"Hey, beggars can't be choosy. I'm giving up the privacy of my bedroom for you." She stuck out her tongue.

"Thank you. I know. I'm just cranky, I guess. I feel guilty putting you in yet another predicament because of my condition."

"Nonsense. I've got this."

"Thanks again. So when is she moving in?"

"Tomorrow."

"Tomorrow! So soon? Dr. Sherman is going to have to check my blood pressure as soon as I get to her office."

"Myra already gave me her first and last month's rent money, so hey. When we come back from the doctor's, I need to clean out my room and my closet. I'm also going to rearrange my bed. That's something I've been planning to do for a while. I may have to store some of my stuff in your closet, if that's okay."

"Sure. You're really going above and beyond what you signed up for when we became friends."

"Girl, we're friends to the end, and don't you forget it."

When they walked through the building to Dr. Sherman's office, Lois was still pitching the benefits of a short-term third roommate. She only had one unspoken concern in the back of her mind. By now, Lois was used to her mood swings, heavy appetite, and restless nights. Would Lois's friend be so forgiving?

"She does know I'm pregnant, right?"

"Of course."

"How come I've never met her?" Talise didn't get an answer. Just then, her name was called and she was shown to a room. Lois trailed.

"So how's Mommy today?" Dr. Sherman greeted Talise, as she came into the room. She and Lois then exchanged greetings. As soon as the doctor placed the stethoscope on Talise's stomach, the baby moved. All three women laughed.

Dr. Sherman went down a checklist of what Talise should expect going into her twenty-second week. "You may experience some slight contractions. Don't be concerned unless they become regular or painful. Otherwise, they're harmless. Braxton-Hicks contractions occur when your uterus begins to practice for delivery."

"This early?" Talise asked.

Her doctor smiled and nodded.

"I'll be so glad when this is over, so I can move on," Talise said, staring up at the ceiling.

Dr. Sherman consoled her before asking more questions. "How's your stress level?"

"Stressful. I just knew my blood pressure would be sky high . . ."

That's when Lois jumped in and informed the doctor of the latest happenings. Listening to her chattering on and on, Talise thought, *If this new roommate is half as irritating as Lois is being at the moment, then I'm in some serious trouble.*

The rest of the examination was uneventful.

———⁓———

At work on Friday afternoon, Talise was relieved when Gabrielle arrived. Talise knew she'd be there because the coworker who was sick actually quit and Gabrielle was in the process of hiring someone.

Even with that stress, Gabrielle was all smiles. The woman truly had a calming effect. Talise wished Gabrielle could be her "temporary" new roommate. The idea had been making her anxious all morning, thinking about another person living with them.

"You are free to move about the cabin," Gabrielle said, as she waited for Talise to sign off her terminal.

Kendall was standing next to them with a slight scowl and an evil eye. She was waiting impatiently for her replacement. Since it was almost time for her shift to end, she asked to be excused for a quick potty break.

All day, her coworker had made comments about Talise's weight. At one point, Kendall stopped just short of coming right out and asking her if she was pregnant. It was obvious for even a blind man to see that her waistline had expanded. Talise was growing increasingly uncomfortable about it. Already under stress, this wasn't the day for her to get into a question and answer period with her coworker.

Watching Kendall walk away, Talise whispered to Gabrielle, "Do you have a few minutes to pray for me . . . silently? I don't want a pilot coming in for a landing to hear us." Her eyes pleaded along with her indirect request that Gabrielle not make a scene.

"I don't do things for show." Grabbing hands, Talise didn't bow her head or close her eyes. Instead, she anxiously scanned the terminal. Very soon, Gabrielle finished with a soft Amen.

Bewildered, Talise stared. "That's it?"

Smiling back at her, Gabrielle nodded. "God is already here. He was waiting for us to petition Him for what He was already going to do anyway. Now you go on and start your weekend."

Gabrielle reached into her purse and felt around for a pen. As a passenger walked up to the counter, she scribbled her number on a piece of paper. "Call me if you need to." Dismissing Talise, she greeted the customer with a dazzling smile.

Talise's bright spot on the way home was her baby moving around more. She found herself smiling when she wanted to frown at the unexpected. Lois was a good judge of character, except for Ace. Actually, Talise blamed that infraction on Cameron.

Getting off at her bus stop, she strolled the short walk to her apartment. When she turned the corner on Durham, a U-Haul truck was double-parked in front of her building. "She's here."

A few minutes later, Talise climbed the stairs to the third level where she could hear hearty laughs and music in the background. She groaned. The only thing she longed for was a quick bite, a shower, and her bed.

"Excuse me," a sweaty, short guy said, passing her on the stairs.

She almost gagged from his odor, as he beat her into the apartment. The door was ajar and Talise pushed it open. Boxes littered the living room. Talise eyed the large pieces of furniture she was going to have to navigate around to get to her bedroom.

A group of three women were chatting near the kitchen. "Hello, I'm Talise, Lois's roommate."

Immediately, all eyes traveled to her stomach. When it looked like her "temporary" guest wasn't going to identify herself, Talise asked, "And which one of you is Myra?"

"Oh. Hey girl, I'm Myra." A petite dark-skinned woman stepped forward and identified herself. Now it was Talise's turn to do the scrutinizing. Myra was definitely not dressed for moving—in her strappy sandal heels, shorts, and tank top. But then, judging from the two taller guys taking orders from the short, musty one, she didn't need to lift a finger.

After politely listening to Myra's mindless chatter for longer than she should have, Talise excused herself to her bedroom and closed the door. Changing out of her uniform, she washed up and slipped on a sundress instead of the pajamas she preferred. Opening her door, she walked hesitantly to the kitchen.

"Help yourself, there's plenty," Myra offered.

"Thank you." At least they brought food. *Maybe, this will work,* she thought. Opening the boxes, Talise would have helped herself if there was something healthy to eat. Thick pan pizza oozing with cheese and various pasta dishes were the only choices. She declined and warmed up some chicken stir fry leftovers.

On Saturday, the chaos remained when she got home from the salon. Lois was usually never home on the weekends. She wondered if Myra was a homebody. However, it did appear that she loved to entertain. To make matters worse, more of Myra's things had arrived.

By Sunday, Talise had to escape. Sitting in her car in the parking lot of Sandra's church Talise needed a good cry but contained herself to sniffles. Rubbing her stomach, she wondered how her mental state was affecting the baby.

She had long ago abandoned those five-minute prayers Sinclaire had suggested. The prayers and Bible reading helped some, but her utopia feelings didn't last very long. Unfortunately, she didn't know what to do to hold on to them.

To be truthful, Talise hadn't expected to return to Sandra's church so soon. However, she had nowhere else to turn to escape the chaos at home. A few minutes later, she turned off her car and repaired her makeup. At least this time she remembered to bring her Bible. Talise got out and started walking toward the church. It wasn't long before she spotted Sandra's minister friend. He stood outside the door, as if he was waiting for someone.

When he glanced her way and recognized her, he left his post and met her halfway. "You came back."

"Yes. I don't really know why, but I'm here."

"God knows before we know." Falling in step with her, Minister Thomas escorted her the rest of the way.

"How are you? Talise, right?"

"You remembered my name," she said, somewhat impressed. By the same token, she didn't know if she was unconcerned or embarrassed that she didn't remember his.

"How could I forget a person so unique and fascinating? How is the baby?" He grinned, which made him more handsome, even though he didn't have a dimple.

Talise almost tripped, but he reached out and steadied her. Forgetting that was the last thing she had told him when she was there a few weeks ago, she replied, "My baby's fine, Minister . . ."

"My name is simple, Richard Thomas. After church, do you mind having dinner with me?"

"Huh?" She stopped and stared. Talise wanted to say *Are you crazy? I'm pregnant,* but he already knew that. "Why?"

"Maybe because I find you lovely, mysterious, and so much more."

"What you should find me is pregnant, dumped, and friends with my child's grandmother. Not to mention I'm hormonal and hostile at times. If that isn't enough to run you the other way, then I don't know what is," she said as Sandra drove by, waved, and turned into the parking lot.

Sandra hurried through the parking lot to meet them. She and Minister Thomas went through their greeting ritual before he smiled at Talise and walked away.

"What was that all about?"

"He wants to take me out to dinner."

"Really?" The color seemed to drain from Sandra's face. She swallowed and held her breath. "What did you say?"

"I didn't."

Chapter Thirty-Seven

*S*andra couldn't believe her eyes. Her heart rejoiced when she drove into the parking lot and saw Talise at the entrance to the church. Although Sandra spoke to Talise during the week, Talise never mentioned she was coming back.

Praise God. Sandra didn't need to know everything God had in store for the young woman. She was just excited to see that Minister Thomas was welcoming Talise back.

Discovering that he asked Talise out, only after the second time he'd seen her, gave Sandra a sinking feeling. The young man of God was like a son to Sandra. But Ace was her son, who she might add, wasn't interested in Talise.

God, I signed up to be a witness for You, but not to witness this. Sandra wanted nothing but happiness for Talise, but Richard didn't know that she was pregnant. While inhaling and blinking several times, Talise seemed to wait for her to recover. Sandra added a swallow and then stuttered, "W . . . w . . . wow."

Talise chuckled. "That's what I said. I wasn't expecting it, especially after I told him I was pregnant."

Sandra's mouth dropped open. She couldn't believe Talise had told him but then realized that she was starting to show. It was only a matter of weeks before it would be obvious to everyone that she was pregnant. "Wow," was all she could say again.

Talise had to know what was going through her mind as Ace's mother, but Sandra dared not to voice it. As they continued on their way through the foyer and up to the second level, neither of them said another word. If only Sandra had telepathy with her son, she would shout, *Ace, get up here and fix this mess!*

This time, an usher met them at the entrance, and Sandra allowed her to find them two seats. As she knelt at her seat to pray, Sandra's heart was heavy.

"Lord, I have led her to You and this is Your plan, but is this Your will?" When Sandra realized she was scolding God for what she considered "getting a wrong end of the stick" deal, she repented.

"Lord, I only ask that You save my son," she whispered, as she stood and stretched out her hands.

The praise team seemed to know just the right song to sing when they began an old spiritual hymn, "What a Friend We Have in Jesus." The words brought comfort to replace the agony in her soul. She wanted to do the right thing for Talise, and for Ace. That meant she could only focus on doing God's will and then step aside.

Sandra didn't know how long the praise team repeated the words, but she found renewed strength by the time the music stopped and the hand claps ceased. Then she took her seat.

"I am not slow in keeping My promises, but everyone must come to repentance." Jesus spoke from 2 Peter 3:9.

"Hallelujah!" Sandra shouted when she heard the voice of the Lord. Talise covered her mouth and smiled.

As Pastor Lane took his time stepping up to the pulpit, the Spirit continued to stir throughout the sanctuary. More "Hallelujahs!" echoed, followed by a series of "Thank You, Jesus!" praises.

The wave of praises swept through the auditorium with such magnitude that the noise was like a hurricane. The pastor stepped back from the podium and instructed the musicians to cease, and then he led the congregation in thunderous hand praises to God.

Minutes later, while the praises quieted down, he made a second attempt to approach the podium. This time he opened his Bible. "Praise is the key. Praise is your strength. Praise will get you out of bad situations. It delivered Paul and Silas. Praise will get God's attention."

A few more "Hallelujahs!" vibrated through the church. Pastor Lane chuckled and said, "It's all right." He turned a few pages. "If you will open your Bibles, I will read one Scripture, Matthew 18:20: *'For where two or three come together in my name, there am I with them'*. In case you didn't know it, Jesus is here. He never misses a praise party."

Chapter Thirty-Eight

*T*alise could feel Him. God was there. While Sandra and others around her were on their feet and caught up in worshipping God, she sat quietly. Although her Bible was open, Talise couldn't read a word. She was too busy dabbing her eyes.

The next thing she knew, Sandra was sitting and had wrapped an arm around her shoulder. "What's wrong, sweetie?"

Shaking her head, the only thing Talise could barely say was, "I want to be saved. If praise has this much power, I want it."

As she continued to quietly sob, Talise heard Sandra mumble something like "hurry, altar call."

But it was a while before Pastor Lane asked the congregation to stand. "God is not slack concerning His promises. If you want to be saved today, it's simple—repent. Acknowledge you're a sinner and confess your sins. Make up your mind that you want to be permanently in the midst of His praise. Next, I ask you to walk down one of these aisles. Our ministers are waiting to pray for you."

"That's your cue, Talise. Do you want me to walk with you?"

"Yes, please."

With Sandra's arm around Talise's waist, they walked together to the altar. Sandra didn't leave her side.

"Have you repented?" the minister asked.

She nodded.

Female altar workers took over and led her and Sandra to the chapel, which was in another part of the church complex. Extra care was given when the women saw she was pregnant.

"Your baby's going to rejoice with you, sweetie," one worker commented.

"That's my grandbaby and you're right, Sister Georgia," Sandra chimed in with pride.

"I love you, Sandra," Talise heard herself say out of nowhere, but she meant it. The woman had truly been sent to her by God.

"I love you too," she responded with tears in her eyes. As God would have it, Minister Thomas came out of nowhere to pray for her. He smiled warmly and said, "You're on the right path, Talise. Your child will rejoice with you." That was the second time she heard that.

Sure enough, she felt her baby leaping and rejoicing inside her.

———ɷ———

Amazing, unbelievable, exciting, were just some of the words to describe her present state of mind as Talise reflected on the complete salvation experience.

Some time later in the prayer room, she couldn't stop crying, praising God, and talking to Jesus. Her emotions were still astronomically high. Sandra had held her hand and softly prayed with her. She encouraged her to commune with God and fellowship with Him in His presence. Whew! Her words ignited the praises in Talise once again, and she released them with a new round of glorious praises.

Finally, she had been able to collect herself. "I told myself that I had to cash in on God's promises. I've been so full of anxiety and stress over my life, but somehow, at the moment, it all seems like a blur. I now believe if I keep praising Him, my situation will change," she said confidently to Sandra, who nodded in agreement.

Neither of the ladies was in a hurry to leave the chapel. Minister Thomas strolled back into the room larger than life and smiled warmly.

"So ladies, dinner? To celebrate?" He glanced from Talise to Sandra.

Talise didn't answer right away. Her thoughts were preoccupied. She was curious why he asked her to dinner when she first arrived. Did he know what God was going to do? Sandra appeared thoughtful for a few moments. She told Talise she liked Richard, so surely she trusted him. When she sucked in a deep breath and exhaled, it seemed as if she had an answer.

"You two young people go on. I'm going to stop by a friend's house." Getting to her feet, Talise followed. Sandra gave her a tight hug and a kiss on the cheek. Turning to Minister Thomas, she repeated her affection.

"Sister Talise?"

Rubbing her stomach, she replied, "My baby is hungry." Wearing a big smile, she let that be her answer.

"All right then." He clapped his hands again. "What's your favorite?"

"Boston Market," she and Sandra answered at the same time. They exchanged glances and laughed.

Sandra handed Talise her Bible and purse and then picked up her own. Walking out of the prayer room together, Talise chatted all the way to the front door. Despite the extra weight she had gained, she felt lighter. It was as if the burdens were no longer significant; they had been truly lifted. She would always remember this day as her Nicodemus moment.

Ace could no longer push her buttons. Donna could no longer condemn her, and Lois's temporary roommate would not be able to irritate her. Her financial situation would be all right. She was free to praise God.

"Congratulations again, baby," Sandra said, as they stopped at Sandra's car. After strapping in her seatbelt, she waved goodbye to Talise and Minister Thomas and drove off.

He turned to her. "Shall I drive?"

Talise may have been delirious in the Lord, but she was still on guard where men were concerned. "Sure, drive your car and I'll drive mine."

He grinned. "Good answer. There's one about ten minutes from here at Tolman and Morrissey."

"I'll follow you."

He opened her car door and waited until she fastened her seatbelt. When Talise started her engine, Minister Thomas jogged across the parking lot to his vehicle. She couldn't help but wonder what drew him to her. But right now, she was too excited to ponder that.

Digging frantically in the bottom of her purse, she grabbed her cell phone and called Sinclaire. The overseas call was pricey, but this was worth the cost. Once Sinclaire's voice mail kicked in, Talise shouted. "I've got great news! Won't tell you until you call me back. Love you, Claire!"

Next, she sifted through the junk in her purse until she found the piece of paper with Gabrielle's number. She got her voice mail too. "I did it! I went to church and repented like a drunken sailor." She laughed. "You probably know what happened next." She laughed again and disconnected.

Where was everybody when she needed them? Punching in her roommate's number, Lois was next on her hit list. When a horn honked, Talise looked up. Minister Thomas had pulled beside her. He was behind the wheel of a sleek GMC vehicle.

"Okay," she said, adding a bob of her head.

"Hey, Lois. Listen, I've got to go. I'm going out to dinner with Minister Thomas."

"Who?"

"Details when I get back." She disconnected and motioned to Minister Thomas that she was ready and he took off slowly. Before pulling away, Talise took another minute to fumble with the radio until she found a gospel station.

"Jesus will work it out . . ." the choir sang and she joined in. The music seemed to startle her baby, causing him or her to move.

She giggled. Her books said the baby would be able to hear by week eighteen and, about a month ago, she discovered it to be true. Paying attention so she could keep up, Talise trailed Minister Thomas down Talbot Ave. They passed Codman Square and then turned onto Ashmont, just past O'Donnell Square. After a few more twists and turns, they arrived at Tolman and Morrissey.

He pointed to a parking space closer to the door for her and snagged a spot farther down in the same row. Talise parked, gathered up her purse, and stepped out. Minister Thomas' long strides met up with her before she left the side of her car.

"We could probably have been here five minutes sooner if you weren't on the phone." He wiggled his brow and his brown eyes sparkled.

"You said that I wouldn't be able to keep it to myself. And you were right," she said with a giddy smile.

"True." He tilted his head and guided her to the entrance. Being a gentleman, he opened the door for her to enter first. Without looking at the menu, she gave him her order and left to use the restroom. Minutes later, she returned and chose a seat.

It didn't take long before he came to the table with their trays. After filling their cups with water, he carefully placed their drinks down and sat across from her. Stretching his legs, Minister Thomas grinned. Giddy once again, this time over the opportunity to pray, Talise waited patiently while he made himself comfortable. She was ready.

Bowing his head and closing his eyes, Talise followed suit as he began, "Jesus, we praise Your name today for Your marvelous acts and unselfish love to redeem my dear sister. I ask that You bless her and her child, bless those who bless her."

He paused. "Now, Lord, we ask that You bless our food, sanctifying it from all impurities. And please provide for those who have not, in the Name of Jesus. Amen."

"Amen, Amen, and Hallelujah," Talise added.

Talise wasn't shy about digging into her sweet potato casserole. He laughed at her gusto, as he started on his meal. After taking a few sips of water, she patted her mouth with a napkin.

"Minister Thomas—"

"Please call me Richard. We're not at church . . . but that doesn't mean I'm not on call 24/7."

"Makes sense. Okay, Richard, what is it about me that made you ask me out to dinner when I arrived this morning? It was only the second time you saw me. Why didn't my pregnancy run you away like it did the father? Did God reveal to you what was going to happen today?" She fired off so many questions that Minister Thomas began to laugh.

"Whoa, Sister Talise, or may I call you Talise?"

Talise wanted him to call her Sister. She enjoyed the sound of that. It made her feel like she belonged in the Body of Christ. But he was right, the dinner was informal. Minister Thomas must have picked up on her hesitation.

"I'm sorry, I meant no disrespect."

"It's okay. I just like to hear you call me Sister Talise," she explained and hoped she hadn't offended him. "It reminds me that I've been changed."

"I understand completely. Then Sister Talise it is." He gulped down his water before answering her questions. "I was glad to see you this morning after you didn't return the Sunday after your first visit. I had thought about you, Sister Talise," he smiled and continued, "and prayed that God would make His presence known in whatever you were going through. And no, I didn't know what God was going to do for you today, but I'm so glad He did. Jesus is awesome!"

"Thank you for praying for me." Talise forked off a piece of her meatloaf. She chewed, waiting for him to answer her other question. "Okay now, about your dinner invitation."

"I asked you to dinner because you are a beautiful, absolutely gorgeous woman—I might add."

"Did you add that I'm pregnant with another man's baby . . . and you are friends with the man's mother?" she countered.

"No, but let me add that Sister Nicholson's son has chosen not to be involved in your life. If he has made no attempts to reconcile with you after these many months, then I'm not out of line to court you."

"I'm pregnant, Richard, with another man's child," she wanted to repeat herself in case he didn't hear her."

Minister Thomas laughed and broke off another piece of his chicken breast. "If you're trying to scare me off, then it didn't work. I'm a product of a stepfather who would take issue with me if he heard me refer to him in such a manner."

He glanced away, as if recalling a memory. "Richard Sr. was there when I was born and I was there at his bedside when he passed away. He never abused me or my mother a day of his life. In fact, Dad taught me to take responsibility in whatever I do. He showed me countless times in the Old Testament how the sons of kings chose their paths by following in their fathers' footsteps to do good or evil. I chose to do good like my dad."

Wow. Talise blinked. Stunned, she was speechless for a moment. There really are good men out there.

"I don't know what to say."

"Talise—I mean—Sister Talise . . ."

She grinned at his endearing blunder.

"I'm a good man. If you allow me to get to know you, then you can see for yourself. When is the baby due?"

"In eighteen weeks."

Nodding, he forked the remainder of his creamed spinach into his mouth. "Hmm, just enough time to see if our friendship could develop into something more permanent."

Sucking in her breath, Talise held it. Flattered, she wanted to cry for happiness that she was still desirable, but mourned that Ace wasn't the man sitting across from her.

Emotionally full, Talise didn't see the harm in giving him her phone number, so she did. She wondered what Sandra would think. Minister Thomas was *like* a son to her, but Ace *was* her son.

Chapter Thirty-Nine

*A*lthough Sandra trusted Minister Thomas, she was going to have to trust God on the young man's attraction to Talise. The minister did have a good reputation, was well-liked, and stayed away from controversy.

She hadn't heard of any reports that he had strung along a sister in the church and then broke her heart. Sandra doubted there was any man more than her own son who could break Talise's heart.

It was Sunday night and she hadn't heard from Talise. She was itching to find out "what happened" between her and Minister Thomas. Sandra had to remind herself that she sought Talise out for friendship before she was really sure if the woman was pregnant, or if it was Ace's child.

She smiled, recalling when Talise told her that she loved her. That came from her heart and so did Sandra's words of affection. If Sandra truly loved Talise, then she had to root for her happiness.

When she knelt to pray before climbing into bed, she made sure to praise the Lord Jesus for the souls that repented earlier, who were buried in His name, and who rejoiced under His anointing. Then she poured out her soul, "God, You said You are not slack concerning Your promises. I reached out to Talise when I heard Your voice's command. But I'm uncomfortable with being the matchmaker to the mother of my son's baby."

Sandra's heart was in distress as she cried out, "God, can't You do something to fix this? Please?" She didn't want her flesh to rise up in rebellion against Talise or Minister Thomas. Clearly, they were innocent in God's plan.

"I am concerned about man's soul; then his happiness will follow," God spoke.

Comforted, but not fully satisfied, Sandra said Amen and then got under the covers. She prayed that God would give her an excuse to call Talise.

The next day at work, she called Eva. Her daughter-in-law was in high praise about Talise's salvation. On the outside, Sandra was praising God too. On the inside, she was hurting, chiding herself for being the cause of drawing Talise even farther away from Ace.

Eva must have suspected something when she ceased her chatter. "What's wrong?"

"Nothing Jesus can't fix. You know how it is when God sends His blessings and the devil is on your heels to snatch your joy."

"Then maybe it's a good thing we plan to come to Boston next weekend for a shopping spree!" Eva said, surprising her.

The news lifted her spirits, yet Sandra sighed with one reservation. "All of us, except Ace, of course."

That's the one who should be coming, she scolded silently.

"The husbands are coming too. Kidd, Parke and his family, Malcolm and his, and maybe even Grandma BB. I'm calling it a school shopping trip."

"Count me in. I wish Aaron would turn his life around and come."

"So do I. But I don't see an end in sight with his refusal to make things right with Talise. I hate to say this, but I think she may need to move on because I don't think Ace will ever make her happy," Eva stated.

Hidden in her office, Sandra stood and walked over to close the door. Tears began to steam down her cheeks. The evidence Eva felt in her heart may already be in the works.

"Do you mind asking Talise if she can handle doing our hair?" Eva paused. "You know what, I'll call her because I want to congratulate her and ask—"

Sandra had an excuse to call now. "No. I'll call. I want to check up on her anyway."

Chapter Forty

*T*alise was in high spirits when she went to work on Monday. She didn't care about the stares, the gossips, or the fake concern from other employees. It was no longer her battle; she had given her life over to Jesus. Nothing could steal her joy of redemption—not even Kendall.

"Girl, I knew something was up with you," her coworker, Kendall, said when Talise broke the news. They were idle and waiting for customers.

"Yep." Talise's mind was somewhere else.

Although no longer hoping for Ace to come to his senses, Talise wasn't sure that anything serious would develop between her and the gorgeous, charismatic Minister Thomas. It was encouraging that a man found her attractive while she was pregnant—and with another man's child—no less.

Any other time, Kendall's remarks, opinions, and backstabbing comments would grate on her nerves. Not today. She and her baby were doing fine in Jesus. *Thank you very much, Lord,* she said in her heart.

"I will keep you in perfect peace with your mind stayed on Me,"

278

the Lord responded from Isaiah 26:3.

Talise was thrilled when the Scripture came to her mind. Hours later, Gabrielle strolled through the airport terminal with an extra pep in her step. She carried a small gift bag in one hand. When she made it to Talise's side, Gabrielle placed the gift on the counter.

"For you," she said with a wide grin. "You are free to move around the cabin."

Kendall peeped over Talise's shoulder. "You're getting baby shower gifts already?"

Gabrielle mouthed, *she knows?*

Talise nodded and shrugged.

Gabrielle spoke up. "Actually, this is a gift for Talise's new birth. I'm sure she talked to you about her experience with Christ. Now she's a new creature in Christ Jesus. Check it out in Romans 6:4; 2 Corinthians 5:17 . . ." She rattled off the passages to Kendall.

What a memory. That was going to be Talise's goal—to know her Scriptures like that. Last night, she couldn't read enough of her Bible before she dozed off. Then Sinclaire woke her, begging for the good news. From the Persian Gulf, her sister praised Jesus for what He had done all the way in America.

When Talise felt Gabrielle slightly bump her, she refocused on what her friend was saying. "That ought to keep Miss Thing busy."

Logging off, Talise gathered her purse and gift. "Thank you," she said through misty eyes. Besides Sandra's madness when she shopped for her, this was the second gift she had received since Ace had been gone. He used to lavish her with presents constantly, just because.

"It's a small token, a salvation gift, to encourage your walk with Jesus." They briefly hugged and then Talise left so she wouldn't miss her bus home.

Her apartment, she thought of the third roommate at home. Besides the clutter, her loud, shrieking voice, and untidiness in the kitchen, Myra wasn't that bad. She could be worse.

279

Talise sighed, getting on the bus and settling into a seat. About three stops later, Minister Thomas called her.

"Hello, Sister Talise, how was your day?" His voice was deep, but compared to Ace's, it didn't make the mark. Still, it was baritone enough to give a woman goose bumps.

"Good. I've been happy in Jesus all day. And a friend at work gave me a 'salvation gift.' She said it was something to encourage me."

"I can't let her outdo me," he said.

Talise rolled her eyes. She hoped he wasn't a man who did things to out-best someone else. She liked things that came from a person's heart, like Ace—she caught herself.

"Richard, please don't buy me any gifts. I need a friend and a listening ear, not a Sugar Daddy."

His roar of laughter made her blush. "I've never been called that before. A Sugar Daddy. Hmm," he repeated with a hearty chuckle. "I wouldn't disrespect you or God. Your friend was very thoughtful. I was only teasing you."

Talise felt bad for scolding him.

"One thing for sure, no matter how hard we try, we can't beat God giving us anything."

Closing her eyes, Talise smiled to herself. She liked him talking about Jesus. Rubbing her stomach, she hoped to wake her baby. It worked.

"I stand corrected."

"You stand to be appreciated," Minister Thomas assured her.

They chatted until she reached her bus stop. He told her to be safe. "Call me for anything, whether it's to explain a Scripture, because you're hungry, or simply for company. I'll make myself available."

"I will. Thank you."

She grinned at the thought that she could thank her ex's mother for introducing her to Minister Thomas. Talise wondered how Sandra felt about her going out with the minister. She did say more than once she wanted to be Talise's friend.

Well, even friends get tested, she thought. Then, just a few minutes later, she was put to the test. When Talise walked into her apartment, she discovered that Myra had left a sink full of dirty dishes instead of loading them into the dishwasher. She and Lois never let that happen.

Talise needed to talk with Lois about their "temporary" roommate. However, she knew she wasn't in a position to complain because Myra was paying a portion of their monthly rent.

Hungry, she changed quickly and then tackled the task of cleaning up behind Myra before she could cook something to eat. An hour and a half later, Talise had prepared enough salad for all of them, along with baked chicken breasts, roasted potatoes, and warm rolls.

When she finished devouring her meal with a tall glass of milk, Talise showered. Afterward, she slipped into her pajamas and grabbed her Bible, remembering one of the passages Gabrielle had fired off to Kendall.

After being physically satisfied, now she was hungry for the Word. Talise couldn't believe she had read five chapters before closing her Bible. Some of the passages she had read off and on before but had never got the understanding she had now. Truly amazed at the transformation that had taken place in her life, she whispered, "Thank You, Jesus."

Lois and Myra strolled through the door as Talise left her bedroom to get a fruit snack from the kitchen.

"Hey, church girl," Lois teased.

"It's Sister Talise to you." She teasingly scrunched up her nose and then nodded at Myra.

"I smell food." Myra dumped her purse and blazer on a nearby chair and rubbed her empty stomach.

Talise exchanged glances with Lois, who shook her head not to say anything. "I made enough dinner for all of us. I'm getting a snack."

"Cool. I'll have some of everything," Myra said.

Talise sliced her apples and washed grapes. She topped it off with a dab of cream cheese dip. When she headed back to her room, Lois trailed behind her.

Checking over her shoulder to make sure Myra was occupied with piling food on her plate, Lois whispered, "How was I supposed to know she was an undercover 'junkie'? At work, she's as neat as a manicured lawn. Five and a half months to go. Just count them down."

"I'm counting down seventeen weeks before my baby arrives, then I'll be back on my feet soon after that."

"Or married, if this Minister Ricky has his way. After you told me what he said . . ." Lois wiggled a brow.

"He does have a lot going for him, with good looks, the right attitude, and a good rep."

"That's what I'm talking about." They exchanged high fives.

Suddenly Myra walked up behind them with her hand up in the air. "Me too," she chimed in.

Talise high fived her too. When Lois steered Myra in the direction of the kitchen, Talise closed her door. Grabbing her phone, she settled on top of her comforter and called Sandra.

"Talise, I was going to call you. How's the first day of being a new saint in Christ going?"

"Amazing." She chuckled and then remembered Gabrielle's gift. Getting up to retrieve it, Talise reached into the bag and pulled out a small box. In it, she discovered a snow globe with a pair of praying hands inside. Smiling, she carefully removed it, shook it, and held it up to the light.

"So how was dinner?" Sandra asked.

"I didn't know if you were going to bring it up or tiptoe around it," Talise said honestly. "I've been wondering how you felt about Minister Thomas asking me out."

Sandra sighed and didn't respond right away. "The flesh was upset, but my spirit overrode it. Your life is in God's hands. He wants the best for you and He knows what that means. Whatever it is, I want that for you too. Just promise me one thing."

Talise held her breath. This could be the moment their friendship ended if she switched personalities on her. "What is it?"

"If Richard turns out to be the man whom God has for you—and I know he is a good man—please don't keep my grandchild from me."

Talise's eyes misted. This woman was truly an example of Christ. She was showing no bias or favoritism on behalf of her son. Like God, Sandra showed no respect of persons. Talise had read that in Romans 2:11. Her opinion of Sandra just moved up a notch.

At that moment, the conversation made Talise question her feelings toward Myra. The woman may not be as tidy as she and Lois, but Myra was helping Talise out. She would definitely have to try harder.

"My child will know the wonderful woman she or he has for a grandmother," she told Sandra with a sober tone.

Once the ice was broken, they talked about the previous day's preaching and the baby.

"Hey, guess who's coming to town next weekend?"

Lord, don't play. Ace is out of the picture, right? "Who?"

"Eva and the girls. You know Eva is a shopaholic after my own heart. She talked Kidd into needing a shopping spree. They also want you to do their hair, if you feel up to it."

"I'll check my client load." She had so much fun with the Jamieson wives. "Is Grandma BB coming too?" Talise still didn't know what to make of that complex woman.

"She might be. Eva didn't know if that's the weekend she's renting herself out as a grandma."

"What?" Talise laughed, startling her baby. She rubbed her stomach.

"Yeah, Eva says she has a franchise where clients contact her for babysitting services from women over sixty. Her marketing strategy is that seniors have more patience than younger women."

"Hmm. I could see that."

"She orders a background check, drug test, and credit history on every candidate. If they pass all of that, the women are also required to have gray hair, whether it's theirs or not. To complete the criteria, every woman has to own at least one pair of Stacy Adams shoes. Otherwise, they can't work for her," Sandra told Talise.

"That woman is a character."

"Yeah, and I want to have her energy and fun when I'm her age."

After getting off the subject of Grandma BB, they returned to the matter of the hair appointments. "Okay, I'll try and fit them in around my regular clients, but I won't be held responsible if I give somebody blonde hair."

They laughed. Since Sandra was now a regular, high-paying customer, Talise knew what hair products to use on her. For the others, she would rely on the products she already has on hand. It'd take time to really assess their hair. That would have to come later.

"It will be nice to see them again, especially since it sounds like I'm going to miss out on the shopping spree."

"Humph. You're probably glad about that! What if I come next Friday? That would be less people on Saturday."

"That may work." When Talise yawned, Sandra hurried her off the phone so Talise could get some rest.

—⁂—

The next day at work, Talise thanked Gabrielle for her gift when she came in early. "I really appreciate the praying hands. It's a lovely gift."

They hugged and Gabrielle told her, "Remember, if you keep your hands together, you'll have strength to make it through anything. Now you are free to move around the cabin."

"I'll remember that. By the way, if you have time, call me when you get a chance. I want to tell you something."

"Will do." Gabrielle said and waved goodbye.

Since Talise had driven to work, she decided to walk to the neighborhood park later that evening for her exercise. She was sitting on the bench when Gabrielle called. Talise filled her in on the dinner with the minister. She told her about his daily phone calls with a Scripture for her to meditate on, accompanied by his commentary.

"I'm honored that you've allowed me to be in your circle of friends. Now allow me to give you my opinion, not advice."

Talise listened.

"You loved Ace, and you haven't had closure. You still need that. You told me that he called you once—"

"And it wasn't a good conversation. Every word became colder."

"Oh, we need to pray for him, Talise."

"I know. I'm asking God to help me with that, but when I think of Ace, it's synonymous with hurt, betrayal, and desertion."

She told Gabrielle how Sandra had treated her warmly when she knew Talise had dinner with another man.

As she listened to Talise's testimony, Gabrielle whispered, "Thank You, Jesus."

When she finished talking, Gabrielle brought the subject of Ace back into the discussion. "This minister sounds like a wonderful man who is willing to step in where Ace stepped out. In a perfect world, you and Ace would patch things up and move forward with a happy ending. Unfortunately, that doesn't seem like it's going to happen."

"You sound as if you are about to cry over a man you've never met."

"I'm a romantic. I believe God can make fairy tales come true. I was hoping Ace would come to his senses."

Talise stood and began to walk back to her apartment as the sun was setting. Before they disconnected, Gabrielle had one last thing to say. "It's easier to replace people when they're out of sight, out of mind, and seemingly out of a person's heart."

In the back of her mind, Talise had an uneasy feeling about her friend's words.

Chapter Forty-One

The Jamieson family game night a few weeks ago had done Ace in. It had nothing to do with the oddest questions known to man that were asked, but the embedded feeling of connection among everyone else besides him and Kidd. The pride in the elder Parke's eyes and voice when one of his family members gave the right answers was priceless.

As much as he loved his mother and Kidd, there was never that type of bonding with any of his cousins on his mother's side. Amazingly, Kidd fit right in with the Jamieson crowd, as if he belonged all along.

What would it take for me to fit in? Ace wondered.

When Eva had slipped—or maybe it was on purpose—and mentioned Talise's name, he left as promised. Not because he wasn't having a good time, surprisingly. It was merely about saving face. He had to prove that once he made up his mind about something or someone, he didn't change it.

Then two days later, it was a shocker to all, including Ace, when he accepted Kidd's invitation to church. It was the first time since he had been in St. Louis that he said yes.

What was it that prompted him now? Maybe it was the feeling of living in isolation that he had been experiencing. Although it would be hard for Ace to admit out loud, his new apartment felt lonely, like something, or somebody, was missing. Perhaps that was increasing his desire to spend more time with his family.

Sunday morning, he met Eva and Kidd at Salvation Temple. Ace chuckled as he parked his car and strolled his way to the front entrance. He was sure Kidd would be waiting for him there.

What exactly did the church name imply? Was it an emergency room where people could go when they were sick and leave bandaged up? Ace had no expectations. Walking inside the vestibule, he nodded to a few who greeted him with "Praise the Lord."

Kidd stepped up to him and shook his hand before giving him a bear hug. He introduced Ace to a few people, bypassing the ladies, and then headed to their seats to join Eva.

Until now, his sister-in-law hadn't given Ace a smile so bright since he first moved to St. Louis. Back then, she wasn't even aware of his motive for relocating. Since she found out, her smiles had been at a premium.

Making himself comfortable, Ace sat through the praise team, the choir, and the announcements. The church wasn't much different than his mother's in Boston. He knew how to go through the motions without letting a sermon change his mind about doing what he planned to do before he walked in.

It wasn't long before Salvation Temple's pastor, Elder Taylor, took front and center. Without much of a preliminary, he opened his Bible and began reading from Acts, chapter nine.

Focusing on verse five from the King James Version, he read, *"And he said, Who art thou, Lord? And the Lord said, I am Jesus whom thou persecutest: it is hard for thee to kick against the pricks."*

Pausing for a slight moment, Elder Taylor began, "My subject today is 'thinking you've got it all right, and in the end, finding out you had it all wrong.'"

"Amen," "Well," and "Preach, Pastor" comments circulated around the auditorium.

"Paul was an honorable man when he was on the road to Damascus. He was a Jew with knowledge and zeal. He didn't take anything off of nobody. Yet God wasn't pleased with what he was doing because it wasn't God's way. Here is the question you need to ask yourself: Are you living your life the way God wants for you?"

Pausing again, he went further, "You see, God doesn't have to persecute you, your ignorance will cause you to persecute yourself . . ."

For the next hour, Ace listened to the message. Finally, although the altar call was stirring, Ace didn't feel a need to make a change in his life. Once the benediction was given, he turned to say goodbye to Kidd and Eva.

"Did you enjoy the service?" Eva asked him.

"I did. When I get a chance, I might visit again." Ace meant it and headed to his car. One thing that stuck with him was their pastor's opening statement, "thinking you've got it all right, and in the end, finding out you had it all wrong." But he really didn't want to consider the consequences of him making bad decisions.

On Monday, Ace was in his office downtown. Things didn't get better for him. He couldn't concentrate because his mind was elsewhere. Instead of Sunday's sermon inspiring him, it bugged him and made him grouchy.

When it came to Talise, who he once felt made him complete, he had miscalculated her intentions. She could definitely be chalked up as a misstep in his life. That thought made him both sad and mad at the same time.

Highly agitated, he snapped at his assistant for opening his office door without knocking. She never knocked before, and it had never been a big deal. Later on that day, Ace gave a store clerk a hard time when she overcharged him fifty cents for a case of beer.

When Kidd called one evening, Ace roared at his brother. Kidd growled back. "Is there anything you want me to get for you while we're there?"

Ace snarled over the phone. "Thanks for rubbing it in that you're taking Eva on a Boston shopping spree."

"I can't help it." Kidd snickered. "Who would have thought when Ma was teaching you how to walk you would become a love stalker on a 'no-fly list'? How many more weeks do you have before you can buy a plane ticket?"

"So you've got jokes, huh?" Clicking off his new high-def TV that he wasn't watching anyway, Ace padded across the carpet of his sparingly furnished living room and went into the kitchen to put his frozen dinner in the oven.

His apartment building was fairly new. Ace could still smell the freshly painted walls and the carpet was brand-new. Eva had offered to decorate, but Kidd declined for him.

"Get your own wife," Kidd had said without a smile or blink.

Ace didn't blame him. He was thankful Kidd let Eva still cook for him. Walking over to the sliding door, he glanced out. A plane coming in for a landing caught his attention and mocked him.

How ironic is that? He couldn't board a plane for a couple more months. Yet the huge flying pieces of metal taunted him several times a day. Their engines seemed to roar louder than usual whenever another one flew over his head. Ace couldn't wait until he was free to clear the security checkpoint again. Planning to be on his best behavior, if he saw anybody he thought he knew, he wouldn't even offer them a handshake.

"I'm sure while you guys are in Boston, Eva will see Tay. Will you tell me how she looks?"

"You mean, if she looks pregnant?" Kidd huffed. "Well, I'm going to tell you right now, if I can't tell at a glance from yards away, I'm not about to be staring. Not when I have a beautiful wife to gaze at day and night. You're on your own."

The joke was on Ace. What he meant was did she look okay health-wise? Or did she seem happy or not? Or was she as miserable as he was because she wasn't in his life? At this point, he was over her, concerning the pregnancy. Ace wasn't about to explain himself.

Kidd softened his tone. "I can't help you on this. I've been your problem-solver all your life. I don't know the details with Talise, but be a man. Don't handle it like the old Ace Jamieson I know would. Pray and God will show you the best way to deal with it."

Ace grunted. "Like mumbling a few words will really change things."

"It doesn't take an hour to talk to Jesus. When your heart is heavy with concerns, God hears you. How do you think He drew me to Him when my mouth said one thing, but God zoomed in on my heart?"

Ace didn't know if he would ever get used to the way his brother talked about the Lord. When Kidd repented years ago, Ace thought he'd lost his mind. Now, adding to his vexation, Kidd always made sense to him.

Closing his eyes, Ace leaned his head back against the wall. "The last time we spoke, it didn't end well. I hurt her when I walked away, but she crushed me with her scheming. We can't get pass that. But I do care about her, so just let me know if she looks well, please." He returned to his spot on the sofa.

Kidd's voice took on a serious tone. "Are you okay? This is the longest conversation we've had in months about Talise. What gives?"

"You all are killing me softly with your double-talk. You don't talk about Talise in my face. But let me turn to the side or turn my back and those Jamieson wives are in cahoots with her."

"Are you accusing my wife of something? If you are, it might be worth getting a speeding ticket to get to you."

"Bring it on, Kidd. Why not let me take out my frustration on your face." They both knew how to street fight. "All I'm saying is Eva and the others are guilty by association."

"The only guilty party on this phone call is you. Handle your business, man. Go talk to her."

"I can't fly, remember?"

"I guess you'd better tie up your hiking boots, Ace, or buy a gas card. Pick your poison."

Drive? Kidd was nuts. No woman was worth a train, a bus, or a twenty-hour car ride.

Chapter Forty-Two

On Saturday morning, Talise wasn't prepared to see three complete Jamieson packages stroll into Sasha's Sassy Salon. Talk about showstoppers, hand blow-dryers seemed to quit on their own accord and all conversations ceased.

She was almost guilty of burning Priscilla's locks with the curling iron. The group was picture perfect. No wonder the Jamieson women were a happy bunch.

"Who are they?" Priscilla asked, angling her neck to get a better view.

"The Jamiesons."

"All of them?" Priscilla followed up.

"I think so."

Since they were paired off, Talise could only assume that the former NBA player turned actor, Rick Fox look-alike, was Cheney's husband, Parke. Kami stood between them, holding on to a toddler's hand. She waved and Talise smiled.

A younger version of Parke stood near his father. He didn't look happy to be in a place where all the clientele were women.

Talise remembered Hallison's husband's name was Malcolm. The brother was built like a linebacker. She supposed he was fine, considering he looked menacing behind a pair of dark glasses. Malcolm's stance and folded arms mimicked a private security agent. His no-nonsense persona was only ruined by a toddler running circles around his legs at will.

Finally, there was Eva. She glowed in her stunning maternity outfit. From across the salon, her makeup looked perfect and her hair didn't need to be touched. The dark hunk standing next to her had to be Ace's older brother, Kidd. The resemblance was uncanny. Kidd was good-looking like the rest, but Ace still was the pretty boy of the bunch.

All of a sudden, a cane wiggled its way between Kidd and Malcolm. Creating an opening, Grandma BB bumped her way to the front and stood in all her fashionista glory. There were only so many seats, so the men stood as the women sat. They were a patient bunch.

"Who is that feisty one?" Priscilla pointed.

"That's their Grandma BB. She's not related, but don't tell her that."

Priscilla was quiet for a few moments, studying the older lady. "Is that woman wearing men's shoes?"

Talise chuckled. "Yep, always top of the line of Stacy Adams. That's what Eva tells me. I guess she didn't have to rent herself out this weekend."

"I'm not going to even ask you to elaborate." Priscilla sniffed. "Oooh! I smell something," she said with alarm.

"Oh, that's the hot curler that I took out a few minutes ago. It's frying my towel, but not your hair."

Finished, Talise was about to spray Priscilla's hair when she stopped her.

"That's not good for the baby," Priscilla whispered.

"Everyone knows now." Talise pointed to her protruding stomach. "It's okay."

"Good, but that spray is still not good for the baby."

Talise removed the cape from around Priscilla's neck. As usual, she overpaid for her services. Learning to accept her blessing, Talise always whispered a grateful thank you.

As she escorted Priscilla to the lobby, Talise brushed off any excess hair strands on her clothes. Her two-piece silver sleeveless top and Capri bottoms were comfortable and, according to "temporary" roommate Myra and her customers, classy. She always hoped to look presentable, especially if she would ever be compared to Ace's other women.

However, that didn't matter anymore. Rather, the bouquet from Minister Thomas on display reminded Talise that she had moved on. Smiling when she thought about him, she knew he really cared about her and the baby. They had already been on three dates.

Kami broke from the group and hurried to her. The young girl engulfed her arms around Talise and spoke to her stomach. "Hi, baby cousin."

Closing her eyes, Talise relished in the warmth of the child's attention. Her baby moved, so apparently he or she did too. Next, Eva followed, and then Cheney and Hallison. The two small boys also clamored for their turn. But the tall, younger version of Parke did not move from his father's side.

Tapping her cane, Grandma BB made them all step aside. "How ya doin', T? I'm going to tell you right now, you ain't touching my hair. I'm getting a pedicure only and I want different colors on every toe."

The Jamieson wives rolled their eyes and some customers chuckled. "I'm sure the manicurist will take care of you." Talise pointed to the nail section of the salon. That was one head she didn't have to wash.

Kami's hair was already washed and freshly braided. So she followed Grandma BB to the nail section. Talise was relieved that she had two less heads to shampoo, leaving the three wives. She hoped Grandma BB wasn't serious about having ten different colors on ten toes.

Swallowing, she waited for an introduction of the Jamieson men.

Knowing she had to be under inspection, she wondered what Hallison's husband was thinking behind those dark glasses. What was going through Kidd's mind? Did they think Ace had made the right choice in dumping her?

They all smiled as Talise shook their hands. Kidd surprised her when he gave her a gentle squeeze. "Thank you," he whispered.

When he released her, Talise returned a questioning look. "Huh?"

"You didn't have to keep that baby and become a single mother, but we are all glad you did," Kidd explained.

"Thank you." Talise's eyes misted. The Jamiesons were a different breed, except for Ace, who would always be a mutt in her book. They were remarkable human beings.

Sniffing, she added. "The past months have been hard, but now—"

"God saved you from your sins, so your slate is clean to start over, sister. Eva told me and all of us," Kidd comforted her with his kind words. "Just so you know, God isn't letting my brother down easy. Keep praying for him."

Talise nodded. It took Sinclaire's emails, Gabrielle's reminders at work, and the Holy Ghost to make sure she did just that.

The moment was surreal. Although they treated her courteously, she couldn't shake the feeling of being an outcast. Even with flowers waiting for her at her station, the realization was she had loved and wanted Ace, but Ace didn't love or want her.

While the men filed out to catch up with Cameron, Eva and Hallison relaxed and mingled with other clients who were waiting for their stylists. Back at her station, Talise started with Cheney, assessing her hair texture and prior hair treatments. Since Cheney needed a press-n-curl, she shampooed and conditioned her first.

Talise was thankful that Hallison had a relaxer applied recently. Because of the fumes, she had handed her chemically treated clients over to Sasha. Not only did the smells make her nauseated, but she developed a headache.

After a shampoo, she rolled and set Hallison's mane. Eva was the last of the trio to get serviced. She had kept her relaxed ends trimmed while letting her natural hair grow out.

"Make me beautiful," Eva joked.

"That's easy. All you have to do is look in the mirror."

Talise loved Eva's hair texture. It was soft, but thick and naturally brown, with strands of light and dark brown variations. Eva chatted about their early morning shopping spree with Sandra and what she bought. Then she switched topics to Talise's salvation, which thrilled Talise.

When it came to styling, Cheney's hair took the longest, but each one patiently waited their turn. As the salon thinned with clients, Eva switched subjects again. "Our husbands like you." Cheney and Hallison nodded.

"I'm glad. I'm so thankful that Sandra reached out to me from the beginning. She has really made a difference in my life, including letting me meet my baby's relatives."

"We love you, and not just as a sister-in-law—"

"Which I'll never be," she interrupted Eva. "And I've accepted that. I'm still making peace as I move on."

"Are those gorgeous flowers from 'Mr. Moved On'?" Cheney pointed.

Smiling, Talise nodded. "He knew I was pregnant when he asked me out." She didn't see any harm in telling them about Minister Thomas. After all, she and Ace were over before she met them.

"Are you happy?" Hallison asked.

Frowning, Talise tilted her head, as she combed out Hallison's wrap. "I'm content and in a safe place. I feel accepted by Minister Thomas instead of rejected by Ace."

"He's a minister?" Eva blinked.

"Yes, too bad you all are flying out early tomorrow and you won't be able to meet him. It's probably for the best anyway. I wouldn't want any of you to feel uncomfortable."

"We're changing our flights," the Jamieson wives said almost in one voice.

"Huh? Just like that?" Talise snapped her fingers.

Four hours later, Talise was the only stylist left in the salon with clients. Cheney and Hallison took care of the sweeping and straightening Talise's work station under the supervision of Grandma BB pointing her cane.

Sure enough, Grandma BB's toes each had different shades of silver until the last color was nearly black. Kami also had the multi-color thing going on, but in shades of pink. Actually, it was cute on her but looked ridiculous on the grandmother.

When everything was put in place, Talise and her guests relaxed in the lounge area, waiting for their husbands to return. The genuine camaraderie brought back memories of their St. Louis tea party.

Talise's night ended when the Jamieson men came back with Cameron. They invited her to dinner, but she was exhausted and declined. However, with five-hundred dollars in her pocket from the Jamieson wives alone, Talise was happy. She could definitely splurge on take out. Most of the money would go into her savings, after she paid her tithes and offering at church the next day.

Back at her apartment, Talise almost wished she had gone out to eat with them. Myra had struck again. The kitchen was a mess—a hot mess. Disgusted, Talise went to bed. As far as she was concerned, the maid was off duty tonight.

The next morning, she woke up tired and struggled to get out of bed. Determined, she slid on her knees for a morning prayer before church. The baby seemed to move all night long, pressing on her bladder, or some other body part.

That made it hard for her to ignore an important point. She definitely wasn't up to driving across town to church, even if Eva and the crew were attending. Talise dialed Minister Thomas to tell him and then she would call Sandra and let her know she wasn't going to make it.

"Good morning, Sister Babe," he would sometimes tease her. And she liked it.

"Mornin'."

"What's the matter?" The alarm in his voice was evident.

"I had a rough night, and I'm dragging this morning. By the time I get ready and drive across town, Pastor may be in the middle of his sermon."

"I'm already dressed. Why don't you take the extra time you need to get ready and I'll pick you up."

Talise's heart warmed at his offer. "But don't you have to be at church early?"

"I think the Lord and anybody else would understand that I have a little lady to take care of. I want to see you and find out how the baby is doing. Plus, I have to feed you . . ."

Laughing, Talise agreed. "I promise to be ready when you get here."

"Will an hour be enough?"

"Richard, I have a little one who did not work with me last night. I can't see him or her cooperating this morning either. I need at least an hour and a half."

"You've got it." When they disconnected, Talise smiled. That man could be easy to love.

Although Talise moved slowly, she was able to dress, eat breakfast, and relax before Minister Thomas arrived.

"I'm here. I can come up or wait for you down here," he announced over his cell phone, almost exactly an hour and a half later.

"I'll be right down." Talise disconnected and walked out of her bedroom into a makeshift storage locker housing Myra's extra large pieces of furniture. Seating in the living room was at a premium. The only exception was the window seat in the front bay where she used to sit and watch for Ace. It dawned on her that it hadn't crossed her mind to do the same for her new friend.

He was leaning against his Enclave SUV when Talise walked out of the apartment building. Minister Thomas hurried to take her hand as she walked down the steps. Suddenly, the gesture reminded her of Ace. She used all of her might to force the memory to the back of her mind. Ace wasn't the only gentleman in the world.

"You look gorgeous," he complimented her. "You mentioned that you modeled as a girl. You should definitely get back into it. You would make a beautiful expecting mother model."

"Thank you." She was touched by him remembering that.

Once she was buckled up, he took off. As they drove along, she asked about some Scriptures, and he explained them to the best of his understanding. After that, they sung choruses of worship songs.

"So how did it go yesterday with Sister Nicholson's daughter-in-law and the ladies?"

"I had a ball. I also met Ace's brother and male cousins."

Minister Thomas glanced at her and then back at the road. "They didn't upset you, did they?"

"Oh, no. They were very nice, which saddened me to know that I picked the bad apple in the bunch. You'll meet them. Eva said they were changing their flight to attend services."

He whistled. "That has to be expensive."

"It can be. If I was working, I would have tried to override much of the fees."

Minister Thomas nodded and tapped the steering wheel. "Do they know about me?"

"Yes, and they know you make me happy." She smiled at him.

"Then I'm sure they'll get their money's worth to see the man who is making you happy."

You can make me happy, but can you make me love you? Talise hoped he could.

299

*A*ce opened his door Monday evening to three fiercely intimidating characters. Kidd, Parke, and Malcolm strolled into his apartment without as much as a greeting.

"What is going on?"

Kidd said he was on his way over, but he didn't say anything about bringing the other two stooges.

They stood in the middle of the floor, as if waiting for an invitation to make themselves comfortable. Ace's sole piece of furniture in the living room—the sofa—would barely accommodate them. Closing the door, he tilted his head. And one by one they flopped down.

With his poker face secure, Ace leaned on the wall. He very seldom received company, so he wasn't in a hurry. He could wait all evening to find out what they were up to. They had families, he didn't. Why did their presence remind him of that fact?

After that game night, he was seriously wishing he did have what they had. Ace wasn't accustomed to living alone. He didn't even have loud, annoying neighbors.

"Your brain must be the size of a pinhead," Kidd started off.

"Your insult must be leading somewhere," Ace said, staring his brother down.

"The sister is fine—and pregnant—if your inquiring mind wanted to know. You should've handled your business better, bro."

"You came over here with backup to tell me something that you could've *handled* with a phone call." Ace folded his arms and tilted his head toward his cousins. "And you brought the Jamieson stooges with you."

Malcolm smirked but didn't say a word. His faux calmness would have scared the average thug on the street. At the moment, only one person instilled fear in him. Ace wouldn't admit it to anyone—not even his brother—that a woman had brought him down.

"Cuz, we all flew to Boston and met Talise. She's very beautiful. Unfortunately—" Parke began.

"Hold up, bro. Let me take it from here." Malcolm widened his smirk and grunted. "Congratulations. It appears that you have succeeded in pushing Talise out of your life completely. She's dating a minister. We met him and he seems very attentive to her." Malcolm paused. "You did it. Game over."

Ace's heart dropped. "So she *was* stepping out on me—and with a minister. Why does every woman I've dated who decides she wants to have my baby, get it from another man . . ." The more Ace rambled, the madder he got.

"Ace!" Kidd lifted his voice. "Wake up! That is not Minister Thomas's child."

"Really?" Fired up, Ace took a deep breath and rested his fists at his waist. "And how do you know that, O wise one?"

"Because Momma introduced them."

"What!" Ace shouted. "My own mother betrayed me?"

The trio's laughter was deafening and taunting. They gave each other high-fives and busted out laughing again.

"I'm glad you think this is funny, but it isn't. My own mother went behind my back and got into my business."

Parke cleared his throat. "Well, that's not exactly true. Here's the footnote to the story. We all went behind your back."

"Okay. I'll bite," Ace said cautiously. With his nostrils flaring, Ace began to pace his living room floor, listening intently. There was nothing else they could say to shock him more.

Kidd picked up from there. "While the ladies primped at the salon where Talise works, Cameron and I took Parke and Malcolm sightseeing. We made a stop at One United Bank in Boston."

"My TV dinner is getting cold while you're giving a play-by-play."

"Our wives cooked, so we're stuffed, but thanks for offering." Parke added and grinned.

Ace was so ready to take his chances and take them all down at one time then force them out of his apartment. "So what that you stopped by the largest Black-owned bank in the country?"

"Well, it appears Cameron already started a savings account for your little tyke. We added to it and gave a cashier's check to Talise after church. She didn't want to accept it, especially in front of Minister Thomas—who by the way—is a real nice guy. I've seen him a few times when Eva and I went back home and attended church with Ma."

Annoyed and hungry, Ace snapped. "Would you just get to the point? Exactly how much money did you give her?"

"Five thousand dollars. It was just a small token to show our love and appreciation for Talise. She decided to give birth to a Jamieson child instead of taking the *cowardly* way out and having an abortion."

Ace noted Kidd's sarcasm.

His brother continued, "Anyway, it turns out that your ex didn't want to accept the gift because she decided that her child was not going to carry the Jamieson name. But we were able to convince her. You might say that the Jamieson charm won out," Kidd said with a confident grin.

That was nothing new. She had even told Ace as much in one of their two abbreviated, heated conversations. "So what?" He folded his arms.

"When she said that, those were like fighting words. Since I wouldn't strike a woman, I came along with your brother to give you a beat down." Parke interjected with his nostrils flaring.

"We're Jamiesons. We take claim our own and take care of our own. Slaves were stripped of their freedom, dignity, and birth name. Some fought for their freedom until their last breath. The Jamieson name has been passed through thirteen generations. Only you want to break that cycle and—"

"Parke," Malcolm called to his brother. "Calm down. Cheney will know if you're upset when you get home."

Ace didn't want to feel anything, but Parke's raw emotion was starting to eat away at him. He already knew how his brother felt about responsibility. But Parke and Malcolm were so far removed as cousins; why they cared was beyond his reasoning.

When Ace was a child, Kidd had taught him to never let another man see him sweat. "That's old news. Her child will carry her last name."

"Let me deliver the punch line." Malcolm cleared his voice. "That was before Minister Thomas. And if it's a boy, he might be called Richard Jr."

Ace had heard enough conspiracy for one night. "Close the door behind you," he said, dismissing them and heading to the kitchen to re-warm his dinner.

A man needed energy to mastermind a plan to block a trespasser on his property—Talise.

Chapter Forty-Four

*Y*ou should have seen them, Gabrielle. They were the most beautiful Black men I have ever seen," Talise chatted while they ate lunch. After working so many days straight, Gabrielle was finally given a few days off. She made a special trip on her off day to come to the airport and meet with her friend.

Talise had to fan herself. "They were like celebrities on a runway—tall, muscular, sexy, and all of them reminded me of Ace. It was agonizing to see that I didn't make the cut. I was envious of what the Jamieson wives snagged but I couldn't. I didn't."

"Did you say Jamieson?" Gabrielle frowned. "That's your ex's name?"

"Yeah, why?"

"Oh, nothing. I went to college with a Jamieson. She's a Rayford now. We were so close. Her name was Giselle and people would call us Gigi." Gabrielle shrugged. "I don't know that many Jamiesons. That's all."

"Oh. Don't get me wrong, I like the wives and would really enjoy spending more time with them. But when I saw their better halves, my mental stability faulted." Talise glanced away and met the eyes of a handsome bystander.

Ignoring him, she turned back to Gabrielle. "Anyway, you can't always have what you see in the window. My wound is deep with Ace. But the Bible says time heals all wounds."

Gabrielle shook her head. "You won't find that in the Bible, but it's a great saying. Try Psalm 147:3: *'He heals the brokenhearted and binds up their wounds.'*"

"How can you quote Scriptures like that?"

Gabrielle laughed softly. "I can give you a Scripture to answer that. The Bible says, 'study to show yourself approved of God.' You'll find it in 2 Timothy 2:15. People don't want to hear Christians talk about Scriptures, but that verse says we should not be ashamed to correctly analyze and breakdown the Word of God. Honestly, the Bible was written for hurting people. Jesus came to save us."

She grinned and leaned closer. "Keep reading your Bible, Sister Talise, and the Scriptures will begin to stick." Gabrielle patted her hand. "Back to the Jamiesons, have you ever thought about breaking ties with them?"

Shaking her head, Talise dipped her French fry into a pile of ketchup. She sighed. "It's too late. They have been more than kind to me and generous with the baby. I'll probably always miss not being a part of their family, but my child won't miss out. They're even planning to set up a trust fund once they baby is born. They, meaning minus Ace, of course."

"God sends some people in our lives for a season. Maybe Ace's season is over and it's time for Minister Thomas."

It hurt to hear Gabrielle say those words, even if Talise's heart knew it was true. "Maybe," she sadly repeated the word.

A few days later, an exhausted Talise opened her apartment door. Several of Myra's guests, who had basically commandeered the living room and kitchen, greeted her. Talise mustered a smile. She was able to say hello after taking a deep breath.

What was that song the choir sang at church? She tried to recall the words. "The Lord will make a way somehow . . ." As the medley began to revolve in her mind, she took another deep breath. Again, she had no right to complain. Myra was somehow making her life easier, as Lois tells it.

She headed for her bedroom and removed her clothes. After Talise showered, she decided to take a quick nap to escape the company. Because the baby wouldn't allow her to hold out forever, later on, she would have to get up and cook something to eat.

Soon enough, she was tossing and turning as voices, music, and a variety of noises outside her door intensified. Talise closed her eyes and tried to recall Scriptures like Gabrielle.

Patience, what was it about patience? *Knowing that the trying of your faith works patience.*

Talise didn't know where to find the verse or if she quoted it verbatim, but at the present time it worked. She got the gist of it—patience comes through having faith. She would have to hold on to that.

When her cell phone rang, she reached for it and answered before it went to voice mail.

"Hello?"

"Did I catch you at a bad time?" Sandra asked.

"You have no idea." Just then, a piercing laugh on the other side of the door must have startled the baby. The kick was a bit forceful. Evidently, her baby was irritable too.

"What's wrong?"

"Put it this way. There's a new renter who is paying part of my rent until basically after the baby is born. My nerves are shot and I don't think the baby likes it either."

Sandra was quiet and then said, "Why don't you come and relax at my place? I have a three-bedroom, empty condo. Pack a few things."

The idea did sound appealing. "I can't. I'm too tired. I don't think I could drive a block. I need a nap."

"Well, it doesn't sound like you're going to get it there. I'll come and get you and bring you back in time for work at the salon."

Good sense wouldn't allow Talise to argue. They disconnected and she gathered a few changes of clothing and some bare necessities. She was finally going to Ace's house, but not by his invitation.

Chapter Forty-Five

*B*etrayal. That's what Ace's family had done to him—his mother, his brother, and his cousins. How could he have been so clueless to what every sneaky Jamieson was doing behind his back? Ace assumed that if he didn't mention Talise's name, they would drop it and forget about her too.

"What a mess," Ace complained, stepping out on his patio as the sun was setting. The night was peaceful and quiet. There were no sounds of planes, trains, or automobiles. He chuckled at the words from the title of an old movie starring the late John Candy.

However, at the present time, his life was anything but a comedy. Women had come and gone in his life until their memories completely faded, but not Talise Rogers.

Talise. If Ace was a sculptor, he couldn't create anything more beautiful. But that regrettable Friday night in May, she had ripped his heart out. Did she or didn't she try and trap him? It was the nagging assumption that had driven him away. Now what? According to his brother and cousins, Talise was indeed pregnant. "With my child," Ace whispered for the first time.

"With my child?" he repeated, not believing himself.

At twenty-eight years old, Ace was scared for the first time in his life. The guns, knives, or jail time hadn't terrified him. Being a father frightened him beyond measure.

His carefree lifestyle was based on his "responsibility is optional" mantra. Now could he handle the responsibility of being a father? Beyond child support, Ace didn't trust himself to be the right kind of role model.

Getting up from the lounge chair, he returned to the house for his cell phone. Lying down on the sofa, he punched in Kidd's number. Ace hoped Eva wasn't close by. He needed to have a heart-to-heart talk with his brother.

"Yeah?" Kidd answered, as if Ace was disturbing him.

"We need to talk."

"Talk."

Ace huffed. "In person, in private . . . and bring your Bible."

"I'm on my way."

While Ace waited for Kidd to arrive, he closed his eyes. Alone with his thoughts, his mind filled with images of Talise's smile and her laughter. No longer able to deny it, he yearned for her. The truth be told, he started to miss her even while packing to leave Boston and never stopped once he moved to St. Louis.

Less than an hour later, the doorbell rang and interrupted his thoughts. When Ace opened it, Kidd stormed through the door, carrying a thick Bible. Wanting to avoid any distractions, Ace didn't comment on the size, but thought, *A pocket Bible would have sufficed.*

He closed the door and joined Kidd at the other end of the sofa. At first, he couldn't look at his brother. Kidd would immediately see the fear in his eyes. Ace chose instead to prop his elbows on his knees and rest his face in the palms of his hands.

"I love her. Talise said she didn't trap me."

"Do you believe her?"

"If I say no, then I've lost my edge of staying on top of my game. If I say yes, then I've lost her for good."

"What does your heart say?" Kidd patted his own chest. "It will never lie. Your mind will lie to you, your eyes will play tricks on you, and your ears will deceive you, but your heart is right on point. That's why God looks at the heart and blesses or judges us based on what He finds. Jesus has no problem showing us our ugly selves. Believe me. He spared no mercy showing me how wretched and lowdown I was."

Ace's next words wouldn't be a shocker to Kidd—he just needed to hear himself say it out loud. "I never wanted to be a father. I wanted to be like our father."

"Humph." Kidd grunted.

"When I was little, Samuel was my idol. He bragged about the places he had been and the fun he had. He came whenever he wanted and brought gifts. As I got older, I thought that was so cool . . . it must be a great life to be free like him . . . to have no responsibility and not have to answer to anyone."

"And we suffered from his lack of responsibility," Kidd snapped and stretched out his legs. "Hey, aren't you supposed to offer your company a glass of water, Kool-aid, or something? And, man, you need to get a coffee table and some chairs in here."

Ace tilted his head toward the kitchen. "You're not company. Get it yourself."

Kidd did and returned with bottled water. "Listen, Samuel lived and died a fool. He gave us his name, but not his heart. He cheated us out of a family. I wish he was alive today, because I would show him how to be a father—a good one."

"Yeah, you had me to practice on." Ace looked Kidd in the eye. "You're a good man and a great brother. You'll be a wonderful father."

"I am the man I am today because of two women, Ma and Eva. Without knowing it, Eva forced me to get past my disappointments, hatred, and stubbornness. She taught me how to give my best. Wanting her love was the reason I tried Christ. Ever since, Jesus has been my Pops and He's had my back."

Ace sighed heavily. "Well, Talise hates me. I made sure of that in our last conversation. In all the materialistic things Samuel bought us, he failed to tell me the price tag on his lifestyle. With eleven children that we know about, from two marriages and one relationship, he was a busy man."

"I can tell you the cost of doing it his way. The Bible says the wages of sin is death."

Leaning back on the sofa, Ace rested the back of his head on the wall. "I already died when I walked away from Talise, knowing she needed me."

"Okay, let's brainstorm. Ace, you did make her happy once—check. But then you hurt her—so repent. Get your sorry, ugly behind in gear and fight for her. Step up to the plate and fight for the Jamieson name." Kidd grinned and puffed out his chest.

"Besides, my daughter is going to need a cousin to play with and long distance won't cut it. Then again, I'm not sure if I want you as a next door neighbor."

"You're having a girl?" Ace was in awe.

Kidd nodded. "Yep, and proud of it! At first, Eva didn't want to know, but our mother talked her into it. If you repeat this, I'll break your nose. Nobody is supposed to know."

"Oh, yeah?

Sitting up straight, Kidd crossed his arms. "I believe you're the one who bears a scar, not me, pretty boy."

Ace rubbed the spot on his nose where the wound had healed, but the scar left a reminder. "You have to admit that was a good fight." He grunted. "Taking down two men for the price of one, they were no match. So what if they drew a little blood? I knocked them out."

Ace paused and regrouped. He didn't summon his brother over to his apartment to reminisce. "That lifestyle ended way before I met

Talise. Although I'm 100 percent male, I'm scared that this is one mind-and-heart game where I'm going to have to fold. I'm out."

"You were always mentally challenged," Kidd joked. "I'll leave this Bible for you to read, but I've got to get back home. So let's pray."

Bowing his head, Ace gripped his brother's hand and waited for some type of miracle to happen.

"Father, in the Name of Jesus, I love You today for so many things. Most of all You put Yourself in harm's way for us. You allowed Yourself to be murdered for us, and You've given us gifts and power to help us to be ready when You come back . . ."

Ace held his breath. The only thing he wanted Kidd to do was recite a powerful prayer and be done with it, not preach.

"Jesus, You are the Father to the fatherless. You know my brother's heart. Help Talise and Ace to forgive each other and be a blessing to their child. Amen."

"That's it? I was hoping God would give you some kind of message that everything would be all right."

"God will get your attention, and when He does, you'd better listen."

Ace slept better that night. Instead of Talise's distraught face haunting him, the laughter of a child soothed him.

—⟋⟋⟋—

Glancing at his watch, it was seven o'clock, eight, on the East Coast. Since his mother didn't normally leave for work this early, he called. Ace needed her help to get Talise back.

"Nicholson residence," the sweetest voice answered.

Ace was momentarily tongue-tied. "Tay?"

"Sandra, telephone," Talise said, without responding to him.

"Tay," Ace repeated, as his mother came on the line.

"Hello?"

"Hey, Mom. Was that Tay?" *How close had they become in his*

312

absence? He wondered. "Can I talk to her?"

"She answered the phone, son. If she wanted to speak to you, then I'm sure she would have. So what's going on?" Sandra switched subjects, as if they were discussing whether he made up his bed or not.

"Can you tell me why Talise is at our house this early . . ."

That was a mistake. "First of all, you moved out. So this is no longer *our,* but *my* house. Now I have to finish dressing to go to work. Is everything okay?"

"It's not until I speak with Tay."

"Then you'll have to call her cell."

"I don't have her number."

"I can't give it to you," Sandra told him. "Sorry, she'll have to give it to you on her own."

Okay, Ace recognized when he was being challenged. He had hoped after Kidd prayed for him last night that things would turn-around instantly. Evidently not. Talise might not want to talk to him over the phone, but she sure would face-to-face.

Unfortunately, flying was not an option. As Kidd had suggested, he had no choice but to buy a gas card and start driving—twenty hours one way—to plead his case.

Chapter Forty-Six

After work on Thursday evening, Sandra strolled through her front door. Unaccustomed smells and sounds greeted her.

The aroma meant Talise had made herself at home and felt up to cooking dinner. *Yummy.* Her sons could cook, but they always burned the first batch of anything. A soft gospel melody serenaded in the background, another welcome home treat. What a contrast to the R&B music Kidd and Ace would blast when they lived there.

After placing her purse and keys on the French side table in the hallway, Sandra rounded the corner into the living room. She stopped and smiled, taking in the sight before her eyes. Stretched out on the sofa, Talise dozed. Sandra hated to wake her, but she looked uncomfortable.

"Hey." Sandra said softly, gently shaking Talise's shoulder until she stirred. Her lids fluttered open. Once Talise seemed to have her bearings, she smiled. "Hey. How was work?" Sitting up, she rubbed her stomach.

"The same every day and every minute—crazy. I'm glad you felt up to cooking. You didn't have to, but thanks." Sandra headed to the kitchen and washed her hands.

314

Talise stood and followed her. "It's the least I could do. You rescued me from the craziness at my apartment. I slept well last night and, as you can see, was in the middle of an afternoon nap. Now your grandchild is hungry." They laughed.

After filling their plates with slices of roast beef, beets, green beans, mashed potatoes, and a roll, the two women enjoyed easy conversation. They chatted about fashion, hair, and baby stuff.

"That was good. You're a great cook," Sandra complimented, putting down her fork.

"You're the one who left me with something to cook—"

The house phone interrupted Talise. Her eyes widened as Sandra stood to answer it. "Hello?" She paused. "You have the wrong number, sweetie."

When Sandra returned to her seat, Talise wouldn't look at her. Instead, she picked with her napkin and said, "Sandra, I appreciate you not only opening your home to me, but reaching out to me in the beginning. You've really become an unexpected friend and I appreciate that. But I have to ask . . ." She took a deep breath. "Are you comfortable with me dating Minister Thomas, really? I know we discussed it briefly."

"I have mixed emotions. As a mother, of course, I want to see my son happy and doing the right thing. I would be ecstatic to have you as a daughter-in-law. You already know that."

Talise nodded.

"But, most of all, I want us to remain close—no matter what. I know how it can be, going at it alone. I was a single parent." Sandra snickered. "I guess I still am. And the title didn't come without sacrifices. I traded in my social calendar for a school calendar, nice lingerie for cartoon underwear, and going back and forth between boy scouts meetings and football practice."

Talise listened quietly as Sandra continued to share from her heart. "Back then, no man wanted an unmarried woman with two little blockhead boys. In hindsight, I guess that was a good thing with so much molestation of our boys going on. It's horrendous."

"I know, that scares me too."

"My sons didn't have a full-time or part-time father. I blindly loved Samuel and let him get away with it. I was one of those silly women who suspected he wasn't upfront with me, but I ignored it."

Tears stained Talise's cheeks as she sniffed. "You make your life sound so sad."

"Children bring you joy—for a little while, anyway." Sandra rolled her eyes. "I'm surprised you didn't make sweet potatoes."

Talise chuckled. "You didn't have any."

"Back to your original question. Richard is a confident man who knows your situation and isn't judging you because of it. He wants to be in your life. That's love."

"I wonder how it might affect my relationship with Eva and the others."

"You have a support system from the entire Jamieson clan. They put their money where their heart is. Although they've already given you some money, their intent is to set up a trust fund as soon as the baby is born and issued a social security number. No strings attached."

Talise shook her head. "When you love someone, there are always strings attached."

Chapter Forty-Seven

On Sunday morning, Ace attended Kidd and Eva's church again. Kidd had given him something to think about last week. Yet, days later, Ace still struggled with accepting what was in his heart. Making him even more uncomfortable, that first sermon he'd heard still lingered in his mind. It challenged him to think about the possibility of being wrong about past decisions. The pastor's words kept gnawing at him. And Ace was compelled to come back.

This morning, Elder Taylor was preaching on the need to surrender. The pastor recited so many Scriptures, Ace couldn't write them all down. He didn't quite get it. He thought that he was surrendering by coming to church, praying, and opening that big, thick Bible Kidd had left at his apartment.

The next day, Ace had come to a decision. On a mission, he walked into his office. Not only was he bent on clearing his desk, but he didn't plan to do any work remotely from Boston. To stay ahead meant doubling up on his projects. For the next couple of days, he came in early and worked late. The end result was on Wednesday night, Ace was packing his bag.

Giving Kidd the heads-up, Ace asked him not to mention his plans to Eva or their mother. Kidd agreed. Next, he called Cameron. Their relationship was still only held together with Band-Aids. Cameron's bottom line was family first, second, and third. He didn't care if the relative was a first cousin or fifteenth. To him, diluted blood was still thicker than water.

"I'm going to make things right with Talise," Ace said when Cameron answered. "I'm driving up."

"You know you're a fool."

Ace had already figured that out. "For driving? Or for Talise?"

"Both. About time the guilt started to corrode your brain, but I've got your back."

"I knew you would. Thanks."

Once they resolved the tension, Cameron brought him up to speed on what was going on back home. Ace hadn't laughed so hard that his side ached in a long time. He hoped that things would go smoothly with Talise.

Thursday morning at five minutes after four, Ace was on the road. "Twenty plus hours," he murmured, setting his cruise control for his own personal road to Damascus. He was determined not to drive over the speed limit. All he needed was to be jailed or have his driver's license revoked for violating his probation. Still, if he had to hitchhike to see Talise, he would.

An R&B music lover, he didn't want any distraction while contemplating what he would say when he showed up at Talise's apartment. His mind and thoughts was his only companion.

The shocker was he had no idea that Talise had become so close to his mother. For any other son, that would be a good thing. Unfortunately for him, his church-going mother had backstabbed him in favor of a church-going brother.

Ace swallowed and slowed. "Lord, am I on the right course?"

Suddenly, he wanted God to talk to him, tell him what he was doing wrong and how he could fix it. With eighteen more hours ahead of him, God had his full attention.

As the hours stretched on, besides pit stops for the restroom and grabbing something to eat, Ace kept driving. He knew he'd spend more time on the road than with Talise, but they had to talk.

After gassing up twice, he was running out of steam. It was five in the evening when he crossed the Ohio border near Youngstown into Pennsylvania. Ace contemplated pressing on while there were still a few more hours of daylight.

He tried to refocus his mind on the things the pastor had said about surrendering and what his brother had told him in their heart-to-heart talk. What did God want from him? At that moment, the question entered his mind that the pastor had asked the first time he attended service: "Are you living your life the way God wants for you?"

Until now, he hadn't bothered to directly answer it. But considering where he was, on the road driving like a man on a mission, Ace had to respond with a resounding "no." Now it was time for him to accept the fact that he'd had it all wrong—and it was time for him to get it right.

Staring into the face of the most important event in his lifetime, he realized this was beyond his control. But how was he supposed to depend on God? His questions were endless to ponder.

Ace always considered himself to be self-sufficient. After his father stopped coming around, he had learned never to depend on another man. Throughout his entire life, he didn't recall asking God for a dime. When he really thought about it, for the first time in his life, he recognized that he needed God's help.

Ace was exhausted—mentally and physically. Finally, deciding to check into a hotel, he fell asleep in his clothes, as soon as his body crashed on the bed.

On Friday morning, he was jolted awake by the sun beaming through the window. Dragging himself out of bed, his body screamed with extreme fatigue and all he could do was groan. The mattress was inflexible and the room air conditioning was faulty.

It was a little past seven when Ace willed himself to the shower and was still sluggish as he got dressed. If only he could hold out until he could collapse in his own bed at home.

A short time later, after two shots of Espresso in a large cup, Ace was ready to hit the road. After gassing up and grabbing some breakfast sandwiches, he was behind the wheel. Otherwise, he would be caught in some serious morning rush hour traffic and hit even more in Boston's evening madness.

Scratching the hairs on his face, Ace wished he had shaved, but it didn't matter. Whether having the semblance of a beard or a clean shaven face, he would look his best when he confronted his ex.

If Talise confessed that her plan to trap him had backfired, Ace didn't know if his heart would recover.

"God." He paused and took a deep breath. "If I really can just ask, then I need You to have my back on this. I'm clueless on how this thing is supposed to play out and even what to say to her."

No answer. Then his next thought was something his mother had told him long ago. "Treat people right, Ace, and you can't go wrong. Right is right—and right will wrong no one."

"Got it."

He would use that and be exceptionally gentle and pleasant with Talise. Unlike how Ace had treated her since he broke off their relationship, Ace was prepared to do a one-eighty. It made sense that God would use something his mother taught him to help him make things right. How could he lose?

Slipping on his sunglasses when the sun began to blind him, it suddenly came to mind about what happened to Paul in Acts, chapter nine. Ace thought, *Jesus, I was just kidding when I called my trip the road to Damascus.* Yet he couldn't deny that his attitude and behavior had taken a turn in the right direction. If only God could put his conversion on hold a bit longer. Right now, it was crunch time for Ace.

Nine hours later, he parked in his mother's complex and stared at "home." The Boston air even smelled fresher. Getting out of the car, he grabbed his duffel bag, stretched his abused muscles, and headed for the stairs.

Turning the key, Ace walked through the front door and took in the familiar setting. Everything seemed the same since his departure months ago.

"Mom, I'm home," he called out.

Sandra peeked her head from the kitchen doorway. Startled momentarily, she recovered with a bright smile. Hurrying toward him with her arms wide open, all she could do was call out her son's name.

"Aaron." Despite the changes and disappointments he had put her through; his mother's embrace was nothing less than welcoming. In her loving way, she hung on to him for the longest time before letting him breathe. Then stepping back, realization must have hit. "What are you doing here?"

"I think I still live here. I have a key." Ace held it up, grinning, and then closed the door behind him. Dropping his duffel bag on the floor, he followed his nose to the kitchen. His mother was on his heels.

"Watch it. I'm still the reigning queen and locksmiths are on call 24/7," she warned and smiled back. "But how did you get here? Aren't you on a 'no-fly' list?"

As if his tired body needed a reminder. "Yes, Mom. I drove. I have seven more weeks on probation and then I can take to the friendly skies again. I'm starved. What ya cooking?" Ace headed to the stove and started lifting lids.

"*Shh.* Stop making so much noise. Talise is upstairs asleep in Kidd's old bedroom. She's caught some type of virus and isn't feeling well."

Time stopped as Ace's jaw became unhinged. "She's what? Tay is here?" His heart pounded. Talk about perfect timing? *Thank You, Jesus.* He couldn't ask for a better scenario.

321

"What exactly is going on between you two?" Ace stared at his mother for an answer, but Sandra Nicholson wasn't easily intimidated.

"Number one, none of your business, because if it was, you would've been here handling it. Number two, Talise is carrying my grandbaby, and it's my responsibility to be there for her. Now if you have a problem with my house guest, then there's a choice of hotels nearby."

"Been there, done that. I drove here to set things right with her."

"Humph. It's about time, but," Sandra started and paused, "I think it may be too late. A woman as pretty and as sweet as Talise doesn't stay unattached for long. Her condition wouldn't deter a good man."

"Yeah, I heard about the preacher." Ace twisted his lips in disappointment. "Mom, whose side are you on?"

"I'm on the Lord's side." Her words were confident, but sadness filled her eyes.

Ace heard movement above his head. Talise was awake. The next thing he heard was the wrenching sound of her throwing up in the adjoining bathroom. He raced up the stairs, taking two or three at a time toward Kidd's room. When Ace busted into the unlocked bathroom, she was on the floor near the toilet. Even in her disheveled appearance and weakened state, he found her beautiful.

"Talise," Sandra called, trying to push past Ace, but he blocked her.

"Tay?" he called softly, as she looked into his eyes. She seemed too weak to respond. "Mom, she's burning up."

"Let's get her in the bed and I'll call her doctor."

"No, I'm taking her to the hospital," Ace said firmly. He reached for a towel, quickly wet it, and began to pat her face. Helping her up to the sink, he pulled back her hair as she rinsed her mouth.

With a little strength, she fussed. "I'm mad at you."

That makes both of us mad at each other. Scooping her up in his arms, he could feel her extra weight as he carried her down the steps. "Mom, grab her purse and whatever else she needs. And get my extra keys to my Charger," he ordered.

Ace was comforted when she rested her head on his chest. *God, You know I really did miss her and I do love her.*

Sandra raced down the stairs with two purses and jingled his car keys. Ace missed his sports car almost as much as Talise. When his mother opened the front door, a tall guy, almost his height stood there with flowers in his fist. Alarm crossed the man's face when he laid eyes on Talise.

"Excuse me. We've got an emergency here." Ace squeezed Talise tighter, as she slept in his arms.

"What's wrong with Sister Babe?"

"Who?" Ace frowned. "Man, step aside. I told you I've got an emergency and you're impeding it."

"Minister Thomas, this is my son, Aaron," Sandra made the necessary introductions.

It didn't matter. "Yeah, and the father of the baby." Ace bulldozed him out of the way and bolted out the door.

"She's got a temperature. Aaron's taking her to the emergency room." Ace heard his mother explain, as she closed the front door and locked it. Then she pointed the remote and deactivated his car alarm.

Carefully, Ace hurried down the steep stairs to the car port where his pride and joy waited for him.

"Then let me pray for her," the minister said, as his long hurried stride caught up with Ace.

Not now, was on the tip of Ace's lips when he felt the slight movement of Talise's stomach against him. *Our child.*

"Please," Ace consented, as Talise snuggled closer to him. He could feel the heat permeating from her body against his chest.

As Sandra held the bouquet, Minister Thomas pulled a small vial of oil from his jacket pocket. Unscrewing the cap, he dabbed a bit on his finger and then placed it on Talise's forehead.

"Can you put some of that on me too?" Ace had to set aside his pride for the safety of the woman in his arms.

Minister Thomas did, and then began to pray, "Father God, in the Name of Jesus, we come boldly to Your throne. We ask that You speak to the condition in Sister Talise's body. Command the sickness to flee and be cast into outer darkness where it belongs. Saved the unsaved and bless the blessed, in the saving Name of Jesus. Amen."

Talise mumbled, "Amen."

"I'll take my car and follow," the minister said.

Placing Talise into the passenger side front seat, Ace carefully secured the seatbelt around her stomach. Before he closed the door, Sandra dabbed Talise's forehead with a cool towel.

"Let's go, Aaron. Take her to Carney Hospital. It's closer," Sandra instructed, as she climbed into the backseat.

After firing up his engine, Ace glanced at Talise. Beads of sweat were forming. He brushed his hand against her cheek and drove out of the complex, heading toward Dorchester Ave.

Unwilling to wait for Minister Thomas, the brother would have to catch up. Ace took his chances pushing the speed limit. Fifteen minutes later, he pulled up to the emergency room entrance and parked. Getting out, he hurried around to the passenger side and unfastened Talise's seatbelt. She moaned.

Scooping her up in his arms, he stormed inside. When a nurse looked up, she scrambled for a wheelchair to assist him. A few minutes later with Talise at his side, Ace answered the intake nurse's questions as best he could, estimating how many weeks along, how long she had been running a temperature, and his relationship to the patient.

"Father of the baby."

When his mother walked in with the minister, Ace realized he had forgotten about them. He had left behind his mother and his car. Another nurse appeared and wheeled Talise into the examination room. Ace dared anyone to keep him from following.

"We're going to get some fluids in her and give her something to bring her temperature down," the nurse advised him.

"What about the—my baby?" Ace was scared.

"We'll monitor the baby's heartbeat as well. Relax dad, everything will be fine."

Yeah, that was easier said than done. It didn't take long for the IV to start pumping fluids through Talise's veins. Once the wires were attached to her swollen stomach, Ace watched the baby's heartbeat, in awe.

Holding Talise's hand, he racked his brain about what to say first and how to say it. As she regained some of her strength, she saved him the trouble.

"Ace, why are you here?" To his relief, her voice was already clearer and stronger.

"I drove here to talk you, but now it doesn't seem like a good time."

He exhaled and told her, "Tay, you are the most beautiful expectant woman I have ever seen."

"Where's Richard? Is he here?"

He was trying to pour his heart out and she insisted on injecting another man into his spiel. "Richard is not your concern—"

"But I'm his. It's nice seeing you, Ace, but you can leave and ask Richard to come in."

Ace tried to regulate his breathing, as he stared into her determined face. He stood. "Tay, I am nowhere as close with God as this man seems to be. But I've always heard that God is for the underdog, so don't underestimate me."

He walked to the waiting room and gave them an update. Ace squinted at Minister Thomas and then took his seat. He wasn't about to tell another man that his woman wanted to see him. Ace was a Jamieson. He may be stubborn, but not stupid . . . well, at any rate, not at the moment.

Completely worn out, he could use some of Talise's fluids to jump-start his adrenaline. Starving, he went in search of a vending machine. A sugar fix would have to give him some temporary energy.

When Ace returned to the waiting room, Minister Thomas was missing. With three candy bars and a bag of chips in hand, he marched back to Talise's room. Sandra couldn't stop him.

The minister was at her bedside, holding her hand. Talise had dozed off again. Stuffing a handful of chips in his mouth, Ace crunched, trying to figure out how God would punish him if he physically ousted the guy from the room.

Ace decided whatever punishment God would hand down probably would be harsh if he messed with one of God's anointed. So he moved to plan B and claimed a chair from the hall. Situating it on the other side of her bed, careful of the cords streaming from the monitor, Ace posted guard there.

Minister Thomas gave him an expressionless look and Ace returned it with his poker face. Taking Talise's other hand into his own, he gently squeezed it and leaned his head against the wall. The last thing he saw before his lids drifted closed was his mother coming into the room and then backing out, shaking her head.

Talise was discharged midday on Saturday and told to get plenty of rest. She was thankful to Sandra and agreed to return to her house for the remainder of the weekend. She needed the respite, but she had one stipulation. Ace had to stay away from her.

Sandra agreed. Ace didn't, and he didn't plan to abide by it.

Talise slept most of Saturday afternoon and evening. Sandra spent the day nursing her back to health, waiting on her and providing nourishing meals. Although his own room was vacant, his mother banished Ace to sleep in the living room on the rollout bed. "I promised Talise that I won't let you near her while she recuperates. We have to abide by that, son."

The sadness in his mother's eyes pricked his heart. But he didn't travel all this way to be denied access to the woman he both loved and disappointed. Ace had a mandatory meeting on Tuesday morning. He had to be at work and on top of his game. His livelihood was at stake, and he couldn't let his out-of-control lifestyle affect that.

"Mom, I know things aren't looking good for me right now, and I deserve Talise's cold shoulder and more. My family turned against me and the only person I have left is God. I do love Talise. I always have, but only God can keep me away from her."

Sandra nodded. "Then I'll pray that Jesus helps you." With that assurance, his mother proceeded to give him an earful about responsibility and the power of love. At one point, it sounded more like Sandra was talking about herself rather than Talise's needs.

That night, he barely got any sleep. The rollout bed was just as uncomfortable as the hotel mattress. Before he drifted off to sleep, Ace prayed, "Lord, help me to get Talise back, please."

Early Sunday morning, Ace was determined to defy his mother and take his chances with Talise. While Sandra was distracted with a phone call, he made a beeline to Kidd's old room. Tapping softly on the door, Ace opened it to find Talise sitting up in bed. She was enjoying the pancakes and fruit his mother had prepared for her.

"Oh, you're still here? Humph." She ignored him and returned to eating and watching her TV program.

"I'm getting ready to head back, but I wanted us to talk. Tay, I want us to clear the air."

"Done. The smoke you left behind dissipated into clear skies," she stated with a hand motion sweeping the air. "Go away. I release you from all responsibility."

Isn't that what he initially wanted? "I may be late coming to this party. But you've forgotten, I got this party started and I'm not leaving."

"You think you can come and go, in and out of my life, and be like your father? Your mother helped me to see the error of her ways. I told you earlier, Ace. I want nothing from you, not even your name."

Ace was trying to keep his temper, but he exploded. "That's where

327

you're wrong! I'm not going anywhere! That baby is a Jamieson—as is his father—me," he exclaimed, pointing at himself. "I'm not my father! I never have and never will cheat on you!"

As their argument escalated, Talise yelled and grabbed her stomach. Fear swept through Ace as he hurried to her side.

"What's wrong?" His heart raced. Moving the tray from her lap, he knelt by the bed.

"The baby kicked me." She continued to rub her stomach.

Ace watched in awe at the baby's slow movement. He was about to reach out and touch her stomach, but Talise stopped him.

"Don't ever touch my body, ever again," she scolded. Her eyes misted.

"God, I deserved that."

"Humph, among other things, Ace."

Ace didn't want to leave her, not like this, but he had to get back to work. He stood. There were no words to say in defense of his actions. Kidd was right. The only thing he had going for him was prayer. And, so far, that wasn't working.

Going to the door, he glanced over his shoulder. "The damage is done to your heart, but God is my witness, I will mend it."

"It may already be too late," she managed to say, as he closed the door.

Once he was back downstairs, his mother gave him a tongue-lashing for upsetting Talise. "I had hoped before you left, you and Talise would talk. But the only thing I heard was yelling. It took all within me not to intervene."

"Thanks, Mom. It's good to know you haven't completely defected to the other side," Ace said, sarcastically. Shaking his head, his tone changed. "She's so beautiful. Thank you for being there for her when I should have been. How is she making it? Does she need anything?"

"She needs to know you love her. That's all a woman ever wants in life, especially when she's pregnant. But Richard has been filling that gap."

"Humph. I'm not worried about that dude."

"You'd better be," she scolded. Then after a brief pause, Sandra filled him in. "Talise hasn't asked for a dime. She's looking ahead and I know she's saving like crazy for the baby. Of course, she wants time off to spend with her child when he or she gets here. Although it's probably best for her, the airline cut back on her hours."

She gave him the full story. "Talise does my hair now—and a good job, but she's had to turn down many of her clients. Her feet swell if she stands too long. Besides, she's not getting any rest at her apartment with an extra house guest. That's why I invited her to spend some time here with me. And, believe me, it's been my pleasure. She is so sweet."

Three people in that apartment? That's way too many, he thought. "I'm surprised Lois would go for that." Ace rubbed the hairs on his face, which had officially become a thin beard. His determination was even greater to get back to Boston and straighten things out. He didn't want Talise suffering at all.

Whipping out his wallet, Ace counted out eight-hundred dollars to his mother. "I'll send a thousand every month. I wish I knew the amount of her share of the rent. Better yet, she needs to get out of that overcrowded place."

Sandra suspiciously eyed the bills she was holding. "Aaron, this is a lot of cash you're carrying. You're not . . . gambling again?" She swallowed. "You gambled on your relationship, and I'm sorry to say you've lost, son."

"I'm traveling, remember? I don't like plastic. And it's not over yet. I don't believe God's going to let me lose. Well," he stretched, "I'd better get back on it. Damascus is a long road."

"Huh?"

"Let the minister know, I will be back—soon." Ace hugged and kissed his mother and left.

Chapter Forty-Eight

*O*nce Talise was back at her apartment, she was able to set up a video chat with Sinclaire. She couldn't wait to give her sister the details of her crazy weekend.

"Let me ask you this. If Richard wasn't around, would you give Aaron another chance?" Sinclaire quizzed.

Shaking her head, Talise didn't have to think over the answer. "This isn't about the minister. It's about Ace devastating and deserting me. He didn't look back."

"Until now. He's a man. They're slow learners, not only in the head department, but with their hearts too."

"So you're pulling for Ace?" Talise couldn't believe her.

Sinclaire gave her a tender smile. "I'm pulling for you."

Sometimes her sister's wisdom was mind-boggling. Their video chat ended too soon but with a much-needed prayer. Afterward, Talise kept praying. Her tears mingled with each petition, asking God to stop the hurting that resurfaced when Ace arrived. When she finished, one thing came to mind: two men holding her hands at the hospital.

A few evenings later, she and Gabrielle had dinner at Church, a popular neighborhood establishment near Fenway Park. One side was the restaurant; the other side was a club.

As Talise savored the taste of her veggie burger sliders with goat cheese and pumpkin seed pesto, Gabrielle enjoyed the fried chicken pot pie dumplings with cranberry chutney.

"I'll tell you, Gabrielle, either it was my hormones or the baby's keen development, but I don't recall the baby kicking so much as when Ace was around."

"Doesn't your book say the baby will begin to recognize voices? Maybe he knew his dad was talking."

Talise stuck out her tongue. "One, the doctor doesn't have to tell me. I know I'm having a girl. Plus, I'm just barely twenty-five weeks and that's not supposed to happen until week twenty-seven."

Gabrielle waved her hand in the air. "Regardless of whether it's a boy or a girl, your baby is ahead of his or her time." She scrunched up her nose.

"I'm taking a poll. What would you do in my shoes?"

Swallowing, Gabrielle took a sip of her tea. "I like happy endings. Remember, I started a romantic handbook, of sorts. The man drove twenty plus hours to see you, left you money, and attempted to apologize. That's a noteworthy entry in my book."

Gabrielle added, "To me it sounds like when the prodigal son came to himself. I think Ace came to himself after wasting time being a lousy boyfriend. That's a fairy-tale ending."

"The past six months have been anything but a fairy tale. It's been a constant rerun of a horror movie."

"I know. I just believe everyone deserves a second chance. At the least, hear him out. Some people are born with stupidity. Others pick it up along the way."

"You haven't even met Ace. Whose side are you on?"

"That precious little baby's side. Whether or not you and Ace resolve your differences and unload your baggage, you're going to have to be cordial. Plus, it appears the Jamiesons are determined to be in your life. Let them. Above everything else, you're a new creature in Christ. Let the Holy Ghost lead you."

"I have gotten closer with his side of the family. Eva and I talk a few times a week. Although she doesn't mention Ace directly, I can hear the whimsical tone in her voice. She's planning activities for our babies like we live next door."

Smiling, Gabrielle's eyes twinkled.

"What?"

When Gabrielle shook her head, Talise continued. "Eva invited me to their next family game night. This time, she couldn't give me her word that he wouldn't be there.

"I really want to go too. I'm piqued by their concept of getting together once a month to play games with an African American theme. I love that idea and being around the Jamieson wives."

"Go. You might as well get accustomed to seeing Ace. Your child is going to want to know his or her father. Besides, you live in Boston, and he lives in St. Louis. It's not like you'll see him every weekend."

Chapter Forty-Nine

I want my old job back." Ace called his former supervisor in Boston after he returned to the St. Louis office.

"Your position was filled not long after you left. As a matter of fact, I had to hire two people to replace you," Melvin said.

"What about another department? I've got to get back home."

"You're stuck in the Midwest for another seven months."

Seven months wouldn't work. If he had to drive to Boston every weekend to make things right, so be it. However, Ace hadn't recovered yet from his recent marathon drive. His bottom still had a hangover when he got behind the wheel of his car. Six more weeks, and then he could fly.

A few hours later, Kidd called him at the office. "Hey, are you coming or not?"

He'd been hounding Ace about attending the upcoming Jamieson family night. Ace hadn't realized that another month had passed since he stormed out, for no other reason but to save face.

This time around it would be at Malcolm and Hallison's house. Between the two brothers, Malcolm was the most sickening. He loved his wife and constantly made sure she knew it, along with everybody else.

Life seemed easy for those brothers. Even Eva stuck by Kidd's side when he was getting his act together. Talise didn't want to be in the same room with Ace, but the Jamiesons had one common trait. They were stubborn.

"Man, the only thing on my mind is convincing Talise that it's worth giving us another try. My first visit didn't go as I had envisioned, and I've got to get back to Boston."

"I hope no time soon, especially not this weekend. Let's hang out at Malcolm's, and the next time you go, I'll drive with you to see Mom."

Ace perked up. Another driver would definitely help. When Kidd committed, he never reneged.

His body said deal. His heart said no, he couldn't wait. But common sense ruled.

"See you Friday night."

———ᗰ———

Friday night, Ace's heart wasn't into playing games. He didn't care how fascinating or educational. His mind was stuck on stupid when he thought about Talise. His actions had cost him dearly. Even if she had trapped him, he still loved her. If he could forgive her for that, then they could move on.

Ace parked behind the row of cars. Judging from those present in front of him, it seemed as if he was the last to arrive again. As usual, whoever hosted the game night had their home shining like a lighthouse, with a light beaming from every window.

He got out and strolled up the walkway. His eyes were fixed on the large, oversized living room window of Malcolm's home. Ace thought back to the Friday nights when he drove to Talise's apartment. She would wait and watch for him, perched high above in her bay window.

His heart ached to turn back the hands of time. As he approached the front door, Ace strained his eyes. His mind was definitely toying with him. Malcolm didn't have a bay window, but the outline of the woman standing on the other side of his cousin's picture window reminded him of Talise. Shaking his head, Ace blinked. If he was starting to have hallucinations, it was time to get some medication.

The screams of the toddlers, laughter of the adults, and overall loud voices greeted Ace when he opened the door. It was kept unlocked until everybody arrived. M. J. and Pace raced to him for attention.

Ace grinned at their antics. The noise hushed as he scanned the room, exchanging greetings with the group. His heart almost stopped when his eyes landed on the woman near the window.

"Tay?" Ace swallowed. What was she doing here at game night? *What do you care? She saved you a long haul*, his mind quickly reminded him.

His steps were slow like a predator, as he made his way toward her. "Tay?" he repeated.

"Hello, Ace," she said, reserved and nonchalant. The stormy eyes he recalled from their last argument were now blank.

Hallison strolled out of the kitchen. "Hey, Ace, you made it. Let's eat. Jamieson children, wash your hands."

Did I walk into the Twilight Zone? he thought. Talise was here in St. Louis and he had another chance.

Ace smirked at that, as he headed to wash his hands. The younger children had beaten him to the restroom. They seemed to be competing to see who could be the first to win the three-minute scrub rule. Rinsing off their germs, they argued and played in the water.

He detoured to the kitchen sink. When he strolled back into the dining room, Kami occupied the seat next to Talise.

"I have a bag of candy, and you can have some, if you let me sit there," he lowered his voice near Kami's ear.

The girl shook her head. "Candy is bad for my teeth."

Couldn't a brother get any help from his family here? With a pleading look, he glanced at his cousins, who were watching him. His brother finally said in a mellow voice, "Eva got Talise here. You're on your own."

Picking up the chair with Kami on it, Ace moved her over and opened up some space. He grabbed a seat and sat it next to Talise. Then he made eye contact with everyone around the table to see if anyone wanted to challenge him on his actions. The men smirked.

"Would you like me to fix you a plate?" Ace looked into her eyes. They were as bright as he remembered them from happier times. Even when she was sick, she was beautiful. Tonight she was gorgeous.

"Nope. Hali is getting it. Thanks." As if on cue, Hallison rested a plate with plenty of vegetables and chicken fingers in front of her. After everyone had served themselves, the family stood to say grace. Ace looked at Talise again. Her head was already bowed. He stared at her stomach—his child.

As the elder Parke, Papa P., began the blessing, Ace refocused.

"Lord, in the Name of Jesus, first, we thank You for dying on the cross for us. It's through Your blood You have wiped our slates clean from sins, lies, deceptions, wrongdoings, and other impurities . . ."

When he finally made it around to blessing the food, Ace relaxed as Amens echoed among them.

"Grandpa, I hope my food isn't cold. That was a long prayer," Pace joked.

"If it is, you can warm it up in the microwave," Cheney advised her eldest son.

Ace couldn't eat. He was getting his fill of Talise. "You look pretty. Thanks for coming."

"Don't flatter yourself. I'm not here for you. I'm interested in the games, and I plan to play undisturbed." The warning in her eyes said she meant it.

He didn't want a repeat of their last argument. Ace would bide his time, but she was on his turf and he wasn't going to let her leave until they talked. Regardless of the game tonight, she would be on his team.

Their vibes had been strong from the first day they met. He was depending on his closeness to unnerve her. Ace wanted Talise to recall all the good memories between them. He only wanted one thing from God—and that was to restore his relationship with the mother of his child.

He tried making small talk. "Do you still crave sweet-n-sour chicken wings?"

"No. I eat healthy now."

He glanced at the veggies on her plate and the chicken fingers, which weren't exactly healthy. But it was a party with party food. "Do you have any cravings now?"

"Yeah, sweet potatoes," she replied then lowered her voice. "Ace, we can't just pick up as if that Friday night never happened. You hurt me and I'm really uncomfortable sitting next to you, knowing how you threw me away." Her eyes misted.

"I know I handled that badly, and I'll always regret that. But I came to your apartment that Friday night to profess my love. When you told me your suspicion about the pregnancy, I felt you had set a trap that you didn't need to set. I was already yours."

Clinching her teeth, her watery eyes now shot daggers. "I told you I don't need to trap any man," she raised her voice.

"You sure don't. I was a fool, baby," Ace looked around. The children were busy eating, but the adults were feigning interest in their food. He didn't care. He wanted her back.

Talise wiped her mouth. "I flew in to spend time with the ladies and play games with the family. After I fly back home, I won't get on another plane until after the baby. Leave me alone."

"I've done that once, I can't do that again!" Ace snapped loudly, drawing everyone's attention.

Papa P. cleared his throat. "Okay, children, you should be finished. Start to clear the table so we can begin."

The little ones obeyed without an argument. Talise finished the last remaining carrots on her plate and downed the reminder of her milk. Ace offered her a refill, but she declined as Hallison took her plate and wiped off the table. Moments later, Malcolm began to spread an oblong board on the table.

"Talise, since this is your first time attending a game night, we decided to play 'Tracking.'"

"It's a fun way for you to learn about your ancestors and how to track them," Cheney explained.

"Sounds like fun," she said with a smile, seemingly eager to get started. "Besides my grandparents, I don't know too much about my family before them."

"Aren't we doing teams tonight?" Ace was ready.

"Nope, not for this one," Malcolm answered.

Ace sighed in disappointment. *Lord, I could use some help here and not to play this game. I need to win Talise back.*

"Before we start 'Tracking,' I'll have my son share what he uncovered about Kidd and Ace's side of the family. They're actually my eleventh generation cousins and Parke, Malcolm, and Cameron's twelfth," Papa P. looked to Parke.

Talise sat straighter and rubbed her stomach. She seemed impressed already.

"Paki Kokumuo Jaja was born in December 1770 in Cote d'Ivoire, Africa," Parke began by rolling his tongue to authenticate an African dialect. Ace rolled his eyes.

"Landing in Maryland, Paki was indoctrinated into servitude. Ironically, he was sold in front of Sinner's Hotel for a couple of hundred dollars. The slave master's daughter, Elaine, became his wife when they ran away together.

"The two adopted the name Jamieson after a Robert Jamieson, who helped them escape along the Underground Railroad. Kidd and Ace's eleventh great-grandfather, Orma, was born in 1780."

Parke slowed down, "Orma was the youngest son after Parker,

Aasim, Sandra, and Fabunni. Orma had an interesting history. His name means 'born free,' yet he sold himself back into slavery for Sashe, a Kentucky runaway. When she was recaptured, Orma went with her, basically giving up his freedom to live with her in bondage."

"You see, it's in my blood, Talise. I'll give up whatever it takes to be with you," Ace whispered.

Turning, Talise gazed into his eyes. As they stared, silence reigned. Everyone seemed to be holding their breaths with him. When Talise broke eye contact with Ace, Parke continued. "Their children were Kingdom, Candy, Paradise, and Harrison."

"Thanks, cuz." Kidd picked up the story. "Kingdom named his firstborn King. For the next sixty years, the firstborn sons kept the name going with King II, III, and IV."

"There won't be any Kings in my family," Talise said, joking.

"Don't be so sure. I plan to have me a queen one day." Ace dropped his voice to the lowest baritone God gave him. It was the only ammunition he could use in front of the children and his family to seduce her.

After a few more tidbits about Ace's family tree, Papa P. suggested that was enough background information for Talise to digest in one night.

"Now, on to the game," he explained. "It involves questions and answers. There are no losers. We pull a card and read the question. On the back, it contains generic information on how to find answers. We, the Jamiesons, prefer to share our personal experience."

"Can I take a potty break first?" Talise began to scoot her chair back.

"Yeah." Everyone chuckled.

Ace quickly stood and pulled out her chair, taking the opportunity to steal a whiff of her fragrance. "I miss everything about you," he whispered near her ear.

Talise didn't respond and headed to her destination. While she was gone, the family turned on him.

"Don't blow this, man," Kidd advised.

"Or you'll live to regret it," Malcolm added.

"She's a hormonal woman scorned. Don't play with her." Cheney lifted a brow.

"If she doesn't become my sister in-law, I am so through with you!" Eva hissed.

"Put your overalls on and be a man, son," Papa P. chimed in.

"I know." Ace rubbed his head in frustration. "I'm trying and praying."

When Talise returned, Ace stood and pulled out her chair again, then gently pushed her up to the table. Kami shuffled the cards and placed the stack in front of Talise to start the game.

Taking the first card, Talise recited the question, "I'm at the funeral of a family member. It's a devastating time for everyone. Should I engage my distant relatives about the family history or wait until another time?" Frowning, she took a few moments to consider her answer. "I would show sensitivity and wait."

Papa P. shook his head. "Yes, to showing sensitivity. But always take advantage of opportunities to ask family members about their aunts, uncles, grandparents, great grandparents, maiden names, where they were born, how many times a relative married, and so on. Get as much information as you can. The next morning is not promised to us. When you bury a loved one, everything they know is buried too."

"Hmm." Talise pondered out loud. "Honestly, that would be the last thing on my mind."

"Understandable," Eva agreed.

The stack was moved to Ace. He pulled the next card and read the question. "Name websites a person can use from a home computer to get free information."

"Ooh. I know." Kami waved her hand in the air. "I know."

Ace squinted at her. He debated if he could trust the little traitor. "I know the answer too."

She pouted as her shoulders slumped. Talise shoved him. "Don't be mean to her."

"Okay, go into the kitchen first and grab some more grapes, apple chunks, and crackers, please." Ace bribed Kami with a grin.

Nudging Ace again, Talise scolded him, "If you want it, go get it yourself."

"It's for you, babe." Ace wasn't there for her earlier, but from now on, he would see that her needs were met.

When she blinked and relaxed, he knew his words had affected her. "I'm not about to play musical chairs when I get up to get something and come back and have one of these guys steal my seat." He tilted his head toward the children.

After doing his bidding, Kami returned and dutifully placed the plate in front of Talise as Ace instructed her. Then he gave Talise an unwelcome hug.

Back at her seat, Kami recited her answers, "HeritageQuest.com, rootsweb.com, Familysearch.org, FindaGrave.com, Our Black Ancestry on Facebook..."

"Okay, show off," Ace told her with a smile.

"I get straight A's," Kami answered proudly.

Almost everyone at the table said in union, "We know."

The stack made its way around the table. Eva announced she was calling it quits after she pulled her card. "How can you track your ancestors from the 1850 and 1860 Slave Schedule?"

"I'll take this one," Cheney answered. "You compare the number of enslaved people on both censuses and carefully note their ages. They may be listed as Black or Mulatto. The larger number of enslaved people will give indication of how big the property."

Cheney reached for her glass and took a sip of water. "Blacks were finally listed as heads of households on the 1870 census. Check to see if your relatives' last name matches the slaveholder's name in the same county. If there's no match, check with the historical society or reference library in that county about any probate papers or enslaved people bills of sales. There's more, but . . ."

"The end," Eva announced.

Talise clapped and others joined her. "Wow. I'm so glad I came."

"Me too," Ace told her.

"Humph. Again, it certainly wasn't for you," she reminded him.

"Malcolm, can I use your home office for a minute?"

When he nodded, Ace didn't waste any time pulling out Talise's chair. Then he gently lifted her up out of her seat.

She screamed. "Ace Jamieson, you better not drop me! I will kill you if you hurt my baby."

The children laughed at the entertainment as murmurs of "It's about time" and "Girl, stay strong" circulated around the table.

"Our baby," Ace corrected, as she gripped his neck, almost shutting off his wind pipe.

Once they were behind closed doors. Ace placed her onto the small sofa and sat next to her. She winced and rubbed her stomach.

"The baby?" Ace asked concerned. "I didn't hurt him, did I?"

"No," she corrected him, smiling. "I prefer to think the baby is a 'she.' Evidently, she seems to know when you're near. She seems to move when you talk."

Ace longed to touch his child. "May I?" When she nodded, he reached out. Talise's soft hand guided his to the right spot. He swallowed and teared at the miracle moving beneath Talise's skin.

He bowed his head in shame. "I'm so sorry for putting you through this."

Her fingers lifted his chin. The smile Talise gave him was tender and encouraging. "Ace, I've forgiven you. I couldn't move on if I didn't. I know you have trust issues in relationships, but I don't. I go into a relationship, trusting and believing. We're at two different places now."

She was too calm and understanding for him. A drag out argument would at least allow him to wrap his arms around her and kiss her. He loved kissing her.

"I want a man who will trust me and love me and receive mine in return. Minister Richard Thomas accepts me as I am—and my child."

Ace grunted, twisting his lips to rein in his temper. He didn't want his child to hear angry words. "Humph. If you think that great-grandfather of mine was crazy those eleven or so generations back, if you think he was insane for selling himself into slavery for a woman, then hold your breath, Talise Rogers. Love created our baby, a misunderstanding separated us—"

"That's not how I see it. You separated us. Richard has already proposed."

Chapter Fifty

*T*alise silently cried the next morning during her flight back to Boston. She had survived the looks, charm, and smell of Aaron "Ace" Jamieson. She had even resisted the temptation to smack him and didn't give in to the seduction of the chemistry between them.

Minister Thomas was the type of man Talise could love and trust. Ace was the kind of man she could love, but was afraid to trust.

When her plane landed Saturday afternoon, she stopped by her ticket counter where Gabrielle was working. Did management think her friend was a work machine? Gabrielle deserved an award for top middle manager/supervisor/regular employee. Talise hoped God would bless her with a different job soon, although she would miss her friend.

"How did it go?" Gabrielle's face lit up when she saw Talise.

"I was civil." Talise chuckled. "When Eva warned me that Ace would probably be there, I had to pray. I wanted to go, but I wasn't up to having a part two of our argument that started when he was here in Boston.

"All the way there, I kept envisioning myself as Bette Midler in that movie with Danny DeVito when she found out her husband tried to have her killed. She pushed him overboard."

Shaking her head, Gabrielle smiled in amusement. She watched as a passenger glanced their way and then apparently changed her mind about approaching the counter and walked on. "How did it go with your heart?"

Thinking that over, Talise didn't say anything. "Richard hasn't stopped proposing to me since Ace stormed back into Boston . . ."

Gabrielle gasped. "Oooh, let me mark that down in my romance handbook." She made an imaginary check mark sign with her pen and laughed.

"I know. He wants my baby—it will be our baby—to have a father at birth. I would never have to doubt his love, Gabrielle. You know Richard was dead set against me going to St. Louis. I repeated to him what you told me about having to deal with my baby's father for a lifetime. He said when I returned, if I felt that I've truly moved on from Ace, then he won't take no for an answer."

"Don't think I'm not aware that you purposely didn't answer my question about how your heart was faring. Don't you dare say anything! We'll talk later." Gabrielle turned and greeted a passenger. "Hi, can I help you?"

When she got back to her apartment, Talise was surprised to see the living room back in order. Myra's furniture was gone and Lois was putting up leftovers.

"She had to go," Lois said before Talise could ask. "I can only deal with messy folks for so long. That definitely was a bad idea. Talk about the Lord working in mysterious ways. I told her yesterday and she was out today." Then, with a wide grin, Lois added, "But wouldn't you know it, just like that—your rent is covered for months to come."

"Thank God for my father. He knows that, besides my mandatory bills, I've been saving almost every dime I get for the baby. And my tithes, of course. Daddy has really been there for me. When did you hear from him?" Tired from her trip, Talise smiled a weak smile, removed her shoes, and rested her carry-on on the floor.

"I'm not talking about Mr. Rogers. It was Ace. He sent the money to me because he knew you wouldn't accept anything from him." Lois stared. "The man must be seriously trying to kiss and make up."

Talise didn't want to think in those terms. She had to fight her feelings. "No, he's getting a jump-start on his child support payments, which I wouldn't ask him for anyway."

Sitting on Talise's bed, Lois crisscrossed her legs. "Well, whatever you want to call it, he overnighted it when I told him why you had to stay at his mother's for a few days."

Whirling her head around too fast, Talise steadied herself as she became dizzy. "You talked to him and didn't bite your tongue?"

"Oh, don't think I didn't give him a peace of my mind, your mind, and the mind of every woman who's ever been wronged. I made him throw in grocery expenses too."

Pondering over everything Lois said, Talise knew Ace was never stingy with his possessions. *God, I love them both: Richard and Ace. How do I know who would give me the greater love?*

Greater love has no one than this; to lay down one's life for one's friends, God whispered in the wind, John 15:13.

*A*ce was fuming as he gripped the steering wheel. There was no way he was going to let another man bring up his child—period. And nobody was going to marry Talise— but him— period.

"So how long do you plan to keep driving home?" Kidd asked, as they began their road trip.

"As long as it takes. I'll be able to fly soon—Hallelujah."

"You do know there's an easier way to handle this?" He waited for Ace to bite, but he didn't.

"Your solution is in Hebrews 11:6. You've got to have faith in God's abilities. Meaning, instead of taking matters into your own hands, give it to God. He's the One who has control over everything. Trust Him to give you what you need."

"How come I have a feeling this talk was planned?"

"Because I've butted out long enough. We could tell Talise still loves you, but if she's anything like the Jamieson women, including my wife, she's not going to make it easy to earn her trust."

"You tell me to trust God, but if a man was trying to take Eva from you, you wouldn't sit back, kick up your heels, and wait," Ace challenged his brother.

Kidd took a long time to answer. "There's no way another man would have come close to her, not even in that nursing home where a man tried to attack her. But since God saved me—and I do go to church and read my Bible—I've learned to kick up my heels, as you say."

Ace didn't want to hear that. "That night, months ago, I was prepared to tell Talise how much I loved her. She just threw me for a loop when she hinted there may be a baby involved."

"You've been coming to church with Eva and me off and on for a few months, but you haven't committed." Kidd grunted. "I held out to the end too with God, but it's not worth it. Save yourself some grief. Go all the way with God. If you've really repented, then you need to get those sins off your plate.

Silently, Kidd was praying that he would get through to his brother. "Jesus won't clean you up without giving you the gifts to help you live a righteous and victorious life until He comes back. All you've been doing is chasing after a woman, instead of God."

It was going to be a long ride to Boston. Ace was already hoping God was working in his favor, but God didn't expect for him to just sit around and wait. He had to make things right.

After a twenty-two hour journey, Kidd rolled into the condo complex and parked next to their mother's car. It was a family reunion, of sorts. The two brothers greeted their mom with hearty hugs and kisses. Sandra embraced them and returned their heartfelt feelings.

Ace hoped Talise would be there again, but she wasn't. Still without her new phone number, he had to convince his mother to call on his behalf.

"Hey sweetie, how are you feeling?" Sandra paused for Talise's response then continued with her task. "Well, Ace is here. Yes, again. He wants to know if he can stop by." Sandra nodded and listened. "I understand. I agree." Sandra hung up and turned to Ace. "She said 'sure.'"

"Sure? You two had more than a 'sure' conversation."

She walked up to her son and grabbed his arms. "I love you, Aaron. I always will, but I see myself in Talise. I also want a better life for her. I'm on her side. If you aren't prepared to stay and make her happy, then walk away. Let her be loved by someone else."

"Aaron Jamieson is back, and I'm playing to win." Shaking his head, Ace made his statement with conviction. He grabbed some fresh clothes from his bag and headed off to shower and change.

———※———

"Didn't we resolve this last weekend in St. Louis?" Talise asked Ace when she let him into her apartment. She couldn't believe her ears when Sandra called her. "You're wasting your time."

"If I have to drive every weekend until I can fly here to make this right, I will, Tay."

Glad that finally she could sit in her favorite living room chair again, Talise made herself comfortable and said, "Look, I'm twenty-eight weeks pregnant and it's taken me this long to find peace. I had to really seek God to get to this point. You need Jesus too."

"I know. That gives me twelve weeks before the baby comes." Folding his arms, Ace leaned against the wall. "That minister man will never fit my shoes in loving you."

"You're right," she agreed, shifting her body in the oversized chair. "Richard has a different shoe size. Listen, Ace, I promise there won't be any baby mama drama, custody concerns, or problems about your name on the baby's birth cer—"

"Don't go there, Tay." He clenched his fists and squeezed his lips shut.

She was having second thoughts about the baby's last name. Maybe she shouldn't have taunted him about omitting his name on the birth certificate. After attending family game night, she recognized the pride they all had in the Jamieson name. Yet Talise was undecided because, if she married Richard, she didn't want her child to have a different last name from hers.

Talise still hadn't given Minister Thomas an answer. Her lips wanted to say yes, but her heart was saying, hold up.

Ace sat on the sofa across from her and looked directly into her eyes. "I'm not bluffing, baby. If you marry another man, you're going to have to buy every house on the block. Otherwise, I'll move next door and, whether you like it or not, we'll be joined at the hip. I'll sue for joint custody and be around every day to bathe my child and read him bedtime stories. I'll pray constantly for God to help make me a better father than the one I had."

Ace stood and began to pace the floor. "God knows I'm putting in the effort, but I'm not making any headway."

He stuffed his hands in his pockets. "I love you, Tay, and I'm sorry I hurt and deserted you. That's a guilt trip I've put on myself." He paused and took a deep breath. "If I walk out that door, will you ever open it again for me?"

"It's barely cracked now. Ace, I appreciate you paying my rent, but I didn't ask you to. I want nothing from you. I've told you that."

"But I want everything from you," he said with all the passion in his heart. Ace then walked out the door and closed it softly behind him.

Talise didn't move. She was numb. Grabbing a throw blanket, she wrapped herself in it and cried herself to sleep.

—⁓—

The next day at the salon, Priscilla picked up on Talise's somber mood. "What's the matter?"

Shrugging, Talise really didn't want to talk about it.

"I'm a good listener," she continued to coax.

"Ace is in town."

"Again?"

"Yeah. He drove up with his brother this time . . ."

Just then, a hush around the salon made Talise turn around to see what was happening. Talk about timing. To her utter surprise, in all of God's glorious creation, Ace stood with balloons tied to a vase of flowers and a boxed lunch like he used to bring her.

He walked up to her station without an invitation, politely spoke to her client, and then handed her his offering. When he noticed the flowers already on her counter, he picked up the vase, flowers and all, and dumped it in her wastebasket.

Stunned, Talise's mouth dropped open. So did Priscilla's.

"I thought you might be hungry. It's your favorite," Ace said without blinking.

As he turned to walk away, out of nowhere Priscilla whipped the belt out of her purse and popped Ace on his behind. He yelped and twirled around, rubbing his backside. "What's your problem, lady?" He scowled.

"Blame it on Tammy."

Chapter Fifty-Two

I've done all I can do," Ace said in defeat to his brother and mother later Saturday night. All his fight had gone out of him when he left Talise's apartment the day before and made one final attempt earlier at the salon.

They sat quietly in Sandra's living room, waiting for Ace to explain.

"With my eyes, mouth, and heart, I've told Tay I'm sorry. I backed it up by paying her living expenses. Twice, I've practically driven across country to show her I'm serious about reconciling. I even started going to church and reading my Bible. Nothing has helped, not even God."

Dropping his head, Ace closed his eyes. His mother had been right. Ace had gambled with her affections and lost.

"Son, we all know you love Talise, but that's where you went wrong. Never go to the Lord for selfish reasons because you want something. You want her back, but what are you willing to give Him in exchange? Have you surrendered your heart to Him? You have to reach out to Jesus for Aaron."

Ace didn't respond right away; instead, he stared over their heads at nothing in particular. Apparently, he had been reading his Bible. The old Ace would never say, "Maybe that's what God was telling me when I read the verse, 'In his heart a man plans his course, but the Lord determines his steps.'" Those powerful words had spoken to him, and he had decided on the spot to commit them to memory.

Then with a loud groan, he admitted, "I guess I was off track big time. But I sure thought God would see that I've changed my ways. My desire has been for Him to help me get Talise back. Was I wrong?"

Sandra interjected, "'One thing I ask of the Lord is that I may dwell in the house of the Lord.'" She paraphrased a portion of Psalm 27:4 and leaned forward. "Ace, your desire must be on a spiritual level for salvation, so you'll be ready when Jesus returns."

Now it was Kidd's turn, as he offered some personal testimony. "Ace, when I first moved to St. Louis, God started dealing with me, but I wanted no part of Him. Eva was truly sent to me by God because she led me to Christ."

Sandra got up and stirred in the kitchen for a few minutes. She returned with three bottles of water and the brothers eagerly accepted theirs. With a solemn expression on her face, she retook her seat and shared Ace's beloved's testimony. "In Talise's case, she was at her wit's end. When she came to church, she was repenting before she even heard the sermon. She was ready at the altar call to get her sins washed away. God's power has kept her ever since."

Of course, Ace heard about that through the grapevine, but he thought her experience was keeping them apart.

"You may think Talise brought you to this lowest point in your life, but the truth is, God did. He's got your attention, and He's more forgiving than Talise. Focus on God."

Nodding, Ace didn't say anything. He was finally getting their point as he processed, digested, and then accepted his misguided attempts to play God's hand. He was guilty of trying to manipulate God as though they were playing a shrewd card game. Clueless about what to do next, Ace sighed and rested his head on the back of the sofa. It was time to give it all up. Closing his eyes, he threw his arms in the air.

"Okay, where do I go from here?"

"Repent, bro. Recognize God for who He is—your Creator, Savior, and Deliverer. Pour out your heart to Him and, this time, leave Talise out of it. This is between you and God."

"Son, I know you and Kidd are heading back to St. Louis tomorrow, but it's nothing like washing away all your spiritual filth. And the Name of Jesus will cleanse you."

That instant, Ace made a decision. Sitting up, he slapped his hands on his thighs. "Okay. I surrender. Kidd, I'll pay for you to catch a plane in the morning. I'm going to be at church with Mom tomorrow."

Tears streamed down Sandra's face. Kidd pumped his fist in the air. Standing, his mother huddled her sons into a hug. While she cried out to God, praying and rejoicing, Ace repented for his irresponsible lifestyle, his selfish attitude, and his deep regrets.

"I'll call Eva and give her the good news, and then I'll have Cheney and Hali check on her until I get back. We're brothers, Ace, we hang together, and I plan to be right there with you. And then we'll drive back together, rejoicing."

Once his mother composed herself and dried her tears, she prepared a snack and they talked some more before retiring to bed. Ace knew he needed to get some rest, but he couldn't. He stayed up most of the night, devouring the Word.

Sunday morning, Ace was packed and dressed for church by the time Sandra got up.

"Aren't you eager this morning." She greeted him with a smile and a hug. Quickly, she teared-up again. "I think I must have praised God in my sleep all night long. He's allowing me to witness both my sons turn their lives around. Hallelujah!"

Ace smiled. "I don't know what's going to happen between Tay and me, but I know I've tried. At the least, I'll be able to tell my child that I gave it my best. I don't blame Tay for not trusting me. A few days ago, I read the whole book of Ephesians. Last night, I think God led me back to Ephesians 6:13 and the words nearly jumped off the page. It says to stand after I've done all I can do."

"As you read Scriptures, be careful not to take anything out of context. I believe the previous verse talks about standing against the spiritual forces of evil. Then verse thirteen tells us to put on the whole armor of God so that we can stand our ground," she explained.

"I'm going to keep studying it, Mom, and even more. I promise you."

A few hours later, Sandra was grinning from ear to ear, as Ace and Kidd escorted her up the steps to Faithful Church. Ace spied Minister Thomas in the distance.

"Talise and I usually sit together, but if you want to sit elsewhere . . ."

"I do. I don't want any distractions."

Once they were situated, Ace closed his eyes. He just wanted to absorb the power of God in the atmosphere. He needed it. In fact, if they skipped the preaching like Kidd said his church does at times when people want to repent of their sins, then Ace was ready.

When the praise team and choir were finally finished, Pastor Lane walked up to the podium. After a few preliminaries, he opened his Bible. "Please turn to the book of Hebrews, chapter 11. This morning, I want to focus on verse six."

Ace and Kidd exchanged knowing nods.

"It says, 'And without faith it is impossible to please God, because anyone who comes to him must believe that he exists and that he rewards those who earnestly seek him.'" When he finished reading, the pastor asked, "Do you hear that, church? God has a reward for anyone who seeks Him. There are a number of ways to describe how a man must seek the Lord; that is faithfully, sincerely, unconditionally, seriously, lovingly . . . and on and on, searching for God."

Pastor Lane removed his reading glasses. "Once you find Him, it pays to trust Jesus. He will not fail you."

Perhaps it was because Ace was listening with a whole new attitude, but Pastor Lane preached from Scripture in a way that was extremely convincing to Ace and, amazingly, he understood the message.

Soon, the pastor began to close out his sermon. "Remember, there are two purposes why Jesus hung on that cross: first, to save us from ourselves—sin will do us in. And second, to come back and redeem those whom He has saved. When you get tired of looking, you'll realize there's nothing this valuable and free today. You don't have to live in your sins and be tormented . . . You don't have to wait. No appointment is necessary. Repent where you're standing and then step out and come to the altar."

Ace turned to Kidd and gripped his hand in a shake and hug. Taking a deep breath, he began the walk that he hoped would change his life. Ministers were waiting in front of the pulpit. One met him halfway and asked what Ace wanted from God.

"I want to be saved," Ace said with determination.

The minister anointed his forehead and then began to pray. Another minister came up beside them to assist. It was Minister Thomas. Once they were face-to-face, Minister Thomas winced when he recognized Ace and then dutifully prayed for him. Ace refused to look at the man as his nemesis. He banished those thoughts and concentrated on giving his life to the Lord.

Too soon, Kidd nudged him. "God manifested Himself in a mighty way, but we'd better head out, so we can make a dent in driving before dark."

He nodded. This was the moment he missed flying the most. Ace truly wasn't ready to leave church yet. Reluctantly, he followed his family out of the prayer room.

Ace had to keep himself from stumbling when he saw Talise and

Minister Thomas talking at the other end of the hall.

What now, God? He thought. *I've used all my options. I'm in Your hands now.*

Surprisingly, they walked toward him. Talise wrapped her arms around Ace and hugged him. Her affection felt so good.

"Congratulations, Ace! I'm so happy you surrendered. Your life will surely change . . ." she encouraged him.

He nodded in agreement. "Beginning now," he said before turning to Minister Thomas. Secure in his standing, Ace told him, "We're on a level playing field. You can't beat me to heaven and I can't beat you. I'm asking you to step aside so I can try and salvage my relationship with the woman I love, the mother of my child."

Ace wanted to add that it wasn't a request, but he held his tongue. with his Nicodemus moment and Damascus he just experienced with God, he didn't want a blemish on his clean garment.

Ace didn't waste another second. Getting on one knee, he reached for Talise's hand and placed his other hand on her stomach. He smiled as the baby moved.

"Talise Shanté Rogers, I love you with all my heart. I'm an imperfect man made perfect by God. And I'm thrilled to say He has perfected my love for you. I'm asking you to marry me. The worst is over and the best is yet to come."

His eyes misted as Talise sniffed. Reaching down to touch his face, she answered, "Yes!"

Epilogue

*A*ce purchased his airline ticket to Boston the day his name was removed from the "no-fly" list.

Since Talise was in her last trimester, her obstetrician recommended that she should not fly. Finally, he had her new cell number. They talked throughout the day and Skyped in between his visits. Ace even convinced her to set up a Facebook account.

On a snowy December evening in Boston, Ace and Talise became husband and wife in Pastor Lane's office. Upon Talise's insistence, their formal wedding wouldn't take place until after the baby was born and Sinclaire returned from her tour of duty—against Ace's protest.

Three weeks later in January, during a Boston blizzard, they barely made it to the hospital in time for Lauren Chaz Jamieson to make her entrance into the world. Lauren and Eva's daughter, Kennedy Solae, became the twelfth generation descendants of Orma Jamieson, the last son of Prince Paki Jaja of Africa.

The rest, as the Jamiesons would say, is history.

BOOK CLUB QUESTIONS

1. Discuss Ace's "responsibility is optional" mentality when it came to learning that Talise might be pregnant.

2. Discuss Talise's initial decision not to put the Jamieson name on her baby's birth certificate. Is it justified if the father doesn't want to claim responsibility?

3. Discuss Sandra's role in Talise's life. Were you for her relationship and interactions with Talise as a friend? (I would really love to hear your answers on this one).

4. Do you feel that the Jamieson family had the right to go behind Ace's back and develop a relationship with the mother of Ace's child?

5. Ace didn't understand why God hadn't acted until his mom and brother explained that he had to go to God in the right spirit, not wanting something. Discuss your opinion on this.

6. What is your opinion of Minister Thomas? Should he have stepped aside as Ace requested, or should he have fought for Talise?

7. Did Ace deserve a second chance?

8. Which character in the book did you most identify with? Why?

9. Have you had a chance to research your family genealogy? Do you plan to?

10. Discuss the pastor's topic: "Thinking You've Got It Right, and in the End, Finding Out You Had It All Wrong."

Please visit www.patsimmons.net or
email me at pat@patsimmons.net

ABOUT THE AUTHOR

*P*at Simmons considers herself a self-proclaimed genealogy sleuth. She is passionate about researching her ancestors, then casting them in starring roles in her novels. She has been a genealogy enthusiast since her great-grandmother died at the young age of ninety-seven years old. She enjoys weaving African American history into local history.

Pat describes her Christian walk as an amazing, unforgettable, life-alternating experience. She is a baptized believer who is always willing to share her testimonies about God's goodness and gifts. She believes God is the true Author who advances her stories.

Pat has a B.S. in mass communications from Emerson College in Boston, MA. She has worked in various media positions in radio, television, and print for more than twenty years. Currently, she oversees the media publicity for the annual RT Booklovers Conventions. She has been a guest on several media outlets, including radio, television, newspapers, and blog radio.

She is the award-winning author of *Talk to Me*, ranked #14 of Top Books in 2008 That Changed Lives by *Black Pearls Magazine*; she also received the Katherine D. Jones Award for Grace and Humility from the Romance Slam Jam committee in 2008. Pat is best known for her Guilty series: *Guilty of Love, Not Guilty of Love*, and *Still Guilty*, which was voted the Best Inspirational Romance for 2010 by the RSJ committee. Her newest release, *Crowning Glory*, has received rave reviews and was noted as the Best Christian Fiction for 2011 by O.O.S.A Online Book club. Her fans are eagerly awaiting the next books in the Guilty series: *Guilty by Association, The Guilt Trip*, and *Free from Guilt* in 2012.

Pat Simmons has converted her sofa-strapped, sports-fanatical husband into an amateur travel agent, untrained bodyguard, and GPS-guided chauffeur. They have a son and daughter.

ACKNOWLEDGMENTS

"Jesus, I'll never forget what You've done for me."

I am so glad for the continuous support of numerous book clubs across the country, including my Guilty captains: readers, church members, including First Lady of Bethesda Temple in St. Louis, Missouri, Sister Juana Johnson, who has been a fan since book one. Thank you, Bishop Johnson, for preaching and teaching the Word of God with no compromises. God Bless you!

My family, as well as the descendants of Coles, Browns, Carters, Wilkerson/Wilkinsons, Jamiesons, Brownlees, Wades, Jordans, Palmers, Lamberts, Thomases . . . and in-laws: Simmons, Sinkfields, Crofts, Sturdivants, Stricklands, Downers . . .

To my wonderful agent, Amanda Luedeke, with the MacGregor Literary Agency. You have been a blessing to me! It's your birthday.

The Jamieson Legacy is brought to readers by Acquisition Editor Cynthia Ballenger; without her enthusiasm, the legacy of the Jamieson men would not have continued. I praise God for the staff at Life Every Voice Books/Moody Publishers for the opportunity to tell this story. May God bless you! Special thanks to freelance editor Chandra Sparks Taylor who has helped get me to this point in my career. Much love!!!!

Thanks for sister-girls/fellow writers Lisa Watson and Vanessa Miller. Who else is willing to pitch in when I have to meet deadlines?

Finally, I thank God for a good husband, Kerry Simmons, and my son and daughter.

O give thanks unto the Lord, for he is good:
for his mercy endureth for ever. —Psalm 107:1 KJV

If you want to know about my connection with the Jamison/ Jemison slaveholders, please visit my website at www.patsimmons.net

362

and click on the genealogy table. Or visit my blog and leave comments at talkgenealogy.blogspot.com.

Prologue

Three months later . . .

*C*ameron Daniel Jamieson wasn't going down like his brothers and cousins. No woman in the world would get him to a prayer altar as a prerequisite to the wedding altar.

As he looked around the room, the common thread among the men was their wives. The culprits all dug their stilettos into the ground, refusing a diamond ring unless their Jamieson man humbled himself to Christ. How ridiculous. That's exactly what happened to Parke, Malcolm, Kidd, and now Ace.

Ace and Talise were moments away from renewing their wedding vows in an elaborate ceremony. They were married two months earlier and three weeks before their precious daughter, Lauren, was born. It was a happy ending to their tumultuous courtship.

Talise had two stipulations to her holdout. She did not want to be pregnant in a wedding dress, and her sister serving in the Persian Gulf, Sinclaire, had to be present. Women and their demands. Still, Cameron took the credit for introducing them.

The photographer knocked before walking in, ready to take snapshots. Cameron slipped on his tuxedo as his oldest brother, Parke, fought with his three-year-old son.

"Paden, be still, so Daddy can get this bowtie right," Parke demanded to no avail. The boy twisted his mouth, body, and feet in order to get a look at his cousin. The three-year-old was bouncing off furniture in the church's dressing room.

"M. J., sit down, or I will tie you down," Malcolm ordered his son from his perch in the corner. The boy froze immediately.

"Oh, the joys of parenthood." Cameron couldn't help but laugh at his nephews. The little Jamiesons were double trouble in the same room. Oddly, the groom was pacing the floor like a nervous wreck.

"Chill, dude. You're already married. It's not like Talise is going to leave you standing at the altar," Cameron taunted his cousin, who was also like a brother to him.

"Today is all about Tay. You have no idea how important this is to my baby," Ace said as he posed, staring down at Talise's wedding band that he cupped in the palm of his hand.

Kidd, Ace's older brother, grunted. "Oh yeah, I do. My wife planned this shindig, so everything better go smoothly."

Ace's cell phone rang and when he answered it, the photographer snapped a picture. Listening to the one-sided conversation, Cameron knew something wasn't going as planned.

"She did what?" Ace began to fume. "You've got to be kidding me?" He paused. "It'll be okay, baby," Ace consoled.

"I'll see you in a few. I love you," he added the words of comfort before disconnecting.

Folding his arms, Kidd looked at his brother and frowned. "That means something is not okay. What's going on?"

"Hold it!" The photographer shouted as the men huddled around Ace. Waiting for the click of the camera, everyone froze, including the boys. "You all can relax now," the man ordered after taking the shot.

Ace glanced around to make sure Talise's father wasn't in the room. He started in on the play-by-play.

"It's Frederick's wife. She's in the bridal chamber, giving Tay her unwelcomed opinion. Basically, she's complaining about the bride wearing pink and not white. Then Donna couldn't understand why we didn't renew our vows from her hometown of Richmond. Next, Grandma BB stepped in—literally in her Stacy Adams shoes—and put Donna in her place when she insisted, as the stepmother, to be escorted down the aisle as part of the wedding party."

"Yikes." Cameron stuffed his hands in his pockets. After the death of her mother, it was a known fact that Talise did not refer to Donna as her stepmother, but only as her father's new wife

"Yikes is right. Grandma BB in all her Sunday best shoved Donna out the door and dared her to see what happens if she walked down that aisle," Ace continued.

Cameron snickered and Parke grunted. "We'd better keep an eye on her, or Grandma BB will be fighting in church."

"I think she earned a brownie point with my wife when Grandma BB volunteered to post guard outside her door." Ace chuckled and soon the men joined in, even the photographer.

"Grandma BB, related to everybody, but not a drop of blood to connect her to any of us," Malcolm described the woman, shaking his head.

The woman had latched onto the Jamieson family years ago. She took her role as grandma seriously.

After taking a few more shots, the photographer walked out as Talise's father was coming into the room.

"Wait until you see her. She's beautiful and happy." Frederick grinned and shook hands with Ace. "Keep her that way and there won't be any problems."

Ace nodded as Parke suggested a prayer for Ace. Linking hands, Parke bowed his head and the others followed.

"Father, in the Name of Jesus, we come before Your throne of grace. We worship You today for this opportunity to witness the love shared between husband and wife. I ask that You bless my cousin's life and marriage, bless his Christian journey, and most of all, bless their precious daughter."

Parke paused, and then added, "Lord Jesus, and please bless every married man and their households represented here today. Help us to never fail You as the strong Black Christian men You created us to be, in the Name of Jesus. Amen."

Amens echoed around the room. One by one, a Jamieson man patted Ace on the back, following after his father-in-law.

Ace tilted his head. "Ah, it appears there's one man standing in this room that isn't hitched. Even Melvin over there just recently got married, so you, my dear cousin, are the Lone Ranger."

"You're going down, Cam, sooner rather than later," Parke taunted his youngest brother.

"I haven't been caught yet."

LIFT EVERY VOICE BOOKS

Lift every voice and sing
Till earth and heaven ring,
Ring with the harmonies of Liberty;
Let our rejoicing rise
High as the listening skies,
Let it resound loud as the rolling sea.
Sing a song full of the faith that the dark past has taught us,
Sing a song full of the hope that the present has brought us,
Facing the rising sun of our new day begun
Let us march on till victory is won.

The "Black National Anthem," written by James Weldon Johnson in 1900, captures the essence of Lift Every Voice Books. Lift Every Voice Books is an imprint of Moody Publishers that celebrates a rich culture and great heritage of faith, based on the foundation of eternal truth—God's Word. We endeavor to restore the fabric of the African-American soul and reclaim the indomitable spirit that kept our forefathers true to God in spite of insurmountable odds.

We are Lift Every Voice Books—Christ-centered books and resources for restoring the African-American soul.

For more information on other books and products
written and produced from a biblical perspective, go to
www.lifteveryvoicebooks.com or write to:

Lift Every Voice Books
820 N. LaSalle Boulevard
Chicago, IL 60610
www.lifteveryvoicebooks.com